PRAISE FOR CHAR...

Hidden Variables

Charles Sheffield

SF
ace books
A Division of Charter Communications Inc.
A GROSSET & DUNLAP COMPANY
51 Madison Avenue
New York, New York 10010

HIDDEN VARIABLES
Copyright © 1981 by Charles Sheffield

An ACE Book
First Ace printing: July 1981

Published Simultaneously in Canada

2 4 6 8 0 9 7 5 3 1
Manufactured in the United States of America

TABLE OF CONTENTS

INTRODUCTION

"Most readers come to see the show, not to watch the stage manager take bows in front of the footlights."
—Stephen King, *Night Shift*.

I'll keep this short.

Story collections present two dangers to the buyer. They may be a re-packaging of old material under new titles, so nearly all the stories can be found in other collections. Or they may contain good stories padded out with unpublishables, dead dogs that no editor would buy. It's easy to find examples of both these ways of cheating the reader.

I can't tell you how good the stories are in this collection—for that you have to read them. But I can guarantee that none of them appeared in the earlier collection, VECTORS, and all of them were bought by respected editors. Maybe I should also add that of the 356 pages in this book, 281 were either unpublished or committed when VECTORS came out, so this is not the sweepings left over from a first collection.

One thing is common to VECTORS. I still believe that a bad story cannot be improved by a self-serving or explanatory introduction to it. I will instead provide brief afterwords that aim to provide perspective on how or why the story came out the way it did. But the story's the thing, the whole thing.

—CHARLES SHEFFIELD, October 8th, 1980

For Ann, Bowler, Deb, Simon, and Jo.

THE MAN WHO STOLE
THE MOON

The line was quite short but it was moving very slowly. By the time they reached the service desk, three hours had passed since they entered the License Office.

"Application number?" The woman behind the desk did not look up at the two young men. She was in her mid-twenties, sloppily made-up and about forty pounds overweight. Her smeared make-up was a perfect match for the cluttered desk top and the battered metal filing cabinets behind her.

"I'm Len Martello." The taller and thinner man was looking about him impatiently. "And this is Garry Scanlon. We've got an Evaluation petition in here, and we wonder what's happened to it."

"Yeah?" The woman looked up at them for the first time. There was no flicker in interest in her eyes as she slowly scanned from one to the other. "I need yer Application number. Can't do nothin' without that. D'ya have it?"

"Here's what we have. But it's not an Application number." Martello handed a slip of paper across the desk. He was thin, dark-haired and nervous, with sharp features and a pale, bony face. An old wound on his upper lip had healed to give him a twisted mouth and a skeptical, sardonic look. "We never received an Application number from you. All that came back to us was this, with a file code and an Evaluation petition acknowledgement. Look here." He leaned forward, trying to communicate his own urgency to the woman behind the desk. "We filed for the evaluation of our propellant *four months* ago, and we've had no answers at all. Not a word from here. What's the delay?"

1

She stared at the yellow slip for a few seconds, rubbing one hand against her pimply cheek. At last she shook her head and handed it back. "You got the wrong office. You shoulda gone to Room Four-forty-nine. You'll hafta go over there."

"But dammit, we asked downstairs, and they *told* us to come here." Martello had crumpled the yellow slip and stood there, fists clenched. "We asked the guard, and he was quite definite about it."

The woman shrugged. "He tol' ya wrong, then. Ya know, we only do applications in here. We *used* to do 'em, evaluations, but not now. I mean, not since I've been here. You'll hafta go to Room Four-forty-nine, nex' floor up."

Her look turned to the clock on the office wall. She began to pull tissues from a box on the desk and transfer them to her shoulder bag.

"Look, we made six phone calls from outside, before we came over here." Martello's voice was furious. "Nobody seemed to be able to tell us where to go or what to do or *anything*. We've taken all day just to get this far."

"Yeah. But you shoulda gone to Four-forty-nine." The woman stood up, showing a thick bulge of fat over her tight skirt. "They do evaluations, we only do the applications. Anyway, I can't stay an' talk now. You know, I gotta car pool."

Garry Scanlon put a restraining hand on Len Martello's arm and stepped forward. He was fair-haired, pink cheeked, and slightly pudgy. "Thank you, ma'am." He smiled at her. "I was wondering, could you maybe call up there and tell them we're on the way? We'd like to see them, and we shouldn't have to wait in line all over again."

"Sorry." Her eye turned again to the clock. "You'll hafta start over anyway. I mean, they close same time we do, in another coupla minutes. They won't see you today. I can't change that, ya know."

"You mean we'll have to begin the whole thing again tomorrow?"

"Guess so, yeah. Offices here open at eight-thirty." She picked up her bag and shepherded them in front of her, out into the corridor, then looked at them uncertainly. "Well, have a nice day,'' she said automatically, and was off, wobbling away on her high heels.

Garry Scanlon slumped back against the corridor wall and took a deep breath. "Christ, Len, there's another whole day wasted."

"Yeah." Martello was paler than ever, with anger and frustration. "God, no wonder we couldn't get any sense out of these turkeys over the phone. If they're all like her, I don't see how Government evaluations ever get done at all."

"So what do we do now?"

Martello shrugged. "What the hell *can* we do? We'll have to come back. We're trapped, Garry. It's going to be the same old crap. If we don't get an approval, we'll never get an industrial group to look at us. And we've agreed that we'll never get the bench tests done without outside financing."

He shook his dark head. "I hope the propellant's as good as we think it is. Another night in this crazy place, and I thought we'd be on our way back to Dayton by now. Come on, let's see if we can check in at the Y again."

He started to walk away, head bowed, along the dingy corridor. After a final, helpless look at the empty office, Garry Scanlon followed him.

"Yes, yes, it's here all right. Martello and Scanlon, right, Evaluation Request 41468/7/80. Now, if you'll wait a minute I'll run a computer search and see where it's got to."

The speaker was small and white-haired. He wore a flowered red vest, opened to show old-fashioned suspenders and a well-pressed white shirt. A carved wooden sign on the desk in front of him read: "Henry B. Delso—the Last One Left." He hummed softly to himself as he carefully entered the data request, pecking away at the keyboard with two gnarled fingers. When it was done he swivelled the display screen around so that they could all see it.

"Be just a few seconds, while it does the search. Rocket propellant, you said?"

"That's right." Len Martello swallowed. "A good one."

"Don't get many of those any more." Delso shook his head.

"Well, here she comes."

The characters that filled the display screen were unintelligible to Len and Garry. They watched Delso, trying to read his expression.

"What's it say?" asked Garry.

"Not much." Delso shook his head again, and looked at his watch. "I'll get a hard copy output of this for you, and tell you how to read it. But I don't think it'll do much for you."

He leaned forward in his wooden, high-backed chair. "Look, how long have you boys been working on this?"

"Here in Washington? Just three days." Garry's pink face was earnest. "But we filed the forms over four months ago."

Delso nodded. "First application, right?"

"Yes. Did we file it the wrong way?"

"Nope. You did it right, evaluation request's on the right form, everything's in order there." He looked again at his watch. "I'm done for the day, just about. Gimme a hand here and I'll boil up a cup of tea for all of us—better for your gut than the stuff in that coffee urn—and I'll tell you what the problem is. Can't tell you the solution, wish I could. You'll have to figure something out for yourselves. Good luck on that."

He carried a battered shiny kettle into the back room, filled it, and came back. "Go bring the teapot and milk through here, would you? And get cups and a spoon while you're there." He plugged the electric kettle into an outlet on the wall behind him. "There we go. Three minutes, and it'll be boiling."

He leaned back. "So, you've got a new propellant? I'll believe you, even believe it might be a good one. But do you know what happens when you file your evaluation form with the Government here?"

Garry and Len looked at each other in bewilderment. Len shrugged. "I guess somebody here takes a look at it. And decides if it's dangerous for us to test it. If it's not, we get a permit from you and we go ahead and do the bench tests."

"Just so." Henry Delso was carefully measuring four spoons of tea into the big brown pot. "Sounds very fair and logical, eh? And you know, it used to be. I've been around this office for thirty-five years—as long as we've had the evaluation procedure. When I first started here, I read *all* the applications—we didn't distinguish in those days between applications and evaluations, that only came in fifteen years ago. I'd take each application, and I'd study it for a day, maybe two days. For something like a propellant I'd dig out the relevant patents, and the engineering handbook. Maybe do a few calculations, see if things seemed to be in the right ball-park. And you'd get an answer, yes or no. It took a week, sometimes two weeks, from start to finish.''

''But we've waited over four months,'' said Len.

''Right.'' A rueful smile. ''That's progress, yer see?''

Delso looked around his office, at the ranks of file cabinets, the computer terminal, and the elaborate multi-channel telephone. ''I had none of this in the old days. Look at what we have to do now. Rocket propellant, see, first thing I have to do is look up the Industrial Codes. I can do it in that book''—he pointed at a three-inch thick volume with a bright red cover—''or I can check through the terminal there. That tells me which Government departments must be involved in the evaluation procedure, where they are, and so on.''

''Hell, if we'd known that we could have contacted them before we sent in the forms,'' said Len. ''We could have saved you a lot of time here.''

''Not the approved method.'' Henry Delso poured tea into three chipped cups and pushed the tray forward. ''Help yourselves to milk and sugar.''

He picked up a cup. ''I can tell you the complete list if you want it, but it wouldn't help you. The law says that they have to be contacted from here, whether you talk to them or not. Let's look at just a few of them. Environmental Protection Agency, naturally—you have to get their approval, because you'll be releasing some substances into the air. It might affect the environment when you do the bench tests. Center for Air Quality, same thing applies to them. Food and Drug Administration''—he looked at them over the top of his thick glasses—''didn't think of them, did you? You'll be working with new compounds, they'll want samples to test for the effects on humans, plants, and animals. Might be harmful effects there. Then there's Defense, they have to be involved on anything that might have defense implications. Then, let's see, Office of Safety are on the list—with a new material test, they have to be sure there'll be no danger to workers who'll be involved.''

"But we're the only two people who'll be involved!" Garry's eyes were bulging. "We don't want their stupid protection."

"Ah, but it's for your own good—you don't have a say in it. Where was I?" Delso leaned back, checking off on his fingers. "Health Department, naturally—they duplicate some of Food and Drug's work and some of the Office of Safety, but they have their own checking system and that has to be followed."

Len Martello's scarred mouth was more twisted than usual. "I just can't believe it. You mean we have to get approval from all those groups before we can get a positive evaluation from you—that we can't do any more testing until that's finished?"

"That's right." Delso handed him a cup. "All those groups—and we're just getting started. Equal Opportunity, there's a dilly for you. They have to be sure that your company will have a positive action program for minorities."

"But there's only the two of us in it!"

"Makes no difference, laws are laws. Then there's the Women's Civil Commission. They'll have to be satisfied that there's no sex discrimination in the operation—that's not considered the same thing as the minority question. Mustn't forget the Department of Transportation, too. You'll need to get a clean bill of health from them, to ship your propellant."

"We won't be shipping any propellant!" Garry slammed the cup down on the old desk. "We'll be making it right where we test it. Damn it, Mr. Delso, these regulations are ridiculous. Why should we have to get approval from a whole bunch of places that won't have anything at all to do with the development?"

Delso pursed his lips and shook his head. "I can't disagree with you. You're five hundred percent accurate. That's exactly what I'm trying to get across to you. I can't change the laws, they've all been passed and we have to go along with them here. I think they're as silly as you do, most of them, but I can't break those laws—not if I want to see my pension in a couple more years."

Len Martello put down his cup and stood up. "Mr. Delso, I don't know all those laws, but I do know how to count, and I think I understand probability. How many negative evaluations from those departments would it take to kill our chances?"

"One is enough, for the evaluation to come out negative. You can always re-file, of course."

"And start all over again? Look, if we have to get, say, twenty independent agencies to approve, and there's just a one-in-five chance that any one of them will say no to us, do you see what that means? The probability that we'll get approval is down to four-fifths to the twentieth—less than one chance in eighty. Am I right?"

"Quite right, I'm afraid." Delso nodded. "Your arithmetic's probably right, and I'm sure about your conclusion. In the past ten years, since the last set of regulations came into effect, I can count the number of successful evaluation petitions from small companies like yours on the fingers of one hand. I tell you, I'm just trying to help, even if it sounds as though all I'm doing is offering bad news."

"So what ought we to do?" Len sat down again and looked intently at the old man.

"You don't know much about law, do you? Either one of you."

"Hardly anything—we've never needed it."

"Well, let me give you some free advice. It's the best I can offer but I don't think you'll like it. If you ever hope to get a positive evaluation nowadays, go and hire a lawyer—a whole bunch of lawyers. And you'd better be ready to spend a year and a lot of money, if the petition involves advanced technology."

He peered over at their cups, buttoning his vest as he did so. "You've not touched your tea, either one of you. How old are you now, twenty-one?"

"Twenty-two." Len laughed without any sign of humor. "Twenty-two, and the more I hear, the older I feel. You're telling us there's no hope—this whole trip has been a waste of time."

"I'm telling you I don't think you have much hope, the way you're doing it now. But you're young, and space-mad from the looks of you. Don't give up."

"So what ought we to do?"

"You've got plenty of energy, and you want to work on the space program. I don't think you can get far these days on your own. Forty years ago, there weren't all these restrictions. Nowadays, you ought to join the Government, or one of the really big corporations. They can afford to hire a whole team of lawyers, and they can afford to sit and wait until all the roadblocks to permits are out of the way. You can't do that, you don't have the resources."

Len stood up again, and this time Delso rose also. He walked over to the door and took an umbrella from the hook behind it, then a heavy and out-of-style overcoat. "You can't wait—and it gets worse every year. I see it happening, right here."

"How long does it take to get an evaluation approved now?" asked Len.

"It varies. But I've never seen it happen in less than two years, recently—and I've got one here that's been ten years and we're still going on it. You have to get yourselves on the right side of the argument, and that means working with the big outfits—maybe even learning law yourselves. But I can tell you, if I were a young man now, and I wanted to have a career in space work, I'd be in the Government. I've seen too many youngsters like you come here and go away disappointed."

He maneuvered them in front of him, so that Garry and Len again found themselves out in the long-dimly-lit corridor. Delso held out his hand.

"Good luck to both of you, however you decide to go. I just wish I had something more promising to tell you, but I don't. You can't beat the system, not the way it is now. Things have just got too complicated these days. So don't beat it, join it."

He locked the door and walked away, a jaunty little man with an overlong overcoat. Len and Garry looked after him in silence until he turned the corner and was out of earshot.

"What do you think, Len? Is he for real?"

Martello scowled at the wall, with its dirty peeling paint and broken light fixtures. "I think he must be. He was trying to help us. Why should he want to make anything up? If we try and get a positive evaluation out of this place, we'll still be working on it when we're as old as he is."

"Then I guess we ought to do what he says." Garry Scanlon was leaning against the wall, his shoulders slumped forward. "I don't want to waste my whole life fooling with those damn-fool regulations. I want to do something *real*, get a real job where I can see results. Let's get out of here. When we get back to Dayton I'm going to write off for an application to the Space Program."

"You'll apply for a Government position?"

"Right. Why don't we both do it?"

"No." Len's face was thoughtful. "Maybe you should do it, Garry. You're the technical brain, and you ought to be producing where you'll be most effective. I'm just not ready to give up yet."

"But what can you *do*, Len? It sounds as though every year there are a bunch of new regulations and a longer approval cycle."

"Sounds like it." Martello shrugged. "Delso sounded pretty convincing, but maybe he only knows his own little area. I'm going to try another approach—I'm damned if I'll give up yet. Not while there's a whole universe up there, waiting for us to get our act together."

Evaluation Petition Request 41468/7/80. (Martello and Scanlon, petitioners). Request denied on the following grounds: Code A3T, Insufficient evidence of affirmative action plan; Code B77G, Failure to comply with Child Welfare Act A-15, Amendment 5; Code G23R, Failure to provide statement of intended uses of Inland Waterways; Code R3H, Insufficient evidence of adherence to Privacy Statute D-04; Code T1TF, Failure to provide evidence of recycling (materials SIC 01,03) in processing of limited supply substances.

Len—the ticket will be waiting when you get here (for the launch viewing, I'm afraid, not for the flight!) If you can get down to the Cape a day early I'll show you the sights. We've got two Orbiters in Maintenance. You'll see how far we've come since last time you were here.

Seen the new Lunar Treaty yet? It's a bummer. NASA's official line is that everything is fine, but you should hear the contract support staff. Nobody's ready to put a wooden nickel into space investment until it's clear who'll own what.

I was up at Wright-Patterson a couple of weeks ago, looking at hi-temp tiles. Know who I ran into in Dayton? Old Uncle Seth. Told him you were off studying law and I thought he'd break down and cry. Looks as though the old stories are right, he really is hooch-peddling on the side. Remember those cases in his garage every Christmas? He's in great shape, must be nearly eighty but you'd never know it. Pickled in his own product, it can't be too bad.

It looks iffy on *Lungfish*. The industrial consortium is backing off, not sure they can raise more money. Macintosh and his committee are against Government assistance, say it's more pie in the sky.

You getting near the end up there yet? Remember, if you can't take New York any more there's always a job here at the Cape. I've got so many equal opportunity quotas round my neck—be nice to have somebody round here who can change a light bulb without an instruction manual. I've never told anyone you're a budding lawyer, they think you're an engineering buddy from way back.

Don't get the wrong idea about this place, it's not all roses. I'll tell you some of my problems when you get here.

Stick in there with the tort and malfeasance. Jennie says hi.

                                Garry.

SUPREME COURT UPHOLDS DECISION ON POWER-SATS. In a landmark decision, the Supreme Court today upheld last July's Superior Court finding that the construction of solar power satellites offers an unacceptably high risk to human life and health. In a seven to two decision, with Justices Stewart and Basker dissenting, the Court ruled that possible future power shortages cannot be used to undermine the force of existing laws. Microwave radiation levels near the receiving rectennas of the proposed power stations would exceed recent Federal maximum levels by a factor of three or more.

In a minority opinion, the dissenting justices referred to the billion dollar investment that has already been made in the powersats, to the overwhelming need to build some independence from imported fossil fuels, and to the poor understanding of the effects of microwave radiation. Justice Basker stated: "We are condemning our children and our children's children to a life of reduced options, in order to satisfy a set of arbitrary standards on radiation levels that is neither clearly understood nor fully supported by scientific experts."

This ruling by the Court confirms similar decisions made by the European, Russian and Chinese Governments. The Japanese Parliament is currently debating the same issue. . . . UPI NEWS RELEASE.

"Assholes." Len Martello slapped his hand down flat on top of the newspaper. "They have no idea what they're doing. Here we are in the middle of the worst set of brown-outs we've ever seen on the East Coast, and those silly old bastards decide to cut off one of the only decent alternatives."

Garry Scanlon looked at him in surprise. Len was even thinner than the last time they had met, and his dark hair was already beginning to show the first strands of grey. The scar on his left upper lip seemed more prominent than before, pulling that side of his mouth up and giving a slightly manic look to his whole face.

"It's not just the Supreme Court in this country, Len—look at the rest of the countries, too."

"I am looking at them. Just because they walk off a cliff doesn't mean we have to. Ah, hell, what's the point." He folded up the newspaper. "I guess they don't care what happens twenty years from now, they'll all be dead."

He looked across the table at his friend. Garry Scanlon was showing his own first signs of aging. The fair hair was receding a trace at the temples, and he no longer looked as though his face had never felt a razor. There was a tough, straw-colored stubble on his chin, and his eyes were tired and black-edged.

Garry slipped a couple of dollars under the glass ashtray and stood up.

"Come on. We might as well get out of here and over to the launch site. I agree with you about the way they're handling powersats, but it's not just an isolated case."

"I know. I've been following the appropriations cycle in Washington. But I thought you'd be free of it down here. Your programs are on the move, aren't they?"

"Yeah. We're on our way up Shit Creek. It's as frustrating here as it was when we were just a two-man show, back in Dayton."

Len was shielding his eyes against the bright Florida sunshine. He whistled.

"Bad as that, eh? I thought you'd got rid of the problems when you joined NASA."

"So did I."

"So what's gone wrong?"

Garry rubbed at his chin and shook his head. "I just wish I knew. Last time I wrote to you we had, oh, I guess fourteen hardware developments stalled. We had four briefs in preparation, and just one piece of gear approved. Know what the score is now? Eighteen in evaluation, and *no* new ones approved. Zero."

They climbed into the buggy and began the short drive back to Launch Control. The half-liter engine had a top speed of less than forty miles an hour, but it was a real miser on fuel oil. Len struggled out of his jacket and held it on his lap as they puttered their way over the heat-soaked roadway.

"Are you telling me it's as hard to get anything done in Government as it is outside it? I thought that was the whole point of the NASA job."

"So did I." Garry shrugged. "We have to fill out all the same bullshit, get everybody and his uncle to say yes. There's only one difference—I don't go broke waiting, the way that we did. That makes it a bit easier to take."

Ahead of them, the eight-wheeled support vehicles had finished their final service and were crabbing away from the foot of the gantry. A mournful siren began its booming call across the flat Florida landscape.

"Five minutes," said Garry. "Come on, we ought to be inside the blockhouse."

"One more minute." Len had descended from the buggy and

was standing on the concrete, drinking in the scene in front of them. His face was excited. "My God, Garry, this is what it's all about. I should be doing what you're doing instead of fucking about up north. It will be years before I take the Bar exams, longer than that before I can do anything useful."

"Don't let this mislead you." Garry took his arm and began to draw him into the protected area. "This launch will look great—they always do. But we're down again by another twenty percent from last year. The Shuttle works like a dream now— whenever we can get approval to do anything useful with it. We've done all the easy stuff"—he waved his arm with its wrist radio—"but there's nothing new about antenna farms. Dammit, they've been around for fifteen years now. We *have* to see some new starts."

The siren had changed to a more urgent, high pitched note as they entered the blockhouse. Len went at once over to the display screen. The silver Orbiter with its solid boosters and external tank looked fat and clumsy, too squat and awkward ever to leave the ground.

"Two minutes," said Garry, sitting down next to him.

"So it's the way we figured it." Len didn't take his eyes from the screen. "We're going to lose out to the other countries—we won't even come in second."

"Maybe not that bad." Garry's voice was baffled. "I thought the way you did, until I went over to Geneva for the last joint meeting. Now, I'm not so sure. Hold it, now, we're on the final thirty seconds."

They sat silent as the last seconds of the countdown ticked away. On cue, the swell of flame appeared at the base of the rocket and the assembly began its first stately lift-off. Inside the concrete block-house, four miles from launch, the noise was still deafening.

Garry flicked in the tracking monitor, split-screen from the rising Shuttle and the down-range cameras. "She's away. Watch that status display, any second now we'll get solid booster separation. We'll have an accurate trajectory back here in a couple more minutes, but from the look of it she's going to orbit with no problems."

He turned away from the screen, swinging his chair to face Len. "That's what makes me sick. See those boosters? Ten years, and we still use solids. We should have had liquid reuseables years ago. The Space Tug's still on the drawing boards, and we're further from nuclear propulsion than we were in 1960. The International Affairs people in Washington are so sensitive about Test Ban agreements that we can't even *mention* nuclear any more, not even for comparative studies."

Len was still hungrily drinking in the displays. *This was the real thing–the action was here, not back in New York fiddling with precedent, regulation, and who won in Soriba versus Rockwell, 1982. What was the point of all that legal effort, if it didn't lead to this?* He watched until the final sign of the ascending Orbiter was gone from all the displays, then turned at last to Garry.

"We *must* be losing out. I've been looking at the patents filed, things are going slower than ever. Our own system is killing us—strangling us. Remember our oath? At this rate we'll never do it."

"I know. But Len, you're wrong on one thing. We're not losing out. Everybody seems to be in the same boat."

"Slowing down?" Len's attention was suddenly all on Garry.

"And how. China, Russia, Japan, Europe, Australia—all over. Everybody has a space program in trouble. We keep trying to move ahead, but there's more and more red tape and bureaucratic bumscratching. You'll find this hard to believe, but we're not doing at all badly here."

"Everyone's strangling? What about the Brazilians?"

"Just as bad. Hell, if there were any place better, I'd go there, but I can't find a cure anywhere in the world."

Len turned back to the displays. On the one showing the launch area, a large black automobile was crawling slowly towards the pad. Windows of tinted glass made it impossible to see the interior, but it looked like a great hearse moving across the concrete. Len stared at it, a sudden speculation showing on his face.

"Maybe there is an answer. Garry, remember the oath? Meet on the Moon, July 20th, 1999, and drink a toast."

"We weren't the only ones that made it, I'll tell you that. Lots of the guys here did the same thing when they were kids. Better face it, Len, something took a wrong turn. A lot of us want space—millions of us, if NASA's mail means anything—but there's no *mechanism* any more. We've got technology, all we need. But we'll never make it through all the control and half-assed regulations. You ought to recognize that, too. Come on down here, there's still a job for you."

"Yeah." Len's eyes were still fixed on the black limousine. "Maybe, if all else fails . . ."

"All else *has* failed. The bureaucrats are in charge, all over the world."

"Not quite. I haven't given up the idea of legal loopholes completely. But if it doesn't work, I have another thought. What's that limo out there make you think of?"

"Eh?" Garry turned to the screen. "The VIP tour car? Beats me. Funeral parlors? Al Capone and Lucky Luciano? Henry Ford?"

"Pretty close with one of those. Look, Garry, I need to bounce something off you. Can we go for another beer?"

Garry looked doubtful. "I told Jennie we'd be home early for dinner."

"Still interested in drinking that toast?"

"All right." Garry sighed. "I'll call and tell her we'll be late. I know a bar where they don't blast muzak down your ear. If we don't get through by eight, though, you'll have to tell me the rest of it over at the house."

The winter storm had surprised everyone with its ferocity. After three days at a standstill, the ploughs were finally beginning to make an impression on the Dayton suburbs. Len stood inside the bitterly cold garage and looked out through grime-coated windows at the blown snow drifts. He had been waiting for almost half an hour in the unheated building.

"All right." The big man had slipped through from the inner

office so quietly that Len had not heard him arrive. "You can come in now. But hold still while I check you over."

"Somebody already did that."

"Yeah." There was a gruff chuckle in the darkness. "But that was twenty minutes ago. Meyer likes people who are thorough. O.K., you're clean. Keep your hands behind you and go on in."

Inside there was more light but no heat. Len shivered and walked forward to the old table. A little man with thick grey hair, carefully styled, sat behind it. Len received a long, measured stare before Sal Meyer again bent his head to the papers spread out in front of him.

"So all right." Meyer was wearing thick woollen gloves with just the fingertips cut away. "So you're Seth's nephew. Yeah, I can maybe see his look there. You're a Martello, you got the nose."

Dark eyes flashed up from their inspection of the papers and fixed again on Len's face. "You got fancy degrees, one in engineering and one in law. Now, you tell me what you want a job with us for. There's lots of other places you could work, no sweat for finding a job for yourself."

Len took a deep breath. "Money. I want to make a lot of it."

"You could do that in a law practice just as easy. Crooks, all of 'em, but you never see one in jail."

"But I don't see why I should work eighty hours a week, just to pay it in taxes."

That produced the first trace of a smile from Meyer. "You got me there. That's what I hated worst of all when I worked in City Transport. The big gouge, I call it." The smile was suddenly gone. "All right, you want a job with us. Now tell me what you got that I can't get better from Jake and Rocky behind you. Do it quick, before we all freeze to death here."

"I've talked to Uncle Seth. He wouldn't tell me much—"

"Bet your ass he wouldn't—not if he wanted to stay well."

"—but he made me think you've probably got problems with distribution, and maybe with quality control. I think I can help with both. I've controlled a fractional distillation line, I know how to check for fusel oils."

Sal Meyer held up his hand. "I talked to Seth, too. Look, I don't care about the quality end of it. If people are willing to drink it, or run their buggies on it, that's not my problem. Distribution is—specially with the way the pay-offs have been screwed up with the new Chief of Police. How greedy are you?"

"Try me and see."

Meyer grinned again. "Let me tell you the rules. I don't care where you make your money, how you spend it—except when it's in my area. I've got drugs, and I've got gambling. Anything that you make in that area, I take a third. If you want to get into booze and pimping, that's up to you. I don't ask for a piece. But remember, you get in trouble in those areas and you're on your own. I won't make one phone call to help you. If it's trouble you get into on my business, you'll have the best lawyers money can buy. You married?"

"No."

"Kids?"

"No."

"All right. For a married man, I look after the wife and kids if he goes inside." Meyer looked at Len curiously. "What do you do for fun?"

"I keep busy." Len cleared his throat. "I gather you're offering me a job, then?"

"I got an opening in Cleveland. Just so you know what's happening, the number two man over there got too greedy, started moving in on the hard drugs action. We've not heard from him for two weeks, and somehow I figure we're not going to. You'd go in as Number Three, and if you do anything decent you can move up fast. You want to ask me about money?"

"Not at the moment."

"O.K. That's the right answer." Meyer stood up and came around the table. He moved to within a few inches of Len and peered closely at his face. "How'd you get that lip?"

"Played ice hockey without a mask, back in high school." Len realized that Sal Meyer preferred short answers—something to file away for future reference.

"O.K." Meyer stepped back and gestured to the men behind Len. "Martello, don't tell the customers how you got that scar.

It's worth money in your bank account. You'll have to organize a little enforcing once in a while—it helps a lot if you look as though you've seen action. If you need to reach me, do it through Seth or Jake here. You'll see me anyway, once a week. O.K. Jake.''

"Thank you, Mr. Meyer.'' Len drew another deep breath as he was shepherded out into the main garage.

"Don't thank me, it's all business. So long, Lips, be seein' you next week. Oh, yeah, one other thing.''

Len turned in the doorway. "What?''

"Tell your Uncle Seth he'll have an extra piece of change coming from me. And if you know any good people, let me know. Competence seems to get rarer and rarer.''

He nodded, and the door closed.

"All right, Lips,'' said Jake. He shivered in the unlit garage. "Give this fucking snow a day or two to clear, and I'll show you round your area. You're part of the operation now. Remember one thing. Once you're in, you can't leave—so take my advice, and don't even think of it.''

LUNAR AGREEMENT SIGNED. At a Special Session of the United Nations, marked by a parade of angry demonstrators along Fifth Avenue, the controversial Lunar Agreement was finally signed. All off-Earth resources of the Moon and all other natural celestial bodies become, under this Agreement, the common heritage of all mankind, and the common property of all mankind. No organization, group, or nation may exploit those resources without paying compensation to all member nations, on a scale to be decided by the General Assembly.

Industrial representatives have pointed out that this Treaty makes it impossible for any corporate enterprise to continue to invest in Lunar development, or to plan the use of Lunar resources, since the basis for compensation to other nations remains unresolved. The Agreement has been defended by the Administration as the natural next step in the peaceful uses of Outer Space. Opponents of the Agreement deride this view, since there is an admitted escalation in particle and laser weapon beam development for use in near-Earth orbit. However, with the signing of the Agreement further debate on the issue now appears of academic interest only . . .

—UN Correspondent, N.Y.

"Yes, I've got it right here." Len looked up from the video screen, where Garry Scanlon's earnest face showed as a diminutive black and white image. He winked at Sal Meyer, waved him to a seat and turned back to the screen. "I read it the same way that you do, Garry—it'll have a bad effect. Remember what the Law of the Sea Treaty did to the industrial investments in deep ocean development? This will be as bad as that, maybe worse. Look, I'll call you tonight and we can talk about it some more. How's Jennie?"

Garry shook his head. "No change."

Len sat silent for a moment. Since the loss of the baby, stillborn, he had a feeling that a thin curtain had come down between him and Garry—the barrier that separated those with families from those without. "Do they think it was the drugs?" he said at last.

Garry shrugged. "Who knows? The Government tests and tests, and still they don't know what's good and what's bad." His voice was bitter. "Len, I feel as though the whole world's going to hell. There's not a thing left working for."

"Stick with it, keep on working." Len's voice was gentle. "Remember the oath. I haven't given up hope, you know—and I may need help soon. Talk to you later."

While Len talked, Meyer had unabashedly been picking up and reading letters and notices that sat on top of Len's desk. That was something worth noting for future reference. Meyer had stopped at the Lunar Agreement article.

"What in hell's name is this doing here? You thinking of putting a few feds into orbit, Lips?"

"Wouldn't be a bad idea. You know they're walking all over our operations?" Len smiled. "It's hard to believe, but they suspect we're not paying all our taxes."

"Are the books all clean?"

"Trust me—*both* sets of them. They won't find a thing wrong. As for that article, don't ignore it. I think it might be very important to us."

Meyer picked it up again and took another look. "This? You're crazy. How could it have anything to do with us?"

"That depends on how good your contacts are. Look, Sal, you know the figures on the drug business a lot better than I do. How much will the new intercountry agreement on drug sources cost us? I don't mean local operations, I mean over the whole world, for us and others like us."

Meyer leaned back and squinted at the ceiling. Len knew what was going on inside that grey head. Figures were being recalled, summed, allocated and compared.

"Fifty, sixty billion a year," said Meyer at last. "That's assuming the sources dry up as completely as we think they will."

"All right. Now look at the taxes on *legal* gambling—forget the other parts for the moment. How much are they, worldwide?"

"Thirty billion a month, maybe forty—depends what you call legal. So what? We can't find a home for drug production—you know they sniffed out and closed down the last three sooner than you could wink—and if we can't find a safe place for gambling activities, then what's the use of talking about it?"

Len reached over to the other side of the desk and pulled out another printed sheet. "I've got a place for drug production—one that won't get raided in a hurry by any government agency. Take a look at that while I get a cup of coffee."

The prose was flowery enough to raise Meyer's eyebrows as he read.

'A ghost still walks above the Earth. Blue-grey and silver, a hundred feet tall, it moves silently through the night and through the day, never pausing above any point. Like an uneasy spirit, it travels on and on . . .

'Who is this spectre? It is the most expensive shade in man's history, a sad reminder of what might have been. It is the unoccupied hulk of *Lungfish,* the empty space shell that still sits up near synchronous orbit. The U.S. and European industrial consortium who funded the launch and assembly of *Lungfish* at a cost of more than two hundred million dollars have declared that the project to make use of it has been abandoned.

'The future of the empty shell (four million cubic feet of working space!) is now uncertain. The consortium would certainly accept any reasonable or even nominal offer—but who is likely to make one?

'Meanwhile, get out your telescope some clear night just after sunset. With a two-inch refractor you'll easily be able to see *Lungfish*. And broken dreams are up there with that ghost.'

''What the hell *is* this, Lips?'' Meyer was still frowning over the piece when Len came back into the room.

''Space for sale—working space.''

''Up *there?* You're out of your mind.''

''Not if you try logic. Point one: you'll be outside the jurisdiction of any Government. They can't come in and close you down, because even if they could ever agree who would do it they don't have a space force in the U.N. Point two: I've looked at the economics of it. We could carry our materials up and our products down for a tiny fraction of their value. It wouldn't add more than a couple of hundred dollars a pound. For what we work with, that's like nothing.''

''You'd never be able to land it.''

''Not true. The Free Trade Zones would welcome a space facility. You'd have to grease a few palms with each cargo, but that's something we already know all about.''

Meyer leaned back in his seat. ''You're *serious* about this! I should live so long.''

''Sure I'm serious—but we can't take step one with that damned Senator Macintosh blocking all movement on space manufacturing.'' Len came over to Meyer's side. ''I'm dead serious. I'm even volunteering to set up the whole thing. Before I can do that, I need some encouragement from the rest of the operations that there's interest. Are you willing to carry it up the line for me?''

Meyer looked up at him sharply. ''What's your angle? You looking for control?''

''I'd never be given it. No, I'm simple-minded. I want one

percent of operations. And I'm willing to wait until everybody else has earned out their investment before I begin taking my percent."

"That keen, eh?" Meyer whistled softly. "You know, Lips, you've come on fast the past four years—some of the local operators say it's been too fast, but I don't agree. Tell you what I'll do. I'll take this over to the Central Council meeting—give me all the facts you have—just to see what reaction it gets. There's no way it'll fly first time around, everybody has to let it stew for a while and look for loopholes. If you rush things, that's the death of 'em."

"I've waited a long time. I can wait longer." Len had automatically reached over into the left hand desk drawer and pulled out an indigestion tablet. Sal Meyer watched the movement, shook his head unhappily.

"Still got the ulcer? You should take a break sometime, go off to Vegas and get laid. When you get to my age, you lose interest in raising hell." Meyer stood up, grunted, and rubbed at his chest. "And the damn doctors won't let you do it anyway, even if you feel like it."

Len was watching him shrewdly. "You ought to be up in *Lungfish* yourself, Sal. You'll add years to your life—that's a nice effect of low gravity, no heart strain."

Meyer didn't speak, but Len saw the change in the hard old face. Converts were sometimes made in the strangest ways. Len spoke as Meyer was turning to leave.

"If we did go ahead with this—in a year or two, I mean—we'll need to put political pressure on a few people. For a start, that Lunar Agreement has to go."

"Well, if that's all we have to do, I'll be surprised." Meyer laughed. "I'll push it along, Lips—but don't hold your breath waiting."

"They'll buy it, Garry. But they want me to prove myself one more time. I don't know how."

Garry Scanlon looked across at Len, slumped in the rocker. The dark hair was grey, as grey as the face beneath it.

Have I aged that much? Garry thought. *God knows, I've had the reasons. The baby, then Jennie.*

"I can help, Len. Just tell me what you need. I didn't get much from the move to Headquarters, but at least I can pull a few strings if I have to."

"Not these strings, Garry. Who do you know over at the Department of Justice?"

"Couple of neighbors are there. You want me to keep you out of jail?"

Len smiled wanly. "It may come to that—I haven't told you what I've been doing, but I've gone a long way past old Uncle Seth. A long way. Right now, I want to arrange a meeting with somebody, as high up as you can get me."

"You're part of the group that's bidding on *Lungfish,* that ought to get their attention. What else do you need from me?"

"Nothing. The less you know, the better. Believe me, when the time comes for a trip out, you'll know the minute that I do."

"How long?"

A weary shrug. "Three years? As my ex-boss says, don't hold your breath waiting. Maybe you'll beat me to it, doing it the regular way."

"Uh-uh." Garry stood up. He was developing signs of a paunch and the rounded shoulders of a desk worker. "You should see the budget for next year. It's a disaster—we spend more in welfare in one week than we do on space in two years. Got a job for me out there, Len?"

Len Martello had closed his eyes. He was silent for so long that Garry wondered if he were in pain.

"Not right now, Garry."

And not this year. It's bad enough that I have to do what I'm doing.

"Maybe when we get the operation going," he said at last.

"You'll need specialists in chemical plants if you're really going into space pharmaceuticals."

"There's a few bridges to be crossed before we're there. Big ones. Got a Congressional Directory? I need to dig out Senator Macintosh's address."

'Most men and women, at their deepest levels, are a complex combination of bravery and cowardice. It is the rare individual who has the pure essence, the complete courage or the true cowardice. Of all the professions, politics draws an unusually high percentage of both pure types. The difficult task is to determine with which one is dealing, since there are strong resemblances in their superficial behavior.

'It is much the same when we look at corruption. Politics presents a strange mixture of high and low ideals, the naturally corrupt and the incorruptible. The 101st Congress is no exception . . .'

Len read on, marking certain passages for future use. At nine p.m., the preset alarm sounded. The sixteen inch refractor set into the roof of his penthouse apartment was ready, computer-controlled on its target. *Lungfish* was rising. Slightly above synchronous orbit, its twenty-seven hour period took it slowly across the star field; it had less apparent motion than any other body in the sky except for the synchronous satellites.

The consortium was ready to prove their statement: *Lungfish* still had working communications with ground-based stations, and enough fuel in the mickey-mouse external thrusters to achieve attitude stabilization.

Len watched closely, but he could see no change. *Lungfish* was still only a point of light. He would have to wait for attitude telemetry to come down and prove that the station was still live and controllable, even though it was no more than the hollow husk of a working space station.

On impulse, he keyed in lunar coordinates. The microcomputer that controlled the telescope tracking took a fraction of a second to compute the relative positions, then swung the system quickly to its new target. The Taurus-Littrow Range was at the center of the field of view. For the thousandth time, Len peered at the image, seeking in his own inner vision the tiny speck of the Lunar Rover from Apollo 17. The last trip out . . .

A sudden razor's edge of pain from his stomach made him gasp, then reach for an antacid pill. They were scattered all over the apartment, never more than a couple of paces away. The ulcer was under control, no worse than it had been a year ago—but no better.

Reluctantly, Len turned from the telescope and sat down to word the next letter.

"Congressman Willis? I think you ought to see this for yourself."

The aide had been waiting patiently outside the Committee Hearings. He passed a sheet of plain white paper across to the Congressman.

"Another one! This is intolerable." Congressman Willis was a big man, close to three hundred pounds, but the suit did a good deal to hide the swelling belly and thick neck. "What's in this one?"

"The same sort of thing—you'll be hearing more in the future, but you ought to look closely at your voting record."

"Hmph. Didn't do a bit of good last time, giving this to the FBI. Let me take a closer look."

"Congressman"—the aide was greatly daring—"Do you think this is genuine? This is the third one, and nothing has happened."

"And nothing will happen!" Willis stuffed the paper into his pocket and patted the young aide with a thick hand. "You go on back to the office, Ron. Don't worry about it, and I'll take care of the whole thing."

"Yes, sir." The aide's face cleared and he hurried off along the corridor, back to the Rayburn Building office. Behind him, Willis put one hand out to steady himself against the corridor wall. A thin line of sweat had appeared up where his forehead met his thinning hair. Another one! The threat was vague, but it was there. And it was not the usual hint of financial pressure, of blackmail for past activities, of defamation. It would be physical violence, broken bones, torn flesh . . .

Congressman Willis had a vivid imagination. He could turn this one over to the FBI and have them again fail to find anything. Fail to protect him, too, when the trouble (the gun, the knife?) came to him. Or else he could take the phone call when it came, vote as he was directed to vote. That was a cheap price for freedom from the terrible fears that had been with him since the first letter. Damn the Free Trade Zone controls—first things first.

He leaned against the wall, white suit blotched with perspiration, and waited for the end of the Hearing Recess.

Len had made the decision personally. Now everything was falling apart, and there was no doubt who would get the blame. Already, Sal had called in and was telling him that the heat was on, that he had better have something worked out.

"I'll do what I can, Sal, but I need more *facts*. What made Mesurier renege on the deal?"

Meyer's voice was quavery over the line, and his video image showed him looking older than ever. He was being eaten away inside, the drugs doing no more than slowing the spread. "He's greedy, Lips. Pure greed."

"How much does he want?"

"I don't know. We promised him a hundred million."

"Right. Damn it, I picked the Cook Islands for the launch and free trade site because it's nicely out of the way, and because the price was less than half we'd have had to pay to Papa Haynes in Liberia. Who's Mesurier's number two man?"

"Bartola." Meyer had caught Len's expression. "He'd maybe be easier to work with, but he's an unknown quantity. You thinking of putting out a contract on Mesurier?"

"No." Len was silent for a few moments. "Make that maybe. I'm not going to let a tin-pot dictator stop us when everything else is going well."

"So what are we going to do?"

Strange how their roles had reversed. Sal Meyer had become the dependent one, looking to Len for guidance . . .

"I think the threat should be more than enough. He'll get the choice, a hundred million for Mesurier, tax-free in a Swiss bank; or a dead Mesurier, and a deal with his second-in-command. He's no fool. The decision shouldn't be too difficult." Len glanced down at his desk. "Not like that damned Senator

Macintosh. I can't see any way round him, and he's too brave to scare and too honest to buy. We need some angle on him.''

"Stick at it, Lips.'' Meyer sounded a lot better now that the decision on Mesurier had been made. ''I'll get the message back out to the Cook Islands. Rocky Courtelle's the right man to deliver it, he looks as though he'd kill his mother for a good cigar. What's the launch date going to be?''

"Two months from now. We've got the boosters for the upper stage, and we'll be taking the first work crew out there on the second mission. I'll be ready to brief the Council in two weeks, but I can already tell you that a lot of the usual production problems will disappear when we've got the Lungfish Station running smoothly. Then I want to hit them with the next step.''

"Next step! I thought we were in business with *Lungfish*.''

"You'll be all right, Sal. We'll have you up there as soon as there's a medical facility running. But I mean the next *big* step. I want Council approval for a Lunar Base.''

"On the Moon! What the hell are you talking about, Lips. You'll never sell them on that.''

"Want a little bet on it, Sal? A hundred thousand, and I'll give you five to one odds.''

"But why, for God's sake? We've got all the production capacity we'll need on Lungfish Station for twenty years.''

"Capacity, but not *total* security. We'll have that when we have a Lunar Base, once we dig in there we'll be out of reach of anybody. We can set up a bigger facility and we'll be able to get the Arabs into the Casino. They say that the Lungfish Station is bad, it's where Mohammad's coffin is supposed to be—but they don't mind the Moon at all. How'd you like to get your hands on a few of those four hundred billion a year petrodollars? We'll make the fanciest Casino in the universe.''

"You think you'll get Arabs to go all the way to the Moon to *gamble*, when they could be doing it at home? Lips, I hate to say this, but you sound all screwed up.''

Len grinned. ''Wait and see, old man. Wait and see. They'll go. Don't you understand, the Moon isn't part of the Moslem earthly universe—it's a place where all the rules can be broken without offending the religion. As far as they're concerned, it'll be *janat*, the garden of paradise. All the vices and none of them forbidden.''

''On the goddammed *Moon?*''

''Why not? You've never been to the Empty Quarter in southern Arabia. After that desert you'd find the lunar surface a pleasant change. Here, before you cut out let me show you my first design. The more you know about this, the easier it'll be to come in hard on my side with the Council.''

Twenty minutes of coaxing, explaining, and summarizing didn't convince Sal Meyer. The financial analysis did that, as soon as Meyer looked over the basic budget and projected returns.

He shook his head as he finally cut the connection. ''Damned persuasive, Lips. And you know what? It's not even an illegal operation.''

''Never mind, Sal. You can't have everything. Who's going to tax us for money we make on the Moon? We don't *have* to be illegal to avoid the tax bite up there.''

Like the Arabs, Sal Meyer had the sudden look of one to whom Paradise has become just a Shuttle ride away.

Len Martello was mortal. Like any mortal he couldn't cover *all* the bases. Development operations had been spread over a hundred separate corporations in thirty countries. Each company had become the instrument that cleared some roadblock standing in the way of *Lungfish's* conversion to production and use. But there were connections between corporations, and that network—given enough time and patience—could be traced. On the day that Sal Meyer made a minimal acceleration ascent to the *Lungfish* medical facility (five thousand dollars a day; Meyer might feel the pinch if he had to stay there more than fifty years) late that same afternoon Len Martello felt the first thread of the noose.

''Len.'' The call was voice only, Garry Scanlon from Washington. ''I can't talk long now but you've got problems.''

''You bet I've got problems.'' Len was lying back in a reclining chair, moodily reviewing the proposed changes to the

Lunar Agreement. "Do you know of a new one? Construction on the Lunar Base looks like being a barrel of snakes."

"Listen. I've been subpoenaed to appear before a Special Commission on organized crime. They sent a set of interrogatories with the notice. They're going to ask me a whole set of questions about you, what your background is, what you've been doing for the past twelve years, how much money you have—everything."

Len jerked upright. "Who's behind it?"

"Senator Macintosh. Remember, I told you once before I'd had his staff aides around to my offices in NASA, wanting to know how well I knew you."

"Damn. I knew in my bones that it was a mistake asking you to go on that check-out trip to the Cook Islands. I was in a box for somebody who really knew his launch procedures, but we should have kept you out of it."

"Len." Scanlon's voice was strained. "I'll protect you if I can. But I have to say this, I won't lie to the Commission. You've only hinted at some of the things you've been doing but I'll have to talk about them if I'm asked."

"That's all right." While Len had become more and more the loner, he knew that Garry had been steadily merging into the Establishment. Over the years there were less protests about the crippling lethargy in Government, more in his casual conversations about the responsibilities of the job of Associate Administrator. "You tell them what you have to. We'll talk when you're free to do it."

Len Martello returned to his work with a cold and furious energy. Macintosh, the old incorruptible. He had always been there on the horizon, a presence that Len couldn't convert or distract with other business. Could he be any more than a nuisance at this stage of the work?

Len reviewed the steps that stood between him and an operating and permanent Moon Base. Thirty of them depended on people and functions based in the United States. Over the next sixty days, one by one, he substituted activities that could be handled by foreign interests.

On the sixty-fourth day, Len's own call to Washington was

delivered by an armed marshal. With it came a lengthy set of written questions.

"But despite all that, Mr. Martello, I believe that I can see a pattern."

The kid gloves and the gentle touch were still in operation. Howard Macintosh, Democrat of Oregon, had handled thousands of witnesses, friendly ones and hostile ones. If he thought that Len was going to refuse to cooperate, that didn't show in his manner.

Len cleared his throat. "The only pattern I can see, Senator, is one of simple industrial development of our only remaining frontier. I have tried to promote our interests in space, that is all."

"And that you have done, remarkably well." Macintosh was short and thin, in his mid-sixties. Len had noticed a strange resemblance to Sal Meyer. They could pass for brothers, both from appearance and style of speech.

"But it raises a question of what you mean by *our* interests," went on the Senator. "Would you agree that the road to space has become strangely clear of roadblocks in the past few years?"

"You might think that way. I believe those 'roadblocks' were just that, impediments to progress. No one should mourn their disappearance."

Len noticed that Garry Scanlon had slipped into the back of the room as he was speaking.

"That is an opinion you are entitled to hold," said Macintosh. "Yet I find that there is, as I said, a pattern. Things went just the way that your group needed. Now we have a private corporation—"

"I don't know of any such corporation, Senator."

"—a corporation, I say, a *single* corporation, no matter how much its integrated nature may be disguised. This entity now occupies the Lungfish Station, and has a permanent base on the Moon. It has passed beyond the control of any national Earth government, passed beyond even the power of the United Nations. I myself have had pressure from this group, attempts to subvert my opinions and my vote.''

He paused. Since these were not public hearings, Macintosh was not indulging in any histrionics or impassioned oratory. He was a single-minded man with a basic objective. Len was suddenly glad that the Base was doing so well.

''I did not hear a question, Senator,'' he said at last, when Macintosh showed no sign of continuing.

''I am coming to it. Mr. Martello, I strongly believe that this *entity*, this powerful corporation which now has more activity in space than any country of the earth, is controlled by and the tool of organized crime.''

He leaned forward, his manner intent. ''I also believe that you, personally, know a great deal about the workings of this organization.'' With an instinctive flourish, he picked up a document from the long table and held it out towards Len. ''If you will cooperate with us—help us to the limit of your knowledge—then I have already arranged that you will be given immunity for any crimes you have personally committed. This document, which you are free to examine, gives that guarantee from the Justice Department.''

He handed it across the table. The room had gone completely silent. Len took the paper with trembling hands, surprised by his own tension, and looked at the Presidential Seal upon it. He read it through carefully.

''And if I do not act as you suggest?'' he said at last.

''We will terminate our questions for today. You may return to your home.'' Macintosh paused. ''For a time,'' he said softly. ''But Mr. Martello, that will not be the end of the story. I will continue to pursue this matter, as long as I have strength to do it. And you will not have immunity.''

''A man who has done nothing wrong does not need immunity.''

''How true.'' Macintosh shook his head. ''But how many of us have done nothing wrong? Will you give me your answer, Mr. Martello?''

''I will give it to you, Senator.'' Len cleared his throat, then sat with head bowed for many seconds. When he at last looked up his face was white. "I decline your offer of immunity. If you have no more questions, I request that I be allowed to leave these Hearings."

The hubbub in the room took a long time to die down. As Len was leaving he caught Garry's eye—an incredulous, troubled eye. Behind him, he could hear the mutter of voices at the table as Senator Macintosh huddled with his aides.

After that last meeting of looks in the Congressional Hearing, Len had seen and heard nothing from Garry for almost four months. His phone calls had not been returned, two letters had gone unanswered. That Garry should arrive, uninvited, at the penthouse apartment that Fall evening was doubly surprising. Even as a youth, Garry had made all his appointments in advance.

"Alone?" Garry looked round and snaked into the apartment almost before the door was open fully.

"God help us!" Len was laughing. "Who's after you, Aunt Wilma?"

"No joking." Garry went over to the window and looked out nervously. "I took an Eastern Shuttle flight to get here—paid cash. Have to be back before anybody knows I've left."

"You can come away from the window—we're thirty floors up. No one's going to be looking in. Garry, what the hell's going on?"

They sat facing each other, Garry with his overcoat still buttoned.

"You're in bad trouble, Len. A week from now, you'll be in jail. Macintosh has enough to put you in for tax evasion—I talked to one of his aides, and he told me a lot more than he ought."

He was short of breath and his words came out in wheezing bursts.

"It's not too late, I know that. If you come back to Washington with me, agree to cooperate—you'll still get immunity. Will you do it, Len?"

His expression was pleading. Len shook his head slowly.

"I *can't* do it, Garry. You don't understand the situation. They'd give me immunity so they could get at the top guys in the operations, right? But I've not been level with you. For the past two years, *I've been the top man*. Think they'd give *me* immunity? Anybody else in the Council, maybe. Me? Never."

Garry's plump face flushed and his mouth gaped open. "You're the top of the whole thing? That was why you walked out of Macintosh's hearings!"

"Not the only reason. Here, you need this." He passed across a tumbler of scotch and soda. "I had an even better reason—not just my own skin. Look, Garry, how's the NASA program doing now? Budget and projects."

"You've read the papers. Since you got *Lungfish* and the Lunar Base operating, we've started a big joint program with ESA and the Russians. I can't quote you all the details yet, but I'm sure my area—Tracking and Data Analysis—will double."

"And the year after that I'll bet it will double again—as soon as Congress finds that our group is going to build a Farside Base and start lunar mining. They'll be so keen to stop us that money won't count." Len lifted his own glass. "Let's drink to crime. Don't you see, people only seem willing to pour money into something when they act out of fear—that's why Defense can get fifty times the budget of the peaceful programs. Well, now everybody has somebody they can mistrust: me."

The light was dawning in Garry's eye. He took a huge gulp of scotch, choked on it, and spluttered, "But that won't do *you* any good, Len. You'll be rotting in jail."

Len Martello stood up and walked over to the telescope setting. He switched on the control for the big refractor and opened the opaque cover on the penthouse roof.

"I'll rot in jail—but they'll have to catch me first. Garry, it's bad news but I've been expecting it for a long time. Look at this, tell me what you see."

"Mm. Serenitatis? Let me get the focus right." Garry bent over the eypiece for a long second. "Yeah. That's Taurus-Littrow there. Long time since I looked at that."

The familiar sight somehow had calmed his excitement. He grinned up at Len, then bent again to look at the lunar image. ''You've put your base there, right? No chance of seeing it with this, though.''

''Not yet. Just wait a few years. We began with the Casino, now we're into low-pressure agriculture, power generation, medical plants. It's beginning to grow. But I'm not just telling you that to show off, you know. How long do you think it will be before there's a U.N. team sent up to try and close down that operation?''

''Couple of years, not much more. You know that they relaxed the ban on nuclear rockets, just in the hopes that we'd come up with something that would make sure you were under control?''

Len operated the switch to close the covers on the telescope. ''Think you'll be on that close-out team?''

''Well . . .'' Garry shrugged. ''I'm a pretty high muck-a-muck these days. If it's an official inspection team, chances are pretty good that I can work my way onto it.'' He grinned. ''You can be sure I'll try like hell to go, but so will a lot of others.''

''Know what they'll find there?'' Len went back to his seat. ''It's a one hundred percent legitimate business venture—no sign of crime. The only reason we needed the crime in the first place was for muscle—to get some of those damn-fool regulations pushed out of the way, and to give the financial base.''

''But it's too late for you, Len.'' Garry's expression was serious again. ''It may be clean now, but it wasn't clean when you started. I know that. We'll be up there, and you'll be in some damned jail down here.''

Len Martello leaned back in his chair. He looked tired, ten years older than his forty years, but his eyes were still bright. ''I deserve to go to jail, Garry. I can't deny it.'' He raised his hand to still the other's protest. ''Sure, I went into the game with good intentions. But I found out one thing very quickly. You can't work up to your elbows in dirt and expect your hands to stay clean. Not just the tax evasion. I had to get into the drug sales, and the enforcement, and the strong-arm tactics. I wouldn't have lasted a month otherwise. But good ends don't justify means.''

He shrugged his thin shoulders, watching the shock spread across Garry Scanlon's face. "I deserve to go to jail, there's no argument on that.''

"Maybe.'' Garry's face was a mixture of emotions. "Maybe you do. I won't judge that. But I know this, Len, if anybody ought to go on the lunar trip, it's not me—it's you.'' His voice was earnest. "You touched dirt, sure you did. Lots of people back in Washington will be happy to crucify you for it. But I just want to say that I'm sorry about it all. If I could give you my place on a trip up to the Lunar Base, I'd do it—gladly.''

"Thanks, Garry.'' Len's voice was so soft that he was only just audible. "I know how much that means to you. Don't think I don't appreciate it, and the fact that you came here to warn me the way you did.

"But you know''—he grinned, and suddenly there was a trace of the youth of twenty years earlier in his smile—"you don't need to give up anything for me. They'll come and get me in a week, right? Know where I'll be then?'' He jerked a thumb upward, toward the unseen orb of the Moon. "If they want me, they'll have to come and get me. I'm betting that I can keep a move ahead of the posse, all the way out. We'll have full mobility over the lunar surface in another four years. You'll have to develop that if you want to catch me. How long will that take?''

He raised his glass. "Come on, drink up and we'll get you out of here before you miss that last shuttle. Know what I feel like? In the old days they'd hang a carrot out in front of a donkey to keep it moving along. That's me. As long as I'm out there, you don't need to worry about the health of the space program— they'll have to keep going and catch me.''

"You're right.'' Garry smiled and picked up his glass. "National pride would never be satisfied to leave you out there. We'll be chasing you.''

"A toast then.'' Len shrugged. "It's not the one we've always wanted, I know, but there's still time for that. It's a few years yet to 1999. I'm betting we'll still drink that one—and we'll drink it where we've always wanted to. For now, let's just drink to the Space Program.''

"No." Hesitantly at first, then with increasing resolve, Garry raised his own glass. "This time, *I'm* going to propose the toast. The Space Program is fine, but I'll give you something better. Here's to the carrot—and long may it hang out there.''

AFTERWORD: THE MAN WHO STOLE THE MOON.

You might think that a writer knows exactly what is in his or her head when a story goes down on paper. I used to think so, but now I'm far less sure of it. Consider this example.

Robert Heinlein's classic ''The Man Who Sold The Moon'' was obviously much in mind when I wrote this story. No surprise there. I had even gone back and re-read the original just before I began, but so far as I knew I had not played any word games within the story beyond the twist on the title itself.

This story was published. A few months later a reader wrote to tell me that he got a kick out of the way that I had secretly inserted a non-hero figure who was a variation of Heinlein's main character. At that point in his letter I had no idea what he was talking about. I read on.

Look at Henry B. Delso, he said. ''Delso'' was a very simple anagram of ''Delos'', and Harry is an informal version of the name Henry. The man Henry B. Delso was therefore none other than Heinlein's Del(os) D. Harri(man).

I wanted to write back to him and say, no, not at all, I didn't do what you think I did. I never wrote the letter. You see, after I thought for a while longer I realized that I had done it. I didn't know I'd done it, but that's a different matter entirely.

Some readers may feel that this story is a piece of preaching about the bureaucratic stifling of initiative in our society, and they may assert that I was trying to sugar a warning by wrapping it in fictional form. Some readers would be quite right.

THE DEIMOS PLAGUE

On the highland heights above Chryse City, where the thin, dust-filled winds endlessly scour the salmon-pink vault of the Martian sky, a simple monument faces the setting sun. Forged of plasteel, graven by diamond, it will endure the long change of the Mars seasons, until Man and his kind have become one with the swirling sands. The message it bears is short but poignant, a silent tribute to two great figures of the colonization: IN MEMORIAM, PENELOPE AND POMANDER: MUTE SAVIORS OF OUR WORLD.

Fate is fickle. Although I don't really mind one way or the other, I should be on that monument too. If it hadn't been for me, Penelope and Pomander would never have made it, and the Mars colony might have been wiped out.

My involvement really began back on Earth. A large and powerful group of people thought that I had crossed them in a business deal. They had put in two million credits and come out with nothing, and they wanted the hide of Henry Carver, full or empty. I had to get away—far, and fast.

My run for cover had started in Washington, D.C., after I had been pumped dry of information by a Senate committee investigating my business colleagues. When the questioning was over—despite my pleas for asylum (political, religious, or lunatic; I'd have settled for any)—they turned me out onto the street. With only a handful of credits in my pocket, afraid to go back to my office or apartment, I decided that I had to get to Vandenberg Spaceport, on the West Coast. From there, I hoped, I could somehow catch a ride out.

First priority: I had to change my appearance. My face isn't exactly famous, but it was well known enough to be a real danger. Showing more speed than foresight, I walked straight from the committee hearings into a barbershop. It was the slack time of day, in the middle of the afternoon, and I was pleased to see that I was the only customer. I sat down in the chair farthest from the door, and a short, powerfully built barber with a one-inch forehead eventually put down his racing paper and wandered over to me.

"How'd you like it?" he asked, tucking me in.

I hadn't got that far in my thinking. What would change my appearance to most effect? It didn't seem reasonable to leave it to him and simply ask for a new face.

"All off," I said at last. "All the hair. And the moustache as well," I added as an afterthought.

There was a brief, stunned silence that I felt I had to respond to.

"I'm taking my vows tomorrow. I have to get ready for that."

Now why in hell had I said something so stupid? If I wasn't careful, I'd find myself obliged to describe details of my hypothetical sect. Fortunately, my request had taken the wind out of his sails, at least for the moment. He looked at me in perplexity, shrugged, then picked up the shears and dug in.

Five minutes later, he silently handed me the mirror. From his expression, a shock was on the way—already I was regretting my snap decision. I had a faint hope that I would look stern and strong, like a holovision star playing the part of Genghis Khan. The sort of man that women would be swept off their feet by, and other men would fear and respect. The face that stared back at me from the mirror didn't quite produce that effect. I had never realized before what dark and bushy eyebrows I have. Take those away and the result was like a startled and slightly constipated bullfrog. Even the barber seemed shaken, without the urge to chat that defines the breed.

He recovered his natural sass as he helped me into my coat. "Thank you, sir," he said as I paid and tipped him. "I hope everything works out all right at the convent tomorrow."

I looked at the muscles bulging from his shortsleeved shirt, the thick neck, the wrestling cups lined up along the shelf. His two buddies were cackling away at the other side of the shop.

"I hope you realize that only a real coward would choose to insult a man whom he knows to be bound by vows of nonviolence," I replied.

It took him a few seconds to work it out. Then his eyes popped, and I walked out of the shop with a small sense of victory.

That didn't last very long. I had changed my appearance all right, but for something much too conspicuous. I still had to get to California, and I still had almost no money. As I walked along M Street, turning my face to the side to avoid inspection by passers-by, the shop windows reflected a possible answer. My subconscious had been working well for me in the barber's shop. On a long journey, in a crowded vehicle, where could I usually find an empty seat? Next to a priest—especially one from a more exotic faith. People are afraid they will be trapped into conversion or contribution. The Priests of Asfan, a shaven-headed, mendicant sect who have no possessions and support themselves by begging, were not a large group. Their total number increased to one in the few minutes that it took me to go into a shop and buy a gray shirt, trousers, and smock. Then off I shuffled to the terminal, practicing a pious and downcast look.

Being a beggar-priest isn't too bad. Nobody expects you to pay for anything, and you receive quite amazing confessions and requests for advice and guidance from the people who choose to sit next to you. In some ways I was sorry to reach Vandenberg—for one thing, that was where my pursuers might be looking for me. It wouldn't be unlike them to keep a lookout there, ready to take their pound of flesh.

The brawl and chaos of the big spaceport was reassuring. In that mess of people and machinery it would be difficult for two people to find each other, even if they were both looking hard. I went to the central displays, where the departure dates and destinations of the outgoing ships were listed. The Moon was rather too close for complete security, and the Libration Colonies were just as bad. Mars was what I wanted, but the Earth-

Mars orbit positions were very unfavorable and I could see only one ship scheduled: the *Deimos Dancer*, a privately owned cargo ship with a four-man crew. She was sitting in a hundred-minute parking orbit, ready for departure in two days' time. It was a surprise to see a cargo vessel making the passage when the configuration was so bad—it meant a big waste in fuel, and suggested a valuable cargo for which transport costs were no object.

I watched the displays for a while, then picked my man with care from the usual mob you find any day of the week hanging around the shipping boards. Any big port seems to draw the riffraff of the solar system. After ten years of legal practice, I could spot the pickpockets, con men, ticket touts, pimps, pushers, hookers, bagmen, and lollygaggers without even try-ing. I'd defended more than enough of them in court, back on the East Coast.

The man I chose was little and thin, agile, bright-eyed and big-nosed. A nimmer if ever I saw one. I watched him for a few minutes; then I put my hand on his shoulder at the crucial moment—ten seconds after he had delicately separated a ticket wallet from the pocket of a fat passenger and eeled away into the crowd. He shuddered at my grasp. We came to an agreement in less than two minutes, and he disappeared again while I sat at the entrance to the departure area, watching the bustle, keeping a wary eye open for possible danger from my former colleagues, and holding hostage the wallet and ID tags of my new ally.

He came back at last, shaking his head. "That's absolutely the only one going out to Mars for the next thirty days. The *Deimos Dancer* has a bad reputation. She belongs to Bart Poindexter, and he's a tough man to ship with. The word is out around Vandenberg that this will be a special trip—double pay for danger money, and a light cargo. She'd normally take forty days on the Mars run, and the schedules show her getting there in twenty-three." He looked longingly at his wallet and ID. "Bart Poindexter has his crew together for the trip—he's picked the toughest bunch you'll find at Vandenberg. Just how bad do you need a quick trip out?"

Double pay for danger money. Thirty days before there would

be another one. What a choice. "I thought you said he's got his crew already," I replied.

"He has, but he wants an extra man to look after the cargo. No pay, but a free trip—so far he's had no takers. If you have no ticket, and no money to buy one, that might be your best chance. 'Course, there's always ways of getting a ticket." He smiled. "If you know how, I mean. I can see that might not sit easy with you, being religious and all."

Decisiveness is not one of my strong points. I might have been sitting there still, vacillating, but at that moment I fancied I caught sight of a familiar and unwelcome scarred face at the other side of the departure area . . .

I signed on without seeing the ship, the captain, the crew, or the cargo. A quick look at any one of them might have been enough to change my mind. My first glimpse of the *Deimos Dancer* came four hours later, as we floated up to rendezvous with her in parking orbit. She was a Class C freighter, heavy, squat, and blackclad, like an old-fashioned Mexican widow. Someone's botched attempt to add a touch of color by painting the drive nacelles a bright pink hadn't improved matters. She seemed to leer across at us in drunken gaiety as we docked and floated across to the lock. Her inside was no better—ratty fittings and dilapidated quarters—and her spaceworthiness certificate, displayed inside the lock, was a fine tribute to the power of the kickback. This clanging wreck was supposed to take five of us, plus cargo, out to Mars in twenty-three days.

The second blow was Bart Poindexter. Considered as a class, the captains of space freighters are not noted for their wit, charm, and erudition. Poindexter, big and black-bearded, with a pair of fierce blue eyes glaring out of the jungle of hair, did nothing to change the group image. He looked at my shaven head, paler than usual because of spacesickness, and hooted with laughter.

"Here, Dusty, come and see what the tug's brought us this time!" he shouted along the corridor leading aft. Then, to me: "I asked them to sign me somebody to handle the cargo, not to sprinkle holy water. What in hell's name is a priest doing on the Mars run?"

What indeed? I muttered something vague about expanding my karma. It would have helped a lot to have known a bit more about religion—any religion. Poindexter was scratching at his tangled mop and pointing down the corridor. "If you're the best they could find, then God help the breeding program on Mars, that's all I can say. Get along down there, Carver, and see Dusty Jackman. He's my number two on the trip, and he'll show you your place with the cargo."

Martian breeding program? There were limits to what I'd do for a free trip. Uneasy in mind and stomach, I floated off along the twenty-meter corridor that led to the rear of the ship. Jackman was there, about half a meter shorter than Poindexter but more than a match in mass. He had the fine lavender complexion that comes only from regular exposure to hard vacuum and harder liquor, and his rosy face was framed by a sunflower of spiky yellow hair. He seemed to exude a nimbus of alcoholic fumes and unwash, in roughly equal parts. I wondered about his nickname.

Two crewmen down, and two to go. I won't even attempt a description of Nielsen and Ramada. Suffice to say that those two crewmen made Jackman and Poindexter seem like Beau Nash and Beau Brummell. After I'd run the gauntlet of greasy introductions, Jackman took me all the way aft to the cargo area and pointed out a waist-high entrance door.

"There's where you'll be bunking, in with the cargo. There won't be much happening around here until it's time to eat, so you might as well settle in and get comfortable." He turned to leave, then turned back, scratching his head. "Anything that you can't eat, by the way?"

"Can't eat?" I looked at him blankly.

"You know, because of your religion. Can you eat any meats?"

I nodded, and it was his turn to look puzzled. "Funny, I'd have thought you wouldn't," he said. "Seeing what your special job is." Without another word, he pushed himself off along the corridor leading forward to the bridge.

Special job? Pondering that, I crawled in through the low door. After the crew area, the air inside here seemed sweeter. I sniffed appreciatively and looked around me for the light switch. Then I ducked as a vast pink shape swooped toward me through the gloom. My shout of alarm was answered by two high-pitched screams, like a steam whistle—two-toned—and a second pink zeppelin shot past me from the other direction. I hurled myself backward through the door and slammed it closed.

Nielsen was floating just outside, thoughtfully scratching his grizzled head with one hand and picking his nose with the other. I grabbed hold of his grimy shirt.

"What's going on in there? Something almost got me as soon as I was inside!"

He nodded dreamily, and fought his usual losing battle with the English language. "Them, just playful. Like free fall, you know. Soon, them get used you, there no problem; you get used them, there no problem."

"Them?" Shades of four-meter ants, rampaging through the cargo hold.

"Cargo. You special priest, no? You special for care this. Man sign you up, say you know all about. Come in."

He opened the low door again and crawled through. Somewhat reluctantly, I followed. As my eyes became accustomed to the poor light, I saw that he was standing by—and patting affectionately—two colossal pigs. They must have weighed a hundred and fifty kilos each, and they were floating peacefully in the center of the big cargo hold.

"This Penelope." He stroked a monstrous sow, who nuzzled his ear happily. "This Pomander." The boar, a few kilos lighter, grunted when he heard his name. Nielsen patted him. "Smart pigs. New breeding stock for Mars protein program. Prize cargo. You have job here, look after. Now, you get to know each other."

A shock, an undeniable shock. On the other hand, as I got to know them they became a welcome alternative to the four crew members. For one thing, they were cleaner in habits. I still had trouble with the logic of it, though. I knew that pigs can handle space travel well—they are about the only animals that do. Cows, sheep, and horses can't take it at all, can't swallow in free fall, and there had been a certain reluctance to ship goats because of other reasons. But why would anyone choose to ship the pigs in the high season, when orbital positions were bad? And why was it a danger-money trip? The crew seemed neither to know nor care.

The next day I had something else to worry about. Four crew members and me, that was supposed to be the full roster. At dinner, though (Ramada's burnt offerings—the pigs dined better!), a sixth man appeared, just before we got ready to pump ion for Mars. Poindexter introduced him as Vladic, a supernumerary and last-minute addition to the roster. From the first, he seemed to show altogether too much interest in me. He seemed to spend most of his time snooping aft, keeping an eye on my every move. When he saw me looking at him, he would hurry away forward—then be back in a few minutes, watching again.

Would they send a rub-out man this far after me? I knew that they never let an old score fade away without being settled. That night I locked the door, wedged it, put a mockup in my bunk, and settled myself down to sleep between the comforting bulwarks of Penelope and Pomander.

I didn't call them that. That's how history knows them, but I thought they were silly names. In my mind, Penelope became the Empress of Blandings. Pomander, after I had seen him at work in his free-fall food trough, was renamed Waldo, in honor of my business partner.

A variety of other names were rejected, some reluctantly. Rosencrantz and Guildenstern, Dido and Aeneas, Fortnum and Mason, Post and Propter (post hog, ergo propter hog), War and Peace, Siegfried and Brünnhilde (not fat enough—the pigs, I mean), Pride and Prejudice—it helped to pass the time.

As the days passed, I realized the pigs were interestingly different in temperament and personality. The Empress demanded her swill well cooked, whereas Waldo turned up his patrician nose at anything that was not *al dente*. They both greeted me with grunts of joy when I came back to the cargo hold after dinner. It was a relief to me too, after seeing the table manners of the crew. If it hadn't been for that damned Vladic, snooping around me all the time, I would have been able to settle into the journey and even enjoy it. But it's not pleasant living under constant surveillance, and I got very edgy.

My fears took on a new dimension when Captain Poindexter called me forward to the bridge and told me Vladic wanted to see me, alone, in his cabin.

I protested, but I could feel the old chill inside my stomach. "Captain, I don't take orders from Vladic. Why should I go?"

"You take orders from me. I take orders on this trip, from Vladic. He's paying for it, the whole thing. Now he says he's sick and can't come out here, so you have to go to him. Move it, and get over to his cabin."

He turned his back to show that the discussion was over. Very puzzled, though a good deal relieved, I went down the corridor to Vladic's quarters. If he was paying for this trip, presumably he wasn't after my scalp. At the door, I hesitated. For some reason, the back of my neck was prickling and visions of death were pinballing around my brain. I opened the door, and knew why. For a peaceful and a cowardly man, I've somehow been exposed to death an awful lot. Enough to recognize the smell of it from a distance. Inside the cabin, lying on his bunk, was Vladic, red-faced and gasping. His neck was swollen and his dark eyes were sunk into pits, far back into his head. He motioned me to his side.

Needless to say, I entered reluctantly. Whatever he had, I didn't want it. He gripped my arm with a burning hand and pulled me closer. I leaned forward—as little as possible—to hear his words.

"Gavver. Afta garga pigs." I leaned closer. His eyes were full of desperate meaning. "Gur ums om pigs. Atta ayve pigs."

It was no good. His lips just couldn't form the words. I patted him comfortingly on his arm, said, "Take it easy, now, I'll get help," and hurried back to Poindexter on the bridge.

"Captain, Vladic isn't sick—he's dying. Get the medical kit and go to him."

Poindexter looked at me skeptically. "Dying? He can't be. He was just fine last night." He hesitated, then shrugged. "All right, Carver, I'll take a look—but I'm warning you, this had better not be a joke."

He grabbed the medical kit—no robodoc on the old *Deimos Dancer*—and we hurried back to Vladic's cabin. He was now motionless on the bunk, eyes closed, face and neck congested and purple. Poindexter grunted in surprise, then crossed to Vladic, felt his pulse, and pinched the skin on the forearm. He opened the shirt and put his ear to Vladic's inflamed chest. One thing about Poindexter, he didn't lack for courage. That, I should explain, is not a compliment. In my opinion, the thing that separates man from the animals is the ability to predict, imagine, and stay away from danger.

"He's a goner," said Poindexter at last. "What did he say to you before he died?"

"He said . . ." I paused. Urgle-gurgle pigs, urgle-gurgle pigs. I couldn't repeat that. "He didn't say anything."

Poindexter swore. "He commissioned the Deimos Dancer for special assignment, on behalf of the Mars government. I know that much, but I have to know more. Jackman and Ramada said this morning that they both felt sick. It looks bad. I never heard of a disease that kills so quickly. Here, hold this."

He passed me the medical kit, opened Vladic's locker, and rummaged through it. He emerged shortly with a bulky wallet. After riffling through it, he pulled out two sheets of paper and a passport, then returned the wallet, with a look of studied absent-mindedness, to the pocket of his own jumpsuit.

"The rest is just money and credit cards," he explained. "But let's see if these tell us anything useful."

The first sheet was simple enough. An official government document, it gave Vladic, citizen of Mars, authority to call on Mars credit in traveling to Earth, performing biological work there, and commissioning a spacecraft for the return to Mars. The second sheet was handwritten in a hasty scrawl, and it was much more disturbing.

Homer—the last colonist in Willis City died this morning. It looks as though we can't stop it. Suko and I are sick now, and the pattern says we can't last more than a couple of days. We are going to put this in a mail rocket, then incinerate the whole of Willis City before we get too weak.

You *have* to get blood samples you took back to Earth and do the work to organize a vaccination program. You were only in here for a few minutes, so I don't think you will have caught it yourself. Remember, keep quiet about what you are doing, or we'll have mad panic in all the colonies here. We *still don't know* how the disease is transmitted, but so far it's been one hundred percent infection. Incubation period averages fifteen days, first symptoms to final collapse less than six.

Godspeed, Homer, and good luck. The colony depends on you.

The note was dated sixteen days before. The passport showed that Homer Vladic had caught a super-speed transport from Mars the following day and had reached Earth nine days after that. He had been a man in a real hurry.

As we read, I had inched slowly farther away from Vladic's body and from Poindexter. He rubbed the back of his head, gave it a good scratch, then turned to me thoughtfully. "It looks bad, Carver. Now I see why Vladic insisted on paying us danger money and wouldn't say why. Jackman and Ramada are sick, no doubt about it. Nielsen and I aren't feeling so good either. You got anything wrong with you?"

It was hard to say. The skin on my bald head was goose-pimpled with fear and foreboding and my stomach was rumbling like Vesuvius preparing for a major eruption. Those were just the familiar symptoms of blue panic. Apart from that, I felt fine. I shook my head.

"Nothing, eh?" Poindexter narrowed his eyes thoughtfully, increasing his resemblance to the Wild Man of Borneo. "Wonder what you've got that we haven't. I'm going to try to get a call through to Mars so we can find out more about what's been going on. It won't be easy. We're close to the Sun on a hyperbolic orbit; it's close to sunspot maximum, and the geometry is bad. I'm afraid we won't be able to get anything but static for another few days. I'll give it a try, and you take a look around this cabin and see if you can find any vials of vaccine."

He left, and as soon as he was out of sight I left also. Search the cabin? Not Henry Carver. I'd been in that disease-laden air far too long already. The Mars colonies didn't know how the disease was transmitted, and Vladic had *touched* me. He'd *breathed* on me. My flesh crawled, and I fled back to the comforting presence of Waldo and the Empress of Blandings. Later, Poindexter and Jackman went over Vladic's cabin and belongings with a fine-tooth comb, looking for vaccine, and didn't find anything. So my decision to leave made no difference to anything.

It's very easy for me to sit here now, safe and comfortable, and say, "Why, it's obvious what was happening. All the evidence was sitting there in front of me, spread out on a platter. All I had to do was put two and two together. How could anyone who prides himself on his intelligence possibly be so dense?"

Unfortunately, my brain refused to operate as logically and smoothly when I was rattling through space in a decrepit, noisy tin can, my bowels constricted with terror of the plague, one man dead from it already, the rest of us liable to go the same way any time, and with no company except for four drunken, filthy crewmen and a pair of giant pigs. In that situation, sphincter control alone merited the Golden Sunburst. No doubt about it, things were bad.

Within twelve hours, they looked even worse. Jackman and Ramada were feeling feverish. Nielsen couldn't hold down any food. Poindexter was complaining of a headache and blurred vision, and he hadn't been able to get through to Mars or to anyone else. We held an emergency meeting on the bridge.

"We have to assume the worst," said Poindexter. I was running well ahead of him on that. "Carver is the only man who doesn't seem to have caught it. Did you ever pilot a spaceship?"

That question, if it hadn't been packed with ominous implications, would have been screamingly funny. I couldn't navigate a bicycle without assistance. I shook my head.

"Then you'd better be ready to learn awful fast. If things go the way they are looking, you may be the only healthy person to dock us on Phobos Station. You should be all right. They design these ships so the orbit matching can be done by complete idiots."

Thank you, Captain Poindexter.

"Now, does anyone have any ideas?" he went on. "For instance, why is it Carver that's immune? We all eat the same food and we all saw about the same amount of Vladic. Is it prayer, chastity, clean living, meditation, or what?"

There was a long silence, which I at last broke—somewhat hesitantly. "Do you think it could be the pigs? I mean, me living in with the pigs." The others seemed blank and unreceptive. "I mean," I went on, "maybe there's something special about the pigs—their smell, or sweat, or manure, or something—that stops the disease. Maybe if we all lived there, the disease wouldn't be able to affect us. Maybe the disease is killed by pig manure . . ."

I trailed off. All right, so admittedly in retrospect my idea was complete nonsense. I still don't think it deserved the reception they gave it. Sick as they were all supposed to be feeling, they found the strength to break into hoots of derision.

"Move in with the pigs!" cried Jackman.

"Lie by pit shit, he says!" Nielsen echoed, guffawing like a jackass.

"Bottle up the smell of 'em and ship it forward!" roared Ramada.

"So, Mr. Carver," Poindexter said finally, with a fine show of sarcasm—as we all know, the lowest form of wit. "We should all move aft, is that it? We should share the cargo hold with you and the two porkers, should we? Lay us down among the swine, eh? What else do you suggest we ought to do? Mutter mumbo-jumbo, shave our heads, and all wear a hair shirt like you, I suppose. I should have known better than to ask—what sort of sense can you expect from a man with more hair aft than he has forrard?"

They collapsed again into laughter, but it was the last laughter for a long time. After a few more hours, it was quite clear that everyone on the *Deimos Dancer*, except for me, had the plague. The Empress of Blandings and Waldo were thriving too, but they were not much help as crew.

There is a horrifying bit in Coleridge's *Rime of the Ancient Mariner*, where all the sailors on the ship, except for the Mariner himself, one by one, drop dead. "With heavy thump, a lifeless lump, they dropped down one by one." I felt just like the Mariner as, one by one, Ramada, Jackman, Nielsen, and then finally Poindexter shuffled off this mortal coil. After five days of horror and useless medical attention, I found I was "alone, alone, all, all alone, alone on a wide, wide sea." The space between Earth and Mars was wider than Coleridge could ever have imagined. It doesn't say whether or not the Ancient Mariner had any pigs or other livestock for company, but I imagine he didn't.

The worst time began. I expected to be struck down by the plague at any moment. All I could think to do was follow my established routine with truly religious fervor—rise and shave my head, live in with the pigs, eat the same dreadful food, and hope that the combination would continue to protect me. For six more days we moved in a ghastly rushing silence between Earth and Mars while I waited for a death that never came.

Finally, I had to act.

Poindexter had given me a rudimentary knowledge of how and when the engines had to be fired to bring us close to Phobos Station. I never did manage to get the communications equipment working, so I was unable to send or receive messages for additional instructions. I strapped myself into the pilot's seat, sent a prayer off into the abyss, and began to play spaceman.

It would have helped a lot if I had thought to confine Waldo and the Empress to the cargo hold before I began maneuvers. They liked my company, and now that I was the only human on board, I let them follow me about. However, the accelerations and changes of direction excited them. They whizzed around the bridge, squealing and honking   ith pleasure, as I attempted the delicate combination of thrusts needed to bring us close to Phobos. The video camera, unbeknownst to me, was switched on, and I gather that the staff of Phobos Station watched goggle-eyed as the two pigs zipped in and out of view. When the thrust was off, and I was trying to determine the next piece of the operation, the Empress would hover just above my head, nuzzling my ear and grunting her approval of the new game.

Engines off at last, after the final boost. I collapsed. We

weren't perfect, but we were good enough. Phobos filled the sky
on the left side of the *Deimos Dancer*. I, Henry Carver, a lawyer
with no space experience to speak of, had successfully flown a
spaceship from inside the orbit of Mercury to a satellite of Mars.
That had to be a solar-system first, so I wasn't in the least
surprised when I saw a large crowd of welcoming figures at
Phobos Station as we were drawn in and landed by tractor beam.
As the three of us disembarked, I began to compose the few
modest words in which I would describe my feat.

The crowd's enthusiasm was tremendous. They surged
toward me, shouting and cheering. Then, ignoring me completely, they grabbed Waldo and the Empress and bore them
away in triumph, crying, "Penelope! Pomander! Penelope!
Pomander!"

The only person left to talk to me was a young, rude reporter
from the *Martian Chronicle*, followed by a whole warren of
health officials. I dismissed the reporter with a few unfriendly
words, but the health people attached themselves like leeches. I
had to describe everything that had happened on the *Deimos
Dancer* from the moment that we left parking orbit around
Earth. The ship was quarantined, and I was placed in solitary
confinement until the incubation period for the plague was over.
I explained my theory of my immunity because of living in with
the pigs, and at last a tall string-bean official took enough time
out from asking me questions to answer a few. He dismissed my
theory with a shake of his head.

"That's not the answer, Mr. Carver. Penelope and Pomander
were carrying plague vaccine all right, as an *in vivo* culture.
That's a very common way of safely transporting a large quantity of a vaccine culure, and that's what Vladic was trying to tell
you with his dying words. But just living in with the pigs
couldn't protect you from the plague unless you had actually had
a vaccination prepared from them. You were saved by something else—something we discovered ourselves only after Vladic had left Mars. When we burned Willis City to stop the
plague's spread, we unfortunately destroyed part of the evidence. Here, take a look at this."

He snapped a holo-cube into the projector and switched on. I gasped and shrank back in my seat as a great crustacean sprang into being in front of me, blind, chitinous, rust-red, and malevolent.

"That's the villain of the piece, Mr. Carver. One of man's old friends, but one we've been ignoring for the past hundred years. Order Anoplura, species *Pediculus humanus capitis*—I'm showing it to you at twenty-five hundred times magnification."

I couldn't stretch my college Latin far enough to make any sense of the names he was giving me. The horrible creature in front of me absorbed my attention completely.

"In short, Mr. Carver," he went on, "we are looking at a head louse. If it weren't such an uncommon parasite these days, we'd have caught on to it a lot sooner. Head lice have been carrying the plague and spreading it from person to person. Confined quarters and lack of proper hygiene make the spread easier. Just the sort of conditions they had in Willis City when the water recyclers broke down, and you had on board the *Deimos Dancer*."

He gestured at my shining pate. "That saved your life, Mr. Carver. You see, the head louse is a very specialized beast. He lives in head hair, and he refuses to live in body hair—another species of louse does that. I suppose the others on the *Deimos Dancer* were not shaven?"

Anything but. I recalled their tangled and filthy locks, and nodded.

"I don't know what made you shave, Mr. Carver, but you should be very glad that you did. Shave your head and the head louse won't look twice at you. Down on Mars, everyone has been shaved, men and women."

They led me away in a state of shock. All my theories had been rubbish—but if the other crew members had lived just as I did, they might still be alive, so my suggestions had been good ones. As I left, the same reporter importuned me, asking again for an interview. I dismissed him a second time with a dozen strong and well-chosen words.

At my age, I should know better than to annoy the press. When I arrived on the surface of Mars, still bald and still broke, the first thing that I saw was a copy of the *Martian Chronicle*. Across the front page, in living color, was a photograph of Penelope, Pomander, and myself, floating into the entrance to Phobos Station.

The bold caption beneath it read, PLAGUE SURVIVORS ARRIVE AT PHOBOS. Underneath that, still in large letters: PENELOPE AND PO-MANDER ARE TO THE LEFT IN THE PICTURE.

AFTERWORD: THE DEIMOS PLAGUE.

When this story appeared in STELLAR 4 I was quite disappointed with the reviews. It was not that they were bad—they were actually fairly complimentary. But none of them, I felt, penetrated to the heart of the matter.

Not until the collection was reviewed in England did the situation change. "Pointless and rather disgusting", said one reviewer. I felt a warm glow. This was exactly the reaction that I had been hoping for and had missed in the U.S. reviews. As readers of an earlier short story collection will already have realized, this is another story (the fourth one) in the "sewage series" featuring Henry Carver and his business partner Waldo Burmeister. Two more specimens, if I may use the word, will be encountered later in this collection.

A French publisher recently bought the right to translate this story and publish it in the magazine UNIVERS. I was pleased that it was the only story in STELLAR 4 that he wanted, but I'm also worried about it. How on earth will they translate "pumping ion" or "Martian Chronicle" into French? Worst of all, what will they do with "Post hog, ergo Propter hog"?

I wait with trepidation.

FOREFATHER FIGURE

"Who are you?"

The words rang around the tiled walls. The naked figure on the table did not move. His chest rose and fell steadily, lifting with it the tangle of catheters and electrodes that covered the rib cage.

"Still no change." The woman who crouched over the oscilloscope made a tiny adjustment to the controls with her left hand. She was nervous, her eyes flicking to the screen, to the table, and to the man who stood by her side. "He's still in a sleep rhythm. Heart and blood pressure stable."

The man nodded. "Keep watching. Increase the level of stimulation. I think he's coming up, but it will take a while."

He turned back to the recumbent figure.

"Who are you? What is your name? Tell me, who are you?"

As the questions went on, the only sound in the big room, the woman ran her tongue over her lips, seemingly ready to respond herself to the insistent queries. She was big-boned and tall, her nervous manner an odd contrast to her round and impassive-looking face.

"Here he comes," she said abruptly.

There was a stir of movement from the body's left arm. It rose a couple of inches from the table, twitching the powerful sinews of the wrist and hand.

"Reduce the feedback." The man leaned over the table, peering down at the fluttering eyelids. *"Who are you?"*

There was a sigh, a grunt, the experimental run of air over the vocal chords. "Ah—Ah'm—Bayle." The voice was thick and choking, a mouthing through an unfamiliar throat and lips. "I'm

56

Bayle. I'm Bayle Richards.'' The eyes opened suddenly, an unfocussed and startling blue.

"*Got it.* By God, I've got it.'' John Cramer flashed a fierce look of triumph at the woman and straightened up from the table. "I wondered if we ever would.'' He laughed. "We don't need the stimulants now. Turn to a sedative—he'll need sleep in a few minutes. Let's see how well it took, then we'll end it for today.''

He leaned again over the table. "Bayle Richards. Do you remember me? I'm John Cramer. Remember? John Cramer?''

The blue eyes rolled slowly, struggling to find a focus. After a few seconds they fixed on Cramer's face.

"John Cramer. Uh, I think so. Don't know what happened. John Cramer.'' He moved his arm and made a weak effort to sit up. "Think I remember. Not sure.''

The eyes focussed more sharply, filled with alarm. "What happened to me? What's wrong with me?''

"Not a thing.'' Cramer was smiling broadly, nodding to the woman. "Bayle, you're going to be better than you ever were in all your life. You'll feel dizzy for a while. Do you have any pain?''

"My mouth, and my chest . . . stiff. What you do to me? Was I in an accident?''

"No. Bayle, you're fine. Don't you remember? This was mostly your idea.''

The woman turned her head quickly at that. "John. That's not what he—''

"Shut up, Lana.'' He waved her to silence with an abrupt chop of his hand and returned his attention to the man. "Bayle, I'll tell you all about this later. Now you ought to get some rest. Just lie there quietly, and we'll get this plumbing off you.''

As the sedatives began to take effect, Bayle Richard's eyes closed again. Cramer began to strip the electrodes and the monitoring sensors off the naked body, his fingers working rapidly and accurately.

"John.'' The woman stood up from the control console and moved to the table. "Don't you think you ought to slow down? I thought we were going to watch the monitors for a couple of hours, see if it was all normal. Suppose we get a new problem?''

"No chance of it.'' Cramer's voice was exultant. "Lana, don't try and tell me my business. This is a *success*, I feel it in my bones. Did you see any sign of instability on those monitors? Let's get him in full control, then we can start the second transfer.'' He laughed again. "We'll pull in those memories as soon as we can hook him up. Twenty-two thousand years, the carbon dating says. He'll tell a story, once we get him started.''

His gaze moved over the figure on the table, revelling in the firm, unblemished skin and the smooth muscles. "Look at that body. Bayle, you never had it so good! Wait until he sees himself in a mirror.''

Lana Cramer was automatically beginning to strip off the sensors and uncouple the I-V's. Her placid face was still troubled.

"John, do you think you're being fair to him? We still haven't explained what caused the trouble in the primary transfer— suppose that produces a complication when we try and connect with the memories?''

Cramer continued his systematic treatment of Bayle Richards, his manner confident and casual. He did not look up at her.

"Don't you worry about that, Lana. Thinking isn't your department. A week from now, we'll know more about Cro-Magnon man than anyone has ever known. Bayle Richards should have known the risks when he got into this. If he didn't, the more fool he is.''

The image flashed up on the big screen, an accurate color reproduction. Cramer adjusted the focus.

"There, Bayle. That used to be you. Now you can see what a good trade you made.''

Bayle Richards fidgeted as he examined the screen. He was dressed now in a grey suit that hung elegantly on his tall, thin frame, but somehow his air of discomfort extended beyond the clothing to the body itself. He moved as though the limbs themselves were a poor fit. He kept looking down at his hands, examining the smooth muscles in the palm and along the base of his thumbs. When he looked at the screen, his eyes were afraid.

"Was that really me? Why don't I have a clearer memory of it? It seems like something I dreamed."

"That was you, all right." Cramer looked at the screen with great satisfaction. The figure shown there was small and thin, with a sideways curve to the spine and a big head that sat crooked on the thin shoulders. Big brown eyes swam myopically out of the screen through thick-lensed glasses.

"You lived in that for twenty-six years, Bayle. You never had a good job, never had a woman. When we've finished and you leave here, you'll have both—but we've got to run a few experiments before that happens."

"Experiments?" The expression of fear mirrored the worldview of the old Bayle Richards. It did not match the tall, poised body, with its clear eyes and regular features. "Dr. Cramer, I don't remember things right. Did I agree to some experiments?"

"You did. As a matter of fact, I could say that body is on loan to you—it won't be yours until we complete the experiments. I'll show you the contract that you signed, if you want it. Don't worry. We're not going to do anything bad to you, just explore some old memories."

"I don't seem to *have* memories, not real ones. I have little incidents in my head, but I can't put them together." Bayle Richards looked again at his hands.

"John." She had been sitting quietly, watching the two men. Now Lana Cramer leaned forward and placed her hand on her husband's arm. "John, do we have to do this now? I was wondering, wouldn't it be better to let Bayle take a couple of weeks to get comfortable first? Pierre will still be waiting, even if we took a month before we began."

The flash of irritation in John Cramer's eyes came and went so quickly that it was hard to catch. After a moment he patted Lana's hand reassuringly, but he did not look at her.

"Now then, dear, you know I can't do that." His tone was mildly reproving. "I told the Paris Institute that Pierre would be back there in thirty days. We have to begin work now, as soon as the equipment is set up. Bayle and I agreed to all this long ago."

"But he doesn't remember it."

John Cramer shrugged. He was of middle height, broad and

well-built, with a heavy chin and thick, barred eyebrows.

"We have it all in writing—on videotape, too. You know we always wondered if all the memories would carry over, that's why we took such complete records."

"And I remember it," said Bayle Richards suddenly. "You showed me what I would look like, and I signed the paper. I can *see* it, see my hand doing it." He shuddered. "I was in pain all the time, from my back and my arm. God, no wonder I signed. I'd have signed anything."

"Maybe." Cramer's voice was soft but insistent. "Maybe you would have signed anything, I can't tell. But you *did* sign, and I approved this work because of that. Now we have to carry through on it, and do what you agreed to do. It's not anything that will harm you, Bayle—even Lana will agree with me there. But we have to get started soon, or we won't be finished in a month."

"But I must know some other things." Richards' voice showed that he had lost any real argument. "I haven't been told what you were doing, and I don't remember it. You said my memory will come back in patches, but when?"

John Cramer shrugged and stood up. "I can't say. We have no history on that. I don't see a problem, though, we can tell you anything you need to know. Or Lana can, I should say. I have to go now and get the equipment ready. We have approval to begin work tomorrow, and I don't want to lose time at the beginning."

"John!" Lana Cramer's voice halted him at the door. "I don't know some of the technical details myself. You're the only one who has the full picture."

Cramer shrugged. "I can't see why you'd want that much detail. If you do, call out some of the files onto the screen. I have a record of everything, and the index is set up to be used by anybody. I'll be back in a few hours."

After he was gone, Lana Cramer smiled uncertainly at Bayle Richards. "I'm sorry. That's just John, he never has enough time for anything, especially explanations. I'll do my best. What is it you want to know first?"

"Who am I?"

"What?" She was confused, suddenly carried back to the

previous day, with Cramer's insistent "Who are you?" ringing through the operating theater.

"I want to know who I am." Richards leaned forward, stunning her with those startling, clear eyes. "I'm Bayle Richards, sure. But this isn't my body, my body was a wreck. I want to know who I am now. Where's the original owner?"

"You don't remember *that*? It was the last thing you talked about with John before we began."

"I'm telling you, I don't remember it. I remember a bit about cloning, how it's done, but I don't remember anything about this body. Did I meet the owner?"

Lana paused. Maybe the personality was Bayle's, but he seemed to be picking up something from the physiology and glandular balance of his new body. The old Bayle had never been so insistent on answers. She looked at him again, seeing the fit of mind and body for the first time.

"I think it would be best if I show you. It may be a shock whatever we do. Come on."

She stood up and led the way out of the room. Moving along the corridor behind her, Bayle Richards seemed to be still experimenting with movement, feeling the flex of muscles in his long legs. She was a big woman, but he was half a head taller. It was a new experience. He could remember the old Bayle Richards, peering *up* at everyone. That sudden memory was so painful that he paused and stretched upwards, savoring the new look of the world.

Lana Cramer had stopped at a door near the end of the corridor and was working the combination, shielding it with her body. Watching her bent over, Richards felt another unfamiliar sensation, a surge of lust more powerful than the old body had ever known. He remembered Cramer's words, "never had a woman." Part of the reason for that was a lack of desire. The old body was too racked by pain and physical malfunction to support a strong sexual urge.

He moved forward as Lana swung open the heavy door. A gust of cold air met them as they entered the long, high-ceilinged room. The white tile walls gave off a breath of formaldehyde and methyl alcohol. The whole far wall was a bank of massive drawers, a couple of feet wide and high. Each of them bore its own neatly typed label.

Bayle Richards shivered with sudden recognition, as Lana turned to him.

"You remember what this is, Bayle?"

"Yes. Now I do. It's a morgue. You made me a clone from a dead man's body, right?"

"Sort of." Lana Cramer moved forward to one of the drawers and placed her finger on the button that would open it. "You don't remember it all yet? Bayle, I was hoping this would trigger it for you. You're a clone from a dead man all right."

"I don't mind that." He seemed relieved. No chance now that he would meet himself in a hospital corridor, or out on the street. "Show me the body; that won't worry me."

"It might." Lana remained with her finger on the button but she did not press it. "Bayle, I want to tell you before I show you, because this may be a shock. You heard John say that we had promised to get Pierre back to the Paris Institute in thirty days? Well, you are Pierre. And Pierre is the body inside here."

"Well? What difference does the nationality make?"

"It's not the nationality that matters, Bayle. John borrowed Pierre from Paris, and over there he's known as 'Vieux Pierre'—Old Pierre. He comes from a sort of peaty salt marsh near the Dordogne River, just east of Bordeaux."

She pressed the button, and the drawer began to slowly slide open with a low hum of an electric motor.

"Pierre died fighting in the marsh, and fell over into a deep part. They found him when they were draining the marsh two years ago. For some reason, the chemical balance there in the marsh preserves animal tissue perfectly. When they got him out, Old Pierre had been lying there for twenty-two thousand years."

The body was a dark, uniform brown, wrinkled deeply all over like a dried fruit. Bayle had managed one long look before he moved back, nauseated, to lean against the wall. There was nothing horrifying in the appearance of the body itself. It was hard to think of it as human tissue. The shrunken skin suggested a model of painted papier mâché, a child's attempt to shape the human form with paste and paper. Bayle Richards' nausea came from a deeper cause, a sudden feeling that he had lurched back through time to the salt marsh where Pierre had met his violent end. A gaping hole in the throat—from man or beast?—told how he had died. Violently, and quickly.

"But how did Dr. Cramer do it?" he asked, looking across the table at Lana and again feeling the comfort of the long, straight spine and well-set head and neck. "I've heard of clones, but how could he clone from a dead man? He would need complete cells to do it—how could he get those from Pierre?"

"He didn't." Lana had seen how shaken he was by the sight of the mummified body. She had taken him back to their rooms in the hospital and given him coffee and brandy—tiny amounts of both. The stimulants were completely new to that body, and there would be no built-in tolerance for them. She felt guilty about how she had handled the situation. There had been no need to *show* Bayle Richards, she ought to have been able to do it all with more indirect explanations. He had taken the shock probably as well as anyone could, but there was still a look of perplexity in his eyes.

"John knew he couldn't do a direct cloning," she went on. "He transplanted the nucleic structures from a diploid cell in Pierre's arm to a denucleated ovum from a host female." She blushed a little as she spoke. "We did forced growth of that to maturity in the vitro-labs in the hospital basement. The chromosome transfer was tedious, but we've done it before with no problems."

"Your ovum?" Bayle had caught her look when she spoke of it.

"Yes. But it could have been anybody—none of my DNA got through to the final cell. You are all Pierre."

"Except for my mind. I have no memories of Pierre."

"Of course not. They are all carried in Pierre's brain, not in his DNA. That was John's next step. He had to do the memory transfer from you, the old Bayle, to the cloned body. That was the hard piece. He had built the scanning instrument to read out from you, and read into the new body, but he had problems with it."

Richards was sipping tentatively at the brandy, his nose wrinkling up in surprise. "If I didn't *know* I could drink this, my body would insist it was poison. Twenty-two thousand years, you say." He shook his head. "Lanta, if I'm a cave man—I still have trouble accepting the idea at all—why don't I *look* like a cave man? The pictures I've seen looked more like my old body, all hunched over and chinless. I'm nothing like that."

"You're probably remembering pictures people drew of Neanderthal man. But you're Cro-Magnon. From all we can tell, he had a better body and a bigger brain than people do now." She looked him up and down as he lounged back in the armchair. It was as if she were doing what he had been doing himself for the past twenty-four hours, taking an inventory of a new property that had been around for a while but had not been previously appreciated. It was impossible to relate the strong, handsome man in front of her with the old Bayle Richards. She could feel his interest in her. With Bayle, she had never been aware of any questions of sexual attitudes. The man sitting opposite her made such a thought unavoidable.

Lana forced herself to continue, to ignore the sudden sexual tension in the room. "Cro-Magnon man is probably what we all descended from, but we don't know much about him. When you feel like it, I'll show you some of the cave paintings that he did. After all"—she smiled, trying to change the mood—"you're a lot closer to him than most of us now."

"Yes. But you haven't told me *why.*"

"I will. But there's one other thing I have to tell you first." She hesitated, knowing that she was going to do something that would enrage John Cramer if he found out about it. Usually she did anything she could to avoid his disapproval, but this was literally a life-and-death issue for Bayle Richards.

"You signed an agreement with John to let him transfer your memories to Pierre's cloned body. You agreed when you signed that he would not be held responsible for any failure, no matter what happened."

"But nothing did happen, did it?" Richards was looking slightly dizzy. Even the small amount of alcohol—less than half an ounce—was producing an effect on him. "I mean, I'm sitting here, in Pierre's body, and I feel fine."

"You look fine. I don't want you to ever tell John that I said this to you—promise me that—but something *did* happen. No one has ever done a successful transfer of memories to a stranger's cloned body before. John is the expert in it, and he had troubles. Everything went smoothly for the first few hours, and we were scanning memories out of your old body and into the one you have now. A couple of hours before we were finished, things went wrong."

"What do you mean, things went wrong? I'm here, and I'm in good shape."

"You seem to be. But before all the memories were transferred, the old body died. We don't know why. Bayle Richards just stopped breathing, and we couldn't start him again."

Lana leaned forward, her calm face full of unusual urgency. "Bayle, you may not think you care about this one way or the other, but your old body doesn't exist now. John won't admit it, but there are things about the consciousness transfer process that no one understands yet."

"So why should I care about that?" Richards was gradually moving to the acceptance of his new status. Cramer had completed the transfer, and the loss of the old body was perhaps a good thing. It was no pleasure to be reminded of that crippled, tormented past.

"So what?" he repeated. "I'm here, aren't I?"

"You're here, Bayle, but you don't understand." She leaned forward, took his hands in hers, then quickly released them. She dare not give the wrong signals to the new Bayle Richards. "You signed an agreement that if you occupied this new body, Old Pierre's clone, you would help John in his experiments with it. Don't you know what he wants to do next? He didn't pick out this old body, and perform all that work on it, for nothing."

She was looking nervously around her, afraid suddenly that John Cramer would appear while she was speaking. "Bayle, John wants to try and do some memory transfer from Old Pierre to *you*, to this body. He failed when he tried to do transfers to another subject, but he thinks that it would be possible with a cloned body form of Old Pierre when it wouldn't work with a stranger. Now do you see why I'm worried? John is going to insist on it, but there are still things about the process that we *know* we don't understand. If we *did* understand, why would the old Bayle Richards have died in the last transfer?''

The French countryside was flat and baked under the hot August sun. In the west the land fell slowly away towards the river. The focus moved in, shrinking the broad landscape view to a narrower scene of moss and isolated clumps of grey-green sedge. That dreary prospect seemed far removed in time and space from the Bordeaux land of vines and lush fruit.

John Cramer paused as he was about to move the scene to closer focus. He looked up in annoyance as the door was opened and light flooded into the darkened room.

''Keep that door shut!'' He squinted up, eyes unable to handle the brighter light. ''Lana, what the hell are you doing. You know I'm not to be interrupted when I'm working here.''

''John.'' She closed the door and sat down next to him. ''I have to talk to you.''

''Not now. I'm micro-viewing some of the French material for tomorrow. We have to have it ready so I can navigate with Pierre.''

''That's what I have to talk to you about, John. You have to give up the experiment. Last night I did as you asked with Bayle, and we went over a lot of things that he should remember from before the transfer.''

John Cramer sighed and switched off the micro-viewer with a gesture of irritation. ''Lana, what's got into you? There's no way I'm going to stop the experiments now—we're almost halfway there.''

She was sitting so close that he could sense her nervous hand movements. ''We're not halfway, John. That's why we have to stop. Look, you think that you transferred most of Bayle's memories, so you still think he's the old Bayle. He isn't. For one thing, he has less memories than we realized—when we looked in detail at what he recalls of his old life, it's mostly blanks and vague emotional recall.''

"Of course it is." John Cramer felt a sudden impulse to violence. A week ago, she would never have dared to press him with this kind of intrusion. His working hours were sacred. "Look, Lana, I'll say one more thing, then I want you out of here so I can get my materials prepared. Bayle Richards is in a new body—one that I still own. The less he remembers of the old body, the better the chance that we can induce memories from Pierre into the new one. He doesn't recall much of the old Bayle *because he doesn't want to*. Can't you see it, the last thing he needs cluttering up his head is the knowledge of what a disaster he used to be? I don't think the experiment went wrong—I think he suppresses the old Bayle's memories, rejects them from his mind."

There was a silence next to him, but he sensed that it was not the silence of acceptance. She was refusing to argue, waiting him out. He felt a rising fury at Richards, at the other man's attitudes. Just as Bayle Richards had been replaced by a new Bayle, the same process seemed to be turning the familiar and pliable Lana to a more obstinate and annoying form.

"Well?" he said after a few more seconds. "Do you agree with me, or don't you? I've got work to do."

She recoiled at the intensity in his voice.

"I'm sorry," she said at last. "Maybe you're right, he can't bear to think of what he used to be."

"Do you wonder?"

"No. I can't bear to think of it, either. John, I'll go now, but tell me one thing. What will you do if he refuses to work with you on the next set of transfer experiments?"

There was a creak from his chair as Cramer jerked forward on it. "Refuses? Now, when we're so committed, and he signed the papers to agree to it? You ought to know the answer to that, Lana. I don't let *anybody* cross me like that, ever. He won't keep that new body of his for a day. I'll trash him, that's what I'll do."

"But his old body died. Anyway, you couldn't condemn him to live in that again—you've seen how he is now."

"Wait and see what I'd do, Lana. I've seen you getting closer to Richards in the past couple of days. Do that all you like, help

him get adjusted to that new body. But remember, *I own that
cloned body*. Legally, it's no more than a piece of experimental
tissue I assembled in the labs. I'll get cooperation from
Richards, or I'll recycle the tissue.''

She stood up abruptly. ''That's murder, John.''

He laughed, a snarl of bitter amusement in the darkness. ''Go
and learn the law, Lana. Until I sign off on it, that body has no
independent status. It's what I make it, that's all. If I have to, I'll
start again with another subject. Now, get the hell out of here.
Go and tell all that to Richards. I have work to do. If you're so
fond of him, you'd better explain what he has to do if he wants to
keep that handsome new body.''

She made a noise between a sigh and a groan, blundering in
the darkness towards the door. Before she reached it he had
turned the micro-viewer back on and was adjusting its focus to
the French scene. His expression in the darkness was of grim
satisfaction. He knew Lana. Now and again, it was necessary to
show her who was in control.

''Do I need to run over it again, or do you have everything
clear?''

John Cramer's voice was dispassionate but not unfriendly.
Now that the experiment was beginning, he had no room for
emotions.

''I know what to do.'' Bayle Richards was lying flat on the
bed, a sheet draped over his naked body. A set of electrodes rose
from his shaven skull to the computer monitor that hung suspended above him like a silver bee-hive. A second tangle of
wires led to the sealed coffin on the table.

''Let's get on with it,'' he said. ''I assume Old Pierre knows
what he's doing?''

His voice, unlike Cramer's, was bitter. He and Lana had
spent many hours discussing the situation, but always they came
to the same conclusion. John Cramer was in control, and all that
he cared about was the continued experiments with Old Pierre.

''Do you think he's doing this because of—us?'' Lana had
asked.

''I don't think he cares what we do.'' Richards still felt

uncomfortable, even though Cramer had made it clear during their discussions that he knew there was something between them. "He as good as told me that you would do whatever he told you to do. I don't think he worries about your body—he wants possession of your mind."

She had clung to him, but neither of them had faced the real question. Did John Cramer control her? Bayle Richards thought so, but Lana would have denied it.

There was one sustaining thought that lessened Bayle's concerns: no matter what John Cramer's views might be of Lana, or what he might know of the affair, nothing would be allowed to stand in the way of the experiments—and Bayle was central to those. Attempts to transfer memories from Old Pierre through random volunteers had all been dismal failures.

Cramer was peering at the array of dials on the outside of the coffin, then adjusting the settings of the controls that ran inside it.

"I think we've reached the best possible temperature in the casket. It's warm enough to stimulate the right brain areas, and it's cool enough to let us keep going without settling up interference reactions in the body. Bayle, just let your mind run where it wants to. If you begin to get visual or auditory images, just talk into the microphone. I've put that there as a stimulus—we'll pick you up anyway, if you begin to subvocalize."

He turned to Lana, who was again at her position as anesthetist and monitor of signal transfer.

"All right. Run a low level sedation rhythm. I think we'll get better response if Bayle's activity level is down from normal. He has to be conscious enough to comment but not to do too much thinking. Can you find that setting?"

Lana nodded. Her wide mouth was firmed to a worried line. Bayle had not only refused to fight against John Cramer's intent—he had displayed a surprising interest in the project himself.

"You don't understand, Lana," he had said. "I want to know all I can about Pierre. It sounds stupid, but he's closer to me than any of the rest of you."

That remark had wounded her. She had done all she knew to

draw him closer, to make him feel that the future would belong to the two of them. Bayle had taken what she offered, but little more than physical attention had been given in return. How much of that was simple physical need? John was unreachable, locked into his world of charts and plans. She sometimes suspected that he had *planned* her affair with Bayle, to give him more control over both of them.

Her attention was suddenly drawn back to the controls in front of her.

"Something's coming through," she said. "I'm getting primary brain rhythm from Pierre."

Cramer grunted. "Predicted. We got that far with the last subject, it's not an information-carrying signal. Watch for that mixture of alpha and beta waves that you saw when we were doing the Richards transfer to Pierre. That's when a real signal will be getting through."

"I'm getting that too."

"What!" Cramer was over by her side instantly, watching the monitors intently. "Damn it, you're right. We never had *that* with the others, not even when we tried for hours." He was as excited as a small child with a new toy. "Keep the signal to Bayle as constant as you can, let him start to soak up the flow. After he's had five minutes, we'll cut off the inputs from Pierre and see what we've got. I don't think we can expect—"

"Sun. Bright sun." The murmured words from the figure on the table cut Cramer off in mid-sentence. He swung around, moved quietly to Bayle Richards' side.

"Keep it going, Lana. Don't cut back on the transfer."

"Some of us." Richards paused, as though somehow looking around him although the form on the table did not move. "Five of us, walking towards the sun. Feels like soft mud under our feet. Skin itches, itches a lot. Something bad there."

Cramer saw that Lana was looking at him, her expression worried. "Parasites. Pierre wouldn't notice them, he was used to fleas and lice. Bayle's too sensitive to feel comfortable in the Stone Age. Keep the signal going."

She looked unhappy, then nodded. "Data rate is up again. Want me to back it off?"

''No. Let's get all the sensory signals we can. I'm tuned in to pick up mainly visuals from Pierre, but I'm going to increase band width and see if we can get audio and tactile—looks as though Bayle has been picking up some of them anyway, he's aware of the skin sensations coming through from Pierre.''

He went to the casket and began to reset the probe levels. After a few moments Bayle Richards began to grunt.

''Hungry. Following scent. Horns went this way, two days ago, must keep following until we can surround them at night. Don't like smell. Danger somewhere near us, not our people.''

He was sniffing the air, turning his head from side to side. Somehow his features seemed to have become more primitive, full of a suggestion of animal awareness. After a few seconds his eyelids flicked open, then closed again.

''Won't find today,'' he said at last. ''Dark coming, country here strange, can't keep going now. Look for safe place, see if can find water and bad food. Hungry. Hungry.''

His voice was trailing off, the words losing clarity.

''All right.'' Cramer turned back from the casket. ''We could keep going and pick up another signal, but there's enough there for me to analyze. I'm cutting off Pierre's inputs. Bring him round, I want to try him with a few visual comparisons.''

Ten minutes later, and the electrodes had been removed. Bayle Richards had sunk into a deep natural sleep.

''Do you want me to give him a stimulant?'' Lana Cramer seemed relieved, as much as her husband was exhilarated.

''No.'' He laughed. ''Let him sleep a while, he has some information processing to do. Then we'll talk to him about what he saw—couldn't get that out while we were working there, but I'll bet he kept most of those visual images that came across from Old Pierre. Just think of it, Lana. He's been looking at the earth today as it was twenty-two thousand years ago—he could tell you the colors of the butterflies, describe the actual weather.'' He took a deep breath. ''God, it's enough to make me want to have myself cloned into Pierre's body form. Do you realize what this means? We have a new way to explore the whole of history, right back to the earliest fossils of man. We can find out when language developed, when writing was invented, when we mastered fire—everything.''

He looked for a long moment at the body on the table, then turned to leave. "Stay with him, Lana. Stay with him, but let me know as soon as he wakes. I want to hear every word.''

"John, what did he mean by 'bad food'?'' Her face was puzzled, while she watched tenderly over the unconscious form of Bayle Richards. "Was that something to harm them?''

He shook his head. "I don't know, but I don't think so. I think that he was talking about grasses and berries—things that they could eat if they had to, just to keep going, but things that didn't really count. They were meat eaters, that's what they wanted. Deer, and cattle, and wild boar—risky business. That's why they had to hunt in groups. We'll know soon enough. Watch him, Lana.''

His words were unnecessary. Lana Cramer was crouched over the body. Everything seemed to have gone well, but she wanted to see him awaken, to hear him talk to her again before she would be convinced.

"We were walking across some kind of—what's the word?—scree? Loose shale and gravel. Funny thing is, I have no idea at all what it *looked* like. Seems as though I've blanked it out.'' Bayle Richards looked up at the ceiling, squeezing his eyes hard shut with the effort of recollection. "Same with the trees and the grasses,'' he said at last. "I don't get much from them—just their smell, and a feeling about some of them.''

"What sort of feeling?'' Cramer was listening intently, the tape recorder by his side silently preserving every word. "Colors?''

"No. Definitely not colors. A feeling for *uses*. That's not right either. A feeling for some special function.'' He shook his head in annoyance. "What's wrong with me? It's as though there are big blank spots in my memory—but I can see a lot of the surroundings when I close my eyes, and I can hear the sound of the birds and the wind. Is it a bad transfer?''

"Bad?'' Cramer laughed, excited and stimulated enough to drop his usual role of the impassive scientist. "It's not bad, it's more than I dared hope for. Bayle, you're doing fine. You have three things working against total recall, and I was afraid that any one of them might make the whole experiment a failure. First, Lana probably told you that Pierre is perfectly preserved, but that's not really possible. There was some decay, there had to be. We were lucky to find as much as we have of preserved chemical memories. Then we had to transfer to you, and *that* has been a big success. You've been getting more sensation than we ever hoped you'd experience.''

"I've had sensation all right." Richards wriggled his shoulders. "Old Pierre had cuts and scratches all over him. He didn't even register them, but they came across to me down below the conscious level. When I woke up I felt as though I had been cut and bitten and stung by every plant and insect in creation. He didn't notice any of it. But what's the other thing working against us?"

"Outlook." Cramer began to flick through the slides in the big projector. "You are trying to see the world through his eyes, but his universe is totally different from the one we have in our heads. Ninety percent of the things that he thought were important are not in your data base at all. You will interpret what he saw, what he did—but the *reasons* he did them? That's something we'll never know. Here, do any of these look familiar to you?"

The slides that flashed onto the screen represented months of careful work in France. John and Lana Cramer had travelled over the whole region, recording characteristic land forms and geological features—anything that might have survived for over twenty thousand years. As image after image passed across the screen, Bayle Richards shook his head.

"Not a glimmer. Dr. Cramer, I guess you're right. Pierre didn't even *see* things like this."

"Keep looking. They must have had some way of knowing where they were, and how to get back from the hunt."

"I'll look, but I think you may be on the wrong track. The one thing that Pierre *always* seemed to be conscious of is the position of the sun. Could he be navigating by that?"

"Maybe. But what about cloudy days?" Cramer shrugged.
"Let's keep looking. What about fire? Did you carry any with
you?"

"Fire." Richards hunched his head forward. "Yeah. That
brings up all sorts of images. But not on the hunt. There was fire
back where we came from—a long way back. Seems to me we
had been farther on this hunt than ever before. They were
worried about getting into enemy territory, some place where
there were other animals or people that would hurt them. Pierre
has a sort of built-in smell reaction, his test for aliens. No fire on
the hunt, though, and a feeling that we were an *awful* long way
from home. Many days. Maybe we were doing more than just
hunting."

"Many days?" Cramer turned to Lana, who had been patiently taking notes of the conversation. "Maybe we spent too
much time in the west when we were over there. Do you have
anything fifty or a hundred miles to the east? I didn't bother."

"Skip to the end." She frowned, uneasy with the role of
decision maker. "You remember, when you went up to Paris I
stayed behind and did some sight-seeing. There may be a few
shots in there."

Cramer began to flick rapidly through an assortment of images, pastoral villages, inns, river valleys, and mountain valleys.

"Hold it." Richards sat upright. "Back up a couple. There.
What's that one? I recognize it, and I've never been to France in
my life."

"This one?" Cramer froze on one slide.

"That's it. That's where we came from. We live in caves
along the side of one of those big ridges. I'm sure of it—I can
even remember which cave I lived in, one with a narrow part that
broadens out again into a second chamber." Richards stood up.
"Where is that?"

Lana Cramer was consulting her notes. "It's Auvergne, in the
hills of the *Massif Central*, a hundred miles east of the Dordogne. We didn't cover that far over—I took that just as a good
view."

"Damn good thing you did." Cramer slapped his notebook

against his knee. "That's frustrating. We didn't expect that Pierre would have been so far away from his home base when he got into trouble. I'll have to call Paris and see if they can ship me a couple of hundred other slides of the eastern area. I want to pin down his travels as much as I can."

"You want to end it for today?" Richards was looking tired, but still stimulated by Pierre's memories. "I'd like to keep going for a while. When you showed that shot, I got a whole bunch of other thoughts. A woman, and a child. I think they may be Pierre's."

"You and Lana can keep going for a while. I want to get these other images ordered, but I don't see any problem if you take notes of everything." Cramer stood up. "Tomorrow, we'll see if we can tap that same area, keep the hunt going and find out how it ends. Make sure you get enough sleep. I think we get better transfer if you are rested."

He left abruptly, his mind already moving on to the next session of the experiment. Lana moved in and turned off the tape recorder. Her calm face had changed, become that of a tormented woman who cannot see any answer to a difficult problem.

"Bayle, I can't go on pretending. It sounds trite, but it's a fact."

"You said you were going to talk to him. Did you change your mind about that?" Bayle Richards did not sound particularly interested in her answer. His eyes were far away, still back in the mesh of alien memories.

"Bayle, I can't face John." Lana sensed the separation but misunderstood the reason for it. "You know he can beat me down, he always could. Can you do it? If I try and talk to him now, he'll ignore me unless he thinks that *you* can affect his precious experiments by refusing to cooperate with him."

"He can force me to."

"No. He can force you to *pretend* to work with him, but he knows that he's at your mercy when it comes to the memories you say you have or don't have. That's your edge, Bayle."

He looked at her uneasily. "What are you suggesting, Lana? What should I tell him?"

"Make the bargain with him. You'll work with him to the end of the experiments with Old Pierre. But set your price for that."

"And my price?" His voice was too cold, she did not think she was persuading him.

"Your price is your freedom." Her voice dropped. "And mine. I could never win it from him without you helping. He's too strong for me."

He shrugged. "What makes you sure there will be an end to the experiments? Suppose that he wants to go on with them forever?"

"No. Not this experiment. You heard what John said, he thinks he has a key that will unlock all human history. There are another twenty preserved bodies scattered in Institutes around the world. If he wants to explore the past with them, he'll need to have other clones developed, give them consciousness from other Bayle Richards. When he does that, we'll be free. He won't care where you go when this experiment is over."

He was quiet for a long time, so long that she thought he was not going to give any reply at all. His face was unreadable in the dim light.

"All right," he said at last. "We need to know how long this is likely to go on, whatever happens after it. He has access to those other preserved bodies?"

"He already made the arrangements. I helped him do it. Bayle"—she moved close to him, touching his head gently as though she was afraid that he would suddenly disappear into the shadows of the room—"when will you do it, Bayle?"

"Tomorrow. Before the experiment. Don't worry, I'll do it. I don't want to stay in this place forever, when I could be out there in the world starting everything over with a decent body."

"Both of us."

He was silent again. Finally he shrugged. "I guess so. If John Cramer agrees. You're his wife. You ought to know him well, but if he says no, what do I do then?"

She put her arms round him. "He won't say no." The words were more like a prayer than a statement. "He won't say no to you."

The images that John Cramer had requested from Paris had

been scanned and transmitted overnight. Lana Cramer, hurrying back with them from the communications office of the hospital, found the lab already a scene of great activity when she arrived there. John Cramer was supervising the installation of a ceiling projector directly above the table where Bayle Richards would again lie during the information transfer from Old Pierre.

"Over there, then get to the anesthetist station." Cramer's manner to her was cold and brusque. She placed the images on the side table, near the projector, and looked across to where Bayle was already connected to the multiple electrodes that would carry the signal for memory transfer. He was staring across at her.

"Did you talk?" she mouthed to him. Her husband was bending over the casket that contained Pierre's body, but she dared not go across to Bayle.

He nodded, and she gave him an exaggerated questioning look and a shrug of interrogation. He turned his thumb up, then down, and returned her shrug. John had listened, but he hadn't given any definite answer at all. She knew that reaction, the steady nodding of his head, then the sudden turn away or the switch of subject.

"Ask him again later?" She mouthed her question, not sure how well Bayle was getting her meaning.

He nodded, then lay back on the table. She would have to wait until this session was over for details--there was no chance that they would be coming from John, and his stony look made her fear the worst.

"Sedation patterns again, same as yesterday," he ordered, abruptly standing up from his position by the casket. "We're set up today so that we can throw scenes for Bayle's inspection while the experiments are still going on. We'll have to bring him in and out of contact with Pierre while that's being done, but I believe we have that degree of control now. Tell me when you are getting first signal transfer."

Lana forced her attention to the control console and watched the pattern of brain waves that was crawling across the oscilloscope. It was establishing itself even quicker than last time, the resonances building between Bayle's brain and Old Pierre's.

"It ought to get easier and easier," Cramer had told her when she expressed surprise at the ease of contact. "Don't forget their brains are structurally *identical*. It's not like trying to establish contact between two dissimilar objects. When these experiments are over, we ought to have sucked out most of Pierre's useful memories. It ought to be a bigger challenge when we leave the Cro-Magnons and try it with *Neanderthalensis* and *Habilis*. I've located well-preserved specimens of both of them."

Put that way, all the complex experiments that had led to Bayle's links with Old Pierre sounded easy and natural. Lana comforted herself with that thought as the transfer signal strength grew on the screen.

"Don't like smell." The words came suddenly from the figure on the table. "Bad smell. Like the others." Bayle Richards' hand moved convulsively, grasping at something by his side. "Will have to fight again, beat the others to the horns."

"He's still on the trail," said Cramer softly. "I've edited the images that came in from Paris. Keep the transfer rate high until I tell you, then push it right down. I want him to look at one of the images."

Lana nodded. Cramer seemed to be the same as yesterday, but she knew from long experience that her own ability to read his emotions was negligible. At least the experiment was going well, that suggested he would be in a good mood later.

"Others ahead," said the figure on the table. Was it Bayle Richards at the moment, or was he no more than a vessel for Old Pierre's memories? "Must fight the others, can't go back without food. Cold, need food."

"Northern France still glaciated." Cramer sounded pleased. "I couldn't understand yesterday, when he said it was hot. Makes more sense for him to feel cold today."

"See many ahead of us. They are not the People, they are others. We get ready, move towards them. Bad place to fight ahead, not covered."

"Now." Cramer gestured across to Lana. "Cut the transfer for the moment, I want to try and get a fix on where he is."

As the signal switched from mildly sedating to stimulating,

Cramer flashed a scene onto the ceiling above Richards' unconscious form.

"Bayle." The eyes flickered open, then closed again. "Bayle, look up there. Do you recognize that scene? Is it one that you've just looked at?"

The eyes flickered open again, stared up at the color image. Bayle Richards shuddered.

"That's it. That's where we are heading, where the others are. Danger, I think there's danger."

"Shall I cut the connection?" Lana sat with her hand poised over the switch that would inhibit all transfer from Pierre to Bayle.

"No." John Cramer's voice was full of some strange satisfaction. "I know what's happening, it's all right. Put him back to full transfer, let's keep this going."

"But what's the scene you showed him?" Lana, poised over the dials, had a poor view of the ceiling display.

"I'll tell you later." He looked at her impatiently. "Lana, get that signal back up *now*. We'll lose transfer, and that would ruin everything."

Automatically she responded to the command in his voice and turned on the full signal again. Bayle Richards jerked spasmodically, strained his head around him.

"See them now, they see us. Go forward now, must win and follow the horns. We all go forward together."

He had begun to pant, his deep chest filling to its maximum capacity beneath the covering sheet.

"John, what's happening?" She could hear the deep grunt of effort coming from the man on the table. "Shall I cut the signal?"

"No." John Cramer had moved to her side, leaning over the control panel. "Keep it like that, maximum transfer rate. I'll tell you when to change it."

"But, John, what's he *doing*." She looked again at the groaning figure on the table. "He doesn't seem to be walking, and look at his arms moving. Do you know what's going on?"

Struck by a sudden thought, she pushed her chair away from the console and leaned far back, looking up at the scene on the ceiling projector. She screamed as soon as she saw the flat plain with its sparse cover of grass and sedges.

"John! That's the salt marsh where Old Pierre was found. If Bayle is there now, it means that he'll—"

She screamed again and threw herself at the control panel. John Cramer was there before her. As the figure on the table thrashed and gargled, the sounds coming from his throat suddenly agonized and blood-clogged, Cramer held the transfer rate switch open to full maximum. He was too strong for Lana to get near it, even though she struggled desperately. The sound from the table took on a new and more terrible urgency.

He came awake in one piece, his muscles flexing him upright at the same time as his eyes opened to the flat white light. Although he was lying up high, he instinctively rolled down to the floor, reaching up to his head to tear away the uncomfortable attachments to his bare scalp.

Naked, he crouched low and looked around him. He had been brought here without the comforting presence of stone axe and spear, without the cheering smells and sounds of the People. The smells that filled his nostrils now were alien and menacing. In front of him, two others struggled together, not seeming to see him at all or to detect his scent. Before they could attack, he had leapt forward to strike hard at the base of the neck, first the man, then the woman. To his surprise, they both crumpled unconscious to the level floor of the white cave.

He bent over and sniffed more closely at the man. Certainly alien, not of the People. With one efficient movement he snapped the neck, then bit the jugular vein to reach the blood. It had been many days since he remembered eating, but for some reason his hunger was satisfied almost at once. He dropped the man's body to the floor, surprised by the peculiar skins that seemed to cover it.

The woman's scent was different. She was not of the People, but it was good to mate outside the People. If he could find his way out of the strange cave, he would take the white-haired woman with her strange mixed smell back with him to the Home. But he wondered if he would find his way Home. If he had been ended in the marsh—his last memory was of the spear in his throat—then he must make a new life for himself here, in the After-Life. First he must possess the woman, to show that she belonged to him.

He knew how to be patient. Looking around the new cave, he squatted next to her on the floor and waited for her to wake. Already her eyelids were moving. It would not take long now.

AFTERWORD: FOREFATHER FIGURE.

Here is a flat, unequivocal statement: I believe that time travel into the past is impossible.

I know that it is one of the standard themes of science fiction, but I still can't swallow it. Stories built around backward time travel are fantasies, embellish them how you will. It's not that such stories violate a law of physics–that happens all the time, whenever we have a new theory. What bothers me is that time travel to the past breaks laws of logic, and that's a far more serious matter. If once we agree that we can throw out logic we have nothing left at all–not even confidence that logic can be rejected, since the basis for rejection must itself depend on some form of logical argument.

Why do I insist that time travel breaks laws of logic? It's that old "grandfather paradox", the one that says if you could send material or information into the past you could arrange for your own grandfather to be killed before your father was conceived. Thus you could not be born, and so you could not kill Grandpa. Simple, and irrefutable. All the parallel universe or trick endings (he wasn't your grandfather at all) or infinite time loops that people have used in stories are attempts to wriggle out of the paradox. Not one of them makes a minor dent in it.

So?

So a few months ago Eleanor Wood sent me an announcement that Fred Saberhagen was looking for stories about time travel, for an anthology. A SPADEFUL OF SPACE-TIME. It was clear that she knew nothing of my aversion to time travel stories. There was no way I could write anything for the anthology, I was sitting down to write and tell her so, and then . . .

In one sense, time travel is more than possible–it is inevitable. We do it with every passing second. Would a story about forward time travel be cheating, not really a time travel story at all? Only, I would argue, if the reader feels cheated.

MOMENT OF INERTIA

"Now," said the interviewer, "tell us just what led you to the ideas for the inertia-less drive."

She was young and vulnerable-looking, and I think that was what saved her from a hot reply. As it was, McAndrew just shook his head and said quietly—but still with feeling—"Not the *inertia-less* drive. There's no such thing. It's a *balanced* drive."

She looked confused. "But it lets you accelerate at more than fifty gees, doesn't it? By making you so you don't feel any acceleration at all. Doesn't that mean you must have no inertia?"

McAndrew was shaking his head again. He looked pained and resigned. I suppose that he had to go through this explanation twice a day, every day of his life, with somebody.

I leaned forward and lowered the sound on the video unit. I had heard the story too often, and my sympathies were all with him. We had direct evidence that the McAndrew drive was anything but inertia-less. I doubt if he'll ever get that message across to the average person, even though he's most people's idea of the 'great scientist', the ultimate professor.

I was there at the beginning of the whole thing. In fact, according to McAndrew I *was* the beginning. We had been winding our way back from the Titan Colony, travelling light as we usually did on the in-bound leg. We had only four Sections in the Assembly, and only two of them carried power kernels and drive units, so I guess we massed about three billion tons for ship and cargo.

Halfway in, just after turn-over point, we got an incoming request for medical help from the mining colony on Horus. I passed the word on to Luna Station, but we couldn't do much to help. Horus is in the Egyptian Cluster of asteroids, way out of the ecliptic, and it would take any aid mission a couple of weeks to get to them. By that time, I suspected their problem would be over—one way or another. So I was in a pretty gloomy mood when McAndrew and I sat down to dinner.

"I didn't know what to tell them, Mac. They know the score as well as I do, but they couldn't resist asking if we had a fast-passage ship that could help them. I had to tell them the truth, there's nothing that can get out there at better than two and a half gees, not with people on board. And they need doctors, not just drugs. Luna will have something on the way in a couple of days, but I don't think that will do it."

McAndrew nodded sympathetically. He knew that I needed to talk it out to somebody, and we've spent a lot of time together on those Titan runs. He's working on his own experiments most of the time, but I know when he needs company, too. It must be nice to be a famous scientist, but it can be lonely travelling all the time inside your own head.

"I wonder if we're meant for space, Mac," I went on—only half-joking. "We've got drives that will let us send unmanned probes out at better than a hundred gees of continuous acceleration, but we're the weak link. I could take the Assembly here up to five gee—we'd be home in a couple of days instead of another month—but you and I couldn't take it. Can't you and some of your staff at the Institute come up with a system so that we don't get crushed flat by high accelerations? A thing like that, an inertia-less drive, it would change space exploration completly."

I was wandering on, just to keep my mind off the problems they had out on Horus, but what I was saying was sound enough. We had the power on the ships, only the humans were the obstacle. McAndrew was listening to me seriously, but he was shaking his head.

"So far as I know, Jeanie, an inertia-less drive is a theoretical impossibility. Unless somebody a lot brighter than I am can come up with an entirely new theory of physics, we'll not see your inertia-less drive."

That was a pretty definitive answer. There *were* no people brighter than McAndrew, at least in the area of physics. He was a full professor at the Penrose Institute, and the System's leading expert on space-time structure. If Mac didn't think it could be done, you'd not find many people arguing with him. A lot of people were fooled by the fact that he took time off to make trips with me out to Titan, but that was all part of his way of working—he said he needed time away from his colleagues, just so he could do his real thinking.

If you deduce from this that I'm not up at that rarefied level of thought, you're quite right. I can follow McAndrew's explanations—sometimes. But when he gets going, my own degrees in Electrical Engineering and Gravitational Engineering don't help a bit. He loses me in the first two sentences.

This time, his words seemed clear enough for anyone to follow them. I poured myself another glass of ouzo and wondered how many centuries it would be before the man with the completely new theory was born. Sitting across from me, McAndrew had begun to rub at his sandy, receding hair-line. His expression was vacant. I've learned not to interrupt when he's got that look on his face—it means he's thinking in a way that I can't follow. One of the other professors at the Penrose Institute says that Mac has a mind that can see round corners, and I have a little inkling of what he meant by that.

"Why inertia-less, Jeanie?" said McAndrew after a few minutes.

Maybe he hadn't been listening to me after all. "So we can use high accelerations. So we can get people to go at the same speeds as the unmanned probes. They'd be flattened at fifty gee, you know that. We need an inertia-less drive so that we can stand that acceleration without being squashed to a mush."

"But that's not the same thing at all. I told you that a drive with no inertia isn't possible—and it isn't. What you're asking for, now, it seems to me that we should be able to . . ."

His voice drifted off to nothing, he stood up, and without another word he left the cabin. I wondered what I'd started.

If that was the beginning of the McAndrew drive—as I think it was—then, yes, I was there at the very beginning.

So far as I could tell, it wasn't only the beginning. It was also the end. Mac didn't talk about the subject again on our way in to Luna rendezvous, even though I tried to nudge him a couple of times. He was always the same, he didn't like to talk about his ideas when they were "half-cooked", as he called it.

When we got to Luna, McAndrew went off back to the Institute, and I took a cargo out to Cybele. End of story, and it gradually faded from my thoughts, until the time came, seven months later, for the next run to Titan.

For the first time in five years, McAndrew didn't make the trip. He didn't call me, but I got a brief message that he was busy with an off-Earth project, and wouldn't be free for several months. I wondered, not too seriously, if Mac's absence could be connected with inertia-less spaceships, and then went on with the cargo to Tital.

That was the trip where some lunatic in the United Space Federation's upper bureaucracy decided that Titan was overdue for some favorable publicity, as a thriving colony where culture would be welcomed. Fine. They decided to combine culture and nostalgia, and hold on Titan a full-scale, old fashioned Miss & Mister Universe competition. It apparently never occurred to the organizers—who must have had minds that could not see in straight lines, let alone around corners—that the participants were bound to take the thing seriously once it was started. Beauty is not something that good-looking people are willing to take lightly. I had the whole Assembly filled with gorgeous, jealous contestants, screaming managers, horny and ever-hopeful newshounds from every media outlet in the System, and any number of vengeful and vigilant wives, lovers and mistresses of both sexes. On one of my earlier runs I took a circus and zoo out to Titan, but that was nothing compared with this trip. Thank Heaven that the ship is computer-controlled. All my time was spent in keeping some of the passengers together and the rest apart.

It also hadn't occurred to the organizers, back on Earth, that a good part of the Titan colony is the prison. When I saw the first interaction of the prisoners and the contestants I realized that the trip out to Titan had been a picnic compared with what was about to follow. I chickened out and went back to the ship until it was all over.

I couldn't really escape, though. When it *was* all over, when the winners had finally been chosen, when the protests and the counter-protests had all been lodged, when the battered remnants of the more persistent prisoners had been carried back to custody, when mayhem was stilled, and when the colonists of Titan must have felt that they had enjoyed as much of Inner System culture as they could stand for another twenty or thirty years, after all that it was my job to get the group back on board again, and home to Earth without further violence. The contestants hated their managers, the managers hated the judges, the judges hated the news media, and everyone hated the winners. It seemed to me that McAndrew may have had advance information about the trip, and drawn a correct conclusion.

I would like to have skipped it myself. Since I was stuck with it, I separated the Sections of the Assembly as much as I could, put everything onto automatic, and devoted myself to consoling one of the losers, a smooth-skinned armful from one of the larger asteroids.

We finally got there. On that day of rejoicing, the whole ghastly gaggle connected with the contest left the Assembly. I said a lingering farewell to my friend from Vesta—an inappropriate origin for that particular contestant—and settled back for a needed rest.

It lasted for about eight hours. As soon as I called into the Com Center for news and messages, I got a terse summons on the com display: GO TO PENROSE INSTITUTE, L-4 STATION. MACAVITY.

Not an alarming message, on the face of it, but it worried me. It was from McAndrew, and it was addressed to me alone—no one else in the System called him Macavity, and I doubt if three people knew that I had given him that nickname when I found he was a specialist on theories of gravity (''Old Possum's Book Of Practical Cats'' didn't seem to be widely read among Mac's colleagues).

Why hadn't he called me directly, instead of sending a com-link message? The fact that we were back from Titan would have been widely reported. I sat down at the terminal and placed a link to the Institute, person-to-person to McAndrew.

I didn't feel any better when the call went through. Instead of Mac's familiar face, I was looking at the coal-black complexion of Professor Limperis, the head of the whole Institute. He nodded at me seriously.

"Captain Roker, your timing is impressive. If we had received no response to Professor McAndrew's coded message in the next eight hours, we would have proceeded without you. Can you help?"

He hesitated, seeing my confused expression. "Did your message tell you the background of the problem?"

"Dr. Limperis, all I've had so far is half a dozen words—to go to the L-4 branch of the Institute. I can do that easily enough, but I have no idea what the problem is, or what use I could possibly be on it. Where's Mac?"

"I wish to God I could answer that." He sat silent for a moment, chewing on his lower lip, then shrugged. "Professor McAndrew insisted that we send for you—left a message specifically for you. He told us that you were the stimulus for beginning the whole thing."

"*What* whole thing?"

He looked at me in even greater surprise. "Why, the high acceleration drive—the balanced drive that McAndrew has been developing for the past year. McAndrew has disappeared testing the prototype. Can you come at once to the Institute?"

The trip out to the Institute, creeping along in the Space Tug from Luna Station, was one of the low points of my life. There was no particular logic to it—after all, I'd done nothing wrong. But I couldn't get rid of the feeling that I'd wasted a critical eight hours after the passengers had left the Assembly. If I hadn't been obsessed with sex on the trip back, maybe I would have gone straight to the com-link instead of taking a sleep break. And maybe then I would have been on my way that much earlier, and that would have been the difference between saving Mac and failing to save him . . .

You can see how my mind was running. Without any real facts, you can make bears out of bushes just as well in space as you can on Earth. All I had been told by Limperis was that McAndrew had left a week earlier on a test of the prototype of a new ship. If he was not back within a hundred and fifty hours, he had left that terse coded message for me, and instructions— orders might be a better word—to take me along on any attempted search for him.

Dr. Limperis had been very apologetic about it. 'I'm only quoting Professor McAndrew, you understand. He said that he didn't want any rescue party setting out in the *Dotterel* if you weren't part of it. He said''—Limperis coughed uncomfortably—''we had a real need for your commonsense and natural cowardice. We'll be waiting for you here as soon as you can arrange passage. The least we can do for Professor McAndrew in the circumstances is to honor his wishes on this.''

I couldn't decide if I was being complimented or not. As L-4 Station crept into view on the forward screen, I peered at it on highest magnification, trying to see what the rescue ship looked like. I could see the bulk of the Institute structure, but no sign of anything that ought to be a ship. I had visions of a sort of super-Assembly, a huge cluster of electromagnetically linked spheres. All I could see were living quarters and docking facilities, and, as we came in to dock, a peculiar construction like a flat, shiny plate with a long thin spike protruding from the center. It looked nothing like any USF ship, passenger or cargo.

Limperis may have spent his whole life in pure research, but he knew how to organize for emergency action. There were just five people in our meeting inside the Institute. I had never met them in person, but they were all familiar to me through McAndrew's descriptions, and from media coverage. Limperis himself had made a life study of high-density matter. He knew every kernel below lunar mass out to a couple of hundred astronomical units—many of them he had visited, and a few of the small ones he had shunted back with him to the Inner System, to use as power supplies.

Siclaro was the specialist in kernel energy extraction. The Kerr-Newman black holes were well-understood theoretically, but efficient use of them was still a matter for experts. When the USF wanted to know the best way to draw off power, for drives or for general use, Siclaro was usually called in. His name on a recommendation was like a stamp of approval that few would think to question.

With Gowers there as an expert in multiple kernel arrays, Macedo as the System authority in electromagnetic coupling, and Wenig the master of compressed matter stability, the combined intellect in that one room in the Institute was overpowering. I looked at the three men and two women who had just been introduced to me, and felt like a gorilla in a ballet. I might make the right movements, but I wouldn't know what was going on.

"Look, Dr. Limperis, I know what Professor McAndrew wants, but I'm not sure he's right." Might as well hit them with my worries at the beginning, and not waste everybody's time. "I can run a ship, sure—it's not hard. But I've no idea how to run something with a McAndrew drive on it. Any one of you could probably do a better job."

Limperis was looking apologetic again. "Yes and no, Captain Roker. We could all handle the ship, any one of us. The concepts behind it are simple—a hundred and fifty years old. And the engineering has been kept simple, too, since we are dealing with a prototype."

"Then what do you want *me* for?" I won't say I was angry, but I was uneasy and unhappy, and there's a fine line between irritation and discomfort.

"Dr. Wenig will drive the *Dotterel*, he has handled it before in an earlier test. Actually he handled the *Merganser*, the ship that Dr. McAndrew has disappeared in, but the *Dotterel* has identical design and equipment. Controlling the ship is easy—if everything behaves as we expected. If something goes wrong—and something must have gone wrong, or McAndrew would be back before this—then neither Dr. Wenig, nor any of the rest of us, has the experience that will be needed. We want you to tell Dr. Wenig what *not* to do. You've been through dangerous times before." He looked pleading. "Will you observe our actions, and use your experience to advise us?"

Uninvited, I flopped down into a seat and stared at the five of them. "You want me to be a bloody canary!"

"A canary?" Wenig was small and slight, with a luxuriant black mustache. He had a strong accent, and I think he was suspecting himself of a translation error.

"Right. Back when people used to go down deep in the earth to mine coal, they used to take a canary along with them. It was more sensitive to poisonous gases than they were. When it fell off the perch, they knew it was time to leave. The rest of you will fly the ship, and watch for me to fall off my seat."

They looked at each other, and finally Limperis nodded. "We need a canary, Captain Roker. None of us here knows how to sing at the right time. Will you do it?"

I had no choice. Not after Mac's personal cry for help. I could see one problem—I'd be telling them everything they did was dangerous. When you have a new piece of technology, it *is* risky, whatever you do with it.

"You mean you'll let me overrule all the rest of you, if I don't feel comfortable?"

"We would." Limperis was quite firm about it. "But the question will not arise. The *Merganser* and the *Dotterel* are both two-person ships. We saw no point in making them larger. Dr. Wenig will fly the *Dotterel*, and you will be the only other person. It just takes one person to handle the controls. You will be there to advise of hidden problems."

I stood up. "Let's go. I don't think I can see danger any better than you can, but I may be wrong. If Mac's on his own out there, wherever he is, we'd better get moving. I'm ready when you are, Dr. Wenig."

Nobody moved. Maybe McAndrew and Limperis were right about my antennae, because at that moment I had a premonition of new problems. I looked around at the uncomfortable faces.

"Professor McAndrew isn't actually *alone* on the *Merganser*." It was Olga Gowers who spoke first. "He has a passenger on the ship."

"Someone from the Institute?"

She shook her head. "Nina Velez is with him."

"Nina Velez? You don't mean President Velez's daughter— the one with AG News?"

She nodded. "The same."

I sat down again in my chair. Maybe the Body-beautiful run to Titan had been an easier trip than I had realized.

Wenig may have come to piloting second-hand, but he certainly knew his ship. He wanted me to know it, too. Before we left the Institute, we'd done the lot—schematics, models, components, power, life support, mechanicals, electricals, electronics, controls, and back-ups.

When the ship was explained to me, I decided that McAndrew didn't really see round corners when he thought. It was just that things were obvious to him *before* they were explained, and obvious to other people afterwards. I had been saying "inertialess" to Mac, and he had been just as often saying "impossible". But we hadn't been communicating very well. All I wanted was a drive that would let us accelerate at multiple gees without flattening the passengers. To McAndrew, that was a simple requirement, one that he could easily satisfy—but there was no question of doing away with inertia, of passengers or ship.

"Take it back to basics," said Wenig, when he was showing me how the *Dotterel* worked. "Remember the equivalence principle? That's at the heart of it. There is no way of distinguishing an accelerated motion from a gravitational field force, right?"

I had no trouble with that. It was freshman physics. "Sure. You'd be flattened just as well in a really high gravity field as you would in a ship accelerating at fifty gee. But where does it get you?"

"Imagine that you were standing on something with a hefty gravity field—Jupiter, say. You'd experience a downward force of about two and a half gee. Now suppose that somebody could accelerate Jupiter *away* from you, downwards, at two and a half gee. You'd fall towards it, but you'd never reach it—it would be accelerating at the same rate as you are. And you'd feel as though you were in free fall, but so far as the rest of the Universe is concerned you'd be accelerating at two and a half gee, same as Jupiter. That's what the equivalence principle is telling us, that acceleration and gravity can cancel out, if they're set up to be equal and opposite.''

As soon as you got used to Wenig's accent, he was easy to follow—I doubt if anybody could get into the Institute unless he was more than bright enough to explain concepts in easy terms. I nodded.

"I can understand that easily enough. But you've just replaced one problem with a worse one. You can't find any drive in the Universe that could accelerate Jupiter at two and a half gee.''

"We cannot—not yet, at any rate. Luckily, we don't need to use Jupiter. We can do it with something a lot smaller, and a lot closer. Let's look at the *Dotterel* and the *Merganser*. At McAndrew's request I designed the mass element for both of them.''

He went across to the window that looked out from the inside of the Institute to raw space. The *Dotterel* was floating about ten kilometers away, close enough to see the main components.

"See the plate on the bottom? It's a hundred meter diameter disk of compressed matter, electromagnetically stabilized and one meter thick. Density's about eleven hundred and seventy tons per cubic centimeter—pretty high, but nothing near as high as we've worked with here at the Institute. Less than you get in anything but the top couple of centimeters of a neutron star, and nowhere near approaching kernel densities. Now, if you were sitting right at the center of that disk, you'd experience a *gravitational* acceleration of fifty gee pulling you down to the disk. Tidal forces on you would be one gee per meter—not enough to trouble you. If you stayed on the axis of the disk, and moved away from it, you'd feel an attractive force of *one* gee when you were two hundred and forty-six meters from the center of the disk. See the column growing out from the disk? It's four meters across and two hundred and fifty meters long.''

I looked at it through the scope. The long central spike seemed to be completely featureless, a slim column of grey metal.

"What's inside it?''

"Mostly nothing.'' Wenig picked up a model of the *Dotterel* and cracked it open lengthwise, so that I could see the interior structure. "When the drives are off, the living-capsule is out here at the far end, two hundred and fifty meters from the dense disk. Gravity feels like one gee, towards the center of the disk. See the drives here, on the disk itself? They accelerate the whole thing *away* from the center column, so the disk stays flat and perpendicular to the motion. The bigger the acceleration that the drives produce, the closer to the disk we move the living-capsule, up the central column here. We keep it so the total force in the capsule, gravity less acceleration, is always one gee, *towards* the disk."

He slid the capsule along an electro-mechanical ladder closer to the disk. "It's easy to compute the right distance for any acceleration—the computer has it built-in, but you could do it by hand in a few minutes. When the drives are accelerating the whole thing at fourteen gee, the capsule is held a little less than fifty meters from the disk. I've been on a test run in the *Merganser* where we got up to almost twenty gee. Professor McAndrew intended to take it up to higher accelerations on this test. To accelerate at thirty-two gee. the capsule must be about twenty meters from the disk to keep effective gravity inside it to one gee. The plan was to take the system all the way up to design maximum—fifty gee thrust acceleration, so that the passengers in the capsule would be right up against the disk, and feel as though they were in free fall. Gravity and thrust accelerations will exactly balance."

I was getting goose bumps along the back of my neck. I knew the performance of the unmanned med ships. They would zip you from inside the orbit of Mercury out to Pluto in a couple of days, standing start to standing finish. Once in a while you'd get a passenger on them—accident or suicide. The flattened thing that they unpacked at the other end showed what the human body thought of a hundred gee.

"What would happen if the drives went off suddenly?" I said.

"You mean when the capsule is up against the disk—at maximum thrust?" Wenig shook his head. "We designed a safeguard sytem to prevent that, even on the prototypes. If there were a sign of the drive cutting off, the capsule would be moved back up the column, away from the disk. The system for that is built-in.''

"Yeah. But McAndrew hasn't come back.'' I had the urge to get on our way. "I've seen built-in safe systems before. The more foolproof you think something is, the worse the failure when it happens. Can't we get moving?''

"Come on." Wenig stood up. "Any teacher will tell you, you can't get much into an impatient learner. I'll give you the rest of the story as we go. We'll go out along the same path as McAndrew did—that's plotted out in the records back here.''

"You think McAndrew went along with the nominal flight plan?''

"We know he didn't." Wenig looked a lot less sure of himself. "You see, when the drives are on maximum the plasma round the life capsule column interferes with radio signals. Fifty hours after they left the Institute, the *Merganser* was tracked from Oberon Station. McAndrew came back into the Solar System, decelerating at fifty gee. He didn't cut the drive at all—just went right through the System and accelerated out again in a slightly different direction. We got the log, but we've no idea what he was doing—there was no way to get a signal to him or from him with the drive on.''

"So they got all the way up to the maximum drive! And they came back here. God, why didn't Limperis tell me that when we were in the first meeting." I went to the locker and pulled out a suit. "He took it up all the way, fifty gee or better. Let's get after him. If he kept that up, he'll be half-way to Alpha Centauri by now. If they're alive.''

The living capsule was about three meters across and simply furnished. I was surprised at the amount of room there was, until Wenig pointed out to me how equipment and supplies that could take higher accelerations were situated on the outside of the capsule, on the side away from the gravity disk.

We had started with McAndrew's flight plan for only a few minutes when I took Limperis at his word that I'd be boss and changed the procedure. If we were to reach McAndrew, the less time we spent, shooting off in the opposite direction to the one that he had gone, the better. He had come right through the

System, and we ought to head in the direction that he was last
seen to be heading.

"I'll take us up to fifty gee," said Wenig. "That way, we'll
experience the same perturbing forces as the *Merganser* did. All
right?"

"Christ, no." My stomach turned over. "Not all right. Look,
we don't know what happened to Mac, but chances are it was
some problem with the ship. If we do just what he did, we may
finish up with the same trouble."

Wenig took his hands off the controls and turned to me, palms
spread. "But then what can we do? We don't know where they
were going, all we can do is try and follow the same track."

"I'm not sure. All I know is what we're *not* going to do—and
we're not trying for top acceleration. Didn't you say you'd
flown *Merganser* at twenty gee?"

"Several times."

"Then take us out along Mac's trajectory at twenty gee until
we're outside the System. Then cut the drive. I want to use our
sensors, and we won't be able to do that from the middle of a ball
of plasma."

Wenig looked at me. I know he was mentally accusing me of
cowardice. "Captain Roker," he said quietly. "I thought we
were in a hurry. We may be weeks following *Merganser* the way
you are proposing."

"Yeah. But we'll get there. Can Mac's support system last
that long?"

"Easily."

"Then don't let's kick it around any more. Let's do it.
Twenty gee, as soon as you can give it to us."

The *Dotterel* worked like a dream. At twenty gee acceleration
relative to the Solar System, we didn't feel anything unusual at
all. The disk pulled us towards it at twenty-one gee, the acceleration of the ship pulled us away from it at twenty gee, and we sat
there in the middle at a snug and comfortable standard gravity. I
couldn't even feel the tidal forces, though I knew they were
there. We had poor communications with the Penrose Institute,

but we'd known of that and expected to make up for it when we cut the drive.

Oddly enough, the first phase of the trip wasn't scary—it was boring. I wanted to get up to a good cruise speed before we coasted free. It gave me the chance to probe another mystery— one that seemed at least as strange as the disappearance of the *Merganser*.

"What were you doing at the Institute, allowing Nina Velez aboard the ship?"

"She heard that we were developing a new drive—don't ask me how. Maybe she saw the Institute's budget." Wenig sniffed. "I don't trust the security at the USF Headquarters."

"And you let her talk her way in, and you forced McAndrew to take her with him on a *test flight?*"

If I sounded mad, I felt madder. Mac's life meant more than the dignity of some smooth-assed bureaucrat in the Institute's front office.

Dr. Wenig looked at me coldly. "I think you misunderstand the situation. Nina Velez was not forced onto Professor McAndrew by the 'front office'—for one thing, we have no such thing. The Institute is run by its members. You want to know why Miss Velez is on board the *Merganser?* I'll tell you. McAndrew insisted that she go with him."

"Bullshit!" There were some things I couldn't believe. "Why the hell would Mac let himself go along with that? I know him, even if you don't. Over his dead body."

Wenig sighed. He was leaning on a couch across from me, sipping a glass of white wine—no hardship tours for him.

"Four weeks ago I'd have echoed your comments exactly," he said. "Professor McAndrew would never agree to such a thing, right? But he did. Putting this simply, Captain Roker, it is a case of infatuation. A bad one. I think that—"

He stopped, outraged. I had started to laugh, in spite of the seriousness of our situation.

"What's so funny, Captain?"

"Well," I shrugged. "The whole thing's funny. Not funny, it's preposterous. McAndrew is a great physicist, and Nina

Velez may be the President's daughter, but she's just a young
newswoman. He wouldn't—''

Now I stopped. I wondered if Wenig was going to get up and
hit me, he looked so mad.

"Captain Roker, I don't like your insinuation," he said.
"McAndrew is a physicist—so am I. You may not be smart
enough to realize it, but physics is a field of study, not a surgical
operation. Castration isn't part of the Ph.D. exams, you know.''
His tone dripped sarcasm. I wouldn't have liked a two-month
trip to Titan with young Dr. Wenig.

"Anyway," he went on. "You have managed to jump to a
wrong conclusion. It was not Professor McAndrew that suffered
the initial infatuation. It was Nina Velez. She thinks he is
wonderful. She came to do an interview, and before any of us
knew what was going on she was in his office all day. All night,
too, after the first week.''

I was wrong. I know that now, and I think I knew it then, but I
wasn't big enough to make an immediate apology to Wenig.
Instead, I said, "But if she was the one that wanted him,
couldn't he just throw her out?''

"Nina Velez?" Wenig gave a bark of laughter. "You've
never met her, I assume? She's a President's daughter, and
whatever Nina wants, Nina gets. She started it, but inside a
couple of days she had Professor McAndrew behaving like a
true fool. It was disgusting, the way he went on.''

(You're jealous, I said, jealous of Mac's good luck—but I
said it to myself.)

"And she persuaded McAndrew to let her go out on the
Merganser? What were the rest of you doing?''

He reddened. "Professor McAndrew was not the only one
behaving like a fool. Why do you think Limperis, Siclaro, and I
feel like murderers? The two women on the team, Gowers and
Macedo, insisted that Nina Velez should not go near the ships.
We overruled her. Now, Captain Roker, maybe you see why
each of us wanted to come after McAndrew. We drew lots, and I
was the winner.

"And maybe you should think of one other thing," he went
on. "While you are looking at our motives, and laughing at

them, maybe you ought to look at your own. You look angry. I think you are jealous—jealous of Nina Velez.''

It's a good thing that we had to follow our flight plan at that point, and prepare to cut the drive, or I don't know what I would have done to Dr. Wenig. I'm a shade taller than he is, and I outweigh him by maybe ten pounds, but he looked fit and wiry. It wouldn't have been a foregone conclusion, not at all.

Our descent into savagery was saved by the insistent buzzer of the computer, telling us to be ready for the drive reduction. We sat there, furious and not looking at each other, as the acceleration was slowly throttled back and the capsule moved away from the disk to resume its free-flight position two hundred and fifty meters behind it. The move took ten minutes. By the time it was over we had cooled off. I managed a graceless apology for my implied insults, and Wenig just as uncomfortably accepted it and said that he was sorry for what he had been saying and thinking.

I didn't ask him what he *had* been thinking—there was a hint that it was much worse than anything that he had said.

We had cut the drive at a little more than one hundred astronomical units from the Sun and were coasting along at a quarter of the speed of light. The computer gave us automatic Doppler compensation, so that we could hold an accurate communication link back to the Institute, through Oberon Station. Conversation wasn't easy, because the round-trip delay for signals was almost twenty-eight hours—all we expected to be able to do was send ''doing fine'' messages to Limperis and the others.

Our forward motion was completely imperceptible, though I fancied that I could see a reddening of stars astern and a bluer burn to stars ahead of us. We were out well beyond the edge of the planetary part of the System, out where only the comets and the kernels lived. I put all our sensors onto maximum gain and Wenig and I settled in to a quiet spell of close watching. He had asked me what we were looking for. I had told him the truth: I had no idea, of what or when.

We crept on, further out. I don't know if you can creep, at a quarter of light speed, but that's the way it felt; blackness, the unchanging stars, and a dwarfed Solar System far behind us.

Our eyes were all wide open; radio receivers, infra-red scanners, telescopes, flux meters, radar and mass detectors. For two days we found nothing, no signal above the hiss and shimmer of the perennial interstellar background. Wenig was growing more impatient, and his tone was barely civil. He wanted us to get the drive back on high, and dash off after McAndrew—wherever that might be.

He was fidgeting on his bunk and ignoring the scopes when I saw the first trace.

"Dr. Wenig. What am I seeing? Can you tune that IR receiver?"

He came alert and was over to the console in a single movement. After a few seconds of adjustment he shook his head and swore. "It's natural, not man-made. Look at that trace. We're seeing a hot collapsed body. About seven hundred degrees, that's why there's peak power in the five micrometer band. We can call back to Limperis if you like, but he's sure to have it in his catalog already. There must be lots of these within a few days flight of us."

He left the display and slumped back on his bunk. I went over and stared at it for a couple of minutes. "Would McAndrew know that this is here?"

That made him think instead of just brooding. "There's a good chance that he would. Collapsed and high-density matter is Doctor Limperis's special study, but McAndrew probably put a library of them into *Merganser's* computer before he left. He wouldn't want to run into something unexpected out here."

"We have McAndrew's probable trajectory stored there too?"

"We know how he left the System, where he was heading. If he cut the drive, or turned after he was outside tracking range, we don't have any information on it."

"Never mind that. Give me the library access codes, and let me get at the input console. I want to see if Mac's path shows intersection with any of the high-density objects out there."

Wenig looked sceptical. "The chances of such a close encounter are very small. One in millions or billions.''

I was already calling up the access sequence. "By accident? I'd agree with you. But McAndrew must have had some reason to fly back through the System, and make the slight course change that you recorded. I think he was telling us where he was going. And the only place he could have been going between here and Sirius would be one of the collapsed bodies out in the Halo.''

"But *why?*" Wenig was standing at my shoulder, fingers twitching.

"Don't know that." I stood up. "Here, you do it, you must have had plenty of experience with *Dotterel's* computer. Set it for anything that would put *Merganser* within five million kilometers of a high-density body. That's as close as I think we can rely on trajectory intersection.''

Wenig's fingers were flying over the keys—he should have been a concert pianist. I'ver never seen anybody handle a programming sequence at that rate. While he was doing it the com-link whistled for attention. I turned to it, leaving Wenig calling out displays and index files.

"It's Limperis," I said. "Problems. President Velez is starting to breathe down his neck. Wants to know what has happened to Nina. When will she be back? Why did Limperis and the rest of you let her go on a test trip? How can the Institute be so irresponsible?''

"We expected that." Wenig didn't look up. "Velez is just blowing off steam. There's no way that any other ship could get out here to us in less than three months. Does he have anything useful to suggest?''

"No. He's threatening Limperis with punitive measures against the Institute. Says he'll want a review of the whole organization.''

"Limperis is asking for our reply?''

"Yes.''

Wenig keyed in a final sequence of commands and sat back in his seat. "Tell him Velez should go fuck himself. We've got enough to do without interference.''

I was still reading the incoming signals from Oberon Station.

"I think Dr. Limperis has already sent that message to the President's Office—not in those words, maybe. We'd better get Nina back safely."

"I know that." Wenig hit a couple of keys and an output stream began to fill the scope. "Here it comes. Closest approach distances for every body within five hundred AU, assuming McAndrew held the same course and acceleration all the way out. I've set it to stop if we get anything better than a million kilometers, and display everything that's five million or closer."

Before I could learn how to read the display, Wenig banged both hands down on the desk and leaned forward.

"Look at that!" His voice showed his surprise and excitement. "See it? That's HC-183. It's 322 AU from the Sun, and almost dead ahead of us. The computer shows a fly-by distance for *Merganser* too small to compute—that's an underflow where we ought to see a distance."

"Suppose that McAndrew decelerated as he got nearer to it?"

"Wouldn't make much difference, he'd still be close to rendezvous—speeds in orbit are small that far out. But why would he want to rendezvous with HC-183?"

I couldn't answer that, but maybe we were at least going to find *Merganser*. Even if it was only a vaporized trace on the surface of HC-183, where the ship hit it.

"Let's get back with our drive," I said. "What's the mass of HC-183?"

"Pretty high." Wenig frowned at the display. "We show a five thousand kilometer diameter and a mass that's half of Jupiter's. Must be a good lump of collapsed matter at the center of it. How close do you want to take us? And what acceleration for the drive?"

"Give us a trajectory that lets us take a close look from bound orbit. A million kilometers ought to be enough. And keep us down to twenty gee or better. I'll send a message back to the Institute. If they have any more information on HC-183, we want it."

Wenig had been impatient before, when we weren't going

anywhere in particular. Now that we had a target, he couldn't sit still. He was all over our three-meter living capsule, fiddling with the scopes, the computer, and the control console. He kept looking wistfully at the drive setting, then at me.

I wasn't having any. I felt as impatient as he did, but when we had come this far I didn't want to find we'd duplicated *all* McAndrew's actions, including the one that might have been fatal. We smoothly turned after twenty-two hours, so our drive began to decelerate us, and waited out the interminable delay as we crept closer to the dark mass of HC-183. We couldn't see a sign of it on any of the sensors, but we knew it had to be there, hidden behind the plasma ball of the drive.

When the drive went off and we were in orbit around the black mass of the hidden proto-planet, Wenig was at the display console for visible wavelengths.

"I can see it!" he shouted.

My first feeling of relief and excitement lasted only a split second. There was no way we would be able to spot the *Merganser* from a million kilometers out.

"What are you seeing? Infra-red emission from HC-183?"

"No, you sceptic. I can see the ship—McAndrew's ship."

"You can't be. We'd have to be right next to it to be able to pick it up with our magnifications." I spun my seat around and looked at the screen.

Wenig was laughing, hysterical with relief. "Don't you understand? I'm seeing the *drive*, not *Merganser* itself. Look at it, isn't it beautiful?"

He was right. I felt as though I was losing my reason. McAndrew might have gone into orbit about the body, or if he were unlucky he might have run into it—but it made no sense that he'd be sitting here with the drive on. And from the look of the long tail of glowing plasma that stretched across twenty degrees of the screen, that drive was on a high setting.

"Give me a Doppler read-out," I said. "Let's find out what sort of orbit he's in. Damn it, what's he doing there, sightseeing?"

Now that it looked as though we had found them, I was irrationally angry with McAndrew. He had brought us haring out beyond the limits of the System, and he was sitting there waiting when we arrived. Waiting, and that was all.

Wenig had called up a display and was sitting there staring at it in perplexity. "No motion relative to HC-183," he said. "He's not in an orbit around it, he's got the ship just *hanging* there, with the drive balancing the gravitational attraction. Want me to take us alongside, so we can use a radar signal? That's the only way he'll hear us through the drive interference."

"I guess we'll have to. Take us up close to them." I stared at the screen, random thoughts spinning around my head. "No, wait a minute. Damn it, once we set up the computer to take us in there, it will do automatic drive control. Before we go in, let's find out what we're in for. Can you estimate the strength of HC-183's gravitational attraction at the distance that *Merganser* is at? Got enough data for it?"

"Give me a second." Wenig's fingers flew over the console again. If he ever decided that he didn't want to work at the Penrose Institute, he'd make the best space-racer in the System.

He looked at the output for a second, frowned, and said, "I think I must have made an error."

"Why?"

"I'm coming up with a distance from the surface of about nine thousand kilometers. That means the *Merganser* would be feeling a pull of fifty gee—their drive would be full on, as high as it's designed to go. It wouldn't make sense for them to hang there like that, on full drive. Want to go on down to them?"

"No. Hold it where we are." I leaned back and closed my eyes. "There has to be a pattern to what Mac's been doing. He went right through the System back there with the drive full on, now he's hanging close in to a high-density object with the drive still full on. What the hell's he up to?"

"You won't find out unless we can get in touch with him." Wenig was sounding impatient again. "I say we should go on down there. Now we know where he is it's easiest to just go and ask him."

It was hard to argue with him, but I couldn't get an uneasy feeling out of the back of my head. Mac was holding a constant position, fifty gees of thrust balancing the fifty gee pull of

HC-183. We couldn't get alongside him unless we were willing to increase Dotterel's drive to fifty gee.

"Give me five more minutes. Remember why I'm here. It's to keep you from doing anything too brave. Look, if we were to hang on our drive with a twenty gee thrust, how close could we get to the *Dotterel?*"

"We'd have to make sure we didn't fry them with our drive," said Wenig. He was busy for a couple of minutes at the computer, while I tried again to make sense of the pieces.

"We can get so we're about sixty thousand kilometers from them," said Wenig at last. "If we want to talk to them through the microwave radar link, the best geometry would be one where we're seeing them side-on. We'd have decent clearance from both drives there. Ready to do it?"

"One minute more." I was getting a feeling, a sense that everything that McAndrew had done had been guided by a single logic. "Look, I asked you what would happen if the drive failed when the life capsule was up close to the mass disk, and you said the system would move the capsule back out again. But look at it the other way round now. Suppose the drive works fine—and suppose it was the system that's supposed to move the life capsule up and down the column that wouldn't work? What would that do?"

Wenig stroked at his luxuriant mustache. "I don't think it could happen, the design looked good. If it did happen, everything would depend where the capsule stuck."

"Suppose it stuck up near the disk, when the ship was on a high-thrust drive."

"Well, that would mean there was a big gravitational acceleration. You'd have to cancel it out with the drive, or the passengers would be flattened." He paused. "It would be a bugger. You wouldn't dare to turn the drive *off*—you'd need it on all the time, so that your acceleration compensated for the gravity of the disk."

"Damn right. If you couldn't get yourself farther from the disk, you'd be forced to keep on accelerating. That's what happened to the *Merganser*, I'll bet my ass and hat on it. Get the designs of the capsule movement-train up on the screen and let's see if we can spot anything wrong with it.''

"You're an optimist, Captain Roker.'' He shrugged. "We can do it, but those designs have been looked at twenty times. Look, I see what you're saying, but I find it hard to swallow. What was McAndrew doing when he came back through the System and then out again?''

"The only thing he *could* do. He couldn't switch the drive off, even though he could turn the ship around. He could fly off to God knows where in a straight line—that way we'd never have found him. Or he could fly in bloody great circles, and we'd have been able to see him but never get near to him for more than a couple of minutes at a time—there's no other manned ship that could match that fifty gee thrust. Or he could do what he did do. He flew back through the System to tell us the direction he was heading, out to HC-183. And he balanced here on his drive tail, and sat and waited for us to get smart enough to figure out what he was doing.''

I paused for breath, highly pleased with myself. Out of a sphere of trillions of cubic miles, we had tracked the *Merganser* to its destination. Wenig was shaking his head and looking very unhappy.

"What's wrong,'' I said cockily. "Find the logic hard to follow?''

"Not at all. A rather trivial exercise.'' He looked down his nose at me. "But you don't seem able to follow your own ideas to a conclusion. McAndrew knows all about *this* ship. He knows it can accelerate at the same rate as *Merganser*. So your idea that he couldn't fly around in big circles and wait for us to match his position can't be right—the *Dotterel* could do that.''

He was right. "So why didn't Mac do that? Why did he come out all this way?''

"I can only think of one answer. He's had the chance to look at the reason the life capsule can't be moved back along the axis, so the drive mustn't be switched off. And he thinks that this ship has the same problem.''

I nodded. "See now why I wouldn't let you take the *Dotterel* all the way up to fifty gee?''

"I do. You were right, and I would have taken us into trouble if you hadn't been along. Now then''—Wenig looked gloomier than ever at some new thought—''let's take the logic a step farther. McAndrew is hanging down there near HC-183 in a fifty gee gravity field. We can't get there to help him unless we do the same—and we're agreed that we daren't do that, or we'll end up with the same difficulty that he has, and we won't be able to turn off the drive.''

I looked out of the port, towards the dark bulk of HC-183 and the *Merganser*, hovering on its plume of high temperature plasma. Wenig was right. We daren't go down there.

''So how are we going to get them out?''

Wenig shrugged. ''I wish I could tell you. Maybe McAndrew has an answer. If not, they're as inaccessible as if they were halfway to Alpha Centauri and still accelerating. We've got to get into communication with them.''

When I was about eleven years old, just before puberty, I had a disturbing series of dreams. Night after night, for maybe three months, I seemed to wake on the steep face of a cliff. It was dark, and I could barely see handholds and toeholds in the rock.

I had to get to the top—something was hidden below, invisible behind the curve of the black cliff face. I didn't know what it was but I knew it was awful.

Every night I would climb, as carefully as I could, and every night there would come a time when I missed a handhold, and began to slide downwards, down into the pit and the waiting monster.

I woke just as I reached the bottom, just as I was waiting for the first sight of my pit beast.

I never saw it. Puberty arrived, sex dreams replaced my fantasy. I forgot all about the cliff face, the terror, the feeling of force that could not be resisted. Forgot it totally—except that dream memories never disappear completely, they lie at some deep submerged level of the mind, until something pulls them out again.

And here I was, back on the same cliff face, sliding steadily to my fate, powerless to prevent it. I woke up with my heart rate higher by thirty beats a minute, with cold perspiration on my forehead and neck. It took me a long time to return to the present, to banish the bygone fall into the pit.

I finally forced myself up to full consciousness and looked at the screen above me. The purple blaze of a plasma drive danced against the black backdrop of HC-183 and its surrounding star field. It hung there, falling forever but suspended on the feathery stalk of the drive exhaust. I lay there for about ten minutes, just watching, then looked across at Wenig. He was staring at me, his eyes unblinking.

"Awake at last." He made a sort of coughing noise, something that I think was intended to be a laugh. "You're a cool one, Captain Roker. I couldn't sleep with that hanging there"—he jerked his thumb at the screen—"even if you doped me up with everything in the robodoc."

"How long did I sleep?"

"About three hours. Ready to give up now?"

I was. It had been my idea, an insistence that we ought to try and get some sleep before we did the next phase of our maneuver around HC-183. Wenig had opposed it, had wanted to go on at once, but I thought we'd benefit from the rest. So I was wrong.

"I'm ready." My eyes felt as though they'd been filled with grit and my throat was dry and sore, but talking about that to Wenig wouldn't do much for McAndrew or Nina Velez. "Let's get into position and try the radar."

While Wenig juggled us over to the best position, sixty thousand kilometers from HC-183 and about the same distance from the *Merganser,* I wondered again about my companion. They had drawn lots to come with me, and he had won. The other four scientists back at the Institute seemed a little naive and unworldly, but not Wenig. He was tough and shrewd, and I had seen the speed of those hands, dancing over the keyboard. Had he done a bit of juggling when they drew lots, a touch of hand-faster-than-the-eye? I thought of his look when he spoke about Nina. If McAndrew was infatuated, perhaps Wenig shared the spell. Something strong was driving him along, some force that could keep him awake and alert for days on end. I wouldn't know if I was right or not unless we could find a way to haul

Merganser back out of the field. The ship still hovered over its pendant of blue ionized gases, motionless as ever.

"How about this?" Wenig interrupted my thoughts. "I don't think I can get the geometry any better than it is now."

We were hanging there too, farther out from the proto-planet than *Merganser* but close enough to see the black disk occulting the star field. We could beam short bursts of microwaves at our sister ship and hope there was enough signal strength to bore through the sheaths of plasma emitted by the drives. It would be touch and go—I had never tried to send a signal to an unmanned ship on high-drive, but our signal-to-noise ratio stood right on the borderline of system acceptance. As it was, we'd have to settle for voice-links only.

I nodded, and Wenig sent out our first pulses, the simple ship I.D. codes. We sent it for a couple of minutes, then waited with our attention fixed on the screen.

After a while Wenig shook his head. "We're not getting through. It wouldn't take that long to respond to our signal."

"Send it with reduced information rate and more redundancy. We have to give McAndrew enough to filter out the noise."

He was still in send mode when the display screen began to crawl with green patterns of light. Something was coming in. The computer was performing a frequency analysis to pick out the signal content from the background, smoothing it, and speeding it up to standard communication rate. We were looking at the Fourier analysis that preceded signal presentation.

"Voice mode," said Wenig quietly.

"*Merganser.*" The computer reconstruction of McAndrew's voice was slow and hollow. "This is McAndrew from the *Merganser*. We're certainly glad to hear from you, *Dotterel*. Well, Jeanie, what kept you?"

"Roker speaking." I leaned forward and spoke into the vocal input system—too fast, but the computer would take care of that at the other end. "Mac, we're hanging about sixty kay out from you. Is everything all right in *Merganser?*"

"Yes."

"No," broke in another voice. "Get us out of here. We've

been stuck in this damned metal box for sixteen days now.''

"Nina," said Wenig. "We'd love to get you out—but we don't know how. Didn't Dr. McAndrew tell you the problem?''

"He said we couldn't leave here until the other ship you're on came for us.''

Wenig grimaced at me and turned away from the input link. "I ought to have realized that. McAndrew hasn't told her the problem with the drives—not all of it.''

"Maybe he knows an answer.'' I faced back to the microphone. "Mac, as we see it we shouldn't put the *Dotterel* up as high as fifty gee thrust. Correct?''

"Of course.'' McAndrew sounded faintly surprised at my question. "Why do you think I went to such lengths to get to this holding position out here? When you go to maximum setting for the drive, the electro-mechanical coupling for moving the life capsule gets distorted, too.''

"How did we miss it on the design?'' Wenig sounded unconvinced.

"Remember the last-minute increase in stabilizing fields for the mass plate?''

"It was my recommendation—I'm not likely to forget it.''

"We re-calculated the effects on the drive and on the exhaust region, but not the magnetostrictive effects on the life-support column. We thought they were second-order changes.''

"And they're not? I ought to be drawn and quartered—that was my job!'' Wenig was sitting there, fists clenched and face red.

"Was it now? Och, your job, eh? And I've been sitting here thinking all this time it was my job.'' For someone in a hopeless position thirty billion miles from home, McAndrew sounded amazingly cool. "Come on now, we can sort out whose doing it was when we're all back at the Institute.''

Wenig looked startled, then turned to me again. "Go along with him on this—I'm sure he's doing it for Nina's sake. He doesn't want her worried.''

I nodded—but this time I was unconvinced. Mac must have something hidden away inside his head, or not even Nina Velez would justify his optimistic tone.

"What should we do, Mac?" I said. "We'd get the same effects if we were to accelerate too hard. We can't get down to you, and you can't get up to us without accelerating out past us. How are we going to get you out of there?"

"Right." The laugh that came over the com link sounded forced and hollow, but that may have been just the tone that the computer filters gave it. "You might guess that's been on my mind too. The problem's in the mechanical coupling that moves the life capsule along the column. It's easy enough to see, once you imagine that you've had a two millimeter decrease in column diameter—that's the effects of the added field on the mass plate."

Wenig was already calling the schematics out onto a second display. "I'll check that. Keep talking."

"You'll see that when the drive's up to maximum, the capsule catches on the side of the column. It's a simple ratchet effect. I've tried varying the drive thrust up and down a couple of gee, but that won't free it."

"I see where you mean." Wenig had a light-pen out and was circling parts of the column for larger scale displays. "I don't see how we can do anything about it. It would take a lateral impact to free it—you'll not do it by varying your drive."

"Agree. We need some lateral force on us. That's what I'm hoping you'll provide."

"What is all this?" It was Nina's voice again, and she sounded angry. "Why do you just keep on talking like that? Anybody who knew what he was doing would have us out by now—would never have got into it in the first place if he had any sense."

I raised an eyebrow at Wenig. "The voice of infatuation? I think the bloom's off the rose down there."

He looked startled, then pleased, then excited—and then tried to look nonchalant. "I don't know what McAndrew is getting at. How could we provide any help from here?" He turned to the input system. "Dr. McAndrew, how's that possible? We can't provide a lateral force on *Merganser* from here, and we can't come down safely."

"Of course you can." McAndrew's voice sounded pleased,

and I was sure he enjoying making the rest of us try and work out his idea. "It's very easy for you to come down here."

"How, Mac?"

"In a free-fall trajectory. We're in a fifty gee gravity field because we're in a stationary position relative to HC-183. But if you were to let yourself fall in a free orbit, you'd be able to swing in right past us, and away again, and never feel anything but free fall. Agreed?"

"Right. We'd feel tidal effects, but they'd be small." Wenig was calling out displays as he talked, fingers a blur over the computer console. "We can fly right past you, but we'd be there and away in a split second. What could we do in so short a time?"

"Why, what we need." McAndrew sounded surprised by the question. "Give us a good bang on the side as you go by."

It sounded easy, as McAndrew so glibly and casually suggested it. When we went into details, there were three problem areas. If we went too close, we'd be fried in the *Merganser's* drive. Too far off, and we'd never get a strong enough interaction. If all that was worked out correctly, we still had one big obstacle. For the capsule to be freed as *Dotterel* applied sideways pressure, the drive on the other ship would have to cut off completely. Only for a split second, but during that time McAndrew and Nina would feel a full fifty gee on them.

That's not quite as bad as it sounds—people have survived instantaneous accelerations of more than a hundred gee in short pulses. But it's not a picnic, either. Mac continued to sound cheerful and casual, mainly for Nina Velez's benefit. But when he listed the preparations that he was taking inside *Merganser*, I knew he was dealing with a touch-and-go situation.

After all the calculations (performed independently on the two ships, cross-checked and double-checked) we had started our free-fall orbit. It was designed to take us skimming past the *Merganser*, with a closest separation of less than two hundred meters. We daren't go nearer without risking crippling effects from their drive. We would be flying right through its region of turbulence.

Four hours of discussion between McAndrew and Wenig—with interruptions from Nina and me—had fixed the sequence for the vital half-second when we would be passing the *Merganser*. The ships would exert gravitational forces on each other, but that was useless for providing the lateral thrust on the life capsule system that McAndrew thought was needed. We had to give a more direct and harder push some other way.

Timing was crucial, and very tricky. Whatever we threw at the other ship would have to pass through the drive exhaust region before it could impact the life capsule column. If the drive were on, nothing could get through it—at those temperatures it would be vaporized on the way, even if it were there for only a fraction of a second. The sequence had to be: launch mass from *Dotterel;* just before it got there, kill drive on *Merganser;* hold drive off just long enough for *Dotterel* to clear area and for the mass to impact *Merganser* support column; and back on with their drive, at once, because when the drive was off *Merganser's* passengers would be feeling the full fifty gees of the mass plate's gravity.

McAndrew and Wenig cut the time of approach of the two ships into millisecond pieces. They decided exactly how long each phase should last. Then they let the two on-board computers of the ships talk to each other, to make sure that everything was synchronized between them—at the rate things would be happening, there was no way that humans could control them. Not even Wenig, with his super-fast reflexes. We'd all be spectators, while the two computers did the real work and I nursed the abort switch.

There was one argument. McAndrew had wanted to use a storage tank as the missile that we would eject from our ship to impact theirs. It would provide high momentum transfer for a very brief period. Wenig argued that we should trade off time against intensity, and use a liquid mass instead of a solid one. Endless discussion and calculations, until Mac was convinced too. We would use all our spare water supply, about a ton and a

half of it. That left enough for drinking water on a twenty gee
return to the Inner System, but nothing spare for other uses. It
would be a scratchy and smelly trip home for *Dotterel's* passengers.

Drive off, we felt only the one-gee pull of our mass plate as
we dropped it to close approach. On *Merganser,* McAndrew
and Nina Velez were lying in water bunks, cushioned with
everything soft on the ship. We were on an impact course with
them, one that would change to a near-miss after we ejected the
water ballast. It looked like a suicide mission, running straight
into the blue furnace of their drive.

The sequence took place so fast it was anti-climactic. I saw
the drive cut off ahead of us, felt the vibration along the support
column as our mass driver threw the ballast hard towards *Merganser.* The brief pulse from our drive that took us clear of them
was too quick for me to feel.

We cleared the drive region. Then there seemed to be a wait
that lasted for hours. McAndrew and Nina were now in a ship
with drive off, dropping towards HC-183. They were exposed to
the full fifty gees of their mass plate. Under that force, I knew
what happened to the human body. It had not been designed to
operate when it suddenly weighed more than four tons. Mem-
branes ruptured, valves burst, veins collapsed. The heart had
never evolved to pump blood that weighed hundreds of pounds,
up a gravity gradient of fifty gee. The only thing that Mac and
Nina had going for them was the natural inertia of matter. If the
period of high gee was short enough, the huge accelerations
would not have time to produce those shattering physical effects.

Wenig and I watched on our screens for a long, long moment,
until the computer on *Merganser* counted off the last micro-
second and switched on the drive again. If the life capsule was
free to move along its column, the computer would now begin
the slow climb out of HC-183's gravity well. No action was
needed from the passengers. When we completed our own orbit
we hoped we would see the other ship out at a safe distance,
ready for the long trip home.

And on board the ship? I wasn't sure. If the encounter had

lasted too long, we might find no more than two limp and broken sacks of blood, tissue and bone.

It was another long day, waiting until we had carried around in our orbit and could try and rendezvous the two ships. As soon as we were within radar range again, Nina Velez appeared on the com screen. The drive was cut back, so we could get good visual signals. My heart sank when I saw the expression on her face.

"Can you get over to this ship—quickly?" she said.

I could see why all the professors at the Institute had lost their senses. She was small and slight, with a childlike look of trust and sad blue eyes. All a sham, according to everything I'd been told, but there was no way of seeing the strong personality behind the soft looks. I took a deep breath.

"What's happening there?" I said.

"We're back under low gee drive, and that's fine. But I haven't been able to wake him. He's breathing, but there's blood on his lips. He needs a doctor."

"I'm the nearest thing to that in thirty billion miles." I was pulling a suit towards me, sick with a sudden fear. "I've had some medical training as part of the Master's License. And I think I know what's wrong with McAndrew. He lost part of a lung lobe a couple of years ago. If anything's likely to be hemorrhaging, that's it. Dr. Wenig, can you arrange a rendezvous with the mass plates at maximum separation and the drives off?"

"I'll need control of their computer." He was pulling his suit on, too. I didn't want him along, but I might need somebody to return to the *Dotterel* for medical supplies.

"What should I be doing?" Thank Heaven Nina showed no signs of panic. She sounded impatient, with the touch of President Velez in her voice. "I've sat around in this ship for weeks with nothing to be done. Now we need action but I daren't take it."

"What field are you in now? What net field?"

"One gee. The drive's off now, and we've got the life capsule right out at the end of the column."

"Right. I want to you stay in that position, but set the drive at one gee acceleration. I want Doctor McAndrew in a zero-gee environment to slow the bleeding. Dr. Wenig, can you dictate instructions for that while we are rendezvousing?''

"No problem.'' He was an irritating devil, but I'd choose him in a crisis. He was doing three things at once, putting on his suit, watching the computer action for the rendezvous, and giving exact and concise instructions to Nina.

Getting from one ship to the other wasn't as easy as it might sound. We had both ships under one gee acceleration drives, complicated by the combined attraction of the two mass plates. The total field acting on us was small, but we had to be careful not to forget it. If we lost contact with the ships, the nearest landing point was back on Oberon Station, thirty billion miles away.

Nina in the flesh was even more impressive than she was over the video link, but I gave her little more than a cursory once-over. McAndrew's color was bad and even while I was cracking my suit open and hustling out of it I could hear a frightening bubbling sound in his breathing. Thank God I had learned how to work in zero gee—required part of any space medicine course. I leaned over him, vaguely aware of the two others intently watching. The robodoc beside me was clucking and flashing busily, muttering a faint complaint at McAndrew's condition and the zero gee working environment. Standard diagnosis conditions called for at least a partial gravity field.

I took the preliminary diagnosis and prepared to act on it even while the doc was still making up its mind. Five cc's of cerebral stimulant, five cc's of metabolic depressant, and a reduction in cabin pressure. It should bring Mac up to consciousness, if his brain was still in working order. I worried about a cerebral hemorrhage, the quiet and deadly by-product of super high gees. Ten minutes and I would know one way or the other.

I turned to Wenig and Nina who were still watching the robodoc's silent body trace. "I don't know how he is yet. We may need emergency treatment facilities ready for us as soon as we get back to the System. Can you go over to *Dotterel,* cut the drive, and try and make contact with Oberon Station? By the time you have the connection we should have the diagnosis here.''

I watched them leave the ship, saw how carefully Wenig helped Nina to the transfer, and then I heard the first faint noise behind me. It was a sigh, with a little mutter of protest behind it. The most wonderful sound I ever heard in my life. I glanced over at the doc. Concussion—not too bad—and a little more bleeding than I wanted to see from the left lung. Hell, that was nothing. I could patch the lung myself, maybe even start the feedback regeneration for it. I felt a big grin of delight spreading like a heat wave over my face.

"Take it easy, Mac. You're doing all right, just don't try and rush yourself. We've got lots of time." I secured his left arm so that he couldn't disturb the rib cage on that side. He groaned.

"Doing fine, am I?" He suddenly opened his eyes and stared up at me. "Holy water, Jeanie, that's just like a medic. I'm in agony, and you say it's a little discomfort. How's Nina doing?"

"Not a mark on her. She's not like you, Mac, an old bag of bones. You're getting too old for that sort of crap."

"Where is she?"

"Over on *Dotterel*, with Wenig. What's the matter, still infatuated?"

He managed a faint smile. "Ah, none of that now. We were locked up on *Merganser* for more than two weeks, in a three meter living sphere. Show me an infatuation, and I'll show you a cure for it."

The com link behind me was buzzing. I cut it in, so that we could see Wenig's worried face.

"All right here," I said, before he had time to worry any more. "We'll be able to take our time going back. How are you? Got enough water?"

He nodded. "I took some of your reserve supply to make up for what we threw at you. What should we do now?"

"Head on back. Tell Nina that Mac's all right, and say we'll see you both back at the Institute."

He nodded again, then leaned closer to the screen and spoke with a curious intensity. "We don't want to run the risk of having a stuck life capsule again. I'd better keep us down to less than ten gee acceleration."

And he cut off communication, without another word. I turned to McAndrew.

"How high an acceleration before you'd run into trouble with these ships?"

He was staring at the blank screen, a confused look on his thin face. "At least forty gee. What the devil's got into Wenig? And what the hell are you laughing at, you silly bitch?"

I came over to him and took his right hand in mine. "To each his own, Mac. I wondered why Wenig was so keen to get here. He wants his shot at Nina—out here, where nobody else can compete. What did *you* tell her—some sweet talk about her lovely eyes?"

He closed his eyes again and smiled a secret smile. "Ah, come on Jeanie. Are you telling me you've been on your best behavior since I last saw you? Gi' me a bit of peace. I'm not soft on Nina now."

"I'll see." I went across to the drive and moved us up to forty gee. "Wait until the crew on Titan hear about all this. You'll lose your reputation."

He sighed. "All right. I'll play the game. What's the price of silence?"

"How long would it take a ship like this to get out to Alpha Centauri?"

"You'd not want this one. We'll have the next one up to a hundred gee. Forty-four ship days would get you there, standing start to standing finish."

I nodded, came back to his side and held his hand again. "All right, Mac, that's my price. I want one of the tickets."

He groaned again, just a bit. But I knew from the dose the doc had put into him that it wasn't a headache this time.

AFTERWORD: MOMENT OF INERTIA.

It's not hard to reconstruct McAndrew's reasoning when he developed the specifications for designing the Dotterel and the Merganser. It must have run as follows:-

Consider a thin flat circular plate of material, uniform in composition. Suppose its mass is M and its radius R, so that the mass density (σ) per unit area is $\sigma = M/\pi R^2$.

At a point P on the axis of the disc, distance z from its center, the gravitational potential is given by:

$$\phi = G \int \frac{\sigma.dA}{\rho}$$

$$= G \int_{O}^{R} \frac{2\pi r.dr.\sigma}{\sqrt{r^2 + z^2}} \times \frac{2GM \cdot}{R^2} \left\{ \sqrt{R^2 + z^2} - z \right\}$$

----(1)

where G is the gravitational constant.

The acceleration at P towards the disc is then:

$$a_z = -\partial\phi/\partial z = 2GM/R^2 \left\{ 1 - z/\sqrt{R^2 + z^2} \right\} \cdot$$

----(2)

and the tidal effect (rate of change of acceleration) is:

$$-\partial a_z/\partial z = 2GM/\left\{ R^2 + z^2 \right\}^{3/2} \cdot$$

----(3)

If we require that the rate of change of acceleration (i.e. the tidal effect) should be one gee per meter when the acceleration is 50 gee, from (2) and (3) we have:

$$50 = 2GM/R^2 \left\{ 1 - z/\sqrt{R^2 + z^2} \right\}$$

$$1 = 2GM/\left\{ R^2 + z^2 \right\}^{3/2}$$

thus $50R^2 = \left\{ 1 - z/\sqrt{R^2 + z^2} \right\} \cdot (R^2 + z^2)^{3/2}$ ----(4)
and this relation between R and z must hold independent *of the mass M.*

An infinite number of (R,z) pairs will satisfy equation (4), and Table 1 lists some of them, together with the mass M, found from equation (3), and the distance, Z, where the gravitational acceleration towards the disc is one gee. Since we may as well use the most compact and lightest of the possible cases, we use the set: R = 50 meters, z = 0 meters, Z = 246.2 meters, GM = 62,500 square meters.

This means a mass plate 50 meters in radius, and projecting from it we have a column at least 246.2 meters long. The life capsule will ride up and down this as the drive acceleration is varied.

The only other thing that McAndrew needed to know was the gravitational acceleration and tidal effects at different distances from the plate. He would use these to decide how far away the life capsule should be positioned for different drive accelerations. Those values are provided from equations (2) and (3) and are shown in Table 2.

This story has worried a number of readers. They say, in summary, how can a ship that can only generate fifty gee of thrust ever escape from a field where it is just balancing a fifty

TABLE 1

Distance when accn. is 50g (meters)	Disc radius (meters)	Disc mass X G (squ. meters)	Distance when accn. is 1 gee (meters)
0	50.00	62,500	246.2
5	54.35	81,294	281.2
10	57.68	100,308	312.8
25	63.56	159,305	395.3
50	63.60	264,747	511.6
75	51.79	378,575	613.6
100	0	500,000	707.1

TABLE 2

Distance from disc (meters)	Acceleration due to disc (gees)	Tidal effect (gees/meter)
0	50	1.0
2	48	1.0
5	45	.99
10.2	40	.94
15.7	35	.87
21.9	30	.77
28.9	25	.65
37.5	20	.51
49.0	15	.36
66.5	10	.22
103	5	.08
246	1	.01

gee attraction? It's a hypothetical question, since the beginning of the story points out that the fifty gee limit applies not to the propulsion system, but to the balancing system that neutralizes the propulsive acceleration. Even so, it's a nice question, and one easily answered.

If you are sitting balanced with a fifty gee thrust and a fifty gee attraction towards some central body, all you need do to escape is to turn the ship and direct the thrust at right angles to the direction of the attracting body. You then fall inwards at first, but the trajectory has a point of closest approach about 5,000 kilometers from the center of attraction–so we can only use this method for orbits about high-density and compact objects. If anyone is interested I can provide the actual trajectory and the profile of the escape spiral.

There is, however, still a problem with the story, and one less easily answered. It concerns the drive itself. McAndrew's ship generates its fifty gee acceleration by expelling reaction mass– necessary for any propulsion system that wishes to satisfies the law of conservation of linear momentum. Unless we wish to throw overboard the most basic laws of modern physics, reactionless drives are out, as are drives that somehow convert angular momentum to linear momentum. We are stuck with a *drive that consumes reaction mass to achieve its propulsive effect.*

Suppose that McAndrew's ship had a photon drive, in which matter is turned to radiation and the radiation, suitably directed, provides the thrust. That's the best we can imagine, if we accept today's physics. With a photon drive, it's easy to calculate that a sustained fifty gee drive will quickly consume the ship's own mass in order to keep on accelerating. Half the mass would be gone in a few days, and McAndrew's ship would disappear from under him.

There is one loophole, a solution based on a known inconsistency between general relativity and quantum theory. To explore that loophole, see "All The Colors of the Vacuum," later in this collection.

THE NEW PHYSICS: THE SPEED OF LIGHTNESS, CURVED SPACE, AND OTHER HERESIES

Listwolme is a small world with a thin but permanently cloudy atmosphere. The inhabitants have never seen the stars, nor become aware of anything beyond their own planet. There is one main center of civilization which confined itself to a small region of the surface until about a hundred years ago, when an industrial revolution took place. For the first time, rapid transportation over substantial areas of the planet became possible.

Orbital velocity at the surface of Listwolme is less than two kilometers a second. The meetings of the Listwolme Scientific Academy following the development of high-velocity surface vehicles are chronicled below. The highlights of those meetings were undoubtedly the famous exchanges between Professor Nessitor and Professor Spottipon.

The first debate: In which Professor Nessitor reveals the curious results of his experiments with high-speed vehicles, and proposes a daring hypothesis.

Nessitor: As Members of the Academy will recall, a few months ago I began to install sensitive measuring devices aboard the *Tristee Two,* the first vehicle to move at a speed more than ten times that of a running *schmitzpoof.* The work was not easy, because it was first necessary to suppress all vibration induced by the car's contact with the surface.

One month ago we achieved the right combination of smooth suspension and vibration damping. It was with some excitement that I placed one of our instruments, a sensitive spring balance, within the vehicle and we began steadily to increase our speed. As you may have heard, there have been reports of "feeling light" from the drivers of these cars when they go at maximum velocity.

Fellow scientists, those feelings are no illusion! Our instruments showed a definite decrease in load on the balance as our speed was increased. There is a relationship between *weight* and *motion!*

(As Nessitor paused, there was a murmur of surprise and incredulity around the great hall. Professor Spottipon rose to his feet.)

Spottipon: Professor Nessitor, your reputation is beyond question. What would arouse scepticism from another in your case is treated with great respect. But your statement is so amazing that we would like to hear more of these experiments. For example, I have heard of this "lightening" effect at high speeds, but seen no quantitative results. Were your balances sensitive enough to measure some relation between the lightness and the speed?

Nessitor (triumphantly): With great precision. We measured the weight shown on the balance at a wide variety of speeds, and from this I have been able to deduce a precise formula between the measured weight, the original weight when the vehicles was at rest, and the speed of movement. It is as follows.

(Here Professor Nessitor went to the central display screen and sketched on it the controversial formula. It is believed that this was the first time it had ever appeared to public view.

In the form that Nessitor used, it reads:

(Weight at speed v) = (Rest weight) $\times$ (1 - v^2/c^2)

When the formula was exhibited there was a silence, while the others examined its implications.)

Spottipon (thoughtfully): I think I can follow the significance of most of this. But what is the constant, c, that appears in your equation?

Nessitor: It is a velocity, a new constant of nature. Since it measures the degree to which an object is lightened when it moves with velocity v, I suggest that the basic constant, c, should be termed the "speed of lightness".

Spottipon (incredulously): You assert that this holds anywhere on Listwolme? That your formula does not depend on the *position* where the experiment is conducted?

Nessitor: That is indeed my contention. In a series of experiments at many places on the surface, the same result was obtained everywhere, with the same velocity, "c". It is almost four times as fast as our fastest car.

(There was a long pause, during which Professor Spottipon was seen to be scribbling rapidly on a scribe pad. When he had finished his face bore a look of profound inspiration.)

Spottipon: Professor Nessitor, the formula you have written has some strange implications. You assert that there is a lightening of weight with speed across the surface. This we might accept, but you have not taken your formula to its logical limit. Do you realize that there must be a speed when the weight *vanishes?* When v = c, you have a situation where an object does not push at all on the balance! Worse than that, if v *exceeds* your "speed of lightness" you would calculate a *negative* weight. If that were true, a car moving at such a speed would fly completely off the surface. You would have created the long-discussed and arguably impossible "flying machine."

Nessitor (calmly): As Professor Spottipon has observed with his usual profound insight, the speed of lightness is a most fundamental constant. My interpretation is as follows: since it is clearly ridiculous that an object should have negative weight, the formula is trying to tell us something very deep. It is pointing out that *there is no way that an object can ever exceed the speed of lightness*. The speed that we can deduce from these experiments, c, represents the ultimate limit of speed that can ever be attained.

(Sensation. The assembled scientists began to talk among themselves, some frankly disbelieving, others pulling forth their scribe pads and writing their own calculations. At last a loud voice was heard above the general hubbub.)

Voice: Professor Nessitor! Do you have any name for this new theory of yours?

Nessitor (shouting to be heard): I do. Since the effects depend only on the motion *relative* to the ground, I suggest the new results should be termed the PRINCIPLE OF RELATIVITY. I think that . . .

(Professor Nessitor's next comments were unfortunately lost in the general noise of the excited assembly.)

Six months passed before Professor Nessitor appeared again at a meeting of the Academy. In those months, there had been much speculation and heated argument, with calls for more experiments. It was to an expectant but still sceptical audience that the Professor made his second address.

Nessitor: Distinguished colleagues, last time that I was here there were calls for proof, for some fundamental basis for the formula I presented to you then. It was to answer those calls that I embarked, four months ago, on a new set of experiments with the *Tristee Two* vehicle. We had installed a new instrument on board our car. It measures distances very accurately, and permits the car's course to be controlled to an absolutely straight line. For it had occurred to me to ask the question, if velocity and weight are so closely linked, could it be that *distance* itself depends on some unknown factors?

Spottipon (somewhat irritably): With all due respect, Nessitor, I have no idea what you mean by such a statement. Distance is distance, no matter how fast you traverse it. What could you hope to find? I hoped that you would have repeated the experiments on speed and weight.

Nessitor: My esteemed colleague, please have patience. Permit me to tell you what happened. We set the *Tristee Two* to travel a long distance at various speeds. And indeed, we confirmed the speed-weight relation. At the same time, we were measuring the distance travelled. But in performing this experiment we were moving longer linear distances over the surface of Listwolme than any other scientific group had ever done.

I therefore decided to conduct an experiment. We travelled a long distance in a certain direction, accurately measuring this with our new instrument. Then we made a half turn and proceeded far along this new line, again measuring distance all the way. Finally, we headed straight back to our original starting point, following the hypotenuse of the triangle and measuring this distance also.

Now, we are all familiar with the Sharog-Paty Theorem that relates the lengths of the sides of a right-angled triangle.

(Nessitor went to the central display panel and scribed the famous Sharog-Paty relation:

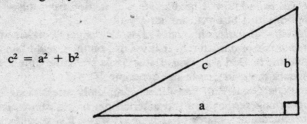

$$c^2 = a^2 + b^2$$

There was a mutter of comments from behind him.)

Impatient voice from the audience: Why are you wasting our time with such trivia? This relation is known to every unfledged child!

Nessitor: Exactly. But it is not what we found from our measurements! On long trips—and we made many such—*the Sharog-Paty relation does not hold.* The further we went in our movements, the worse the fit between theory and observation.

After some experiment, I was able to find a formula that expresses the true relation between the distances a, b, and c. It is as follows.

(Nessitor stepped again to the display panel and wrote the second of his famous relations, in the form: $\cos(c/R) = \cos(a/R) \times \cos(b/R)$.

There was more intense study and excited scribbling in the audience. Professor Spottipon alone did not seem to share in the general stir. His thin face had gone pale, and he seemed to be in the grip of some strong private emotion. At last he rose again to his feet.)

Spottipon: Professor, old friend and distinguished colleague. What is "R" in your equation?

Nessitor: It is a new fundamental constant, a distance that I calculate to be about three million paces.

Spottipon (haltingly): I have trouble saying these words, but they must be said. In some of my own work I have looked at the geometry of other surfaces than the plane. Professor Nessitor, the formula you have written there already occurs in the literature. It is the formula that governs the distance relations *for the surface of a sphere*. A sphere of radius R.

Nessitor: I know. I have made a deduction from this—

Spottipon: I beg you, do not say it!

Nessitor: I must, although I know its danger. I understand the teachings of our church, that we live on the Great Plain of the World, in God's glorious flatness. At the same time I cannot ignore the evidence of my experiments.

(The Great Hall had fallen completely silent. One of the recording scribes dropped a scribe pin in his excitement and received quick glares of censure. It was a few seconds before Nessitor felt able to continue. He stood there with head bowed.)

Nessitor: Colleagues, I must say to you what Professor Spottipon with his great insight realized at once. The distance formula is identical with that for distances on a sphere. My experiments suggest that *space is curved*. We live not on a plane, but on the surface of an immense sphere.

(The tension crackled around the hall. The penalty for heresy (smothering in live toads) was known to all. At last Professor Spottipon moved to Nessitor's side and placed one hand on his shoulder.)

Spottipon: My old friend, you have been overworking. On behalf of all of us, I beg you to take a rest. This "curved space" fancy of yours is absurd—we would slide down the sides and fall off.

(The hall rang with relieved laughter.)

Spottipon: Even if our minds could grasp the concept of a curved space, the teachings of the Church must predominate. Go home, now, and rest until your mind is clearer.

(Professor Nessitor was helped from the stage by kind hands. He looked dazed.)

For almost a year, the Academy met without Nessitor's presence. There were rumors of new theories, of work conducted at white heat in total seclusion. When news came that he would again attend a meeting, the community buzzed with speculation. Rumors of his heresy had spread. When he again stood before the assembly, representatives of the Church were in the audience.

Professor Spottipon cast an anxious look at the Churchmen as he made Nessitor's introduction.

Spottipon: Let me say how pleased we are, Professor Nessitor, to welcome you again to this company. I must add my personal pleasure that you have abandoned the novel but misguided ideas that you presented to us on earlier occasions. Welcome to the Academy!

Nessitor (rising to prolonged applause, he looked nervous but determined): Thank you. I am glad to be again before this group, an assembly that has been central to my whole working life. As Professor Spottipon says, I have offered you some new ideas over the past couple of years, ideas without fundamental supporting theory. I am now in a position to offer a new and far more basic approach. *Space is curved, and we live on the surface of a sphere!* I can now prove it.

Spottipon (motioning to other scientists on the stage): Quick, help me to get him out of here before it's too late.

Nessitor (speaking quickly): The curvature of space is real, and the speed of lightness is real. But the two theories are not independent! The fundamental constants c and R are related to a third one. You know that falling bodies move with a rate of change of speed, g, the "gravitational constant". I can now prove that there is an *exact* relation, that $c^2 = g \times R$. To prove this, consider the motion of a particle around the perimeter of a circle . . .

(The audience was groaning in dismay. Before Nessitor could speak further, friends were removing him gently but firmly from the stage. But the representatives of the church were already moving forward.)

At his trial, two months later, Professor Nessitor recanted all his heretical views, admitting that the new theories of space and time were deluded and nonsensical. His provisional sentence of toad-smothering was commuted to a revocation of all leaping

privileges. He has settled quietly to work at his home, where he
is writing a book that will be published only after his death.

And there were those present at his trial who will tell you that
as Nessitor stepped down from the trial box he whispered to
himself—so softly that the words may have been imagined
rather than heard— "But it *is* round."

AFTERWORD: THE NEW PHYSICS.

Sir Arthur Eddington, who will be quoted elsewhere in this collection, once remarked that one mystery of the universe is the way that everything in it seems to rotate—*planets, stars, galaxies, they all do it. Surely Listwolme too would rotate on its axis.*

This is a worrying thought. What would it do to Nessitor's observations? Well, he would have found that his "speed of lightness" was a function of direction; it would be lower if he travelled in the same direction as the planet's spin, higher if he went opposite to it. From this he would have concluded that his universe lacked perfect symmetry–there was a preferred direction to it, the direction of the spin axis of the planet.

That seems to ruin the analogy between his physics and ours, since our universe appears to exhibit no preferred direction. It is assumed to be isotropic, the same in all directions. Except that . . .

In 1949, Kurt Gödel published a strange solution of the Einstein field equations of general relativity. It describes a universe in which there is a preferred direction, an "axis of rotation" for the entire cosmos. People usually reject Godel's model by saying it is "non-physical" and does not represent anything in physical reality. But one other way to look at it is to say that we happen, by accident, to live in a non-rotating universe. Most universes, like most other objects, may rotate– we are the odd man out. Or perhaps, as our observational methods become more and more sensitive, we will conclude that this universe is not perfectly isotropic. Maybe with better instruments we and Nessitor would both find evidence of a slow overall rotation.

FROM NATURAL CAUSES

Like droplets of acid, envy had eaten slowly into the soul of John Laker. On the day that the shell of his soul was completely eroded he killed Alan Gifford; and on that day the time of true suffering began.

The murder occurred in late September but the first taste of acid had come on a perfect June day more than twenty years earlier. Laker saw the world then through a dark haze. Tight bands of pain were closing about his chest as he went round the final bend and on into the straight, clenching his jaws and pushing towards the finishing tape. As he passed it his senses could record only one thing. Alan Gifford, on his right—and half a pace ahead. The friendly arm that held his panting body after the race was Gifford's.

That scene set the pattern for the school years. Alan Gifford and John Laker, tracks stars—but always in that order. It didn't help Laker to know his times easily beat those of champions of previous years. Somehow that made it worse. In the single year when Laker swept the board in track events, the sight of Gifford in the crowd, weak from an appendicitis operation but cheering Laker on, turned victory to ashes. Next year Gifford was again an agonizing half stride ahead.

College brought no relief. John Laker was a good engineering student and he did well, very well. But Gifford was an engineer too, and seemed always to win the top design prize or get extra credit for originality. By the time they left college John Laker was an obsessed and tormented man.

"What next, John?" asked Gifford on the last day of school.

"Probably a government job. AEC maybe. That's my strongest suit. How about you?"

"Still not sure. I've had a good offer from the Bureau of Standards. See you in Washington, by the look of things." He slapped Laker on the back and headed off across the noisy campus.

In the years that followed the two men ran across each other about every couple of months. Alan Gifford had no idea how closely John Laker followed his career—raises, promotions, new responsibilities. He didn't know there was an unannounced and one-sided competition. Laker resented every success Gifford achieved, was wounded by each sign of his progress. Each year the burn went a little deeper.

The murder when it came was unplanned, almost an accident. Laker, walking from the bus stop to his house, met Gifford in the street. On an impulse he asked him in for a drink.

"This your place?" said Gifford in surprise as they turned into the driveway. "I'd no idea you lived in such luxury. How much land do you have, a couple of acres?"

"A bit more." Laker looked at Gifford, hoping at last to see a sign of envy. There was only simple pleasure at the beauty of the handsome red brick Colonial and well-kept garden.

They went on into the house. Laker saw their reflection in the full-length mirror by the hall coat stand. Greyhaired, lined with bitterness, he looked the older man by ten years. Envy and grinding work had taken their toll. Gifford went to the living-room window and stood looking out over the smooth lawn and carefully tended flower beds.

"You do a first-rate job out there, John," he said. "Wish I could get my garden to look like that."

Laker came over to the window and looked out absently. "That's my gardener. He comes in every day. I don't seem to find the time to do much there myself." He had forgotten the breadth of Gifford's interests. Gifford was an enthusiastic amateur gardener, as he seemed to be an enthusiastic everything else. "What are you doing over this side of town, Alan? I thought you were still living in Arlington."

Gifford nodded. "I am. Right on the approach path to National Airport, I think. I came over here to see Don Thomson at the Arboretum. Remember him from the University? He was mad about plants even then. Has the ideal job and spends all day playing about with new varieties of flowers.''

Laker smiled. ''Sure, I remember him. All teeth and top-soil.'' He poured their drinks and shrugged. ''Should get over there myself, but you know how it is—something's only half a mile away, you figure you can see it anytime—so you never do.''

''You should. There's no place like it for plant collections. Don would love to show you round.''

As he spoke, Gifford was strolling slowly round the room, sipping his drink and admiring the furniture and elegant china. He shook his head ruefully. ''You've got taste *and* money. You know, Jean's illness used up most of my reserves.''

His wife had died three years before after a long illness. Gifford had cared for her until the end, giving his days and nights to the struggle. Childless, he lived alone. Laker, driven from within, had never married and also lived by himself. The furnishings of the house had been decided by his married sister, indulging a taste beyond her own means.

Gifford looked at his watch. ''Better begin the trek home. No, I won't have another, I've got to fight the Beltway traffic. But I'd like to take a look at your garden on the way out.''

''Sure. Pity the gardener's not here. He could tell you what everything is a lot better than I can.''

In the big front garden they walked slowly from one flower bed to another in the early evening sunshine. Gifford kept up a running commentary.

''That's going to be a great show of chrysanthemums in another couple of months. These dahlias are show standard. Ah, now. Here's the sign of a real professional.'' He stopped before a flower bed set back about fifteen yards from the front double gates. ''He's double digging there. Must be two feet deep, that trench. I always swear I'll do that but I never get round to it. It makes all the difference to the soil.''

As they approached the hot-house Laker felt a lump in his chest. When they paused before a tray of seedlings the truth hit him like a hammer blow. He had bought the house to compete with Gifford, to show the world he was richer, more successful.

But Gifford was finding more pleasure there in one evening than Laker had ever found.

The world turned red, the last drop of acid found the center of his soul. He lifted a heavy claw hammer sitting by the boxes of seedlings. Alan Gifford fell. John Laker's real torment began.

The first hours were a frenzy of activity. When darkness fell he carried Gifford's body in a wheelbarrow to the deep trench in the front garden. A crescent moon gave just enough light to drop it in and cover it with a foot and a half of topsoil. Then he went again and again over the house and garden to remove all evidence of Gifford's visit. The cleaning woman arrived at eight the next morning and found him slumped in an armchair in the living room, eyes fixed on the flower beds. He roused himself to call his office and explain he was sick, then call his gardener and give him a month's wages in lieu of notice. He had, he explained, a relative down on his luck who needed the job. No need to come by, he would have the gardener's tools sent over to him.

The next few days were spent in mindless waiting. Nothing happened. After a week he had a new problem. He could allow no one to work on the garden, especially the front flower beds.

"When's the gardener coming back?" asked his cleaning woman. "It's getting really raggy out there."

"I'll be doing it myself. Doctor's idea. Thinks I can do with the fresh air and exercise."

That was easily accepted. He did indeed look terrible. First thing in the morning and last thing at night his thoughts went to the flower bed and the hidden body. At four in the morning he would wake from a recurring dream. Alan Gifford's arm had risen from the home-made grave and was pointing up, visible from the street. Each time he had a compulsion to get up and go out into the garden. It was no more than a nightmare—but sleep came hard after it.

Fall turned slowly to winter. He was forced to work on the garden himself, raking leaves, cleaning up withered raspberry canes and dry iris stems. At first he was clumsy and inefficient. He read books and consulted his acquaintances on the theory

and practice of gardening. For the first time since early youth
envy and work were not the twin centers of his life. In their place
had come concealment of his crime. This meant constant tend-
ing of the garden and private grave.

Evenings and week-ends now were spent working outside.
"It's doing him a lot of good, working in the garden," the
cleaning woman told her sister. "He's getting some color in his
cheeks. The best advice his doctor could have given him, I'd
say."

Winter came and work on the yard slowed. Then the first
promise of spring and renewed frantic activity. Little by little,
the slow pulse of the seasons was marking its rhythm in John
Laker. His mental agony grew less, fear of discovery gave way
to understanding of the motive for the crime and remorse at his
actions. Spring became summer and the garden exerted its heal-
ing influence. Alan Gifford's grave was a bright mass of flowers, planted and tended by Laker's careful hands.

Eleven months after Gifford's death, in mid-August, it came.
A polite, neatly-dressed man was waiting for Laker when he
returned from work one Friday evening.

"Mr. John Laker? My name is Porson." He presented his
credentials. "With your permission I'd like to ask you a few
questions regarding the disappearance of Alan Gifford."

Laker felt the lifting of a long-held burden. "Let's go inside. I
think I can help you in your inquiry."

When they came out half an hour later John Laker stopped by
the coat rack to pick up a jacket. He expected to be away some
time. His reflection in the full-length mirror showed a greyhaired, tanned man, relaxed and fit. On their way to the front
gate the two men stopped briefly by the front flower bed, soon to
be disturbed by police officials.

"Tell me one thing would you," said Laker. "How did you
find out? And what took you so long?"

"You can't rush Nature, Sir." Porson turned again to the
flower bed. "The day he disappeared Alan Gifford had visited a
friend, Mr. Donald Thomson, at the Arboretum down the road
from here. Thomson knew Gifford liked gardening so he gave

him a couple of bulbs from the flower he'd been developing. A new variety of stem-rooting lily—dwarf, with crimson flowers.

"Thomson never saw that flower growing anywhere outside the Arboretum test beds—until he walked past your house last week on a lunchtime stroll. He knew Gifford had disappeared. After stewing on it for a few days he called us.

"A stem-rooting lily likes to be planted good and deep." Porson pointed at the flower bed, where a brilliant Turk's Head contrasted sharply with the array of bright annuals. "As you see, it comes up through eighteen inches of good soil with no trouble at all."

As they left Laker took a last look round. His eyes had an inward-looking and peaceful expression.

"I hope the prison has a garden, Mr. Porson," he said.

The years of contentment were beginning for John Laker.

AFTERWORD: FROM NATURAL CAUSES.

I'm afraid this is not a very American story. "Le vice Anglais", the English vice, was believed in France to be homosexuality. It is actually gardening. Until you have been trapped in the west rose garden by an English enthusiast explaining the virtues of Mermaid over Dorothy Perkins, or have experienced the prize leek contests in Northumberland, you have never seen real passion.

One nice thing about gardening, its vocabulary is the best in the language. In no other hobby will you meet names as beautiful as Jasmine, Love-in-a-mist, Columbine, Snowdrop, Larkspur, Honeysuckle, Forget-me-not, and Canterbury Bell, or as evocative as Soapwort, Snapdragon, Witch Hazel, Quickthorn, Purple Loosestrife, Red Hot Poker, Toadflax, and Bleeding Heart.

If I could live parallel lives, one of them would be as a full-time gardener.

LEGACY

The monsters first came to public attention off the coast of
Guam. They stood quietly on the sea bed, three of them abreast,
facing west towards the Guam shore. Behind them, plunging
away rapidly to the abyssal depths, lay the Mariana Trench.
Faint sunlight fled about their shadowy sides as they stirred
slowly in the cold, steady upwelling.

To the startled eyes of Lin Maro as he cruised along in his new
gilled form, they seemed to be moving forward, slowly and
purposively breasting the lip of the coastal shelf and gliding
steadily from the black deeps to the distant shore. Lin gasped,
forgetting his long months of training and bio-feedback control,
and pulled a pint of warm sea water into his lungs. Coughing and
spluttering, with gills working overtime, he surged one hundred
and fifty feet to the surface and struck out wildly for the shore
and safety. A quick look back convinced him that they were
pursuing him.

His glance caught the large, luminous eyes and the ropy
tendrils of thick floating hair that framed the broad faces. He
was in too much of a hurry to notice the steel weights that held
them firmly and remorselessly on the sea bed.

The reaction onshore was somewhere between amusement
and apathy. It was Lin Maro's first time out in a real environment with his gilled form, and everybody knew there was a big
difference between simulation and the real thing. A little temporary hallucination, a minor *trompe l'oeil* from the central
nervous system; that wasn't hard to believe on the first time out
with a new BEC form. BEC guaranteed against physical mal-
functions but sensory oddities weren't in the warranty. It took
long, hard arguing before Maro could get anyone to show even

polite interest. The local newsman who finally agreed to take a look did so as much from boredom as from belief. The next day they swam out, Maro in his gills, the reporter in a rented scuba outfit.

The monsters were still there all right. When they swam down to look at them, it became clear that Lin had been fleeing from three corpses. They swam around them, marvelling at the greenish scaled skin and the great dark eyes.

When the story went out over the ComSat connections, it was still a long way down the news lists. For three hundred years, writers had imagined Monsters of the Deep coming out of the Mariana Trench and tackling human civilization in a variety of nasty ways. Silly season reports helped to fill the blanks between famines and the real crises, but they got scant interest from the news professionals. Nobody reported panic along the coast, or fled to the high ground.

The three monsters got the most interest from the Guam aquarium and vivarium. A party of marine biologists inspected them on the sea bed, lifted them—shackles and all—to the surface, quick-froze them and whipped them back to shore on the Institute's hovercraft. The first lab examinations showed immediate anomalies. They were land animals, not marine forms, lung breathers, with tough outer skins and massive bone structure. As a matter of routine, tissue microtome samples were taken and a chromosome I.D. run for matches with known species. The patterns were transmitted to the central data banks.

At that point every attention light on the planet, figuratively speaking, went on, the whistles blew and the buzzers buzzed. The computer response was unambiguous and instantaneous. The chromosome patterns were human.

The information that moves ceaselessly over the Earth, by cable, by ComSat Link, by Mattin Link, by laser and by microwave, is focused and redistributed through a small number of nodes. At one of these nodes sits the Office of Form Control; and in this office, delicately feeling the vibrations and disturbances of the normal patterns that flow in along the strands of the information web, sits Behrooz Wolf. The spider analogy would not displease him, though he would point out that his is only one of many webs, all interlocking. Not by any means the most important one: Population, Food and Space Systems all have much bigger staffs and bigger webs. But he would argue that his problems have the shortest response times and need a reaction speed that the others can manage without.

Take the Marina Monsters—the Press dubbing—as an example. As soon as the chromosome patterns were revealed as human, the Form Control office was alerted. It looked as though a group of humans had been using the bio-feedback machines in unsuccessful formchange experiments. Were the experiments authorized, and were the resulting forms on the forbidden list? Was quick action needed to stop the appearance of a new illegal form?

Behrooz Wolf sat in his office as the data began to flow in. None of the official and approved formchange experiments was anything like the one found off the shore of Guam. In addition, cell tests were looking strange in both chemistry and structure. The lungs were modified, showing a change in alveolar patterns, as though the creatures were adapting to high pressure. And the big eyes, although sensitive to low light levels, were most sensitive in the near infrared wavelengths that are cut off almost completely under water.

Bey Wolf liked to approach his job using very basic questions. What was the objective of a form? Where would it operate most effectively? From those answers, he could usually guess the next step in the form-change sequence. The Marina Monsters were breaking the rules. They did not seem to be adapting to any environment at all.

All right, let's try another tack. The Monsters hadn't got there by themselves. After they had died, apparently of asphyxiation, they had been weighted with steel, then dropped, probably from a ship, to the sea bed. Where had they come from? Bey had a complete list of the world's form-change centers at his fingertips, especially the ones that were elaborate enough to need special life support systems. That offered no clues either.

Wolf's unsuccessful initial probing was interrupted by the arrival of his assistant John Larsen, back from a routine meeting on the certification of new BEC forms. He poked his cheerful face in the door, then stopped, surprised by the mass of new listings and piles of formchange tabulations that had appeared in Bey Wolf's already cluttered office.

"Come in, John." Wolf waved an arm. "What did you pick up at your meeting? Anything interesting?"

Larsen dropped into a chair, pushing a pile of listings out of the way and marvelling as usual at Bey's ability to operate cleanly and logically in the middle of such a mess.

"Two good ones," he replied. "C-forms, both of them, adapted for long periods in low gravity. They'll revolutionize asteroid work. There were the usual formal protests from the Belter representatives."

"There'll always be Luddites." Bey Wolf had a weakness for outmoded historical references. "That law will have to change soon. The C-forms are so much better than the old ones that there's no real competition. Capman has changed space exploration forever, as soon as the Belters will let his work be accepted. Here, let me fill you in on our latest headache."

He ran rapidly over the background to the Mariana discoveries, finishing with the question of where they had come from.

"I suspect that they got into the general area of the Marianas through one of the Mattin Links. The question is, which one? We have twenty to choose from."

John Larsen went over to the wall display, which was showing the locations of the Mattin Link entry points.

"We can rule out a few of them; they're open ocean and only act as transfer points. Have you correlated the form-change lab locations with the Mattin Link entry points?"

"I'm waiting for that to come back from the computer. I've also asked for an identification of the three individuals whose bodies were found on the sea bed. I don't know why that's taking so long. Central Records knows that it's a high priority item."

He joined Larsen at the wall charts, and they reviewed the locations of the Mattin Links that serve as the twenty pivot points for the global transportation system. When the communicator screen beeped for attention Larsen went to it, leaving Wolf engrossed in the wall charts. He watched the first words of the message scroll onto the screen, then whistled softly.

"Come and look at this, Bey. There's the reason Records took a while to get us an I.D. from the chromosome pattern."

The message began: 'I.D. Search completed and identification follows: Individuals are: James Pearson Manaur, age 34, Rationality U.S.F.; Caperta Leferte, age 26, Nationality U.S.F.; Lao Sarna Prek, age 30, Nationality U.S.F. Continue/Halt?'

Wolf hit 'Continue' and the detailed I.D. records appeared—education, work history, family. But their attention was already elsewhere. The three dead men were all members of the United Space Federation; that spelled out a mystery.

The United Space Federation had declared its sovereignty fifty years earlier, in 2142. With headquarters at the Tycho lunar base, it represented the interests of all the humans living off-Earth, in the Belt, on the Moon, and in the Earth-Moon Libration Point colonies. U.S.F. citizens were rarities on Earth, and the disappearance of three of them should have roused an outcry long before their changed bodies had been found off Guam.

The two men looked at each other. Wolf nodded at Larsen's puzzled expression. "It makes no sense. The U.S.F. has an out-and-out ban on form-changes. If they won't accept the C-forms, it's even less likely they'd be doing independent development of new forms. One thing is for sure, I'll have to get a U.S.F. man in here—it's too sensitive now."

He looked gloomy. The investigation had just grown two orders of magnitude. There was no way to go further without involving U.S.F representatives. Already they were on the verge of an interplanetary incident.

The communicator continued to pump out information, in display and hard copy. Wolf noticed that it was giving the correlation he had asked for between form-change centers and Mattin Link entry points. It was going to be a long and confusing day.

Not surprisingly, BEC was getting into the act too. An incoming news release set out their official position on the Mariana Monsters.

'Biological Equipment Corporation (BEC) today released a
formal statement denying all knowledge of the human bodies
discovered recently off the coast of Guam. A BEC representative said that the bodies had clearly been subject to form-change,
but no BEC program developments, past or present, could lead
to forms anything like those found. In an unusual procedure,
BEC released records showing forms now under development in
the Company and invited Government inspection of their
facilities. BEC is the pioneer in and world's largest manufac-
turer of purposive form-change equipment utilizing biological
feedback control methods.'

Bey read the release through and passed it to Larsen.

"It looks as though BEC is in the clear but running scared.
I've been waiting for them to plead innocent or guilty. That's
another prospect off the list of possibles."

Larsen trailed out with yards of listings. Bey Wolf sat back
again to wait for a pattern to emerge. The facts were suggestive.
One name kept coming into his head, haunting him out of the
past. Robert Capman, inventor of the C-forms, recognized
without dispute as the greatest-ever expert on form-change
methods. Robert Capman, ex-Director of Central Hospital and
advisor to the Planetary Coordinators. But also Robert Capman, branded as a mass murderer and officially dead for six
years.

Top U.S.F. men, like top kanu players, are usually on the
small skinny side. It was a surprise to greet a wrestler, two
meters tall, and find he was the U.S.F. man assigned to work
with Form Control on the Guam case. Bey Wolf glanced up at
him and bit back the question on the tip of his tongue.

Park Green was regarding him closely, a smile on his big,
baby face.

"Go on, Mr. Wolf, ask me," he said. "Most people do
eventually. In fact, let me answer you in advance. No, I don't
use the bio-feedback equipment and formchange myself this
way. It's completely natural. But it makes life hard when you're
trying to act as representative to the U.S.F., and form-change is

illegal off-Earth.''

Bey Wolf nodded appreciatively. ''On the mark. I didn't think I was so easy to read.''

''I've had lots of practice on that question. Let me ask you some. What's new on the Guam case? I've got to give a report back to Tycho City tonight. Do you know the time and cause of death yet?''

''Three days ago. They all died within about twelve hours of each other, of asphyxiation—and here's the strange part. Their lungs were full of normal air. No gaseous poisons, no contaminants. They shouldn't have choked. They were dropped off Guam about twenty-four hours after they died, almost certainly at night. My guess is that they died somewhere a long way from there.''

''Excuse my ignorance of the case, but I don't follow your logic.''

''Well, it is conjectural. But I think they were intended for the bottom of the Mariana Trench. Five miles down, they'd never have been found. I think they were accidentally dropped a few miles too far west—by somebody who didn't know the local geography too well. I'd say they died by accident, and somebody was keen to hide the evidence as far away as they could. You don't look very surprised,'' Wolf added, seeing that Green was slowly nodding agreement.

The big man squeezed himself into a chair and rubbed his chin with an eleven-inch hand.

''It fits with some of the things I know myself,'' he replied. ''What else did you find out about the three dead men?''

''Not much,'' replied Wolf. ''They were Belters, all off the same ship, the 'Jason.' They arrived here on Earth three weeks ago with plenty of money. Nobody heard of them again until they were found off Guam. We don't trail U.S.F. citizens unless we get a request from you for it.''

''That's all correct as far as it goes,'' agreed Green. ''You are missing a few things that make a big difference. First, you say they were Belters, and technically you are right. But in U.S.F. wording, they were really Grabbers. They had been out in space on the 'Jason' for over two years. . . .''

Caperta Laferte, spotter for the U.S.F. Class B cargo ship 'Jason,' was watching the scope of the deep radar with mounting excitement. By his left hand, the computer print-out was chattering with increasing speed as it performed the final orbit match and confirmed the tracking of the find.

Laferte wiped the perspiration from his face with a dirty cloth.

"It matches exactly," he told the other two. "And it looks like a big one. I'll be able to get us a radioactivity reading from it in a couple of minutes. But it's a piece of old Loge, no doubt about it."

The others hovered about in impotent excitement. Until they had matched and docked it was one man's work and they could do nothing more useful than speculate on their trophy. Grimy and worn, all three looked like men who had endured more than two years of solar flares and radiation storms, celibacy and grinding boredom. It would all be worth it. If this were the big one, it would pay for all of it. Wine, women and song were on the way.

"Radioactivity count coming in now," announced Laferte. "I've tuned it for the 15 MeV dipole transition from Asfanium. Keep your eye on the counter. If it hits forty or better, it's the jackpot."

The digital read-out was climbing steadily. At twenty they lost it for a second. Laferte swore, bent back over the control panel, and recalibrated. It climbed again, past twenty, to thirty, to forty, and was still moving steadily upwards. They all shouted and James Manaur and Lao Sarna Prek joined hands and began a curious Walrus-and-Carpenter dance. It was the best that could be managed in the combination of free-fall and confined space. The future was a rosy glow, full of wealth, high living and excitement. Old Loge had been gone a long time, but enough of him had come back to gladden a few hearts.

"—looking for transuranics," said Green. "Maybe you know, the only natural source in the Solar System is still the fragments of Loge that come back into the System as long-period comets. The Grabbers just sit out there for years and monitor using deep radar. One decent find and they are made for life. The 'Jason' caught a good one about three months ago, packed with 112 and 114, Asfanium and Polkium. They extracted the transuranic elements from the fragment and rolled into Tycho City a month ago, rich as Karkov. They started to celebrate and three weeks ago they came to Earth to continue the spree. After that we lost touch with them and don't know what they did. We expected them back when the fleshpots palled. Want me to make a guess on what they did?''

Wolf nodded. "I think I see where you are leading, but go on.''

"They came to Earth," continued Park Green. "Now, I saw them just before they left Tycho. They looked terrible. A couple of years of hardship in space, then a celebration that you wouldn't believe when they reached the Moon. If you came to Earth in that condition, wouldn't there be a big temptation to do something a bit illegal—and hookup for an intensive session with a bio-feedback machine, set to get you back to tip-top physical shape as fast as legally possible—or faster?''

"There certainly would," Wolf agreed. "I know a thousand places where it could be done. What you say makes perfect sense. Now let me pick up on my side of it.''

He pressed the inter-office communicator and asked John Larsen to join them. When Larsen entered the room, Bey Wolf turned again to Park Green.

"Before I get John's opinions, tell me what you know about Robert Capman. I assure you it's relevant," he added, seeing Green's puzzled look.

The big U.S.F. man thought for a moment before he replied.

"All I can really tell you is what I've heard in Tycho City," he said finally. "Capman was a great man here on Earth, a genius who invented the series of form-changes that we now call C-forms, adapted for life in space. He did it using human children as the subjects for form-change experiments. Some of them died. He was found out a few years ago and died himself trying to escape. Is there more to know?''

"I think there is, but I may be biased," replied Wolf. "For

one thing, it was John and I who handled the case and blew the whistle on Capman. Now let me ask you, do you have strong feelings about Capman, personally?''

Green hesitated again. ''That's really a tough one. I know his reputation for great genius. And honestly, I don't know enough to say if he was fairly treated when he was accused of using human children in his work. But I will tell you, as a representative of the U.S.F. I have to be against Capman. After all, he was the man who invented the forms that are supposed to make me and my fellows as obsolete for life in space as the dinosaurs—the forms he came up with don't need much air, they're radiation tolerant, and they can adapt to run at high or low metabolic rates. I've no reason to like the man, for those reasons alone. Why do you ask?''

''I have a reason,'' said Wolf. He turned to Larsen. ''John, you were there when Capman died. Did he die?''

''I thought so at the time.'' John Larsen sighed and shrugged his shoulders. ''Now, I'm not so sure.'' He turned to the U.S.F. man. ''Bey is convinced it was a set-up, and I must admit it had the makings of one. He hasn't been heard of for the six years since then, but I'll tell you, in the last day I've been thinking about him. These Guam formchanges have just the marks of Capman.''

Wolf looked at Larsen with relief and increased respect. ''I'd been thinking that, John, myself, but it seemed too unlikely to come right out and say it.'' He turned again to Park Green. ''Now, you see how our thoughts have been running. Earth's greatest expert ever on form-change, Robert Capman. Maybe still alive, in hiding, somewhere on Earth. And along comes a set of form-changes that defy all logic, that conform to no known models. It could be Capman, up to his old tricks again. Either way, if Capman *is* alive, he'd be just the man to talk to about this. John or I could have added one other thing—neither of us ever met a man, before or since, who impressed us as much with his sheer intellectual power.''

Green moved about uneasily in his seat. ''It's clear you're selling me something, but I still don't know what it is. What are you leading up to?''

Bey Wolf nodded vigorously. "Only this, I want to find Robert Capman. And I have a very strong suspicion of my own. I think he's *not* on Earth—hasn't been for the past six years. Will you help me reach him, if he's somewhere in the U.S.F. territories? I don't know if it's the Moon, the Belt, the Libration Colonies, or where—but I do know I can't get messages out there without U.S.F. help!"

Green looked speculative. "I can't give you an instant answer," he said. "I'll have to discuss it in person with Ambassador Brodin, and he's in Argentina." He stood up. "What's the best way to get me there?"

"Through the Mattin Link system. There's an entry point in central Argentina. We are only ten minutes away from the Madrid link—two jumps and you'll be there. Come on, I'll show you how to use it."

They hurried out, as Green explained that he was having trouble getting used to the complexity of the Earth system. The Moon had only four link entry points. The Earth had twenty and he had heard there would be more added. Was that true?

It was not, and it would never be. The Mattin Link system offers direct and instantaneous transmission between any adjacent pair of entry points. But the number of entry points, and their placing, is very rigid. Since it requires perfect symmetry of any entry point with respect to all others, the configuration must fit one of the five regular solids. Plato would have loved it.

The dodecahedral system, with twenty vertices on the surface of the Earth, is the biggest single system that can ever be made. The Lunar system, with its four entry points at the vertices of a regular tetrahedron, is the simplest. And Mattin Links away from planetary surfaces are impractical because of changing distances.

Gerald Mattin, who had dreamed of a system for instantaneous energy-free transfer between any two points anywhere, died a disappointed man. The present system is far from energy-free—because the Earth is not a homogenous perfect sphere, and space-time is slightly curved near it. Mattin had an energy-free solution defined for an exact geometry in a flat space-time. He died twenty years before the decision to build the

first Mattin Link system, twenty-five years before the first
university was named after him, thirty years before the first
statue.

"We have a go-ahead, but I had to bargain my soul away to
get an agreement from the Ambassador. Now, where do we go
from here?"

Park Green was back in Bey Wolf's office, shoes off, long
legs stretched out and adding to the general appearance of
confusion. Wolf and Larsen were again over by the wall display,
plotting the Mattin Link paths from the Mariana Trench entry
point and the Australia entry point near the spaceport where the
crew of the 'Jason' had arrived on Earth. Wolf read off the
results before he replied to Park Green.

"The North Australian entry point connects directly to the
Marianas, Southern New Zealand and an Indian Ocean transfer
point. The Mariana entry point connects directly to North
China, Hawaii and back of course to North Australia. None of
those connections looks promising, there's no big form-change
lab near any of them. So either my guess about the use of the
Link system is wrong, or the people who moved the Monsters
did more than one jump in the system. Two jumps takes us a lot
further afield—to almost anywhere. Up to the North Pole, to
Cap City at the South Pole, or into India, or up to western North
America."

He looked over at Park Green. "It's a mess. I'm more
convinced than ever that we need to find Robert Capman and
develop some idea what was happening when the three men
died. They obviously started on some form-change program and
somewhere along the line it got fouled up. How? I wish I could
ask Capman that question."

"So let me repeat my question," said Green. "What do we
do next, and where do we go from here? Advertising for Capman won't solve the problem—he'll be treated as a mass murderer if he ever does show up alive."

"I think I can produce a message that Capman will recognize
and be intrigued by, but others won't," answered Wolf. "As for
protecting him if he does show himself, I'm not worried about

that. I'm sure that he'll have found a way to cover himself in the past six years. I've got another worry of my own. We have no way of knowing how urgent this thing is. It could be a once in a lifetime accident or the start of a general plague. Until we know which, I have to look on it as the hottest thing on my list of problems. Let me take a cut at the message to Capman."

The final announcement was short and simple. It went out on a general broadcast over all media to the eight billion on Earth, and by special transmission to the scattered three million members of the United Space Federation.

'To R.C. I badly need the talents that caused me to pursue you six years ago through the by-ways of Old City. I promise you a problem worthy of your powers. Behrooz Wolf.'

Troubles were mounting. Bey spent a couple of hours with a representative of BEC, who insisted on presenting more confidential records to prove that the company had no connection with the monster forms found in Guam. The Central Coordinators sent him a terse message, asking him if there would be other deaths of the same type, and if so, when and how many? Park Green was getting the same sort of pressure from the U.S.F. Unlike Bey Wolf, the big man wasn't used to it and spent a good part of his time in Bey's office, gloomily biting his nails and trying to construct positively worded replies with no information content.

Two days of that brought a stronger response from Tycho City. Bey arrived in his office early and found a small, neatly dressed man standing by the communicator calling out U.S.F. personnel records. He turned at Bey's entry, with no sign of embarrassment at his intrusion, and looked at Bey for a second before he spoke.

"Mr. Green?" The voice was like the man, small and precise.

"He'll be in later. I'm Behrooz Wolf, head of Form Control. What can I do for you?" Bey was somewhat conscious of his own casual appearance and uncombed hair.

The man drew himself up to his full height. "I am Karl Ling, special assistant to the U.S.F. Cabinet. Here are my credentials.'' The tone was peppery and irascible. "I have been sent here to get some real answers about the deaths of three of our citizens here on Earth. I must tell you that we regard the explanations given so far by your office and Mr. Green as profoundly unsatisfactory.''

"Arrogant bastard," thought Bey, while he looked for a suitably conciliatory answer.

"We have been doing our best to provide you with all the facts, Mr. Ling," he said. "It seemed unwise to present theories until they can be definitely verified. I'm sure you realize that this case is complex and has features that we haven't encountered before.''

"Apparently." Karl Ling had taken a seat by the communicator and was tapping his thigh nervously with a well-manicured left hand. "For example, I see that you are giving the cause of death as asphyxiation. But you tell us also that the dead men had plenty of air in their lungs, and that there were no poisonous constituents. Perhaps you would like to present your theory on that to me.''

Dealing in the past with officious government representatives, Bey had found an effective method of subduing them. He thought of it as his saturation technique. The trick was to flood the nuisance with so many facts, figures, reports and data that he was inundated and never seen again. He went over to his desk and took out a black record pad.

"This has the data entry codes that will allow you to pull all the records on this case. I suggest that you use my office here and feel free to use my communicator to reach Central Files. Nothing will be hidden from you. This machine has a full access code.''

The little man stood up, a gleam in his eyes. He rubbed his hands together.

"Excellent. Please arrange it so that I am not disturbed—but I do want to see Mr. Green when he arrives.''

Far from being subdued, Ling was clearly delighted at the prospect of a flood of information. Bey escaped with relief and went to give the bad news to Park Green.

"Karl Ling?" Green looked impressed. "Oh, I know him—

not personally, but by reputation. He's the U.S.F. leading expert on Loge. He's a fanatic on the subject, really. I saw a holovision program he made a couple of years ago where he traced the whole history of Loge. He began way back, five hundred years ago—.''

(Cameras move from model and back to Ling, standing.)

''School-capsules give the 1970's as the first date in Loge's history. We can find him much further back than that. All the way back in 1766, when a German astronomer came up with a scheme to define the distances of the planets from the Sun. Johann Titius' work was picked up and made famous a few years later by another German, Johann Bode. The relation is called the Titius-Bode Law.''

(Cut to framed lithograph of Bode, then to table of planetary distances.)

''Bode pointed out that there was a curious gap in the distance formula, between Mars and Jupiter. When William Herschel discovered Uranus in 1781—''

(Cut to high resolution color image of Uranus, with image of Herschel as insert on upper left. Cut back to Ling.)

''—he found it fitted Bode's law also. The search for a missing planet began. In 1800 the asteroid Ceres was discovered at the correct distance from the Sun. The first piece of Loge had been found.''

(Cut to high resolution image of Ceres. Zoom in on Ceres City. Cut to diagram showing planetary distances, then back to Ling.)

''As more and more asteroids were found, the theory grew that they were fragments of a single planet. In 1972 the Canadian astronomer Ovenden provided the first real proof. Using the rates of change in the orbits of the planets, he showed they were consistent with the disappearance from the Solar System of a body of planetary mass, roughly sixteen million years ago. He estimated that the missing planet was about ninety times the mass of the Earth. Loge was beginning to take on a definite shape.''

(Cut to image of Ovenden, then to artist's impression of the size and appearance of Loge, next to image of the Earth on same scale.)

"The next part of the story came just a few years later, in 1975. Van Flandern in America integrated the orbits of very long period comets backwards in time. He found that many of them had periods of about sixteen million years and had left from a particular part of the Solar System, between the orbits of Mars and Jupiter. Parts of Loge were coming home."

(Cut to diagram showing cometary orbits, intersecting Solar System diagram at point between Mars and Jupiter. Cut back to Ling.)

"We now had the modern view of Loge. A large planet, a gas-giant about ninety Earth masses, disintegrated about sixteen million years ago in a cataclysm beyond our imagining. Most of Loge was blown out of the Solar System forever. A few parts of the planetary core remain as the asteroids, other fragments from the outer crust drop back into the Solar System from time to time as long-period comets."

(Move in to close-up of Ling, face and shoulders only.)

"That looked like the end of the story, until we picked up the first pieces of the long-period cometary fragments in the twenty-first century and found they were high in trasuranic elements. The mystery of Loge remains. Why should Loge, alone of all the Solar System, contain transuranic elements? Their half-lives are less than twenty million years. Were they formed in the explosion of Loge? If so, how? To those questions, we still do not have answers."

(Cut to image of Loge, feed in beginning of fade-out music, low volume.)

"One final and tantalizing fact. Sixteen million years is like yesterday on the cosmic scale. When Loge disintegrated there were primates already on the Earth. Did our early ancestors look into the skies one night, and see the fearful sight of Loge's explosion? Will other planets ever suffer a similar fate?"

(Fade out as image of Loge swells, changes color, breaks asunder. Final music crescendoes for ending.)

"—but it puzzles me why Ling should be appointed to this

investigation. He writes his own ticket, of course. Maybe he knew one of the dead Grabbers—he certainly knew everything and everyone connected with Loge in any way." Green fell silent, then shook his head. "I suppose I'd better get in there and find out what he wants me to do. I hope I'm not being demoted to messenger boy."

Together Green and Wolf went back into Bey's office. Karl Ling was oblivious of their entry, deeply engrossed in his review of autopsy records of the three dead crew members of the 'Jason.' Wolf's saturation technique didn't work on Ling. He became aware of them only when Bey Wolf spoke.

"Mr. Ling, we are ready to give you a briefing when you want it. This is Mr. Green, from U.S.F."

Ling looked up briefly, then returned his attention to the medical records. "Good. Answer one basic question for me. The three dead men have clearly been through a form-change process. Where are the bio-feedback machines located that were used for that?"

"We don't have an answer to that, Sir," replied Wolf. "Though of course we recognize its importance."

Ling looked up again. For some reason it seemed to be the response he was hoping for. "No answer, Mr. Wolf? I thought that might be the case. Would you like me to enlighten you?"

Bey felt a minor urge to go over and choke Ling but managed a cool reply. "If you can. Though it is hard for me to imagine that you could have reached a conclusion on such a brief inspection of the records."

"I did not. I knew before I left the Moon." He smiled briefly and stood up. "You see, Mr. Wolf, I have no doubt that you and the other members of Form Control here on Earth are proficient in your work. But this particular situation requires something that by definition you do not possess—the ability to think as a U.S.F. citizen. For example, if you were a millionaire, where on Earth would you choose to go for your entertainment? Remember, you may choose freely without thought of cost."

"Probably to the Great Barrier Reef, in a gilled form."

"Very good." Karl Ling turned to Park Green. "You are a Belter, Mr. Green, and suddenly a millionaire. Where on all of

Earth would you want to go—what is the Belter's dream of a place for all the most exotic delights?''

Green scratched his chin thoughtfully. "Why, I guess it would be Pleasure Dome. That's the place we hear about, though I've never been there."

"Of course you haven't," responded Ling impatiently, "and neither has anyone else who is not extremely rich. But it's the Belter's idea of Paradise—and part of the reason you would want to go there would be to prove how rich you were."

He went over to the large map display on the far wall and called out a South Polar projection.

"Let's take this a little further. Look at the geography. The crew of the 'Jason' landed here at the Australian space port. Within easy ground transport distance of the North Australian Mattin Link. One transfer gets them to New Zealand, a second one puts them to Cap City in Antarctica. Now Pleasure Dome, as I am sure you know, Mr. Wolf, though perhaps Mr. Green does not, lies directly beneath Cap City in the Antarctic ice cap. Total travel time from the space port—an hour or less."

Park Green nodded slowly. "I guess so. I'm not yet used to the number of Link entry points you have here. I don't see where that gets us, though. We need a place with sophisticated form-change equipment. I didn't see Cap City or Pleasure Dome on any list of labs that Mr. Wolf showed me."

Karl Ling smiled ironically. "I'm sure you didn't. You saw the legal list." He turned to Bey, who had some idea what was coming and felt a growing excitement. "Pleasure Dome offers *all* pleasures, does it not, Mr. Wolf? Even the most exotic. Would it be safe to assume that a number of those pleasures involve the use of form-changes?"

"It certainly would. We know there are illegal form-changes going on there, for some of the more debauched physical tastes. But we've never had trouble with them, and they are very discreet. We keep a kind of informal truce. I don't have to tell you, Mr. Ling, how much power the managers of Pleasure Dome have when it comes to silent influence in high places."

Ling touched the map display control and a new image appeared. "Then this must be our next stop—Cap City and Pleasure Dome. We still have not answered the basic question: how did those three men become three dead monsters? Mr. Green, you should remain here and be available to answer the inquiries from Earth and Moon authorities. Please make travel arrangements now for Mr. Wolf and myself. Don't worry, Mr. Wolf,'' he added, seeing Bey's questioning look. ''I can call on the full financial resources of the U.S.F. in pursuing this enquiry.''

''That's not my worry at the moment, Mr. Ling. I was wondering why the Mariana Trench was chosen to dispose of the bodies. Can you explain that also?''

''I have a speculation, certainly. After the crew of the 'Jason' died, I think the proprietors of Pleasure Dome looked at their identifications and realized they were in trouble. They know the U.S.F. looks after its own. The plan was to get the bodies off-Earth. They were taken to Australia through the Mattin Link. When the Pleasure Dome people found that security regulations on space access are very tight, that plan was dropped and they were forced to improvise. One further transfer through the Link System took them to the Marianas. Hasty planning— and an inadequate knowledge of local geography—led to a botching of the disposal job.''

Ling looked pleased with his analysis. ''It is only a deductive argument, I admit. But I suspect it has a very high probability of being right.

''Now, quickly, have preparations made and let us be on our way.''

Green hurried out, but Wolf lingered a moment. Ling looked at him questioningly.

''You have further business, Mr. Wolf? I have a great deal of work still to do on the records and not much time to do it.''

Bey nodded. ''I want to make one comment. I've spent my life studying form-change, and I believe I understand it as well as anyone. One man is my master in the theory, but when it comes to seeing through exterior changes I match myself against anyone. I believe that we have met before, Mr. Ling, and under very different circumstances. I do not propose to do anything about it, but I want you to know that I can tell the lion by his paw.''

Karl Ling's acid look seemed to soften briefly. Bey Wolf thought there was the trace of a smile on his lips. "I'm sorry, Mr. Wolf, but I really have no idea what you are talking about. Would you please let me get down to this biological work—help me, if you wish. I want to be in Cap City four hours from now."

After Bey Wolf and Karl Ling had left, Park Green and John Larsen went for a drink and a sharing of dissatisfaction. By the third one Larsen had become more morose and militant.

"Just our luck. Those two go off to sample Pleasure Dome and leave us here to handle the brainless bureaucrats," he complained. "It's always the same, we get all the dog work, they get all the excitement."

He had never met or heard of Ling until that day, but fine points of logic were beneath him.

"I'd like to show those two," he went on. "I'd like to show them what we can do without them. Solve this whole thing while they're gone." He slid a little lower in his seat. "That would show them."

Green and Larsen had been going drink for drink, but with twice the body mass Green was in much better shape. He watched Larsen sink lower yet.

"Come on," he said. "Let's do it." He lifted the limp figure of Larsen easily to a standing position and held him there while he paid the bill. "Just let's get a shot of de-toxer in you and we'll be all set. Let's go and work over the full records and see if we can come up with something new. It would do me a lot of good to beat that smarmy supercilious midget to the answer."

Fifteen minutes later they were both cold sober and deep into the case records.

There was a long period of sifting before John Larsen sat back, looked up at the ceiling for a spell and finally said:

"Question: what is there about the crew of the 'Jason' that made them very unusual? Answer: they had recently been handling large quantities of transuranic elements, probably experiencing high levels of radioactivity. So here is my second question: did the autopsies look for radioactivity in the bodies? My bet is that they didn't. So, final question: is what happened the effects of transuranic elements in their central nervous systems? I doubt if anyone knows what a substantial amount of transuranics could do. It's a long shot, but it's a new line.''

Green shrugged. "It's a long shot, but we should check it. Do you know where the bodies are now?''

"In the Form Control center in Manila.''

Green stood up. "Come on. We'll need authorization for another autopsy and a pathologist.''

The exit point from the Mattin Link system is in the upper levels of Cap City, almost at the surface itself. Bey Wolf and Karl Ling came out of the Link and looked about them for the elevators that would take them down to Pleasure Dome, four thousand feet below in the polar ice. As they stood there, a soft voice spoke in their ears:

'Come to Pleasure Dome, satisfy your heart's desires.'

Ling looked at Wolf and smiled. "An omni projector. What a waste of a technology. We'd give millions for that system in Tycho Base.''

The soft voice continued. 'In Pleasure Dome, you can shed the cares of the world and feel free again. Visit the Caves of Ice and swim in the Pool of Lethe. Win a world in the great Xanadu Casino, or spend a day as part of the Coupling Loom. Be free, be with us in Pleasure Dome.'

Free, at a price, thought Wolf, as the omni advertising went on. Finally, a useful comment came.

'Follow the blue lights to the temple of earthly delights.'

Following the blue lights as directed, they were soon dropped swiftly, deep into the polar cap. The entrance to Pleasure Dome was a great sparkling chamber, lined with perfect mirrors, like the inside of a giant multi-faceted diamond. The effect was shattering. Walls, floor and ceiling were all perfectly reflective. Images of the room marched off to infinity in every direction. Bey looked about him, struggling to orient himself.

"Better get used to it. Mr. Wolf,'' remarked Ling coolly. "Pleasure Dome is all like this.''

"I didn't realize you'd been here before.''

"Long ago. These walls are a necessity, not a luxury, you know. When they cut this city beneath the ice cap, twenty years

ago, the big problem was the heat. People produce heat, from
themselves and their equipment. The ice walls would have
melted in no time. These walls—all the walls in Pleasure
Dome—are coated with Passivine. It's perfectly reflecting and
has a very low coefficient of thermal conductivity. A negligible
amount of heat passes through the ice walls, and a modest
refrigeration system takes care of that easily."

Bey looked at Karl Ling ironically. "For one who is from
off-Earth, Mr. Ling, you have an amazing knowledge of Earth
affairs."

"The long lunar nights give us plenty of time for reading."
There was a definite hint of humor in Ling's formal reply.
Before Bey could comment further, a third person had joined
them.

"Welcome to Pleasure Dome, Sirs." The speaker was a tall
woman dressed all in white. Her skin was pale and flawless, her
hair a fine white cloud. She looked at them quietly with cool
grey eyes. A Snow Queen. Bey wondered how much of it was
natural, and how much she owed to form-change.

"I will be your hostess and help you to arrange your pleasures. Do not be afraid to ask, whatever your tastes. There are
few wishes that we cannot accommodate. Before we begin,
there are a few formalities."

"You want our identifications?" asked Bey.

"Only if you wish to give them, Sirs. We do need proof of
adequate means, but that may be cash if you prefer to use it."

"We are together," said Ling. "My credit will serve for
both. Do you have a bank connection?"

"Here, Sir." The Snow Queen produced a small silver box,
onto which Ling placed his right index finger. In a few seconds,
the I.D. was established and the central bank returned a credit
rating. As she read the credit, the Snow Queen lost her compo-
sure for the first time and became a young woman. Bey suspected that Ling's credit rating was that of the entire U.S.F.

"What is your pleasure, Sirs?" Even her voice seemed
changed. It was now uncertain, nervous, almost childish. With
that much credit available, Bey realized, there was nothing,
literally nothing, that could not be bought at Pleasure Dome.

That included the body or soul of their hostess, and she knew it. It was dangerous to be in contact with such financial power. She could never know when one of Ling's whims might include her as a purchased pleasure.

Ling's businesslike manner helped to reassure her. "We want to talk to the man who controls the form-change tanks. The one who handled the three off-worlders recently. Don't worry, you may not know what I'm referring to, but he certainly will."

She hesitated. Ling's request fell far outside the usual list of fancies.

"One moment, Sirs."

She slipped quietly out through a glittering arch. Karl Ling looked at Bey quizzically.

"I thought the direct approach would be best," Ling said. "If necessary, can you threaten these people enough to make them worried—say you'll close down their illegal form-change services if they don't cooperate?"

"I can threaten all right—but I'm not sure what I can really do if the threats don't work. With any luck they won't want to find out either."

The Snow Queen had brought reinforcements. An equally striking blond haired man, again dressed in white.

"Sirs, your credit is enough to purchase any pleasure," he began. "But certain things in Pleasure Dome are not available at any price. The detail of our operations is one. Please state your wishes again, so that we can see if we are able to accommodate them."

"We have no intention of causing trouble here," replied Ling. "But if we wished to do so there is no doubt that we could. This is Behrooz Wolf, the head of Form Control for Earth. I am Karl Ling, special assistant to the U.S.F. Cabinet. All we are looking for is information. Three men died recently during form-change. We believe that they died here. We want to speak to the man in charge of that operation, and we want to see the full records of the monitors that were recording and supervising the form-changes."

The man made no attempt to deny the charge. He was silent for a few moments, then asked:

"If we cooperate, you will take our involvement no further, here or elsewhere?"

"You have our word."

"Then come with me." The blond man smiled. "You should be pleased. You are obtaining a service free of charge. To my knowledge, this has never happened before since Pleasure Dome was first created."

The three men walked through a maze of ice caves, fairy grottoes lit by lights of different colors, and came at last to a door that led to an ordinary office with panelled walls and a functional looking desk.

He motioned to them to sit down.

"I will return in a moment. This, by the way, is the luxury that we aspire to in Pleasure Dome—normal walls and furniture, and privacy. Our lives here rarely permit us either."

He returned a few minutes later with his identical twin. That seemed to answer Bey's question about the use of form-change on Pleasure Dome staff. The ultimate bondage: someone else dictated the shape of their bodies.

Ling wanted the man to be at ease and displayed a new side of his personality—warmth and kindness. Bey noted it and marked up one more data point on a growing list. The examination began. The man was at first ill-at-ease, but soon relaxed and became more talkative.

"All those three wanted was a full-speed reconditioning program. The only thing we did for them here that is in any way illegal was the speed. We used the bio-feedback machines twenty-four hours a day, and provided nutrients intravenously. So it looked like a completely straightforward request and we didn't give them any special monitoring, the way we would if a customer was to come in and ask for a special change. The full program they'd asked for takes about a hundred and fifty hours, nearly a week of changing if you run it continuously, the way we do."

"You've run this course many times before?" asked Ling.

"Often, especially for offworlders. Of course, we never ask their origins, but we can make a guess from clothing and speech. Since Capman's form-change work, a straightforward program like this has been completely automatic. The tank has automatic monitors that control air supply and nutrient supply and regulate the pace of the process. The subject has to be conscious at some level, since it is purposive form-change that's involved. But the unit's completely self-contained and the only way we know what's happening inside the tank is through looking at the automatic monitor tell-tales on the outside.''

"And how often do you do that?"

"In a simple case like this, once a day. We never have anything to do, but we check anyway. In the case of these three off-worlders, they all began at the same time and they all asked for the same reconditioning program. Needed it, too. They looked done in when they arrived here.

"The evening of the third day, I took my routine look at the tell-tales. All three men were dead. I couldn't believe it. At first I suspected the tell-tales were lying, or there'd been a programming error, or something. Then we opened the tanks. God, it was awful. Like a nightmare. They had changed, they weren't men anymore. They were monsters, with great glowing eyes and thick skin, like a horror holo. We confirmed that they were dead, then we looked at their I.D.'s and realized they were off-worlders. Then everybody around here really panicked, and we tried to get them off-Earth. When we found we couldn't do that, we tried to put them deep at sea. That apparently failed too.''

The man fell silent and there was a long pause.

Ling was too engrossed even to give Bey Wolf a look of triumph. He was bound in a spell of concentration so intense that he looked blind, his eyes unblinking and focused on infinity.

"Did you do any chemical analyses of the bodies?" he asked.

"God, no. We wanted to get them out of here. But there will be records on the tapes that were made by the monitors and tell-tales, and there should be continuous monitoring of some cell chemistry and blood chemistry.''

"Right. I want to examine those now. Bring them here or take me to them.''

"We'll get them. But they'll be in raw form. Only a form-change expert can read them.''

Ling caught Bey Wolf's look "Bring them in. We'll manage somehow," he said. "It's a skill you never lose once you've mastered it completely."

John Larsen looked at the spectrograph output, then at Park Green.

"It's not as much as I expected," he said. "But there are traces of Asfanium in all three bodies. There's slight radioactivity because of that, but it's not enough to make a strong physical effect. I wonder, do you think that it could be a *chemical* effect of Asfanium that did it? We don't have a good understanding of that aspect of the transuranics in the island of stability up around element 114."

"That's quite possible," Green replied. "You know, we are still doing a lot of work on Asfanium and Polkium and are finding some odd chemical properties, up in Lunar Base. One other thing occurs to me, the crew of the 'Jason' had never encountered form-change before. Do you think that they let things get out of control, maybe, due to their inexperience? Then they ran into something new, like the effect of a trace of Asfanium?"

Larsen slapped the spectrogram output sheet against his thigh. "Park, I bet you're on to something. With inexperienced people in purposive form-change, anything might happen. Now, we can test that. Asfanium concentrates in the thymus gland. If we take an extract from one of these three, we can conduct a controlled test and see if there is a tendency to form-change the way they did."

Park Green frowned. "I didn't realize you had suitable test animals. Isn't it true that humans alone can achieve purposive form-change? After all, that's the basis of the humanity tests."

Larsen laughed confidently. "Exactly right. You want to see the test animal? Here it is." He tapped himself on the chest. "Now, don't get the wrong idea," he added, as Park Green began a horrified protest. "One of the things we get in Form Control is many years of training in form-control methods. If anything starts to happen, I'll have no trouble stopping it and reversing it. Don't forget, it's a purposive process. Come on, let's get a thymus gland extract made here and then back to the form-change tanks at Headquarters. We'll really have something to show Bey and your boss when they get back.''

The jaunt to Pleasure Dome was becoming a grind. The staff employees looked on in amazement as Wolf and Ling worked their way through the monitor tapes at express speed, reading raw data, swapping comments and analyses as they went. The tapes contained a mixture of body physical parameters, such as subject temperature, pulse rate and skin conductivity, with nutrient rates. Programs in use as they were swapped in and out of the tank control computer, plus chemical readings and brain activity, were recorded in parallel on the same tape. Reading one required many years of experience, plus a full understanding of the processes—mental and physical—of the human body. Ling was tireless, and Bey was determined not to be outdone.

"Who is he?" whispered the Pleasure Dome form-change supervisor to Bey, at one of their brief halts. "I know you are head of Form Control, but where did *he* learn all this?"

Bey looked across at Ling, who was deep in thought and probably would not have noticed an explosion in the room.

"Maybe you should ask him yourself. I've had that conversation already."

Then more tapes arrived and the question was pushed aside.

After thirty-six hours of intense work, the basic analysis was complete. They had an incredible array of facts available to them, but one of them dominated all others. The crew of the 'Jason' had died well before their form-change was complete. They had died because the forms they were becoming were unable to live in and breathe normal air. The final form they would have become remained unknown. The reason why they were changing to those forms, under the control of a reconditioning program that had been used successfully a thousand times before, was equally unknown.

Karl Ling sat motionless, as he had for the previous two hours. Occasionally he would ask Bey a question, or look again at a piece of data. Rather than disturb him Bey decided that he would go into another room to call back to Headquarters and check with John Larsen on the general situation. Ling was voyaging on strange seas of thought, alone, and Bey Wolf had developed a profound respect for Karl Ling.

Park Green answered the communicator instead of Larsen. He looked very uncomfortable.

"Where's John?"

"He's been in a form-change tank since yesterday morning."

To Green's great relief, Bey Wolf didn't seem at all concerned. Even when he had explained the whole story to Bey, the latter seemed interested but not at all worried.

"John's been around form-change equipment for a long time. He knows how to handle it as well as anyone on Earth. But honestly, Park, I'm sceptical about his theory. Why, injured Belters have been using form-change equipment for years. They call it regeneration equipment. But it's the same thing exactly. It's only form-changes to forms that are not your *original* shape that are illegal to off-Earthers."

Park Green looked as though a big weight had been lifted off him.

"Thank God for that. I thought I might have let John talk me into a deal where he was taking a big risk. I don't know enough about all this to argue with him. I'll go off to the tanks, and see how things are coming along there."

Bey smiled at the honesty of the big man's concern for Larsen and signed off. He strolled back to join Ling, who had now come out of his trance and accepted a cup of syncaff, 'compliments of Pleasure Dome.' Having let them in free of charge, the staff of Pleasure Dome seemed to have adopted them. Ling had just politely refused a Snow Queen's offer of an age-old technique to relax him after all his hard work. He seemed mildly annoyed when she made the same offer to Bey.

"I think I have it, Mr. Wolf, and it's fascinating. More than I dreamed. If I'm right, this is a special day in history." He sat back, relishing the moment.

"Well, Park Green and John Larsen think they have it too," said Bey. "I just had video contact with them."

"They do? Without the evidence that we have here?" Ling was openly surprised. "What do they believe it is?"

Bey sketched out Larsen's theory, and summarized the situation back in Headquarters. He mentioned finally that Larsen was putting it to a practical test.

"Larsen injected an extract from one of the dead men, and got into a form-change tank?" Ling's self-possession had failed him, and he had turned white. "He's a dead man. God, why didn't they consult us here?"

He sprang to his feet, hurled the papers to one side and grabbed his jacket.

"Come, Mr. Wolf. We have to get back to Headquarters as fast as we possibly can. If there is a chance now to save John Larsen's life, it depends on our efforts."

He ran out of the room. Bey Wolf, bewildered and alarmed, followed him at top speed. When Karl Ling lost his dignity so completely, it was time to worry indeed.

In the elevator, on ground transport and through the Mattin Link, Ling explained the basics of his discoveries to Bey Wolf. By the time they reached Headquarters it was hard to say which man was the more frantic. They went at once to the form-change tanks.

Park Green, alerted as they travelled, was waiting for them there. He looked at Ling in trepidation, expecting an outburst of insult and accusation. It did not come. Ling went at once to the tank containing John Larsen and began to read the tell-tales. After a couple of minutes he grunted with satisfaction.

"So far everything is stable. If he follows the same pattern as the others, we have about twenty-four hours to do something for him. The one thing I daren't do is stop this process in the middle. We'll have to let the process run its course, keep him alive while it happens, and worry afterwards about reversing it. Bring me the tank schematics. I need to know how the circuits that control the nutrients and air supply work for this model."

Park Green went for them and came back in bewilderment. He took Bey Wolf to one side after he had given the schematics to Ling.

"Mr. Wolf, does he know what he's doing? He's a Loge expert, he doesn't know about this stuff, does he? Are we risking John's life by letting him do this?"

Wolf put his hand up on Green's shoulder. "Park, believe me he does know what he's doing. If anyone can help John now, he can. Let's help all we can here. I'll tell you what my view is when this is all over."

Ling interrupted their conversation. His voice had a reassuring authority and certainty. "One of you come over here and make a note of the equipment changes we have to put on this tank. I'll read off settings as I find them on the charts. The other one of you, call BEC. I want their top man on interactive form-change programs. Ramo Wold if he's still with them, the best one they have if he isn't. Top priority. Tell them it's codeword circuits, if that'll move them faster."

The equipment modification began. At every stage, Ling rechecked the tell-tales. Larsen's condition inside the tank remained stable, but there were definite changes occurring. Pulse rate was down, and there was heavy demand on calcium and sodium in the nutrient supply. Skin properties were changing drastically.

"They would have noticed all this in Pleasure Dome if they'd have looked closely," grunted Ling. "Give them their due, they had no reason in the world to expect anything peculiar. But look at that body mass indicator. It's up to a hundred kilos. What's Larsen's usual weight?"

"Eighty." Bey was absorbed, watching the indicators. He longed to see inside the tank but there was no provision for that in the system.

After many hours of equipment change and work on program modification with the BEC program engineer, Ling finally declared that he had done all he could. The real test would come in a few hours' time. The records of the crew of the 'Jason' had begun to go wild then. It remained to be seen if the equipment changes would keep Larsen's condition stable as the change proceeded further.

As Ling made the final checks on the tell-tales, Bey realized the mental anguish and confusion that Park Green was going through.

"Mr. Ling, have we done all we can here?" Bey asked.

"For the moment. The rest is waiting."

"Then if you will, for my benefit and Mr. Green's, I would appreciate it if you would explain this to us, from the beginning. I got a quick overview on the way here, but Park is still in the dark."

Ling looked at Green as though seeing him for the first time. He finally noddded sympathetically.

"From the beginning, eh? Well, that's a long story and I'll have to tell it the way I imagine it. Whether it is true or not is another matter."

He sat down and put his hands behind his head.

"It begins sixteen million years ago, on the planet Loge. Loge was a giant, about ninety earth masses, and Loge was going to explode. Now for something you may find hard to accept. Loge had living on it a race of intelligent beings. Perhaps too intelligent. Maybe they were the reason that their planet disintegrated. We'll probably never know that.

"The race had nuclear energy, but not spaceflight. How do I know that? Well, I know they had nuclear energy because they made transuranic elements. Any natural source of transuranics would have decayed by natural process in the past several billion years since the creation of the Solar System. The only way we could have a source of transuranics on Loge—and only on Loge—would be if they were being created there, by nuclear transmutation. We can't do that efficiently yet, so there's good reason to believe the Logians had an advanced nuclear technology—more than we have today.

"How do I know they didn't have spaceflight? That's harder. The main reason: they couldn't get off Loge, even though they knew it was going to disintegrate. They must have had some years' warning and time to plan, so I imagine it wasn't a nuclear war. Perhaps they had found a way of making large-scale interior adjustments to the planet, and lost control. Again, we'll never know.

"They looked around them in the Solar System. They were going to die, personally, but was there a way their race might survive? To a Logian, the natural place for the survival of the race would be Jupiter or Saturn. They probably never even thought of Earth, a tiny planet, too hot, oxygen atmosphere, a metal ball crouched too near the Sun. No, Jupiter or Saturn was their hope. That's where they turned those big luminous eyes—adapted for life in a methane-heavy atmosphere.

"Their scientists calculated the force of the explosion and gave a grim report. No life form, even single celled ones, could survive it. Parts of Loge would be thrown in all directions. Some would undoubtedly hit Jupiter and its satellites—and Earth too. Could anything survive that transit?

"If anything could, it would be a virus. There's no 'life-support system' in a virus, it's just a chunk of DNA. To grow and multiply, it needs a host cell. The Logians took a chance, and packed their genetic material as a viral form.

"Maybe it worked. We've never had a ship down to the surface of Jupiter or Saturn, and perhaps there are Logians down there, created by viral growth of Loge genetic material in host bodies. We do know there are no Logians on the satellites of either planet.

"Some of that viral material was on fragments of Loge that were blown far out and became part of the long-period comets. That didn't matter. A virus lasts indefinitely. Sixteen million years later, some of those fragments fell back into the Solar System and men began mining them—not for their Loge DNA, not at all. For their transuranic elements.

"Humans are very poor hosts for Loge development. The Loge virus could get into the human body easily enough, and even take up residence in the central nervous system. But it couldn't thrive in such unfamiliar surroundings. Wrong atmosphere, wrong chemical balance, wrong shape."

Ling paused and looked at the other two. He had ceased to be the irritating special advisor and become the great scientist, lecturing to an audience of laymen.

"You may find it hard to believe, but I was already convinced of the existence of a Loge civilization before I ever came to Earth for this investigation. The transuranic elements proved it, to my satisfaction. Otherwise I would never have been led down this train of thought so quickly.

"The crew of the 'Jason' picked up Loge DNA from the Logian fragment. Nothing happened. Then they came to Earth and got into the form-change machines; and at last the virus could begin to act. It stimulated their central nervous systems, and the purposive form-change began to create a form that was optimal—for Logians, not for Earthmen. When that change had proceeded to the point where the changed form could not survive in the atmosphere of Earth, the creatures died. Asphyxiated, in normal air.''

Park Green was now looking in horror at the tank containing John Larsen.

''Does that mean that will happen to John, too?''

''It would have. He injected himself with Loge DNA, along with the Asfanium. The work we've been doing this past day has been to modify the life-support system of the tank, so that it follows the needs of the organism inside it. If you go and look at the tell-tales now, you'll find that the nutrients and the atmosphere are ones that would kill a human.''

Park Green hurried over to the tank. He looked quickly at the monitors and came back.

''Body mass, one hundred and sixty kilos. Oxygen down to eight percent. Mr. Ling, will John live?''

''I believe he will. Can we ever return him to the shape of John Larsen? That is a harder question. If we can, I suspect that it will not be for some time.''

Karl Ling looked at Bey Wolf and caught a reflection of his own excitement.

''We must look on the positive side,'' he said. ''We've dreamed for centuries about our first meeting with an alien race.'' He nodded towards the tank. ''The first representative will be in that tank, ready to meet with us, a day or two from now.''

AFTERWORD: LEGACY.

Writers sometimes become ingenious in finding methods to avoid the actual process of writing. I managed to waste a full week on this story, moving a home-made string dodecahedron about over the surface of a large globe. I said that I was determining where to place the Mattin Link system's exit points. When I had a set of locations that best fitted to world geography, I made a list of them. By the time I wrote the story, I had lost the list.

This one was plotted on British Airways Flight 520, between London and Washington. You can't beat a long plane trip as a place to work out ideas–there's nothing to do but eat, drink, and think. But you can't really type there, even if you have the tiniest of portables. Typing requires that you stick your elbows out to the sides and even if you travel first class you become a hazard to passers-by. It is better to stick to scribbles of plot and dialog.

I wanted to call this story, ''His Flashing Eyes, His Floating Hair.'' I gathered that Jim Baen, then editor of GALAXY, didn't think much of that when he asked me in the politest possible way whether perhaps I didn't have an alternative title in mind. He was almost certainly right, but you'll never persuade a writer that the title he thought of is not at least as good as any other. Note to the historians of the field. *Although this story forms part of the novel SIGHT OF PROTEUS, it was never conceived as such. The novel came much later. When I wrote this, I couldn't imagine how anybody managed to write more than about fifteen thousand words on* any *fictional subject.*

THE SOFTEST HAMMER

Fires fascinate me, always have. I had stopped to watch a big one in Silver Spring, and it was ten o'clock before I headed round the Beltway to Dave Bischoff's apartment.

I was very late, but as it turned out I needn't have hurried. Some year we'll have to get organized, but until we do it's either feast or famine. Half the time four or five people bring manuscripts to read, other weeks we have nothing to do but play cards, drink, smoke, and swap the latest facts and rumors from New York.

This was one of the dry weeks. The game of Hearts was going so well that I didn't get more than a look and a nod when I came in. I had to wait until the round ended with George Andrews dropping the Queen of Spades on Rich Brown in the last trick (poetic justice—Rich had given it to him on the pass). Then I put my beer in the icebox, found another chair, and got down to the serious business of dumping on George, who had been doing well all evening and was fifty points in the lead.

"I'm late because I stopped to watch a fire," I explained, while George was shuffling and dealing.

"House?" asked Rich. After a couple of beers he gets terser and terser. I think I can tell how long a meeting has been going just from Rich's words-per-minute statistics.

I shook my head. "Apartment building, over in Silver Spring."

There was silence for a few seconds, while everybody sorted their cards and decided what they would pass, then Jack Locke leaned back against the couch and looked across at me.

"How many floors?" he asked.

He's an odd duck, Jack is. You can never tell what he's going to say. Sometimes I blame the Scots accent that makes even normal statements come out sounding strange, but mostly I think it's inside his head.

I thought for a moment.

"About twelve floors, I'd say. The whole building went before I left. The fire trucks were there, but the hoses couldn't pump water in fast enough to stop the spread."

Jack nodded, as though my statement confirmed some point he had been making. "Often the case, that is. D'yer know, half the fires in big buildings stay out of control just because the flow rate isn't big enough through the hoses?"

"So what?" That was George, with a miffed look on his face. He takes his card games seriously, and he had just missed picking up the Jack of Diamonds. "They couldn't handle hoses bigger than the ones they have now—they'd be too heavy to move around."

Jack nodded, and sipped his beer. "Aye, true enough. But d'yer know, a few years back I came this close"—he held up finger and thumb, an inch apart—"to having my hands on something that would have solved that problem. If things had worked out a bit differently, I'd be a multi-millionaire today."

Nobody spoke, but George sniffed and I don't think it was allergies. About one meeting in four, Jack brings in a story for us to read and criticize. We tear them to pieces. He's one of these people who can tell a story over a beer in the most natural way in the world, but the typewriter does something to him and his written prose comes out like a bad marriage of Jacqueline Susann and Bertrand Russell. We keep telling him to write out some of the yarns he spins us, and then he gets mad and swears they're all the truth, not stories at all.

George followed up on his sniff. "I presume this was after your experience with the hurricane down in the Caribbean?"

Last time, Jack had told us of a treasure hunt with a British group, looking for sunk galleons on the Spanish Main. George had spotted an inconsistency in the range of Jack's ship, and he had pointed it out with considerable pleasure. Jack pointed out, with just as much pleasure, that he had been quoting tank capacities in *Imperial* gallons, natural for a British ship, and they are twenty percent bigger than U.S. gallons. It made his story possible—just.

"After I got back from Trinidad, that's right," said Jack seriously. "I'd seen enough of the sea after that hurricane, so I took a job as a lab technician in a little town in upper New York State."

George growled, but this time he didn't challenge. We've had some pretty odd jobs between us, and lab technician was one of the more mundane ones. It didn't compare with two years with a circus, or eight years in a mental hospital (as a nurse, not a patient). Myself, I've been a builder's laborer, a private tutor, a cook in a holiday camp, and a tour guide for European charter parties. Jack's in his early forties, but he must have had a different job every three months to explain all the places he says he's been and the people he's worked with.

"I wouldn't think you'd get much fire-fighting in upper New York," said Dave from the kitchen. He'd dropped out of the game to make popcorn, and given Melanie his hand to play. "I wouldn't think you'd get much of *anything* up there. I spent a summer up in the Finger Lakes area when I was a kid, and it was the dullest place I've ever been in my whole life."

"But that's because you *were* a kid," said Jack over his shoulder. He turned to the rest of us. "Who was it, Conan Doyle or Chesterton, who said there's more wickedness in the middle of the country than you'll find in the big cities? It didn't take me long to find out that was true. In a couple of weeks, I realized I was seeing the worst eternal triangle I'd ever run across."

He was dealing out cards slowly, not looking up at us. When nobody spoke he knew he had us and went on. "It was an absolutely traditional set-up. Beautiful young wife, stuck away from the city life where she was brought up and looking for something a bit more exciting than she could find in Lundee, New York. And the two men, one of them tall, handsome and impressive, the other short, balding and nearsighted. Funny thing was, it was the handsome one, Vic Lakman, who was married to glamorous Ginny. And it was little Dieter, Dr. Dieter Mahler, who came in to seduce her and break up the happy home.

"After you'd been around him for a few days you could see how Dieter Mahler could do it. He never thought for a moment that he was under-sized and funny looking. He was cheerful, very bright, and fascinated by women. He just assumed that they would find him as attractive as he found them. They might start out laughing at him, but pretty soon they would begin to accept him at his own evaluation. Surprising, isn't it, how much the view we hold of ourselves conditions the way that others view us?"

"People must think you're wonderful, then," said George sourly. He had just picked up the first trick, and from his comment I thought that it might have the Queen of Spades in it. I decided to play the hand accordingly. (I was right, but it didn't help me much—I never win at cards.)

Jack ignored George's acid.

"Vic Lakman couldn't blame anybody but himself for Mahler's arrival in Lundee," he went on. "He and Dieter Mahler met at a conference in Atlanta on fire-fighting equipment, and Vic decided that it would be worth a lot to have Mahler come north for the summer. Did I mention to you that Vic Lakman's lab was doing research in fire-fighting?"

"I missed it if you did," said Dave. He was back in the game, and the cards were beginning to grease up with the butter from the popcorn. We're a disgusting lot, we got through a deck a week that way. "What were they making, hoses?"

Jack shook his head. "Chemicals. The stuff you put in fire extinguishers. And they were just getting into slippery water."

He paused and looked around the table. "I suppose you all know what slippery water is, don't you?"

There was a long silence, while we all waited for somebody else to be the first to admit ignorance. It rang a faint bell with me so I took a shot at it.

"Isn't it the same as 'wet' water, water with detergents added to it to make it spread more quickly? I've seen that used at a couple of fires."

"Not quite the same, but you're close." Jack paused and played a card with a look of deep concentration, then laid his hand face down on the table. "Slippery water has an additive, yer see, same as wet water does, but for a different reason. You use it to increase the amount of water that will pass through a hose. What you do is, you take a polyethylene oxide polymer and add about a pound of it to every four thousand gallons in the water tank. That's not much additive, but it lowers the viscosity and doubles the flow rate through the hose with no increase in head pressure.''

Jack's always trotting out strings of facts like that, and we have a devil of a time contradicting him. As it happens, in this case I took the trouble next day to look up what he said in the 'Brittanica' that Linda bought me for my last Christmas present, and what Jack told us is quite true about slippery water. But I didn't know it at the time, and we all started to look at him and at each other, wondering if this was the point where he was beginning to stray away from the strict and absolute truth.

Jack ignored the looks and took a big handful of popcorn.

''Mahler was an expert on fire-fighting chemicals,'' he said in a corn-garbled voice. ''Usually he taught at some rinky-dink college down in the south, and an upper New York summer must have been a rare treat for him. He turned up at the lab one day with his silver cigar case and his patent medicine for the gout, and Vic Lakman settled him into a little beach house by the side of the lake. That part of the State has lakes all over, thousands of them. The Lakmans had a nice bit of beach property, clean and private, and Dr. Mahler liked to have a quiet place to call his own. For what he got up to, he needed the privacy.''

Jack rubbed his hands on his pants and picked up his cards. ''Vic Lakman was a big, handsome man with blond hair and a fair beard. Remember what George looked like when he grew a beard last year?''

We nodded, and George looked self-conscious.

''Well, that's what Lakman's beard was like. Except that on him it looked good.

''He was a self-made man, somebody who grew up in Long Island City in the Greek or Italian section. I don't think that Lakman was his original name, he started out with something with a bit more of a spaghetti-and-garlic ring to it. But nobody in Lundee was going to suggest that to him. He had a tough

reputation, and he'd come up a long way. Somewhere along the
road to the top he'd collected Ginny and he was as proud,
doting—and jealous—of her as a man can get. His work habits
didn't show it much, because next to Ginny that lab was his
pride and joy. He put in twelve-hour days, six days a week, and
on Sunday he played golf with the bankers who were financing
his expansion plans.

"Ginny was a bird in a gilded cage. It took little Dr. Mahler
about two seconds to see that and to make up his mind what he
was going to do about it.

"I was there the first time they met, one afternoon when I was
cleaning up after a messy lab experiment. Ginny came by to see
Vic, and she was wearing a pale pink sun dress, off the shoulder.
As usual, Vic was off in one of his endless meetings, but I
thought that Dieter was going to leap on her at first glance.
Within five minutes of the first introduction he had her admitting
that she missed access to swimming at the lake, now that he was
living in the beach house, and a minute after that he had invited
her to come out there, any time she wanted to, for a swim and
maybe a drink. She smiled a little—she was about four inches
taller than he was—and she thanked him, but she didn't commit
herself one way or the other. I thought that was the end of it.

"The following week, Vic sent me out to the beach house one
afternoon to drop off some research papers that Mahler had
asked for. He did a lot of his work, all the theory part, away from
the lab, and only went in there when there were experiments to
be done.

"Dieter Mahler was in the outside shower when I got there.
Lakman had installed a solar-heated water tank to feed the
shower so when somebody came in from the beach—Lakman
had imported tons of sand for that—they could take a warm
rinse. Most people needed it, too, because that lake water was
freezing.

"The big water tank was up on the roof, up where it would
catch the most sun, and when I got there I could hear Mahler,
singing in a horrible cracked tenor inside the shower stall. And I
was very surprised to find Ginny Lakman sunbathing on the
beach, lying on a big pink air mattress about seven feet square.

"She was quite a sight. Her little green bikini showed an even, all-over tan, and if she was pale in parts they must have been awfully private ones. I couldn't help goggling. Everything was in the right place, and there was plenty of it. I don't know when I last saw so much smooth, warm flesh. But I think the thing that I noticed most of all was the little heap of cigar ash next to the air mattress.

"I dropped off the papers and left. It wasn't the sort of scene I wanted to tangle with. I'd seen Vic when he was angry, one day when he chewed me out for screwing up a telephone message he was supposed to get and didn't. What would he do if he thought his precious Ginny was playing the two-backed beast with Mahler? I didn't even want to think about it.

"That was all I knew of it for another couple of weeks. At least they kept away from the lab, and I was too busy with the work there to stick my nose in where it wasn't wanted, whatever those two were up to."

Jack paused. We all waited patiently while Dave examined his hand with excruciating care and at last played an apparently random card from it. I always feel that when Dave is stoned you can tell just what he will be like when he's a hundred years old. He gets slow, tremulous, and not quite all there.

We watched while George dropped the Queen of Spades on Dave's lead, and Jack nodded knowingly.

"Aye, you can go badly wrong if you don't watch what other people's hands are holding," he said. "That was Dieter Mahler's problem. He had his eye too much on Ginny, and he underestimated the way that Vic could work like a fiend at the lab and still keep his eye on her too. I didn't know it at first, but Dieter had set another lure for Vic Lakman, one that he expected would hold all his attention. The first I heard of it was late one afternoon, when they were sitting talking in the lab.

" 'It won't be expensive to make,' Mahler was saying. He was puffing on one of his Pittsburgh stogies, and he had unbent far enough to loosen his tie a little. 'You'll need an initial investment in equipment, then it will get cheap. And it will be a lot better than any of the polymers we use now. Not just twice as good—a *lot* better.'

"Vic Lakman was leaning across the bench towards him. He looked about twice as tall as Mahler, like a Viking god looming over a Nibelung dwarf. 'How good, Doctor?' he said. 'You're suggesting that I ought to invest a lot of money in new equipment, but how good will this new stuff be?'

"Dieter Mahler waved his cigar in a circular smoke pattern. 'A hundred times as good as what we have now, at the very least. Probably more like a thousand times better. I assure you, it will revolutionize fire-fighting. Invest in this now, and in five years time we'll be the only people in the business.''

"Lakman pulled a pad of paper over to him and began to scribble numbers. I don't think he saw his wife enter, or the quick look that passed between Ginny and Mahler. Nobody took much notice of me—low-priced lab technicians didn't seem to count in business or pleasure.

"'No good,' said Lakman when he finally finished figuring. 'According to this estimate, I'd have to find a hundred and fifty thousand for a working prototype plant. I can't do that without something to show people. Sure you didn't drop a decimal point somewhere?'

"Mahler shrugged. 'What can I say? Error is always possible, and I can't prove I'm right unless we do some kind of small demonstration and make the new polymer. I could do that on a small scale for, oh, say five thousand. That would give us just a couple of pounds of it—but it would be enough to show off what it can do.'

"Lakman crumpled his sheet of calculations up into a ball and looked around the lab—right through me, as I said I didn't count for much. He looked at Mahler again, then from him to Ginny. Finally he nodded. 'All right. I can find five thousand. How soon will you be done if you begin today?'

"'Two weeks,' said Mahler. Then, too cocky, he made what I thought might be a bad mistake. He added. 'I'll make this my top priority,' and he gave Ginny another quick look, one that was a good deal more direct and was probably meant to reassure her that one of his priorities wouldn't go any lower. She didn't blush, but not many women can do that after they reach thirty—even when they have a lot more to blush about.

"Neither Mahler nor Lakman was going to tell me anything, of course, but it was obvious enough for me to piece it together for myself. Mahler had dreamed up some new super-additive, something that would make water *really* slippery. With that super-slippery water, a fire-fighting unit would be able to pump maybe a hundred times as much water through a hose with no extra equipment."

"Now, just a minute, Jack," broke in George. He was looking pleased with himself. Just last week, Jack had told him that a story he had brought to be read was a piece of mindless flatulence. We don't pull punches in the group, but George thought that was going too far and he had been waiting to get even with Jack since then.

"You're making up this whole thing," he said. "What you just said is a pure physical impossibility. It's absolute nonsense. Water has inertia, like everything else. There's no way you could increase flow without overcoming the inertia, and that would mean completely new equipment to pump the water."

Jack looked at him gravely. "You're quite right, George," he said. "I was overstating. It's not like me to exaggerate, and I'm glad you cut me off when I began to do it. What I meant was, all the work that you'd usually do against *frictional* forces would be avoided when you were pumping water through the hose. You would still have to accelerate the water, and if you were sending it up to a high floor you'd still have to give it enough speed to get it up there. Even so, Mahler's super-slippery water would make a huge difference—most of the problem with the high-velocity hoses comes from fighting the frictional losses—especially when you're using a very long hose.

"Let me go on, and I'll make sure I don't exaggerate anything else. After the meeting with Lakman, Mahler began to come into the lab every day and stay until after midnight. He had a private room in the back, and he locked it when he went in and when he came out. It was easy enough to see how things were going in the experiments from the look on his face when he came out for coffee or to go to the john. Sometimes he'd walk right past me as though I didn't exist, and on other days he'd come out with his cigar lit, and he'd stop and chat and puff away, and swell up with satisfaction like a contented little rooster.

"A couple of times Ginny was at the lab at lunch time, and she and Dieter went off to eat lunch together. They were circumspect enough, but Ginny was looking different these days. It's hard to say how, but she seemed kind of *sleeker* when she was with Mahler, and I almost expected her to rub up against his shoulder and purr.

"I felt sorry for Vic Lakman. He was working harder than ever, juggling his finances to squeeze out cash that he needed for the experiments, and all the time his wife was playing games behind his back. But he must have been a lot more aware of what was going on than I gave him credit for. Late one afternoon, when he was in the back room with Mahler, a fellow in a tweed jacket stopped by with a sealed envelope for him. He wouldn't leave it with me until Lakman called through from inside to tell him that it would be all right, and that he would pick it up in just a few minutes.

"Before Lakman came out, Ginny showed up. She was pale, and her hair was a mess—very unusual for her.

" 'Is someone in there with Dr. Mahler?' she asked.

" 'Mr. Lakman. Go on in, I'm sure they won't mind,' I said.

"She turned paler than ever. 'No, it's all right,' she said, then she turned and ran out.

"I said that she was pale, but she was nowhere as pale as Vic Lakman when he opened that envelope and read what was inside it. He crumpled the message and thrust it into his pocket as Mahler followed him out of the back room.

"Dieter seemed blind to Lakman's mood. He was bubbling over with excitement and high spirits.

" 'Tomorrow I'll be able to show you the whole thing on a larger scale,' he said. 'But I think you'll agree after that demonstration that we are there. How much did I say we had, five hundred and forty grams? I ought to make a note of that.'

"He pulled out a thin blue notebook, wallet size, opened it and scribbled something in it with an old-fashioned ink fountain pen. Then he turned to Lakman. 'Would you care to have a drink to celebrate?'

"I could hardly stand to look at Lakman's face, but Mahler

didn't seem to notice anything. After a few seconds he repeated his question.

" 'No,' said Lakman at last. 'I'm not in the mood for that.' And he hurried off out without another word, leaving Mahler to puff on his reeking cigar and talk me—without too much trouble—into going over to a bar and having a few bourbons. Most of his mannerisms were European, but his time in the south had taught him a proper respect for good U.S. liquor.''

Jack stopped talking and picked up his cards. He frowned at his hand, then looked over to Rich, who was keeping the scores. "How am I doing?"

"You're in last place with eighty-three. Followed by me and Dave with seventy-eight.''

"And I'm leading with thirty-eight,'' said George happily. "No wonder you fall behind, Jack, when you talk so much.''

Jack looked at him calmly. "Aye, that's probably true,'' he said, and passed three cards on to Rich.

"But what about Mahler and the Lakmans?'' I said. I didn't know about George, but I wanted to hear the rest of it. The others muttered agreement with me.

Jack shrugged. "There's not too much more to tell. I left Mahler and went back to my apartment about nine o'clock. Next morning, Vic Lakman came in to the lab about eight-thirty. He looked terrible, as though he hadn't slept a wink. Usually he was all business, but that morning he just seemed to want to sit around and chat to me. I thought to myself, poor bastard, he can't even think straight with what she's doing to him, and we chatted all morning about everything under the sun. I couldn't get my work done, either, but he was the boss and if he wanted to pay me to talk to him that was his option.

"We went and had lunch together, and we were still eating when the police arrived. Dieter Mahler was dead. He had been found by Ginny Lakman about noon, when she went down to the beach house for her morning swim—or whatever it was she enjoyed there when Dieter was alive.

"Mahler's head had been bashed in. According to the police surgeon, he had been dead only an hour or so when Ginny found him.

"They ruled her out early. First, she had almost collapsed when she found the body, and second, the police surgeon did not believe that any woman could have delivered the blow that killed Mahler. He had been hit so hard that his cervical vertebrae had been crushed as his head was driven downwards.

"Vic was ruled out, too, as soon as the police found he had been with me for the whole morning. I could swear to that, and anyway to leave the rear part of the lab we would have had to pass through three rooms full of people, plus a receptionist. After half an hour of answering questions about Mahler, and what he knew of his past, Vic was allowed to go home. He went to their house, where Ginny had been taken under sedation. I don't know what they said to each other there."

Jack paused to play a card. He seemed in no hurry to say more. I slapped down a card of the same suit and said, "Come on, that can't be the end of it! What happened next? You said you were almost a millionaire, but all you've told us about is an unsolved murder."

Rich was nodding agreement. "Give," he said—a moderately long speech for him so late in the evening.

Jack shrugged. "Well, that was the end of Mahler's experiments. Lakman never mentioned one word about super-slippery water to anyone else. I would have accepted the police verdict—Mahler's death was the act of some vagrant looking to rob him—if it hadn't been for a couple of odd reports.

"The first was the official description of Mahler's death. It had come while he was actually in the outside shower. They never did find the murder weapon, but the police said they were looking for the traditional 'blunt instrument', some kind of massive, padded club. The second thing was Mahler's blue notebook. The police had brought it back to the lab for identification. It had been found about thirty feet from the body, but they didn't seem to attach any significance to that.

"When I realized what must have happened, I went out to the beach house myself and had a good look round there. I found what I expected—but it wasn't evidence that you could ever offer in court."

Now we were all looking at Jack, with our mouths more or less gaping open.

"Come on, then," said George at last. "Don't leave us hanging. What had happened to Mahler?"

Jack played another card casually before he answered. "Just what you should have deduced, the way that I deduced it. I told you, Mahler was making super-slippery water—and he had succeeded. He had five hundred and forty grams of the additive, made the day before he was murdered. Enough to treat a couple of thousand gallons of water. It was locked in the lab, and that was off limits—but not to Vic Lakman. He had access to everything. And he'd seen a demonstration the same day as he was given real proof as to what Ginny and Mahler were up to.

"He wasn't a man to stand for that. Where he grew up, adultery was probably considered justifiable homicide. Mahler had to die."

"But you said Lakman had a perfect alibi," protested Dave. "You gave him one yourself."

"Of course I did." Jack picked up another trick and led a high club. "He *arranged* it so he'd have a perfect alibi. Isn't it obvious what he did? He went to the lab that night, took the sample of super-slippery water additive out of the lab, and went to the beach house. While Mahler was sleeping, he climbed up to the roof of the house and dumped the additive in the water tank, the rain-fed one that supplied the outside shower. The additive made the water flow a hundred times as easily—maybe a thousand times as easily, if Mahler's estimate was correct.

"Next morning, Mahler took his usual swim, then went into the outside shower and turned it on. A couple of hundred gallons of water—well over half a ton—came out of the shower head in a couple of seconds. It smashed Mahler, just as though a sixteen-hundred pound weight had been dropped down on him from ten feet up. That was the police's 'blunt instrument'—no wonder they never found it."

"But I still don't understand," said Dave. "You said that you found evidence. Why didn't you take it back and show it to the police?"

"I told you, it wasn't the sort of thing they would accept," said Jack gently. "I found what I thought I would find—the faucet of the outside shower still turned on, as it was at the moment when Mahler died. And all around the shower, forty feet in all directions, the marks of a big splash in the sand. A few hundred gallons hitting all at once makes a big spread, much bigger than you'd ever get from the same amount coming down in a slow trickle. I thought that's what I'd see, when I first had the chance for a good look at this. Remember, the police found it thirty feet from the shower."

He pulled a thin blue notebook from his pocket, wallet size, and handed it to me. I opened it and stared at the pages.

"What's it say?" asked George.

I shook my head. "I don't know. It's unreadable, all you can see is a lot of runny blurs. This could say anything at all."

"Aye, true enough," said Jack. He sighed. "That was Mahler's notebook, the one where he kept the details of all his experiments. It was over near the air mattress, where he'd left it when he went in for a swim. When the super-water smashed him, the book got thoroughly soaked by the splash, even though it was thirty feet away. It's a great pity, but as I told you Mahler's notes were all kept in ink. It ran so much that I've only been able to make out odd words of it, here and there. But if I ever do decipher it, the whole thing, I'll know Mahler's secret of slippery water, and that will make me rich. I can't see Vic Lakman ever talking about it, or working on it again."

"Hold on," said George suddenly, while the rest of us were still staring at the water-run pages of the notebook. "We've not been watching what we were doing here, and Jack has taken all the tricks so far. If we don't watch out he'll take the lot."

"Too late, I'm afraid," said Jack quietly. He laid the rest of his cards, face up, on the table. "I think you'll find these are winning cards for the last three tricks. Let's see, shooting the sun like this takes my score down by fifty-two points, right? I think that puts me nicely in the lead, just ahead of George."

He stood up and picked up the blue notebook, weighing it in his hand and looking at it thoughtfully.

"Aye. Might be a good time for me to call it a day, and maybe have one more look at this before I turn in. Drive carefully, all of you, and I'll see you all next week.''

He turned back for a second in the doorway. ''Aye, and don't any of you take chances when you're in the shower. After all, you never know when some smart man will re-discover Mahler's invention.''

AFTERWORD: THE SOFTEST HAMMER.

The "slippery water" described in this story is real enough. It's made by adding a polyethylene oxide polymer to ordinary water to reduce the viscosity, and that allows more water to flow through a hose—not a thousand times more, but perhaps twice as much.

The writers' group is real, too. It's called the Vicious Circle, a moveable feast where every Wednesday night George Andrews, Peter Altermann, Dave Bischoff, Ted White, Steve Brown, Paul Halpine, Rich Brown and other regulars meet to read and comment on each other's stories. Criticism is severe—we argue that encouragement and stroking are readily available from family and friends. What we aim to do is to make any subsequent disparaging comments from editors and reviewers seem mild by comparison.

When I first wrote this story I had the whole writers' group in there, but I was forced to omit some people when I sent it out for submission to a magazine. No reader could be expected to keep track of a dozen different characters in a story of less than five thousand words.

I was going to apologize here to those who have been left out of the published version. After some thought, I have decided that my apologies must go to those who were left in.

HIDDEN VARIABLE

The beginning of the Scorpio meteor shower was estimated for 19.00 hours. Already there had been a couple of bright flares far below in the Earth's atmosphere, as early members of the shower signalled their arrival.

Jose Perona had trained the big scope downwards, turning it from its usual work of planetary observation. From the synchronous station, twenty-two thousand miles above the equator, he could easily see the lights of Quito, geometrical patterns of white points beneath them. After a few minutes he grunted and turned to his companion.

"What do you think, Mackie? That's the fourth meteor I've seen burn up in two minutes down there."

Mack Johnson glanced over at the wall display. He frowned. "Still over an hour to go, if that 19.00 hour estimate is any good. Where did it come from?"

Jose had pushed himself lightly from his seat by the telescope and floated over to the computer console. He made a rapid data entry and looked at the display console before he replied.

"Pretty old data. The Scorpio's are a long-period group— ninety years since they were here. I bet we're seeing some spreading in elements, even though Outer Station has been tracking them for a month now. We'd better assume we'll need the screens up early."

Mack Johnson sighed. "That's going to make us unpopular, I know for a fact that Lustig has an X-ray observation going that he'd like to hold for another two hours. All right, better safe than sorry."

He picked up the phone and accessed public address. "Attention, all personnel. The Scorpio shower seems to be here early. The Wenziger screens will be switched on five minutes from now. Repeat. The Wenziger screens will be switched on in five minutes. Secure all external materials and prepare for communication blackout.''

He disconnected and grimaced. "I give us thirty seconds, Jose, then listen to the complaints come in. I bet that interrupts a hundred experiments up here."

Even as he spoke, the phone had begun to buzz angrily. He ignored it and coded in an Earth-link circuit. The Quito station cut in at once. They could see the com technician turning back from the window to face their communicator screen.

"Been expecting you," he said. "I've been watching the shower start—it's early, right?"

"Looks like it." Mack nodded. "We'll be cutting in the Wenziger's in about four minutes. The shower is supposed to last about fourteen hours. We'll talk to you again when we're shielded by Earth—six and a half hours from now, maybe a little more. Anything need saying that can't wait?"

The technician shook his head. "I have a pile of messages, nothing urgent. Talk to you again when you switch off the Wenziger's."

They cut the connection and began the final count-down and turned on the Wenziger screen. Everything went dead on the display, instantly. Mack leaned back in his seat and looked again at the phone. The complainers had all given up their efforts to reach him.

"Ever wonder what would happen if the Universe were to end while we've got the Wenziger's on?" he said. "Think we'd know about it?"

Jose shrugged. "Not until we came back out again. *Nothing* gets through, if the theory's right. Perlman tried a neutrino detection experiment a couple of years ago, and he thought a couple of those were penetrating the screen, but he couldn't get the same result when he tried it again.'' He switched off the dead displays. "Won't need these 'til we come out again. You know, there's a funny thing about these Wenziger screens."

Mack was running through all the input receiver systems. There was nothing but thermal noise on any of them.

"Funny thing?" He turned back to face Perona. "The whole idea of the screen's funny to me. I had years of the theory in school, and I still don't understand any of it. Just be thankful we have 'em, that's all—we'd have fried in that last solar flare without 'em."

"Yeah. Sure. I don't know how they work, either. But there's still something funny about them," Jose persisted. "They have the wrong name."

"Wenziger? What's wrong with that?"

They had settled back in their seats, secure in the knowledge that there would be—could be—no incoming or outgoing signal until the screens were switched off.

"Back when we had the theory, back when I was in school, we had to do a paper on the screens." Jose shrugged. "I was keen in those days. I went back to the original reference papers. Couldn't understand them, but I'll tell you one thing. *None* of those original papers was by Wenziger. Not one."

Mack was frowning, running his fingers over the channel selectors. "That's dumb. You must have missed something. I think I even remember reading papers by Wenziger in my physics course—long time ago, now, but I remember the name."

"Yeah, Wenziger was a physicist. But all the papers with the theory in them were by Nissom."

"*Laurance* Nissom?"

"How many others do you know?"

"None. But if that's true, why are they always called the Wenziger screens?"

Jose Perona was smiling smugly. "My question, let me point out. I told you there was something funny about the Wenziger's. All right then, Mackie, stop fiddling with those keys and listen. I'll tell you how they got their name—even a lump like you ought to know this one. *Nissom* named 'em that . . ."

It was dark when he reached the wall; pitch-dark, moonless, with stars hidden by a heavy overcast. He squatted down and felt carefully for his first marker, a sticky blob of resin dabbed on the smooth stone surface. He felt his way down from the resin patch to the groove at the base of the wall, then traced a line outward to the small pebble of his second marker.

The darkness was complete. Everything had to be done by touch, by carefully rehearsed and precise movement. Slowly, carefully, measuring a line down past his braced fingers, he pushed the length of sharpened piano wire into the soft soil beneath the pebble.

After five time-consuming failures, he on the sixth attempt felt a faint pulse returned along the stiff wire. He had struck the coaxial cable that took the signals from the eyes on the top of the wall back to the house.

He straightened up, breathed deeply, and carefully brushed the loose earth from the knees of his trousers. The high wall, invisible, loomed beside him. He knew its exact height and the shape of the concave overhang that led to its top. The surface, cold in the summer night, felt smooth and seamless to his outstretched hand.

He placed his back square to the wall to give him direction, then using the lights of the distant house as a second guide he walked ten measured paces away from the wall. He bent forward. Plunging his hands through the upper branches of an azalea bush, he felt his way down to the cache hidden at its base. One by one, he pulled objects out from it and carried them back to the base of the wall.

Ten trips, and he had the whole collection. He ran his hands over them slowly, noting their exact positions.

They made a strange assortment, a rusting and jagged heap of junk on the dry earth. He picked up the heaviest one first, a four-foot length of thick iron pipe scavenged from the boiler room. The rope tied around its jointed end was old and frayed, a discarded clothesline from the garden shed, but he had tested it carefully and knew it would be strong enough. Placing his foot on the rope end, he swung the pipe around and with a grunt of effort hurled it upwards and over the wall. There was a heavy thud as it struck the earth on the other side.

He waited a full minute, looking back towards the big house for signs of extra activity there. All remained quiet, but that was little reassurance. If the eyes on top of the wall were also tuned to thermal wavelengths, a cold object would pass where a man could not.

He bent to pick up his second find, a massive iron wheel from a derelict washing machine. He secured the end of the rope tied to it, then it too went over the wall to join the iron pipe.

One by one, the roped objects were thrown up and over. He fingered the final one for a few seconds before he swung and heaved. It was a heavy bronze statue of Mars, God of War, clad in helmet, armor, and massive metal leggings. He had seen and hated it every day in the library. Removing it that afternoon had been a pleasure.

Ten lengths of rope trailed upwards from his feet into the darkness. He picked up the whole bunch and began to twist them together into a single braided cable, turning until each one merged with its companions. Then he began to climb, feet braced against the wall. When he reached the top he paused and looked back at the house. Still no sign of increased activity.

He peered down. This was the unpredictable part. He had not been able to determine what lay outside and now he would have to jump blind. A ten-foot drop onto sharp fencing would end everything.

Bracing himself, he pushed off hard with his hands and dropped into the darkness.

"Come on in, Wenziger. I'll be through here in a minute."

The man behind the desk nodded his visitor to a chair and went on with telephone dictation. His jacket was off and his shirt sleeves rolled up, to reveal strong and tanned forearms. A cigarette, lit but unsmoked, smoldered in the gunmetal ashtray in the middle of the big desk. The man who had entered the room received no further attention from him until a full page of dictated memorandum had been completed.

"Right," he said at last, dropping the telephone back onto its stand. "That should hold them for a day or two. You heard, did you, that our bird has flown?"

The other man nodded. He had been patiently sitting, knees together and heavy briefcase resting on his thighs. In contrast to the relaxed and casual man behind the desk, the newcomer was stiff and formal. He looked pressed and polished, from the shining surface of his black shoes, past the charcoal-grey suit to the glistening top of his bald, domed head.

"I was told as I came to the outer office. In view of this, General, perhaps our meeting will not be necessary?"

His voice was soft and husky, with a faint trace of an accent. Not quite German, somewhere a bit farther east.

The man behind the desk picked up his neglected cigarette and inhaled a long drag.

"Like hell. We need to talk *more* now. They had Laurance Nissom in a maximum security hospital and he got out. Before this he could have been just a kook. Now I need to know all about him." He tapped the thick dossier on the desk in front of him. "Lots of stuff in here, but nothing about this new work. Did you get through the stuff I sent to you?"

The bald head nodded again. Zdenek Wenziger opened his briefcase and took out a thick sheaf of xeroxed pages.

"I read it in some detail." He hesitated, biting at his thin upper lip. "General Greer, I really wonder if I can give you a useful evaluation."

He stopped as though there were more to say. The other man looked up quickly from the dossier. His eyes, bright and blue, seemed too young for the grey crew-cut hair and lined face.

"You need more time? Hell, this is supposed to be a top priority item. What have you been doing all week?"

Wenziger flushed at the tone of voice. "I have spent almost all my time on this since it came to me, General. Time is not the problem. The difficulty is one of full understanding."

"You telling me you don't understand what Nissom wrote?" Greer slapped the dossier onto the desk. "I can't buy that. You're our top physics consultant, aren't you? Whistler over at DARPA warned me that getting evaluations out of you was like pulling teeth. I *have* to have an answer. Is there a chance—any chance—that Nissom's work could produce the effects he claims?"

"If you put it that way, I will have to say no. Almost certainly, no."

"*Almost* certainly! What the hell use is that to me? What's the doubt, you're the one with all the fancy awards, not Nissom. You shouldn't have any trouble sorting out what he's saying.''

Zdenek Wenziger had closed his briefcase and placed it on the floor beside his chair. He sighed. ''General Greer, you insisted on a one-word answer to a complex question. I was foolish enough to try and provide one. Will you give me five minutes to try and explain?''

Greer looked at his watch. ''Take five, take ten—but give me an answer I can use. You know I've got forty men out there trying to trace Nissom?—and they're all coming up cold. There's a lot of classified stuff locked up inside his head.''

''I believe you. There is also a lot of unclassified stuff.'' Wenziger took off his glasses and began to polish them with a spotless white handkerchief. His eyes were revealed as a mild and watery grey. ''The content of the paper you sent was new to me, but not the style. I have been dealing with Laurance Nissom since he was a graduate student. If anyone can claim to have a fair understanding of how his mind works, I suppose that I am he. And I tell you that I have at best an imperfect understanding of that process.''

''You mean he's smarter than you are?'' The tone was sceptical. ''You're the one with all the awards, not him.''

Wenziger smiled faintly. ''Yes, General. I have all the awards. I am also sixty-seven years old, and Laurance Nissom is thirty-one.'' He leaned forward. ''Do you realize that Einstein himself did not win a Nobel Prize until he was well into his forties? And that when he did win it, it was not given for his most profound work? If Nissom were to be right—and I do not believe that he can be—it would be another five or ten years before the implications would be understood. I could draw you almost an inverse correlation. The more profoundly original the work, the longer it takes to reach a point where a Nobel Prize Committee is ready to accept and recognize it.''

''I hear you.'' The cigarette had been stubbed out to join the ashtray litter of stubs, and Zdenek Wenziger had the full attention of those bright eyes. ''You're telling me that Nissom is smart. I know that. I want to know, *how* smart. I mean, the way you're talking, is he likely to win a Nobel Prize some day?''

"I think so. But you are still asking the wrong question." The careful polishing of the eye-glasses had continued, though any speck of dust had long since disappeared from them. "This may sound ridiculous to you, General, but at the highest level of creativity the award of a Nobel is not an adequate measure. There is as much spread among Nobel Laureates as there is among—how shall I put it?—professional quarterbacks. All are good, but some are pre-eminent. Do you by any chance speak German?"

"A few odd words. I was stationed in Frankfurt for three years, but that was ages ago."

"Three years?" Wenziger registered surprise for the first time. "Didn't you find it most inconvenient to be unable to speak the language?"

"Hell, no." Greer laughed. "Anything I needed, I just waved a mark at 'em. That always worked." He leaned forward. "I'll let you in on a little military secret. You don't get two stars in the Air Force for learning foreign languages. They're about equal to a big fat zero on your promotion rating. Any spare time I had on watch over in Europe, I used it reading Clausewitz on war, or Machiavelli on using a power structure. If I want a Ph.D. in languages, I just call it some over-educated major. Whatever it is, say it to me in English."

"Very well, General, we will do it in English." The old man looked resigned, shaking his massive head slightly. "Bear with my translation. For almost forty years, Albert Einstein and Max Born—both Nobel Laureates in physics—kept up a friendly correspondence in German about work and other things. In describing their correspondence, many years later, Born talked about his first exposure to Einstein's work. Remember now, this was many years before Einstein was famous, many years before he won a Nobel Prize. He did not even hold a university appointment. But Born, recalling the first time that he saw Einstein's work, says: 'We all knew at once that a genius of the first order had arisen.' I'm translating his words, but do you see my point?"

"I think so." Greer's head was cocked to one side, his manner sober and thoughtful. "If I can see past your funny way of putting it, you're telling me that it takes one to know one. Great physicists can recognize super-great ones before anyone else can—including the fellows who award the Nobel Prizes. Right?''

''You have it exactly. In my opinion Laurance Nissom is one of those rarities, even among Nobel Laureates, the 'genius of the first order' that Born recognized in Einstein.''

''So dammit, you're telling me that he's *right* in this cock-eyed theory!'' Greer sat up straighter in his chair. ''We've got to get our hands on him. Do you know what this could mean to the defense of the country?''

Wenziger replaced his glasses. He held up a carefully mani-cured hand to the other man. ''Gently, General. Let me finish. I had to tell you all that, to explain why I would be forced to view *any* of Nissom's work with great respect. Having said that let me now say something else. I am almost certain, as certain as I can be about any theory, that Laurance Nissom's latest work is not correct.''

''My God, you're choosing a funny way of telling me it.'' Greer leaned to the side of the desk and pressed the Intercom buzzer.

''Yes, General?''

''Get Major Merritt over here with the mission progress report.'' He turned back to Wenziger. ''You'd better be right. If you mess this up and give us the wrong evaluation, you can forget your clearances and my career. You'll lose your industry consulting too. I tell you, we're playing hard ball on this thing.''

He walked over to the window and looked east towards the Potomac. Behind him, Wenziger had gone rigid in his chair.

''All right,'' said Greer at last in a quieter tone. He did not look round. ''So why is Nissom wrong? I couldn't read that paper, it'd all be Greek to me. But I've seen the memo that he sent to Colonel Perling saying that he was onto a development that would make all our defense systems obsolete as chain mail. You don't agree with that?''

There was no answer. He turned from the window to the older man.

''What's up? Lost your tongue?''

Wenziger shook his head slowly. "I'm sure that you have your dossier on me, too, General. There must be information in there on my financial position." His accent had thickened. "I am not fortunate enough to share in your generous pension systems. Even with the government's assistance medical expenses are heavy. I will do my best for you on this matter—as always—and in exchange I hope that you will not seek to deprive me of my livelihood."

Greer walked back to the desk and sat down behind it. He leaned back in his chair. "We'll see. I'm not making promises until I see how this works out. Now tell me about Nissom's paper."

"I will do my best." Wenziger reached again for his briefcase, a slight tremble in his thin hands. "But again I must have time to explain. We are dealing with complex ideas, and even with my best analysis Laurance Nissom's paper seems incomplete. I would have expected more on tests, more on applications. That is his style, the style I know . . ."

He looked across the desk, waiting for some word from Greer. The other man looked back at him impassively.

"The basic idea is not new," went on Wenziger at last. "It is a variation on the old 'hidden variable' theories of quantum mechanics. In that field, there are certain combinations of quantities, conjugate quantities, that cannot be known simultaneously beyond a certain precision."

Greer nodded. "Heisenberg's uncertainty principle." He grinned at Wenziger's poorly disguised look of surprise. "Don't assume too much. Science background *is* one of the things that count on our evaluations. I've had physics courses, more than you'd think."

"That will help this a lot." Wenziger looked around him as though vaguely seeking the familiar blackboard.

"The Heisenberg principle," he went on. "That is Nissom's starting point. It reflects the fact that the fundamental processes of quantum phenomena must be interpreted using *probabilities*. We cannot predict how certain events will turn out, only the *chance* that they will result in one of several outcomes. That idea was developed sixty years ago, back in the twenties—mainly by

Born. But many people found it hard to accept. Einstein himself was one of those. From him, and others who felt the same, came another idea: that we have not been observing 'reality' at the most fundamental level in quantum experiments.''

''You've lost me.'' Greer's face was intent, and another lit cigarette was smoldering unattended in the ashtray. ''What do you mean by 'observing reality'?''

''The easiest analogy for you might be with the behavior of an ordinary gas. We seem to have well-defined quantities like temperature and pressure for a gas, right? We can measure them, they are smoothly varying functions. Now look at a very small quantity of gas, and you start to see the effects of individual molecules. The idea of a single pressure, or a single well-defined temperature, disappears. In its place we have to think of the separate gas molecules, and their motion. They are the hidden variables of the system, the ones that control its basic behavior. Pressure, temperature—they have become *statistical* ideas.''

Wenziger was surprised at the intelligence in the other's tanned face. Greer was nodding slowly, concentrating on every word.

''I'm with you again. You're suggesting that the probabilities you find in quantum theory are like fluctuations in gas pressure. They only seem like chance because we can't observe the smaller things that decide them—the 'hidden variables'. Couldn't you look more closely and see what's missing from the picture?''

''It's not that simple. I'm making it too easy, to get the point across. Nissom starts from a subtle problem in quantum mechanics, what's usually called the paradox of Einstein, Rosen and Podolsky. Most people dismiss that. He accepts it and uses it to introduce new basic variables.''

''You mean smaller particles, things that are too small to observe?''

''Not that.'' Wenziger seemed easier, back in the familiar role of teacher. ''Not particles. Nissom introduces a new set of field equations. Those are his variables. The four conventional fields—strong, weak, gravitational and electromagnetic—and

the elementary particles, they arise as interference effects from
the new fields. It is very elegant, and beautifully developed.''

"So why don't you believe it? I don't track you fully, but it all
sounds pretty plausible to me." Greer picked up his neglected
cigarette, took one long puff, and ground it out.

"If Nissom's as smart as you say," he went on. "Isn't he sure
to be right? Would he take a thing that far and still be wrong? I
still don't see how you get from where you are to particle and
field *deflectors*. That's what Nissom was talking about to Perling, practical defense against anything you can think of—for an
individual. That's what got me excited.''

"With a radical new theory you can expect a lot of new
physical results—if it is correct.'' Wenziger's glasses had come
off again and his eyes seemed to be focused on infinity. ''But
only if it is correct. I'm not objecting to Laurance Nissom's
ideas because of the theory, you know.''

"Then why do you think he's wrong?''

"The experiments. It's the experiments that he wants to do
that let him down.''

He hesitated, then replaced his glasses and looked at Greer.
''Did any of your physics courses ever mention Eddington,
Arthur Stanley Eddington?''

"No. Physicist?''

"Yes, but astronomer and mathematician might be a better
description. He was a leading relativist, and also the key figure
in the development of modern astrophysics.''

Greer shook his head. ''Don't know him. Was he another
'hidden variable' man?''

Zdenek Wenziger frowned and thought for a moment. ''Not
to my knowledge, but he might have been. That's not why I
mention him. Eddington had a brilliant career in England from
about 1910 onwards up through the thirties. Then about 1940 he
came up with a whole new theory—one that was supposed to
explain all the main physical constants of nature with purely
mathematical arguments.''

Greer sniffed. ''He's one up on me. I never managed to
explain *anything* using math.''

''It was impressive. Eddington had great mathematical ability and superb physical intuition. Physicists and astronomers all over the world took his 'fundamental theory' very seriously. It was profound, and it was very difficult to understand. Unfortunately, it had one deadly flaw.''

"It wasn't right?''

"In one crucial respect. It did not describe the physical world that we live in.''

Greer swung his chair forward. "Damn you, Wenziger, you have the most back-assed way of getting to the point. Are you trying to tell me Nissom is doing an Eddington? That he's got his head up his ass with this new theory? I thought you said it makes sense to you. Why are you saying now that it's wrong?''

"I told you.'' Wenziger's beaten expression was back. "I thought I was being very clear. It's the experiments. He's proposing a whole set of them—nothing wrong with that, but he's suggesting that they will give results that are inconsistent with the best-established ideas of twentieth century physics. If you need examples I can give you plenty. The Uhlenbeck and Goudsmit experiment on electron spin. His experiment would give a slightly different result. The measurement of the Lamb shift. Conserved vector current measurements. Non-conservation of parity. How many do you want? We'd have to turn QED upside down.'' He caught Greer's puzzled look. "Quantum Electrodynamics—I'm not quoting Euclid at you.''

"But why couldn't those experiments be wrong?''

"If just *one* of them were, it would shake modern physics to the bottom. All of them wrong? Unthinkable.'' Wenziger shook his head firmly. "You see, General, we theoretical physicists are free to argue with everything in the world—except experimental measurement. In my opinion Laurance Nissom has gone a little unstable. He is beginning to fantasize—which means that I must commend the astuteness of the man, whoever it was, that realized his behavior was peculiar and confined him to the hospital.''

Greer looked at him. "Don't step outside your area of competence, Doctor.'' He leaned over to the intercom again. "Major Merritt here yet? Send him on in.''

He leaned back in his chair. "I'm the one who put Nissom in

the hospital, up in Gaithersburg. He's unstable, but I wasn't worrying about his mental health. I wanted him locked up safe while we checked out those theories.'' He laughed. ''Don't look shocked, Wenziger. That third star is hard to get. You can't afford to sit back and wait for it, you have to take the initiative. I'm kind of glad to hear that Nissom's wrong, though. If he'd been right I'd have done my best to keep him in that hospital for the rest of his life. Did you know that he talked in one memo about *personalized* defense fields against anything? He even had the scheme in there that would make the whole of DOD irrelevant. I don't much care for the offices here in the Pentagon, but I'd sure be sorry to see us put out of business.''

He turned to the young major who had appeared in the doorway and exchanged a brief salute. ''At ease, Major. Dr. Wenziger, I would like to introduce Major Merritt of OSMS. He was up there in Gaithersburg yesterday.''

The pink-cheeked major was looking uncertainly at the elderly figure in the chair. Although the visitor had the appearance of a possible VIP, with no rank as a guide it was hard to know what relationship to assume. He nodded at Wenziger, but did not offer his hand.

''We have been discussing Laurance Nissom, Major,'' went on Greer. There was an edge in his voice. ''Dr. Wenziger was asking me about the events in Gaithersburg—how it was that an unarmed civilian could escape unassisted from a maximum security military hospital. I thought you might be good enough to provide him with some of the details.''

Wenziger had started up briefly at Greer's statement, then subsided wearily in his chair. Merritt would have to fight his own battles with Greer.

''Yes, sir.'' Despite the 'At Ease' command, the Major remained at attention. ''I have discussed the matter in detail with the staff at the Gaithersburg facility. So far as we have been able to ascertain, the prisoner Nissom incapacitated his personal guard just after midnight by means of a blow on the head with a metal bed brace.'' He swallowed. ''There had been no prior suggestion of violence. Dr. Rosenbloom was inclined to regard Nissom as a model patient.''

''Then he's an absolute damned fool.'' Greer's tone was acid.

"If Rosenbloom weren't a civilian employee I'd be looking for a court-martial. Didn't he have the sense to realize that a patient who cooperates when he has no reason to shouldn't be trusted one inch? Get on with it, Major, tell us their next failure."

"Yessir. Nissom had been allowed to move freely inside the house, as long as he had a guard with him. He walked in the grounds every day. They believed that would be safe enough, because of the high wall and the electronic sensors along the top of it. It was too high for him to reach the top and too smooth for him to climb."

"So how did he get out?"

The young major hesitated and looked at Greer in perplexity. "I thought you had already been briefed on that, sir."

"Of course I have. Don't be an ass. I want you to tell Dr. Wenziger."

"Yessir." Major Merritt flushed and gazed straight in front of him. "Nissom had collected a group of heavy objects. They were old bits and pieces of metal, left over from the time before the building became a sanitarium. The night before last he penetrated the underground cable and inhibited the electronic eyes along a section of the wall. Then he threw the roped objects over. He used them as a counterweight so that he could scale the wall and climb out."

Greer looked at Wenziger. "Sound like Nissom?"

The older man shrugged. "I don't know the intelligence of your usual prisoner, General, but to Laurance Nissom such an operation would be a trivial exercise in planning and scheduling." He turned to Major Merritt. "The night before last was moonless. I'm sure that he planned on it. What was he wearing when he escaped?"

"Hospital pajamas. We think he may have dyed them black in the hospital studio, so they would be hard to see at night."

"And they'd pass as work clothes if he were seen the next morning," added Greer. "He didn't want people to notice him and give us any idea where he was headed."

"Yessir. He had no shoes, just hospital slippers, but we think he found a pair of old rubber overshoes in one of the gardening sheds, and put them on."

"What have you been able to find out today?" asked Greer.

"He had no money, no credit cards. He must have found himself miles from anywhere, in the middle of the night."

"Yessir." There was a long pause, while Merrit cleared his throat several times.

"We have been unable to ascertain any reliable information on that subject," he said at last in a wooden voice. "We have therefore been obliged to conclude that he must by now have managed to obtain assistance from some acquaintance of his in the Washington area. At this point in time, we have no information that might lead us to his whereabouts."

"In other words, Wenziger, we don't know a damned thing." Greer swung back to Merritt. "That right, Major?"

"That would appear to be the case, sir."

"All right. Dismissed."

"Yessir."

Greer waited until the Major had left the room. He nodded his head after him. "I don't know how well up you are on Air Force types, but there goes a terminal Major."

"Was any of it his fault?"

"Not directly. His career's ruined, though. The system will squeeze him flat." Greer picked up the empty cigarette pack and crumpled it in his fist. "You don't make it far in the Air Force with anything but a perfect record."

Wenziger gave a thin smile. "I don't need your symbolism to get the point. You may find it hard to believe, General, but the same is becoming true in modern academia."

Greer gave a barking laugh of surprise. "That right? You know, I'll go for that. Dog eat dog everywhere, eh?" He opened a drawer of his desk and pulled out another pack of cigarettes. "I wasn't just thinking of Merritt. It's even more true for me. I have to turn this crap with Nissom into a personal success, or I'm screwed just as much as our friend the Major." He cracked the pack open with a blunt thumbnail and offered it across the desk. "You've known Nissom for a long time, right?"

Zdenek Wenziger looked warily at the outstretched cigarettes. He nodded. "I was on his dissertation committee—as I am sure your dossier reveals. You now have my evaluation of his recent work, which I will amplify in writing. I do not smoke.

If we have finished our business here, I would like to leave.''

"We're not through.'' Greer took out a cigarette and balanced it, filter end up, on the desk in front of him. "Not quite. It's obvious that Major Merritt is right, Nissom had help from a friend in this area.'' He looked up suddenly into Wenziger's troubled eyes. "By now he could be anywhere in the country. Agreed?''

"I see no reason to doubt it.''

"And he'll be staying with a friend? Or do you think that Nissom is the type to hole up in a motel?''

"I take your point, General.'' Wenziger sighed. "In my opinion Laurance Nissom is certainly staying with one of his friends. I agree with you. When can I go?''

Greer was nodding silently, staring at the balanced cigarette as though Wenziger had suddenly proposed a difficult and abstract problem. He opened the folder in front of him. "So, Nissom will be staying somewhere with a friend. We agree on that, don't we? But who are his friends? That's a question I can't answer. Not alone. Let me read you this, from one of Nissom's letters to a friend in Europe—you knew, of course, that we monitored his correspondence?''

"I could have guessed it.'' Wenziger's voice was weary.

Greer looked up briefly. "And you never read Machiavelli? Listen to what Nissom wrote. 'In my opinion, Wenziger's work on the use of resonance concepts to study modes of vacuum polarization is the prettiest piece of analysis in the past decade.' An odd choice of word, wouldn't you say? 'Prettiest'.''

A touch of color flushed Wenziger's grey countenance. "Nissom wrote that? I am surprised and gratified. He has read out my own secret thoughts. 'Prettiest' is not at all an odd choice. To a theoretical physicist, it is an *exact* choice.''

Greer closed the folder. "You are adding weight to my idea. You speak the same language. I do not. Let me ask you another question. When I travel around the world, where do I stay?'' He waved his hand. "Don't bother to try and answer that, I'll tell you. I stay with my old comrades. Naturally. After all, we share the same values and the same past experiences. Pick any country you like, and I'll have an old friend or an old enemy there.''

He had lit the cigarette in front of him and now seemed to be concentrating his attention on the thin column of blue-grey smoke as it spiralled towards the ceiling. Wenziger did not speak, but sat, eyes down and head forward.

"So I have to ask myself," went on Greer at last. "Are scientists any different? Don't they have their old campaigns, their old comrades-in-arms? Isn't there an 'old comrades' network of scientists, in any city and any country? Don't they prefer to stay with their own kind?"

"You know the answer. Of course we do."

"Of course you do." Greer's intense blue eyes came back to Wenziger, lifting the other's gaze by some unseen force between them. "Of course. And of course, Laurance Nissom would be helped by the people in your network. We all look after our own kind if we can. It's dog eat dog if we have to, but it's dog eat cat first."

He drew thoughtfully on his cigarette, deliberately extending the moment. "So we have only one problem, don't we? Your network is like mine—it's for insiders only. I couldn't crack your circle, any more than you would be at home in the Army-Navy Club. But if there were someone—"

"No." Wenziger sat up straighter, his lips trembling. "I am not a fool, and I say no. It is clear where you are heading. I am not a fool and I am not a . . . a *Judas*."

"Easy now." Greer held up his hand. "Keep cool. I haven't asked you to do anything at all. What I'd like you to do is to go away and think about this whole thing. Look at it this way. If you wanted to, you could probably find out where Nissom is staying. We both agree that he needs help. He *has* been behaving oddly, more than the things you know about. If you doubt me, you can read the whole file on him. He's sick, and he needs help—he won't get that in hiding. You could reach him, persuade him to come back here—for his own good."

"To be incarcerated as a common madman?"

"Not at all. I've got clout, you've seen that already. I'd make sure that he got the best of treatment while we checked out his condition and all those wild theories he's been having. You've already assured me that they're wrong, so what's the loss? Anyway, think about it, that's all."

Greer's voice dropped suddenly in pitch and volume. "And while you're thinking about Laurance Nissom," he said softly. "Think about Zdenek Wenziger. Think about medical bills, and clearances, and finances, and the trouble there would be if you were blacklisted. I know you could get a position abroad—but could you get the medical treatments?"

"You would try this? It is blackmail, worse than blackmail."

Greer smiled pleasantly and stubbed out the cigarette in the full ashtray. "Now you're over-reacting, Professor. Since when was patriotism called blackmail? Nissom is dangerous to the country, and to himself. He should be in safe hands. Check me out. You'll find that I'm known as a good friend to people who help me, and a bad enemy to ones who go against me." He stood up and walked around the big desk. "Why don't you call me this week-end? I'll be off at my farm, up in Thurmont, and we can talk better there than here—more informal."

As Zdenek Wenziger rose from the chair, Greer placed a muscular hand on the old man's stooped shoulder. "One other thing. This is just between us, right? Help me, and I swear that your friends—and the people here—will never get to hear about it. It will be our secret, no paperwork, no records of how you were involved."

He led the older man to the door. "I know how you feel now, but who knows? Something may happen in the next few days to make you think differently."

July 28th, 1980. POST WITH MAIN GATE
                    PERSONNEL.
Attention: ODR Security.
Subject: D. Z. Wenziger.
Please be advised of a delay in renewing OSU Clearance for the above. Pending resolution of situation, access to base cannot be granted.

July 28th 1980.
Dear Dr. Wenziger,
   We have been advised of a delay in procurement. Since your consulting contract with us is contingent upon contract award,

no charges should be incurred and no work should begin until you receive written notification from us.

> Yours sincerely, G. Bayes, Contracts Officer.

Memo to: Dr. Z. Wenziger   From: Travel Department
Subject: IAF Congress   Date: July 29th, 1980
Previously approved authorization to attend this conference is withdrawn because of new budget limitations. You will be informed promptly should this situation change.

July 30th 1980.   Walter Reed Army Hospital,
                        Outpatient Department
From: ODR Records   Reference: AST-422
                        Wenziger, Z.

From: ODR Records Reference: AST-422 Wenziger, Z. Please note that Andemil is an experimental drug and its use is currently restricted to volunteer military personnel. Continued participation by the above subject in this program is prohibited pending renewed Special Exemption from ODR Central Office.

"General Greer?"

"Speaking."

"Wenziger here." The voice over the line was hoarse and muffled. "I have located Laurance Nissom. I have also met with him. What should I do next?"

"Well, Hallelujah. It sure took long enough. Where is he?"

"He would prefer that I not divulge that to you yet."

"Don't worry, I'll hold up my end of the deal. Could you bring him out to the farm?"

"I'm not sure." The voice was diffident. "I would need travel funds."

"You'll have them. When can I see him."

"Saturday? And a promise that you will be alone?"

"Just the three of us. I'll expect you about fourteen hundred hours. Pick up a road map from my secretary."

"And the injections?"

"Go on over to Walter Reed right now. I'll clear it while you're on your way there."

The old farmhouse had been set well up on the hillside, out of reach of floodwaters. With the aid of a pair of binoculars it was possible from the upper windows to see cars as soon as they came over the southern rise, two and a half miles away. The heat shimmer on the road made it hard to be sure, but there seemed to be only one person in the blue VW with the Maryland license plates. Greer frowned. He walked down the stairs into the dirt yard and was waiting when Wenziger stepped from the car.

"What gives?"

"We came separately. He had to pick up a book. I expect him in about twenty minutes." Despite the heat, Zdenek Wenziger was dressed in a dark suit, tie and tight collar. His high, bald head was covered with a film of perspiration. Greer peered at him closely before he finally nodded, turned around and led the way into the thick-walled building. Wenziger followed him slowly, still lugging his heavy briefcase as they climbed the narrow stairs.

"Beer? It's home-brewed." Greer held up two bottles. He was shirt-sleeved, in denim patch-pockets and loafers.

"No. Thank you, no."

"Well, here's to Laurance Nissom anyway, the Invisible Man." Greer drank straight from the bottle. He seemed to be in high spirits. "How did he seem when you left him?"

"Under great stress, as you might expect. But sane. I think sane."

"But you didn't manage to talk him out of his pet theory?"

"I think not." Wenziger's manner was restless. He had placed his briefcase by the side of his chair and was staring out of the high window at the valley beyond with a strange intensity.

"And he couldn't talk you into it, either?" Greer watched Wenziger's fidgeting with a cool amusement. "Look, you can't be comfortable like that. Why not take your jacket off?"

"Thank you, but no. You are right, he could not persuade me. I still believe that he is wrong." He turned from the window. "You were not completely honest with me when we met in your office. You did not show me Laurance Nissom's *second* paper."

"No, I didn't." Greer was unabashed. "I knew that if you ever got to Nissom you'd hear about it first-hand. It didn't change his theory any. He showed it to you?''

"Of course. You are right, it makes no difference to the actual theory.'' Wenziger was still looking urgently out at the road winding away from the farm. "But it took us down to the nuts and bolts—the applications that I had looked for in the first paper and couldn't find.''

A nod. "Right. The personalized defense field against all forms of attack? See what turned me on to it?''

"Defense against everything. You do not realize it, but that idea has a special meaning to me.''

"I realize it. I told you, I know you.'' Greer was looking out of the window also, searching the road for a second car. "I know you a lot better than you'd ever believe. I've looked at your background, all the way from Czechoslovakia in the 1920's.'' He flashed a quick sideways look at Wenziger. "What's keeping him? Damn it, man, take that coat off before you boil.''

"He will be here. I had a twenty minute start on him. He may have met more traffic than I did. Be patient.'' Wenziger's own manner showed no patience. A nervous tic moved under his left eye.

"You know,'' he said at last. "I didn't need the help of the 'network' to find Laurance Nissom. Not really. He was running. I have been running all my life—from Germans, from Russians, then from Nixon and McCarthy. I know just where people run to, where they hide.'' He looked across at Greer. "I wonder if I might change my mind. I would like a beer.''

The other man uncapped a bottle and handed it across without speaking. Their eyes turned again to the quiet road.

"That's one thing they drill into us early.'' Greer's tone was reflective, abstracted. "Don't run. An army gets cut up worse running than standing firm. Face the enemy and hold your front.'' There was a curious smile on his tanned face. "So. This week you decided you'd had enough running. Too old to run any more. Right?''

Wenziger swung around. Beer splashed from the bottle onto the thick rug. "Why do you say that?''

Greer's gaze was still on the world outside the window. "I told you. I know you. I've seen men like you and watched your ways for forty years. Sometime last week you decided you'd had it, you couldn't take this thing any longer. You made up your mind that the only answer was to come here and kill me. Nissom didn't have to be right, it was the principle of the thing." He laughed. "Like to see the sales slip for the gun you bought down on Fourteenth Street? It's in my desk over there."

"You know about that? Why didn't you have me arrested then, instead of getting me here to taunt me with it?"

"No law against buying a gun." Greer shrugged. "I own five or six of them. And I have to have Nissom. You're my key to him. But you've changed, haven't you? A couple of weeks ago you were convinced that his ideas were wrong—even *one* week ago you thought that."

"I think it still."

"You don't convince me. You changed your mind, a few days ago, and decided that Nissom had to go free. I want to know what changed you."

He leaned over and picked up Wenziger's briefcase. "I'll lay you any odds you like that you don't have the gun in here. See, I know you too well. No matter what you think of Nissom—or of me—there's no way you could pull out a gun and shoot me cold. 'Ambition should be made of sterner stuff', don't you think?"

He opened the case and looked casually at the jumble of papers and books inside. "Did you ever fire a thirty-eight in your whole life? Any handgun at all?"

Wenziger had settled back in his seat. After an instinctive gesture when Greer picked up his case, he had relaxed. "Never in anger. At fairground shows a few times."

"So I'm still looking for an answer. What made you change your mind, even if you don't have the guts to follow through with it? Something that Nissom told you?"

"Nothing from my meeting with Nissom. I learned from a dead man." Wenziger flicked a glance at his watch, then back to the road. "Do you remember that I quoted Eddington to you, as evidence that genius is no protection against a wrong theory? I ought to have quoted something else that he wrote, but it only came back to me a few days ago—just before I bought a gun. Eddington said, 'The world that we observe is the world of our theories'. *That* changed my mind about Nissom. You understand the significance of what he was saying?"

"No." Greer put down the briefcase without looking into it further. Like Wenziger, he had become obsessed with the thin ribbon of the road leading to the farm. "What does Eddington have to do with Nissom?"

"He meant that scientists become married to their theories. We look only for the things that our theories lead us to expect. Unless we think we'll find a result, why perform the experiment? Especially today, when experiments are very expensive. Let me ask you something, General. Did you ever look into Laurance Nissom's personal finances?"

"Sure I did, early on. I wanted to see if somebody could buy him."

"They could not. He is a rich man, right?"

"He's loaded. He inherited millions from his father."

"So why did he work for the government at all? Especially when he had his own theory to develop."

Greer lowered the bottle from his lips without drinking. He looked puzzled. "You've got me. Strange, I've asked every question about him except that one. He didn't need money, not the way that you do. Do you have an answer?"

"Equipment. He needed access to equipment that millions of dollars can't buy, but billions can. You see, he wanted to test his theory fully, in every branch. That would be hugely expensive—take huge resources. The world that his ideas describe is so different from the one we see that he had to build a whole new structure."

"But he's wrong." Greer moved uneasily in his chair, sensing that somehow the control was moving to the other man. "You said he's wrong, and you still think so."

"I do. All of me believes that, as strongly as I believe anything." Wenziger looked again at his watch and grimaced with concern.

Greer could see the tension building on the other's face. "He ought to be here by now. You're not trying to cross me? I hope not, for your sake."

"He's on his way. I think he's wrong—but *suppose* he were right. I had to admit that possibility, even if I didn't believe it. Suppose that Nissom is right, that he is seeing a different and more valid world picture. Could there be a chance—one in ten thousand, even—that he's right?''

"I've assumed all along that there is." Greer had stood up and leaned closer to the window. "That's why I can't let him run free. That thousand-to-one shot is too dangerous. Our balance of power analyses wouldn't mean a thing if Nissom's defense screen could be built."

"Too dangerous to you." Wenziger was perspiring again. "To me and my kind, it might mean an end to running. That's why I bought the gun."

"That you'll never use. It takes training to face death, you know. I wondered for a while if you'd find the idea of killing both of us easier to take. Then I decided you couldn't even manage that. You can't face certain death, a hundred percent guaranteed. You're not unusual. When we send men on a suicide mission, we always try and build a long shot that they could get out alive. Otherwise some of them can't take it."

"I thought of a double killing, you, then myself. It was no good." Wenziger's breath was fast and shallow. He seemed hypnotized by the moving sweep of his watch. "I called Nissom. I asked him if a certain kind of test of his theory were possible—a crude one. He confirmed it."

"You mean you could do a test? Damn it, a minute ago you were telling me that tests would cost billions. Are you saying that's not true?"

There was a long silence. When Wenziger spoke at last his voice was so soft that Greer could hardly make out the words. "You make me over-simplify, then you are angry at the result. A real test—a *full* test—of Nissom's ideas, with all their subtleties, would cost billions. But a test at the grossest level, one that was qualitative more than quantitative, that could be done cheaply. Nissom confirmed it, but he was not interested."

"You mean you could prove if Nissom's right or wrong *cheaply?*" Greer had seized Wenziger by the arm, straightening him up in his chair. "Why the hell didn't you tell me that? If you're trying to cross me it's all over for you."

"I'm not crossing you. It would be a crude test. Let me give you an analogy. The atomic bomb could be thought of as a test of

Einstein's theory of special relativity, but it would give no detailed measurements, nothing for exact confirmation." Wenziger sighed. "You saw through me, General. I could never pull the trigger on final doom, for you or for me. But I would accept a *statistical* risk. We live with those every day, when we cross the street or leave our apartment. Do you understand the process of radioactive decay?"

"Of course I do." Greer shook him. "Wenziger, don't change the subject. What in God's name have you been up to?"

"In a group of a trillion radioactive atoms"—Wenziger's voice had become calm and professorial again—"some will disintegrate in the next twenty minutes. But which ones? We cannot say. That depends on fate—or on Laurance Nissom's hidden variables. You see, for certain situations—Nissom can specify some of them—his theory predicts radioactive breakdown of certain atoms faster than conventional theory." He stared at his watch face. "I have been here now for twenty-eight minutes. The odds are getting worse. You see, General, I could never have dreamed up Nissom's theory. Never. But I am not stupid. From that theory, I can certainly calculate probabilities."

He smiled, a thin-lipped crack in the old, grey face. "So I decided that we ought to let the statistics make the decision. I have primed a bomb—a small one, as these bombs go—to explode if decay from a radioactive source that has been subjected to certain resonances reaches a certain level. According to conventional theory, that level will be reached with fifty percent probability in one hour. According to Nissom's theory, fifty percent probability was reached eight minutes ago. When he drives over that hill"—he nodded at the road outside the window—"I will disarm it."

"Damn you, Wenziger, you've gone mad." Greer's face was white. He rushed to the briefcase and turned it upside down. A torrent of books and papers poured out onto the rug. "The bomb. Where's the fucking bomb? Wenziger, tell me, I'll keep you out of trouble. I swear it."

Wenziger was laughing, the tic under his eye distorting his

face. "General, General. You have too much faith in technology. Be reasonable. Not even the best scientists have been able to make a zeta small enough to fit in a briefcase—and we know the best, don't we?"

He picked up the bottle from the window sill. His tension suddenly seemed to drain from him. "Sit down. Have another beer, and have faith in the hidden variables. They will make the decision for us, if Nissom is right or if he is wrong. He should be here any minute now. I predicted that he would arrive thirty minutes after I did. That is twenty seconds from now—but of course, traffic is another hidden variable, is it not?"

Greer was still on his knees on the floor, rummaging desperately through the briefcase. His face was sweaty. "The car. If it won't fit in here, it *has* to be in the car. You bastard, you armed it before you got out and came up here." His eyes glared with sudden triumph. "You missed one thing, Wenziger, something you didn't count on. *I don't need you to disarm that bomb*. I had three years with disposal and security. I can take it apart in ten seconds."

He threw the briefcase to the floor, jumped to his feet and rushed from the room.

"And you know, General, you missed one thing, too." Wenziger's tone was quiet and conversational, as though the other man were still in the room with him. "I couldn't shoot you, but you confused ruthlessness and courage. I have read Clausewitz—yes, and Machiavelli, too, in the original languages. You and I differ in the uses that we would make of power, that's all."

He lifted the bottle and took a leisurely sip of beer.

It was hot in the car, eighty-five degrees or more. Normally a long drive was pleasant, it gave plenty of time for unhurried thought and calculation, but this time there was too much else to think about.

How much had Wenziger been keeping to himself? There had been disturbing undertones in their last conversation, a suggestion that crude tests were the way to go.

He peered ahead at the long incline, shimmering in the heat.

Not more than a mile to go, if the sketch map were right.
Laurance Nissom was almost at the brow of the hill when the
valley ahead of him lit with a glow that eclipsed the sun.

AFTERWORD: HIDDEN VARIABLE.

"I was having dinner with the Astronomer Royal, and he said that Eddington . . ."

It's a nice way to begin the conversation but it needs to be put in context. I was a summer student at the Royal Observatory, one of a dozen or more, and he invited all of us to dinner—once each. "He" at the time was Astronomer Royal Richard van der Riet Woolley, later Sir Richard Woolley, and it is my secret opinion that he tolerated summer students not for their value as workers, which was marginal, but for their usefulness as country dancers.

That too needs to be put in context. When the Royal Greenwich Observatory moved from Greenwich, where it had been since 1675, to Herstmonceux Castle in Sussex, there were far more women workers than men, mostly doing calculations for the production of the Nautical Almanac. Actually, there were a fair number of males, but they tended to be senior astronomers and were not the types to be readily persuaded by the AR to leap about in country dancing. Whereas the women, thanks to sexual discrimination or what-have-you, had duller jobs and were ready for evening frivolity. But they had to have male partners, and that's where students came in useful. Once a week we all had a rousing session of dancing. I have long since forgotten the wavelength of the Lyman Alpha line, but if pressed I might well be able to dance a round of Gathering Peascods or Sir Roger de Coverley.

And between dances, before and after dances, and on non-dancing evenings, we would hear personal anecdotes from Woolley's youth about the distant stars of twentieth century astronomy, of Hubble and Baade, Oort, Milne, Hoyle and Struve. And we would hear first-hand accounts of the arguments between Sir James Jeans and Sir Arthur Eddington at the monthly meetings of the Royal Astronomical Society. Eddington

217

was a superb mathematician, and he had an unmatched and almost infallible physical intuition about the way that a star or galaxy would behave. But Jeans was a superb mathematician, too, perhaps even a better one—and in debate he was quicker and more persuasive than Eddington. So as we heard it, Eddington was usually right, but it was Jeans who mostly won the verbal arguments.

I feel much more at home writing than giving speeches, so I have had a soft spot for Eddington ever since those days at the Royal Observatory. It is unfortunate that this story happens to quote a case—a very rare case—where his theories were wrong.

A CERTAIN PLACE
IN HISTORY

"This is really rather nasty. Why did you let it go so long without attention? You should have come in for treatment weeks ago."

The dentist who was working on my ripely abscessed upper molar had a habit, common to his profession, of trying to conduct a conversation with a patient whose mouth was wedged open like a yawning hippopotamus. An accurate answer to his question would take twenty minutes and involve—at a minimum—mushrooms, space warps, high finance, aliens, the asteroid belt and my personal reputation. I rolled my eyes and said "Aa-gn-hng-aa," or words to that effect. The answer seemed to satisfy him and he turned the conversation to local politics.

It really isn't easy to know where to begin. With the aliens? According to common myth, it isn't really possible to hate an alien. If and when we meet up with some, the argument goes, we should get on with them very well. Our hatred is reserved for our own kind. I happen to know that idea is wrong. No human has ever met a Kaneelian, we don't know where or how they live, or even what size and shape they are. But they cost me a million credits, they gave me the worst three days of my life, and they may make the name 'Henry Carver' go down in history as a big joke. I have a strong and personal hatred of Kaneelians, the whole wretched species.

That's obviously the wrong place to begin. I get carried away. Let me begin, objectively, with the tooth.

It was a left upper molar that had been filled a couple of times already, and it was beginning to give me trouble again. Two hundred years ago, in the bad old days before medical science was perfected, a tooth was pulled out when it gave trouble. It is now possible, thanks to partially effective nerve-regeneration techniques, for the same tooth to cause periodic anguish for a good fifty years, with enormous associated cost. The ache was getting bad enough for me to consider and put off a visit to the dentist when I had a videophone call from Izzy Roberson.

Izzy was always worth talking to. An old friend of my partner, Waldo Burmeister, he had suggested some profitable deals for us in the past, and wasn't a man to waste your time with small stuff.

"Got something good for you, Henry," Izzy's cheerful image began. "Know what agaricus campestris is?" He was a tiny, bouncy man, hopping up and down as usual in front of the screen. He had a great fondness for tall women, who loomed high above him and always made me think of the old story of the midget and the showgirl.

I groped vaguely after law-school Latin. "Campestris. Something-or-other of the fields?"

"Not bad, Henry, not bad at all. Agaricus campestris—it's mushrooms, meadow mushrooms. Hold on a second, I'm going to put the scrambler on."

The screen became random color for a second, then cleared again as the unit on my phone picked up the coded unscrambler.

"Safe to talk now," he went on. "Henry, we want you to be a front man. We're all set to develop a mushroom monopoly. If we pull this off, you'll get all the commissions."

A mushroom monopoly sounded about as valuable as a corner in yak-wool hats. Cut off the supply of meadow mushrooms, and it seemed to me that people would happily eat something else. I mentioned this to Izzy.

"Henry, don't you ever look at the science sections? They don't grow the damn things for eating, they use them to extract the transplant catalysts. There are only three companies in the business, and my clients now control two of them. We want the third, but we have to work through an intermediary."

I understood that easily enough. Laws on monopolies were

getting stricter all the time. It was a situation I'd been involved in before and I knew the main limiting factors.

"How much of the stock do you need, Izzy? Where's it traded, and what do I use for money?"

"It trades right here, on the Tycho City Board. If we can get twenty-seven percent of the voting stock, we'll have clear control. We already bought eight percent through a holding company and we've been promised votes on another eleven percent on a trade-for-favors base. We want you to get the other eight percent any way you can."

"Expenses?"

"Sure. But you only get the commissions if you buy us all we need. Finish with seven percent and you get nothing. Here are the credit number and stockholder positions you'll need to do the buying."

I pressed 'Record' and he flashed me a stock I.D. list and a fourteen-digit code on the Tycho City Central Bank.

"One other thing, Henry. We've got a deadline. Midnight, U.T., twelve days from now. Think you can make it?"

It would be tight, maybe, but it should be possible. I thought for a moment, then nodded just as the door behind Izzy opened and a tall blonde walked in. He glanced around, waved a quick farewell to me and cut the connection on the tableau of Snow White and Happy. I was glad to see him go so I could get started at once. I forgot my nagging tooth and began to check the stock prices.

If you've ever been involved in a quiet stock purchase, you know there are two main factors: A low profile, and fast action. If people think there is a take-over in the wind, they get greedy and hold on to what they have. The last percent always costs the most. And if you don't do it fast enough, the professional market analysts will move when they see a lot of quick transactions in a quiet stock, and start buying against you on a speculative basis.

After eight days, I had things moving along nicely. Six percent of the stock I needed was committed to a forward buy, held for three days, and I was expecting a call or a visit on the remaining two percent. I sat in my Tycho City apartment, one ear tuned to the phone and the other to the door chime. Visions of sugarplums danced in my head, and when the door rang, I leaped to answer it.

I've become used to some unusual intermediaries in financial deals, but the man who ducked his head in through the doorway was the strangest yet. Huge, straw-haired, jutting-jawed, steely eyed—you can supply the other adjectives yourself. It added up to the cliche hero of a space opera. He came in, looked at me, past me, and around the apartment. Finally he shrugged slightly and looked at me again.

"Henry Carver?" There was surprise in his voice.

"Yes. You're from Securities Investment?"

He made himself at home on my couch. "Never heard of them. Look, let me make sure there's no mistake. Are you Henry Carver, the man who worked with Gerald Mattin on the development of the Mattin Link?"

Hospitality and politeness have their limits. Anyway, that episode with the Mattin Link is not one of my favorite memories. "I don't know who you are, or what you're doing here. But I have an important business visit due any minute now. If you are not from Securities Investment, I'm afraid I must ask you to leave at once."

"Sorry, Mr. Carver. I can't do that." He fished in his coverall pocket and pulled out a mag strip I.D. "Check that out, then let's talk."

He was depressingly sure of himself. I fed the strip through the phone connection and watched the I.D. appear on the screen: Imre Munsen, Special Investigator, United Space Federation; authorized to commandeer the use of equipment, services and personnel for Level Four System Emergencies; classification of current assignment (you've guessed it): Level Four.

"Now you know who I am, Mr. Carver. Before we go on, I have to be sure that I know who you are. Are you in fact the man who worked on the original Mattin Link—the man who survived those first experiments?"

"I am, but that was a long time ago. I don't know anything about the Links they have nowadays."

"That's all right. We need help from someone with a fresh

mind, not tied to current theory. First, I must swear you to strictest secrecy. A situation of unprecedented danger to the human race has arisen. If you reveal what I tell you to a third party, you will be guilty of endangering the public welfare and will be charged accordingly. You know the penalties.''

I did indeed. Anything the court chose to inflict. It was rather like the old military court-martial. No appeals, and the prosecutors, jury and judge were all the same people. My stomach began a rumble of anticipatory fear.

"Mr. Carver," Munsen went on, "it will be simplest if you listen to me first without asking questions. I have studied your file, so I know your capability and pattern of rapid response. But hear me out, please, before you begin.''

What was the man talking about? I wondered what was in the file. And what about my business appointment? Munsen had better get on with it and go away quickly. There were a million credits waiting for me—if I could conclude my mushroom stock purchases in time. I decided to let him have his say, then tell him at once that I couldn't help.

It's best if I summarize what he said to me. Munsen was just the sort of starry-eyed, deep-chested idiot he looked. Patriotic, fearless, decisive, clean-living—we seemed to have absolutely nothing in common, the two of us. His explanation was full of irrelevant stirring speeches about our future, and the need for all of us to give our utmost to human advancement. It was enough to make a rational man sick.

Six weeks earlier, as Munsen told it, a party of six had chartered a space yacht for a scenic tour of the inner Solar System. Milton Kaneely, the holovision star, had made the rental. Three men and three women were on board—and with Milton Kaneely, for 'scenic tour' you could safely read 'drunken orgy.' They had careered randomly around the Moon and off past Mars into the asteroid belt. Blundering along there, they had landed on a rock fragment less than a kilometer long—and stumbled across the first evidence of an alien race. On the asteroid, in a big rock chamber, sat the space warp. Kaneely and friends didn't know it was a space warp—or even that they had found evidence of aliens. They thought they'd found an un-

manned USF Navy station. They sent a joking message back to
Tycho City, complaining about the lack of a station emergency
grog supply, and rocketed off for Chryse City.

The USF Communications Group would have written the call
off as a joke, except that on the way to Chryse City the Kaneely
party had encountered another asteroid—this time at a relative
velocity of five kilometers a second. The accident, so far as
anyone could tell, had nothing to do with their earlier landing,
but the investigation group had taken a look at that asteroid too,
to make their report complete. They found the space warp. Not
knowing quite what it was, they were still smart enough to
recognize it as an alien artifact. That was when Imre Munsen
had been called in.

"The most irritating thing," he said to me, "is the complete
randomness of it. The Kaneelians didn't try to hide the space
warp from us, but they didn't give it any kind of beacon, either.
For all the help we had from them, it could have been another
thousand years before we stumbled across it. We still have no
idea how long they were on that asteroid, what they were doing
in the Solar System, or when they left. They might come back
any time."

He looked gloomy and irritated. I stole a glance at my watch.
It was getting late, my tooth was aching again, and there was
still no sign of my mushroom man.

"This whole matter is really interesting, Mr. Munsen," I said
to him, polite and insincere. "But I'm a lawyer, you know, not a
scientist. I can't think why you want me involved in all this—
unless you are planning to sue the aliens for negligence."

He cheered up a little and smiled at me. "You underrate
yourself, Mr. Carver. I like to see that in a man. Our computer
selected your file from millions, as the best person we could get
for this job. I read your background myself before I came here,
and I won't be fooled by a modest appearance. The first man to
transfer through the Mattin Link—and the only survivor of those
early experiments. The man to whom Peter Pinton entrusted the
secret of Pintonite, and one of two men to come out of that alive
when Pinton was killed. The only man to survive the Deimos
Plague."

Munsen shook his head admiringly. "It's not just a question

of hard work and intelligence, Mr. Carver. Lots of people have those. You also have good luck—and you've got guts.''

Not only that, I fully intended to keep them. I had no idea where Munsen had got all that information—accurate, as far as it went, but it didn't go far enough. I felt like saying, ''No, no, you've got it all wrong. I'm not brave at all. I'm a certified coward.'' But I didn't think it would make any difference. Munsen looked like a very determined man. Instead, I said, ''I only wish I could help you, Mr. Munsen. But really I have no idea what I could do for you. I have pressing business obligations, and I know nothing about the aliens.''

''You know as much as we do, Mr. Carver. I want you to take a look at that space warp and use your intuition and experience.''

My intuition and experience told me to stay as far away from it as I could.

''It has our group baffled,'' Munsen went on. ''It provides instantaneous transfer, the same as the Mattin Link, but it's a lot more flexible. For one thing, it seems as though the exit points can be anywhere. For another, you don't need Link equipment at the exit. We've been able to send signalling devices—not people—through it, and they come out some place in the Solar System. Some random place. Two disappeared, and we think they must have gone into the Sun.''

Worse and worse. So far, it sounded riskier than the Mattin Link, and I'd had my fill of that long ago. ''You tried to send people?'' I asked.

He nodded. ''Volunteers. But there's some kind of a sensing device on the side of the warp chamber. It won't send living multi-celled organisms. Just sits there humming when we try it. It's very disappointing. The Kaneelians built in some kind of control on it and we have no idea how to change the settings.''

''Why not take it apart?''

''We'd love to. As soon as we know how it works, we will. At the moment we're afraid we may ruin it completely if we tamper with it. We'd like to study the separate pieces. For one thing, it seems as though there are all-temperature superconductors in the control box.''

What was an all-temperature superconductor? I shook my

head firmly. "There's not a thing I could do for you, Mr. Munsen. It's outside my field."

Munsen turned three moods meaner. "Mr. Carver, I don't think you understand the situation. I am *requesting* your cooperation. But I am not really offering you a choice. We need you. If you persist in your attitude, I will be forced to send you for a hearing—on Earth." He smiled a horrid smile. "Your record suggests that you prefer not to visit Earth. In any case, I expected you would welcome a chance to serve humanity."

A hearing on Earth. I shuddered at the thought. There were people there who'd love to get their hands on me. Whatever Munsen's project, I couldn't imagine it would be worse than that. Even so, I wasn't prepared to give up my million credits without a struggle.

"Don't get me wrong, Mr. Munsen. I'd be only too happy to go with you and take a look at the alien machines. But I have big responsibilities here. I can't spare the time, particularly just now."

His manner warmed a little. "Of course, I know you're a busy man. What I have in mind wouldn't take long. I want you to take a quick look at the alien equipment, then you can come back here to the Moon and think it over, see what ideas it suggests to you. If necessary, we'll arrange a second trip later—but that might not be needed, if we can use your ideas without your presence."

"But can't that first trip wait a week?"

He shook his head. "I'm afraid not. Time is important. Every day wasted could mean danger to us all. Until we understand the space warp, we won't feel safe—the Kaneelians could come back any day, and we'd be helpless. I will guarantee you that if we leave tonight, I'll have you back from this trip in forty-eight hours. That's the best I can offer, and I tell you that I'm stretching the rules to promise that."

Two days away would leave only two more days to finish the stock deal. I didn't like it at all, but I sensed that it was the best offer I'd get. For a Level Four emergency like this one, Munsen could have me shot, and no one would ask him for the reason until it was too late.

"Give me the time to make one videophone call," I said.

"Then I'll be ready to go. What do I need to bring with me?"

"Not a thing—we'll fit you out at Headquarters." He looked pleased with himself, and what he probably thought of as his subtle powers of persuasion. "I must say, Carver, I'm feeling relieved to know you'll be working on this job."

I postponed my mushroom meeting for two days—much to my contact's surprise, who knew something tricky was going on financially. Timing on these deals is everything. Then I swallowed a pill for my aching tooth, and off we went. It made me very pessimistic for the future of humanity, to think that they had to rely on people like me to handle their emergencies.

Two hours later we lifted away from Tycho Base on a high-speed USF Navy cutter. Free fall never did agree with me, and never will. I was all right during the eight-hour trip to Kaneely's asteroid, a forlorn chip of rock in the middle of nowhere, because the ship was under acceleration all the way. But the temporary station that the Navy had set up on the rock itself had no gravity to speak of.

We didn't bother to dock in the usual way—there was only a big pressure dome, on the surface of the asteroid. We hovered close to that, and went across to it in our suits. Inside the bubble about forty men and women had assembled. Munsen, like the ham he was, made a fool of both of us.

He made a stand-up speech. "Men," he said—ignoring the women completely. "We've had a hard time of it, this last month. Now there's a ray of hope, a light at the end of the tunnel. Here is the man we've all waited to see, Henry Carver. Henry Carver, the only man—." And away he went.

I endured it, averting my eyes from the audience, which seemed to be lapping it up. After Munsen dried up, they went into a very long and—to me, at any rate—completely meaningless briefing on the work that had been done so far to explore the Kaneelian chamber in the rock. I nodded occasionally, but the technical discussion was beyond me.

Boiling off the jargon and gibberish, what was left seemed to be simple enough. The asteroid chamber was completely empty except for the space warp, and nobody had any idea at all how that worked.

You put a signalling beacon, or some other object, inside it and then pressed a bar on the outside. Instantly, the beacon or whatever appeared somewhere else, anywhere from ten thousand to five hundred million miles away. The beacons that had been recovered—they had lost another since Munsen briefed me—were all intact and apparently unscathed by the jump. But their positions when they appeared were completely random. Put a man or an animal inside the warp cylinder, and press the bar again. Nothing at all happened, except a slight hum from the machine.

They had tried men in twos and men in threes; men in lead suits to screen testing radiation; men in suspended animation; men who had been knocked unconscious; and—Munsen would try anything—dead men. Of these, only the last were accepted for transfer and as usual they told no tales.

The Navy still had plenty of volunteers, going dutifully into the space-warp enclosure and then, hours later, floating back out again when it was clear that nothing was going to happen. There was no doubt that they were all getting discouraged.

I wasn't keen to go near the Kaneelian machine—you never knew when it might suddenly decide to work, explode or otherwise do something drastic. On the other hand, I very much wanted to get the thing over with and go back to Tycho City for my unfinished business. When the briefing ended, Munsen and I floated together down into the big chamber under the surface of the asteroid.

It was actually three big spaces, inter-connected through tall archways. Two were completely empty and in a corner of the third sat a solitary, dull-grey metal cylinder, about two meters wide and three meters high. The space warp. You climbed in through the open top, and on the outside there was a gray bar that activated the system—or failed to if there was a man inside.

"Why are the arches so big?" I asked Imre Munsen over my suit radio. "Were the Kaneelians all ten meters tall?"

"We don't know. They might have been. On the other hand, they should have been our size, or near to it, to fit into the warp. For all we know now, they may come in a variety of sizes. Why do you ask?"

A good question. I was just making conversation to put off the next step. Then I had an idea. "You say it will send single-celled animals through. Is it possible that the Kaneelians were single-celled? Could a single cell grow to the size of a man?"

"I don't see why not. It wouldn't solve our problem. It would explain why a single-celled animal *can* get through—but not why multi-celled animals can't. Why would they want to stop a transfer?"

I shrugged. Since I don't understand human behavior at all, it seemed presumptuous to guess at the motives of the aliens. Munsen gestured at the top of the warp cylinder.

"I'm going to take a look at the inside, Henry. Coming?"

"Best if I stay outside, I think," I said casually. "The control unit's out here. I want to watch what happens to it when you go inside."

Munsen had made it quite clear that at some point he expected me to take a look inside that ghastly cylinder, but I saw no reason to rush in. He nodded at me. "Makes sense. Once I'm inside, press the bar. You never know, I might get lucky."

He floated up, then down into the open top of the cylinder. After a couple of seconds, his voice came over the suit radio. I worked the bar, and hoped. There was a low, steady humming from one of two square boxes on the side of the warp. It went on for about five seconds, then stopped. I waited.

After twenty seconds I heard Munsen's disappointed voice. "No good. I might as well come out again. There's a sort of metal piece inside here that moved backwards and forwards when I was waiting for the warp. I think it's the scanner. Let's change places and you can take a look."

It was the moment of truth. If one of the boxes contained the scanner control, then the other box was presumably the warp mechanism itself. While Munsen was getting out of the cylinder, I took a multi-purpose belt attachment from the waist of my suit and opened up a long dur-steel spike. Its use had always mystified me—it looked like an ice pick, but presumably wasn't. I drove it as hard as I could into the soft-plastic middle of the box that I thought contained the warp mechanism. Then—a bad mistake, as I later realized—to be on the safe side, I drove it just as hard into the other box.

There was a satisfying sizzling noise, like a damp onion ring dropped into very hot fat. Feeling much reassured, I put the spike away and waited for Munsen to join me.

"Let me stand here and watch what happens," he said. "Did you see anything at this end when I was inside?"

I shrugged, then realized he couldn't see that well inside my suit. "Just the hum you told me about—from that box."

I hoped my efforts to gain a little insurance would not be visible to Munsen. With the old butterflies in my stomach, I pushed gently off from the floor, floated up and then, with a slight down-boost from the jets, dropped slowly into the warp cylinder.

Despite my steps to deactivate the warp, I had the feeling that I was in trouble: I think the thing that separates a real coward from ordinary men is an extra sense that provides him with a continuous stream of information on all dangers, real or imaginary. To my eye, the open top of the cylinder gaped beneath me like the mouth of Hell.

I touched the warp floor, and stood there breathless. After fifteen long seconds, when nothing at all had happened, I drew air into my complaining lungs. It felt good.

"It's no good, Munsen," I said, hoping my relief didn't show in my voice. "Nothing's happening. I might as well come out."

He didn't answer. I straightened my legs to push off from the floor of the warp cylinder. They made no contact. I looked down, then up. In both directions, there was a featureless gray nothingness—and it was the same on all sides.

I was baffled. I couldn't be in the warp transfer—that was instantaneous. Then where was I? The question became more and more relevant as time went by and seconds became minutes.

It would be misleading to say that I panicked when I realized the fix I was in. I had been in a state of terror ever since Munsen made it clear that he expected me to go inside the warp chamber. I couldn't get much higher on the panic scale. Even so, I didn't at all relish the prospect of starving to death inside my suit, or maybe popping out inside the Sun. My water and air recycling were almost perfect, but I would run out of food in a week.

After an hour of these cheerful thoughts, a new factor entered.

My tooth erupted again. It had been sitting back, quietly throb-bing, ever since we reached the asteroid. Now it woke up with a vengeance and began to poke red-hot needles down through the top of my head. I couldn't get a finger in my mouth because it was in the suit, but I ran my tongue over the left side of my inner gum and was rewarded with a bolt of lightning through my left temple. The gum felt squishy and I had a peculiar taste in my mouth. The pain grew steadily worse.

There seems little point in a detailed recapitulation of the next three days, If—as seems unlikely—you've been through a simi-lar experience, you know what it was like. If not, no words describe it. Fortunately or unfortunately, the infection from my tooth distorted my time sense. I ran a high fever and was delirious for at least part of the time. Teeth were much on my mind. I remember saying, out loud, "the tooth, and nothing but the tooth," and "uneasy lies the tooth that wears the crown."

One thing is clear. Somehow, the combination of solitude, fear, pain and fever worked a strange synthesis. Just after I had said, "But why put the warp controls on the *outside*, not the inside?" I understood, from nowhere, the purpose, logic and practice of the Kaneelian space warp. I knew why we couldn't see a pattern in the points of exit, and why we hadn't been able to send living things through it.

The knowledge did me no good. My misery went on. Then, long after I had died, gone to Hell, and been sent on from there to a worse place, the gray ambience suddenly vanished and I popped out into the black, dazzling vacuum of normal space. My suit emergency signal switched itself on and four hours later a USF transfer vessel picked me up. I had been warped almost two million miles away from the asteroid. The ship's robodoc clucked over me and pumped me full of antibiotics, tranquiliz-ers and happy pills. By the time we reached Tycho Base I was stoned out of my mind and feeling pretty good.

The trip took twenty hours. When we finally got there, I saw from my watch that my mushroom-deal deadline was a thing of the past. Goodbye million credits, I thought cheerfully. Hello Imre Munsen.

He had arrived at Tycho shortly before I had. Would you

believe it, he wanted to pump me for information before we'd exchanged two words? He was in a fine state of excitement.

"Henry, you did it! We knew you would. What was the trick to it? How did you know what to do?"

I had a clear choice. I could tell the truth, and probably be shot for sabotaging priceless equipment. Or I could explain that I had intentionally disabled the space-warp selection mechanism to make it accept living things—and I had, of course, bravely put myself through it as a test.

No prizes for guessing what I told Munsen and his cohorts.

Naturally, I was the hero of the hour. USF dignitaries kept coming to see me, more and more important ones, finally capped by a visit from the eminent President Dinsdale himself.

After two days of steady adulation, I'd had more than enough and wanted to go and attend to my long-neglected tooth. I had guarded my secret of the space warp closely, after I heard what had happened when I had left the asteroid. Munsen had tried to send himself through and the machine wouldn't do it. Maybe my transmission had been its last dying gasp, or perhaps it was self-repairing and had restored itself to its original selective condition.

I left Tycho Base with their praises ringing in my ears and went back to the City. I hated it. God knows what they'd put into my computer file about this one. I didn't want to be dragged out again next time they needed a hero.

Back in my apartment came the unkindest cut of all. I'd been answering questions and shaking hands for two full days at Tycho Base, in no real hurry because my mushroom monopoly deal was dead. But when I arrived back home and switched on the holovision, the date was three days earlier than my watch showed. The warp *was* instantaneous, but only to the outside observer. No wonder my delirious moans had been completely ignored when I was picked up—no one understood that I'd spent three subjective days in that suit.

If I'd known the real date, I'd have had time left to sew up my stock deal and get my commissions after we got back to Tycho. Instead, I'd sat about for days as a USF showpiece for their VIPs. Most annoying of all, I might have guessed that the warp might not be instantaneous for the transferred object—because I knew what the warp had been used for.

The Kaneelians had come to the Solar System for a while, then packed up their furniture and moved on. They were ten meters tall, but like humans in one respect—who bothers to take the empty trash cans with them when they move house? Who cares whether their garbage-disposal unit sends the trash a million miles or a billion miles, or how long the garbage believes it is in transit? The scanner made good sense too. The Kaneelians were like humans in some other ways—household appliances had to be safe and child-proof.

Imre Munsen had declared, in one of his more inflated introductions, that I had a sure place in history. I could imagine it, ringing down the ages. Henry Carver, the only man since time began to be accepted by, and transferred through, an alien garbage-disposal unit.

I sat in front of my holovision, thinking of my lost commissions and wondering how long it would be before anyone else came to the same conclusion about the function of the Kaneelian space warp. At last I reached for the videophone and made a dental appointment.

AFTERWORD: A CERTAIN PLACE IN HISTORY.

The science fiction literature has many heroes and villains but far too few anti-heroes. The anti-hero (male or female) can never become either hero or villain except by sheer accident. He lacks the dedication to pursue great good, great evil, or great anything-at-all. He is pretty much a total loss if you are looking for a doer of great deeds.

In spite of this, stories with anti-heroes as central characters remain very popular. There are good examples for readers of any age—Mr. Toad, Huck Finn, Holden Caulfield, Flashman, The Ginger Man, Yossarian, Major Bloodnok, Falstaff and Uncle Silas. There are still too few of them, and fewest of all in science fiction, where sense of wonder and sense of humor seem to pull in opposite directions.

Ideally, I should have made Henry Carver a woman, because while there are few male anti-heroes there are even fewer female ones. We need Henrietta Carver—cowardly, a little larcenous, slothful, and lecherous when it implies no danger or real commitment.

I'm enough of an anti-hero myself to be afraid to write about Henrietta. She deserves to exist, but I'm sure some readers would infer sexism when all I intended was entertainment. It would need a woman writer to get away with it. When are we going to achieve sexual equality for writers?

ALL THE COLORS OF THE VACUUM

As soon as we got back from the mid-year run to Titan I went down to Earth and asked Wesley for a leave of absence. I had been working hard enough for six people and he knew it. He nodded agreeably as soon as I made the formal request.

"I think you've earned it, Captain Roker. But don't you have quite a bit of leave time saved up? Wouldn't that be enough?" He stopped staring out of the window at the orange-brown sky and called my records onto the screen in front of him.

"That won't do it," I said, while he was still looking.

Wesley frowned and became a little less formal. "It won't? Well, according to this, Jeanie, you've got at least . . ." He looked up. "Just how long *do* you want to take off?"

"I'm not exactly sure. Somewhere between nine and sixteen years."

I would have liked to break the news more gently, but maybe there was no graceful way.

It had begun, as many of the events in my life have begun, with McAndrew. He was best known—when he was known at all—as the mild-mannered, studious star of the Penrose Institute. To his colleagues he was the best combination of theorist and experimenter that physics had seen since Isaac Newton. And to me he was many things, but one of them was a man who could attract trouble and danger without lifting a finger.

I hadn't seen him in person since the first test of the McAndrew balanced drive, which the general public always referred to, to his huge irritation, as 'McAndrew's inertialess drive'. During that test I had extracted a promise from him that I would be on the first interstellar run. He had been full of drugs and painkillers when he agreed to it, but I wouldn't listen to that as an excuse. I called him as soon as I got back from the Titan run.

"Yes, she's ready enough to go." He had a strange expression on his face, somewhere between excitement and perplexity. "You've still got your mind set on going, then, Jeanie?"

I didn't even reply to that.

"How soon can I come out to the Institute?"

He cleared his throat, with the only legacy I had ever detected of his Scots ancestry. "Och, if you're set on it, come as soon as you please. I'll have things to tell you when you get here, but that can wait."

That was when I went down and made my request to Wesley for a long leave of absence. McAndrew had been strangely reluctant to discuss our destination, but I couldn't imagine that we'd be going out past Sirius. Alpha Centauri was my guess, and that would mean we would only be away about nine Earth years. Shipboard time would be three months, allowing a few days at the other end for exploration. If I knew McAndrew, he would have beaten the hundred gee acceleration that he projected for the interstellar prototype. He was never a man to talk big about what he was going to do.

The Penrose Institute had been moved out to Mars orbit since the last time I was there, so it took me a couple of weeks of impatient ship-hopping to get to it. When we finally closed to visible range I could see the old test ships, *Merganser* and *Dotterel,* floating a few kilometers from the main body of the Institute. They were easy to recognize from the flat mass disc with its protruding central spike. And floating near them, quite a bit bigger, was a new ship of gleaming silver. That had to be the *Hoatzin,* McAndrew's newest plaything. The disc was twice the size, and the spike three times as long, but *Hoatzin* was clearly *Merganser's* big brother.

It was Professor Limperis, the head of the Institute, who greeted me when I entered. He was putting on weight, a middle-aged man with a guileless, coal-black face that hid a razor-sharp mind and a bottomless memory.

"Good to see you again, Captain Roker. I haven't told McAndrew this, but I'm very glad you'll be going along to keep an eye on him.'' He gave what he once described as his 'hand-clapping nigger laugh'—a sure sign he was nervous about something.

"Well, I don't know that I'll be much use. I'm expecting to be just a sort of passenger. Don't worry. If my instincts are anything to go by there won't be much danger in a simple stellar rendezvous and return.''

"Er, yes.'' He wouldn't meet my eye. "That was my own reaction. I gather that Professor McAndrew has not mentioned to you his change of target?''

"Change of target? He didn't mention any target at all.'' Now my own worry bead was beginning to throb. "Are you suggesting that the trip will *not* be a stellar rendezvous?''

He shrugged and waved his hands along the corridor. "Not if McAndrew gets his way. Come along, he's inside at the computer. I think it's best if he is present when we talk about this further.''

Pure evasion. Whatever the bad news was, Limperis wanted me to hear it from McAndrew himself.

We found him staring vacantly at a completely blank display screen. Normally I would never interrupt him when he looks as imbecilic as that—it means that he is thinking with a breadth and depth that I'll never comprehend. I often wonder what it would be like to have a mind like that. Humans, with rare exceptions, must seem like trained apes, with muddied thoughts and no ability for abstract analysis.

Tough luck. It was time one of the trained apes had some of her worries put to rest. I walked up behind McAndrew and put my hands on his shoulders.

"Here I am. I'm ready to go—if you'll tell me where we're going.''

He turned in his chair. After a moment his slack jaw firmed up and the eyes brought me into focus.

"Hello, Captain.'' No doubt about it, as soon as he recognized me he had that same shifty look I had noticed in Limperis. "I didn't expect you here so soon. We're still making up a flight profile.''

"That's all right. I'll help you.'' I sat down opposite him, studying his face closely. As usual he looked tired, but that was normal. Geniuses work *harder* than anyone else, not less hard. His face was thinner, and he had lost a little more hair from that sandy, receding mop. My argument with him over that was long in the past.

"Why don't you grow it back? It's such a minor job, a couple of hours with the machines every few months and you'd have a full head of hair again."

He had sniffed. "Why don't you try and get me to grow a tail, or hair all over my body? Or maybe make my arms a bit longer, so they'll let me run along with them touching the ground? Jeanie, I'll not abuse a bio-feedback machine to run evolution in the wrong direction. We're getting less hairy all the time. I know your fondness for monkeys"—a nasty crack about an engineering friend of mine on Ceres, who was a bit hairy for even my accommodating tastes—"but I'll be just as happy when I have no hair at all. It gets in the way, it grows all the time, and it serves no purpose whatsoever."

McAndrew resented the time it took him to clip his fingernails, and I'm sure that he regarded his fondness for food as a shameful weakness. Meanwhile, I wondered who in the Penrose Institute cut his hair. Maybe they had a staff assistant, whose job it was to shear the absent-minded once a month.

"What destination are you planning for the first trip out?" If he was thinking of chasing a comet, I wanted that out in the open.

McAndrew looked at Limperis. Limperis looked at McAndrew, handing it back to him. Mac cleared his throat.

"We've discussed it here and we're all agreed. The first trip of the *Hoatzin* won't be to a star system." He cleared his throat again. "It will be to pursue and rendezvous with the Ark of Massingham. It's a shorter trip than any of the star systems," he added hopefully. He could read my expression. "They are less than two light years out. With the *Hoatzin* we can be there and docked with the Ark in less than thirty-five ship days."

If he was trying to make me feel better, McAndrew was going about it in quite the wrong way.

Back in the twenties, the resources of the Solar System must have seemed inexhaustible. No one had been able to *catalog* the planetoids, still less analyze their composition and probable value. Now we know everything out to Neptune that's bigger than a hundred meters across, and the navigation groups want that down to fifty meters in the next twenty years. The idea of grabbing an asteroid a couple of kilometers across and using it how you choose sounds like major theft. But it hadn't merely been permitted—it had been *encouraged*.

The first space colonies had been conceived as utopias, planned by earth idealists who wouldn't learn from history. New frontiers may attract visionaries, but more than that they attract oddities. Anyone who is more than three sigma away from the norm, in any direction, seems to finish out there on the frontier. No surprise in that. If a person can't fit, for whatever reason, he'll move away from the main group of humanity. They'll push him, and he'll want to go. How do I know? Look, you don't pilot to Titan without learning a lot about your own personality. Before we found the right way to use people like me, I would probably have been on one of the Arks.

The United Space Federation had assisted in the launch of seventeen of them, between ninety and forty years ago. Each of them was self-supporting, a converted asteroid that would hold between three and ten thousand people at departure time. The idea was that there would be enough raw materials and space to let the Ark grow as the population grew. A two-kilometer asteroid holds five to twenty billion tons of matter, and a total life-support system for one human needs less than ten tons of that.

The Arks had left long before the discovery of the McAndrew balanced drive, before the discovery of even the Mattin Drive. They were multi-generation ships, bumbling along into the interstellar void with speeds that were only a few percent of light speed.

And who was on board them when they left? Any fairly homogeneous group of strange people, who shared enough of a common philosophy or delusion to prefer the uncertainties of

star travel to the known problems within the Solar System. It
took courage to set out like that, to sever all your ties with home
except occasional laser radio communication. Courage, or an
overpowering conviction that you were part of a unique and
chosen group.

To put that another way, McAndrew was proposing to take us
out to meet a community about which we knew little, except that
by the usual standards they were descended from madmen.

"Mac, I don't remember which one was the Ark of Massingham. How long ago did it leave?"

Even mad people can have sane children. Four of the Arks, as
I recalled, had turned around and were on their way back to the
System.

"Seventy-five years ago. It's one of the earlier ones, with a
final speed a bit less than three percent of light speed."

"Is it one of the Arks that has turned back?"

He shook his head. "No. They're still on their way. Target
star is Tau Ceti. They won't get there for another three hundred
years."

"Well, why pick them out? What's so special about the Ark
of Massingham?" I had a sudden thought. "Are they having
some problem that we could help with?"

We had saved two of the Arks in the past twenty years. For
one of them we had been able to diagnose a recessive genetic
element that was appearing in the children, and pass the test
information and sperm filter technique over the communications
link. The other had needed the use of an unmanned high-
acceleration probe, to carry a couple of tons of cadmium out to
them. They had been unlucky enough to choose a freak asteroid,
one that apparently lacked the element even in the tiniest traces.

"They don't report any problem. We've never had a response
to any messages we've sent to them, so far as the records on
Oberon Station are concerned. But we know that they are doing
all right, because about every three or four years a message has
come in from them. Never anything about the Ark itself, it has
always been scientific information."

McAndrew has hesitated as he said that last phrase. That was
the lure, no doubt about it.

"What kind of information?" I said. "Surely we know everything that they know. We have hundreds of thousands of scientists in the System, they can't have more than a few hundred of them."

"I'm sure you're right on the numbers." Professor Limperis spoke when McAndrew showed no inclination to do so. "I'm not sure it's relevant. How many scientists does it require to produce the work of one Einstein, or one McAndrew? You can't just sit down and count numbers, as though you were dealing with—with bars of soap, or with poker chips. You have to deal with individuals."

"There's a genius on the Ark of Massingham," said McAndrew suddenly. His eyes were gleaming. "A man or woman who has been cut off from most of physics for a whole lifetime, working alone. It's worse than Ramanujan."

"How do you know that?" I had seldom seen McAndrew so filled with feeling. "Maybe they've been getting messages from somebody in the System here."

McAndrew laughed, a humorless bark. "I'll tell you why, Jeanie Roker. You flew on *Merganser*. Tell me how the drive worked."

"Well, the mass plate at the front balanced the acceleration, so we didn't get any sensation of fifty gee." I shrugged. "I didn't work out the maths for myself, but I'm sure I could have if I felt like it."

I was, too. I have degrees in Electrical Engineering and in Gravitational Engineering, for my job I have to. I was a bit rusty, but you don't lose the basics once you have them planted deep enough in your head.

"I don't mean the balancing mechanism, that was just common sense." He shook his head. "I mean the *drive*. Didn't it occur to you that we were accelerating a mass of trillions of tons at fifty gee? If you work out the mass conversion rate that you will need with an ideal photon drive, you'll consume the whole mass in a few days. The *Merganser* got its drive by accelerating charged particles up to within millimeters a second of light speed, that was the reaction mass. But how did it get the energy to do it?"

I felt like telling him that when I had been on *Merganser* there had been other details—such as survival—on my mind. I thought for a few moments, then shook my head.

"You can't get more energy out of matter than the rest mass energy, I know that. But you're telling me that the drives on *Merganser* and *Hoatzin* do it. That Einstein was wrong."

"No, I'm not." McAndrew looked horrified at the thought that he might have been criticizing one of his senior idols. "All I've done is build on what Einstein did. Look, you've done some quantum mechanics, you must have. You know that when you calculate the energy for the vacuum state of a system you don't get zero. You get a positive value."

I had a hazy recollection of a formula swimming back across the years. What was it? ½hw, said a distant voice.

"But you can set that to zero!" I was proud at remembering so much. "The zero point of energy is arbitrary."

"In quantum theory it is. But not in general relativity." McAndrew was beating back my mental defenses. As usual when I spoke with him on theoretical subjects, I began to feel I would know less at the end of the conversation than I did at the beginning.

"In general realtivity," he went on, "energy implies space-time curvature. If the zero point energy is not zero, the vacuum self-energy is real. It can be tapped, if you know what you are doing. That's where *Hoatzin* draws its energy. The reaction mass it needs is very small. You can get that by scooping up matter as you go along, or if you prefer it you can use a fraction—a very small fraction—of the mass plate."

"All right." I knew McAndrew. If I let him get going he would talk all day about physical principles. "But I don't see how that has anything to do with the Ark of Massingham. It has an old-fashioned drive, surely. You said it was launched seventy-five years ago."

"It was." This was Limperis again, gently insistent. "But you see, Captain Roker, nobody outside the Penrose Institute knows how Professor McAndrew has been able to tap the vacuum self-energy. We have been very careful not to broadcast that information until we were ready. The potential for destructive use is enormous. It destroys the old idea that you cannot create more energy at a point than the rest mass of the matter residing there. There was nothing known in the rest of the System about this use until two weeks ago.''

''And then you released the information?'' I was beginning to feel dizzy.

''No. The basic equations for accessing the vacuum self-energy were received by laser communication. They were sent, with no other message, *from the Ark of Massingham.*''

Suddenly it made sense. It wasn't just McAndrew who was itching to get in and find out what there was on the Ark—it was everyone at the Penrose Institute. I could sense the excitement in Limperis, and he was the most guarded and politically astute of all the Members. If some physicist, working out there alone two light-years from Sol, had managed to parallel McAndrew's development, that was a momentous event. It implied a level of genius that was difficult to imagine.

I knew *Hoatzin* would be on the way in a few days, whether I wanted to go or stay. But there was one more key question.

''I can't believe that the Ark of Massingham was started by a bunch of physicists. What was the original composition of the group that colonized it?''

''Not physicists.'' Limperis had suddenly sobered. ''By no means physicists. That is why I am glad you will be accompanying Professor McAndrew. The leader of the original group was Jules Massingham. In the past few days I have taken the time to obtain all the System records on him. He was a man of great personal drive and convictions. His ambition was to apply the old principles of eugenics to a whole society. Two themes run through all his writings: the creation of the superior human, and the idea of that superior being as an integrated part of a whole society. He was ruthless in his pursuit of those ends.''

He looked at me, black face impassive. ''From the evidence available, Captain, one might suggest that he succeeded in his aims.''

Hoatzin was a step up from *Merganser* and *Dotterel.* Maximum acceleration was a hundred and ten gee, and the living capsule was a four-meter sphere. I had cursed the staff of the Institute, publicly and privately, but I had got nowhere. They were obsessed with the idea of the lonely genius out there in the void, and no one would consider any other first trip for *Hoatzin*. So at least I would check out every aspect of the system before we went, while McAndrew was looking at the rendez-vous problem and making a final flight plan. We sent a message to the Ark, telling them of our trip and estimated arrival time. It would take two years to get there, Earth-time, but we would take even longer. They would be able to prepare for our arrival however they chose, with garlands or gallows.

On the trip out, McAndrew tried again to explain to me his methods for tapping the vacuum self-energy. The available energies made up a quasi-continuous "spectrum", correspond-ing to a large number of very high frequencies of vibration and associated wavelengths. Tuned resonators in the *Hoatzin* drive units selected certain wavelengths which were excited by the corresponding components in the vacuum self energy. These "colors", as McAndrew thought of them, could feed vacuum energy to the drive system. The results that had come from the Ark of Massingham suggested that McAndrew's system for energy extraction could be generalized, so that all the "colors" of the vacuum self-energy should become available. If that was true, the potential acceleration produced by the drive would go up by a couple of orders of magnitude. He was still working out what the consequences of that would be. At speeds that ap-proached within a nanometer per second of light speed, a single proton would mass enough to weigh its impact on a sensitive balance.

I let him babble on to his heart's content. My own attention was mostly on the history of the Ark of Massingham. It was an oddity among oddities. Six of the Arks had disappeared without trace. They didn't respond to signals from Earth, and they didn't send signals of their own. Most people assumed that they had wiped themselves out, with accidents, wars, strange sexual practices, or all three. Four of the Arks had swung back towards normalcy and were heading in again for the System. Six were still heading out, but two of them were in deep trouble if the

messages that came back to Oberon Station were any guide. One
was full of messianic ranting, a crusade of human folly prop-
agating itself out to the stars (let's hope they never met anyone
out there whose good opinion we would later desire). The other
was quietly and peacefully insane, sending messages that spoke
only of new rules for the interpretation of dreams. They were
convinced that they would find the world of the Norse legends
when they finally arrived at Eta Cassiopeia, complete with
Jotunheim, Niflheim, and all the assembly of gods and heroes. It
would be six hundred years before they arrived there, time
enough for moves to rationality or to extinction.

Among this set, the Ark of Massingham provided a bright
mixture of sanity and strangeness. They had sent messages back
since first they left, messages that assumed the Ark was the
carrier of human hopes and a superior civilization. Nothing that
we sent—questions, comments, information, or acknowledge-
ments—ever stimulated a reply. And nothing that *they* sent ever
discussed life aboard the Ark. We had no idea if they lived in
poverty or plenty, if they were increasing or decreasing in
numbers, if they were receiving our transmissions, if they had
material problems of any kind. Everything that came back to the
System was science, delivered in a smug and self-satisfied tone.
From all that science, the recent transmission on physics was the
only one to excite more than a mild curiosity from System
scientists. Usually the Ark sent "discoveries" that had been
made here long ago.

Once the drive of the *Hoatzin* was up to full thrust there was
no way that we could see anything or communicate with anyone.
The drive was fixed to the mass plate on the front of the ship, and
the particles that streamed past us and out to the rear were visible
only when they were in collision with the rare atoms of hydrogen
drifting in free space. We had actually settled for less than a
maximum drive and were using a slightly dispersed exhaust. A
tightly focussed and collimated beam wouldn't harm us any, but
we didn't want to generate a death ray behind us that would
distintegrate anything in its path for a few light years.

Six days into the trip, our journey out shared the most common feature of all long distance travel. It was boring. When

McAndrew wasn't busy inside his head, staring at the wall in front of him and performing the mental acrobatics that he called theoretical physics, we talked, played and exercised. I was astonished again that a man who knew so much about so much could know nothing about some things.

"You mean to tell me," he said once, as we lay in companionable darkness, with the side port showing the eldritch and unpredictable blue sparks of atomic collision. "You mean that *Lungfish* wasn't the first space station. All the books and records show it that way."

"No, they don't. If they do, they're wrong. It's a common mistake. Like the idea back at the beginning of flight itself, that Lindbergh was the first man to fly across the Atlantic Ocean. He was more like the hundredth." I felt McAndrew turn his head towards me. "Yes, you heard me. A couple of airships had been over before him, and a couple of other people in aircraft. He was just the first person to fly *alone*. *Lungfish* was the first *permanent* space station, that's all. And I'll tell you something else. Did you know that in the early flights, even ones that lasted for months, the crews were usually all men? Think of that for a while."

He was silent for a moment. "I don't see anything wrong with it. It would simplify some of the plumbing, maybe some other things, too."

"You don't understand, Mac. That was at a time when it was regarded as morally wrong for men to form relationships with men, or women with women."

There was what I might describe as a startled silence.

"Oh," said McAndrew at last. Then, after a few moments more, "My God. How much did they have to pay them? Or was coercion used?"

"It was considered an honor to be chosen."

He didn't say any more about it; but I don't think he believed me, either. Politeness is one of the first things you learn on long trips.

We cut off the drive briefly at crossover, but there was nothing to be seen and there was still no way we could receive messages. Our speed was crowding light speed so closely that anything from Oberon Station would scarcely be catching up with us. The Institute's message was still on its way to the Ark of Massingham, and we would be there ourselves not long after it. The *Hoatzin* was behaving perfectly, with none of the problems that had almost done for us on the earlier test ships. The massive disc of dense matter at the front of the ship protected us from most of our collisions with stray dust and free hydrogen. If we didn't come back, the next ship out could follow our path exactly, tracking our swath of ionization.

During deceleration I began to search the sky beyond the *Hoatzin* every day, with an all-frequency sweep that ought to pick up signals as soon as our drive went to reduced thrust. We didn't pick up the Ark until the final day and it was no more than a point on the microwave screen for most of that. The image we finally built up on the monitor showed a lumpy, uneven ball, pierced by black shafts. Spiky antennas and angled gantries stood up like spines on its dull grey surface. I had seen the images of the Ark before it left the System, and all the surface structures were new. The colonists had been busy in the seventy-seven years since they accelerated away from Ganymede orbit.

We moved in to five thousand kilometers, cut all drive, and sent a calling sequence. I don't remember a longer five seconds, waiting for their response. When it came it was an anti-climax. A pleasant-looking middle-aged woman appeared on our screen.

"Hello," she said cheerfully. "We received a message that you were on your way here. My name is Kleeman. Link in your computer and we'll dock you. There will be a few formalities before you can come inside."

I put the central computer into distributed mode and linked a navigation module through the comnet. She sounded friendly and normal but I didn't want her to have override control of all the *Hoatzin's* movements. We moved to a position about fifty kilometers away from the Ark, then Kleeman appeared again on the screen.

"I didn't realize your ship had so much mass. We'll hold there, and you can come on in with a pod. All right?"

We called it a capsule these days, but I knew what she meant. I made McAndrew put on a suit, to his disgust, and we entered the small transfer vessel. It was just big enough for three people, with no air lock and a simple electric drive. We drifted in to the Ark, with the capsule's computer slaved through the *Hoatzin*. As we got nearer I had a better feel for size. Two kilometers is small for an asteroid, but it's awfully big compared with a human. We nosed in to contact with a landing tower, like a fly landing on the side of a wasp's nest. I hoped that would prove to be a poor simile.

We left the capsule open and went hand-over-hand down the landing tower rather than wait for an electric lift. It was impossible to believe that we were moving at almost nine thousand kilometers a second away from Earth. The stars were in the same familiar constellations, and it took a while to pick out the Sun. It was a bright star, but a good deal less bright than Sirius. I stood at the bottom of the tower for a few seconds, peering about me before entering the air lock that led to the interior of the Ark. It was like a strange, alien landscape, with the few surface lights throwing black angular shadows across the uneven rock. My trips to Titan suddenly felt like local hops around the comfortable backyard of the Solar System.

"Come on, Captain." That was McAndrew, all brisk efficiency and already standing in the air lock. He was much keener than I to penetrate that unfamiliar world of the interior.

I took a last look at the stars, and fixed in my mind the position of the transfer capsule—an old habit that pays off once in a thousand times. Then I followed McAndrew down into the lock.

'A few formalities before you can come inside.' Kleeman had a gift for understatement. We found out what she meant when we stepped in through the inner lock, to an office-cum-schoolroom equipped with a couple of impressive consoles and displays. Kleeman met us there, as pleasant and rosy-faced in the flesh as she had seemed over the comlink.

She waved us to the terminals. "This is an improved version of the equipment that was on the original ship, before it left your System. Please sit down. Before anyone can enter our main

Home, they must take tests. It has been that way since Massingham first showed us how our society could be built.''

We sat at the terminals, back-to-back. McAndrew was frowning at the delay. ''What's the test, then?'' he grumbled.

''Just watch the screen. I don't think that either of you will
have any trouble.'' She smiled and left us to it. I wondered what
the penalty was if you failed. We were a long way from home. It
seemed clear that if they had been improving this equipment
after they left Ganymede, they must apply it to their own people.
We were certainly the first visitors they had seen for seventy-
five years. How had they been able to accept our arrival so
calmly?

Before I could pursue that thought the screen was alive. I read
the instructions as they appeared there, and followed them as
carefully as possible. After a few minutes I got the knack of it.
We had tests rather like it when I first applied to go into space.
To say that we were taking an intelligence test would be an
over-simplification—many other aptitudes were tested, as well
as knowledge and mechanical skills. That was the only consolation I had. McAndrew must be wiping the floor with me on all
the parts that called for straight brain-power, but I knew that his
coordination was terrible. He could unwrap a set of interlocking
multiply-connected figures mentally and tell you how they came
apart, but ask him to do the same thing with real objects and he
wouldn't be able to start.

After three hours we were finished. Both screens suddenly
went blank. We swung to face each other.

''What's next?'' I said. He shrugged and began to look at the
terminal itself. The design hadn't been used in the System for
fifty years. I took a quick float around the walls—we had
entered the Ark near a pole, where the effective gravity caused
by its rotation was negligible. Even on the Ark's equator I
estimated that we wouldn't feel more than a tenth of a gee, at the
most.

No signs of what I was looking for, but that didn't mean
much. Microphones could be disguised in a hundred ways.

''Mac, who do you think *she* is?''

He looked up from the terminal. ''Why, she's the woman

assigned to . . ." He stopped. He had caught my point. When
you are two light years from Sol and you have your first visitors
for seventy-five years, who leads the reception party? Not the
man and woman who recycle the garbage. Kleeman ought to be
somebody important on the Ark.

"I can assist your speculation," said a voice from the wall.
So much for our privacy. As I expected, we had been observed
throughout—no honor system on this test. "I am Kal Massingham Kleeman, the daughter of Jules Massingham, and I am
senior member of Home outside the Council of Intellects. Wait
there for one more moment. I will join you with good news."

She was beaming when she reappeared. Whatever they were
going to do with us, it didn't seem likely they would be flinging
us out into the void.

"You are both prime stock, genetically and individually,"
she said. "I thought that would be the case when first I saw
you."

She looked down at a green card in her hand. "I notice that
you both failed to answer one small part of the inquiry on your
background. Captain Roker, your medical record indicates that
you bore one child. But what is its sex, condition, and present
status?"

I heard McAndrew suck in his breath past his teeth, while I
suppressed my own shock as best I could. It was clear that the
standards of privacy in the System and on the Ark had diverged
widely in the past seventy-five years.

"It is a female." I hope I kept my voice steady. "Healthy,
and with no neuroses. She is in first level education on Luna."

"The father?"

"Unknown."

I shouldn't have been pleased to see that now Kleeman was
shocked, but I was. She looked as distressed as I felt. After a few
seconds she grabbed control of her emotions, swallowed, and
nodded.

"We are not ignorant of the unplanned matings that your
System permits. But hearing of such things and encountering
them directly are different things." She looked again at her
green card. "McAndrew, you show no children. Is that true?"

He had taken his lead from me and managed a calm reply. "No known children."

"Incredible." Kleeman was shaking her head. "That a man of your talents should be permitted to go so long without suitable mating . . ."

She looked at him hungrily, the way that I have seen McAndrew eye an untapped set of experimental data from out in the Halo. I could imagine how he had performed on the intellectual sections of the test.

"Come along," she said at last, still eyeing McAndrew in a curiously intense and possessive way. "I would like to show you some of Home, and arrange for you to have living quarters for your use."

"Don't you want more details of *why* we are here?" burst out Mac. "We've come nearly two light years to get to the Ark."

"You have been receiving our messages of the advances that we have made?" Kleeman's manner had a vast self-confidence. "So why should we be surprised when superior men and women from your system wish to come here? We are only surprised that it took you so long to develop a suitably efficient ship. Your vessel is new?"

"Very new." I spoke before McAndrew could get a word in. Kleeman's assumption that we were on the Ark to stay had ominous overtones. We needed to know more about the way the place functioned before we told her that we were planning only a brief visit.

"We have been developing the drive for our ship using results that parallel some of those found by your scientists," I went on. I gave Mac a look that kept him quiet for a little while longer. "When we have finished with the entry preliminaries, Professor McAndrew would very much like to meet your physicists."

She smiled serenely at him. "Of course. McAndrew, you should be part of our Council of Intellects. I do not know just how high your position was back in your System, but I feel sure you have nothing as exalted—and as respected—as our Council. Well"—she placed the two green cards she was holding in the pocket of her yellow smock—"there will be plenty of time to discuss induction to the Council when you have settled in here.

The entry formalities are complete. Let me show you Home. There has never been anything like it in the whole of human history.''

Over the next four hours we followed Kleeman obediently through the interior of the Ark. McAndrew was itching to locate his fellow-physicists, but he knew he was at the mercy of Kleeman's decisions. From our first meeting with others on the Ark, there was no doubt who was the boss there.

How can I describe the interior of the Ark? Imagine a free-space bee-hive, full of hard-working bees that had retained an element of independence of action. Everyone on the Ark of Massingham seemed industrious, cooperative, and intelligent. But they were missing a dimension, the touch of orneriness and unpredictability that you would find on Luna or on Titan. Nobody was cursing, nobody was irrational. Kleeman guided us through a clean, slightly dull Utopia.

The technology of the Ark was simpler to evaluate. Despite the immense pride with which Kleeman showed off every item of development, they were half a century behind us. The sprawling, overcrowded chaos of Earth was hard to live with, but it provided a constant pressure towards innovation. New inventions come fast when ten billion people are there to push you to new ideas. In those terms, life on the Ark was spacious and leisurely. The colony had constructed its network of interlocking tunnels to a point where it would take months to explore all the passages and corridors, but they were nowhere near exhausting their available space and resources.

"How many people would the Ark hold?" I asked McAndrew as we trailed along behind Kleeman. It would have taken only a few seconds to work it out for myself, but you get lazy when you live for a while with a born calculator.

"If they don't use the interior material to extend the surface of the Ark?" he said. "Give them the same room as we'd allow on Earth, six meters by six meters by two meters. They could hold nearly sixty million. Halve that, maybe, to allow for recycling and maintenance equipment."

"But that is not our aim," said Kleeman. She had overheard my question. "We are stabilized at ten thousand. We are not like the fools back on Earth. *Quality* is our aim, not mindless numbers."

She had that tone in her voice again, the one that had made me instinctively avoid the question of how long we would be staying on the Ark. Heredity is a potent influence. I couldn't speak about Jules Massingham, the founder of this Ark, but his daughter was a fanatic. I have seen others like her over the years. Nothing would be allowed to interfere with the prime objective: build the Ark's population on sound eugenic principles. Kleeman was polite to me—I was 'prime stock'—but she had her eye mainly on McAndrew. He would be a wonderful addition to her available gene pool.

Well, the lady had taste. I shared some of that attitude myself. 'Father unknown' was literally true and Mac and I had not chosen to elaborate. My daughter had rights, too, and her parentage would not be officially known unless she chose at puberty to take the chromosome matching tests.

Over the next six days, McAndrew and I worked our way into the life pattern aboard the Ark. The place ran like a clock, everything according to a schedule and everything in the right position. I had a good deal of leisure time, which I used to explore the less-popular corridors, up near the Hub. McAndrew was still obsessed with his search for physicists.

"No sense here," he growled to me, after a meal in the central dining-area, out on the Ark's equator. As I had guessed, effective gravity there was about a tenth of a gee. "I've spoken to a couple of dozen of their scientists. There's not a one of them would last a week at the Institute. Muddled minds and bad experiments."

He was angry. Usually McAndrew was polite to all scientists, even ones who couldn't understand what he was doing, still less add to it.

"Have you seen them all? Maybe Kleeman is keeping some of them from us."

'I've had that thought. She's talked to me every day about the Council of Intellects, and I've seen some of the things they've produced. But I've yet to meet one of them, in person." He shrugged, and rubbed at his sandy, receding hairline. "After we've slept I'm going to try another tack. There's a schoolroom over on the other side of the Ark, where I gather Kleeman keeps people who don't seem quite to fit into her ideas. Want to take a look there with me, tomorrow?''

"Maybe. I'm wondering what Kleeman has in mind for *me*. I think I know her plans for you, she sees you as another of her senior brains.'' I saw the woman herself approaching us across the wide room, with its gently curving floor. "You'd like it, I suspect. It seems to be like the Institute, but members of the Council have a lot more prestige.''

I had immediate proof that I was right. Kleeman seemed to have made up her mind. "We need a commitment from you now, McAndrew,'' she said. "There will soon be a vacancy on the Council. You are the best person to fill it.''

McAndrew looked flattered but uncomfortable. The trouble was, it really *did* interest him, I could tell that. The idea of a top-level brains trust had appeal.

"All right,'' he said after a few moments. He looked at me, and I could tell what he was thinking. If we were going to be on our way back home soon, it would do no harm to help the Ark while he was here. They could use all the help available.

Kleeman clapped her hands together softly; plump white hands that pointed out her high position—most people on the Ark had manual duties to keep the place running, with strict duty rosters.

"Wonderful! I will plan for your induction tomorrow. Let me make the announcement tonight, and we can speed up the proceedings for the outgoing member.''

"You always have a fixed number of members?'' asked McAndrew.

She seemed slightly puzzled by his question. "Of course. Exactly twelve. The system was designed for that number.''

She nodded at me and hurried away across the dining area, a determined little woman who always got her way. Since we first arrived, she had never ceased to tell McAndrew that he must become the father of many children; scores of children; hundreds of children. He looked more and more worried as she increased the suggested number of his future progeny.

The next morning I went on with my own exploration of the Ark, while McAndrew made a visit to the Ark's oddities, the people who didn't seem to fit Kleeman's expectations. We met to eat together, as usual, and I had a lot on my mind. I had come across an area in the center of the Ark where power supply lines and general purpose tube inputs increased enormously, but it did not seem to be a living area. Everything led to one central area, and that was accessible only with a suitable code. I puzzled over it while I waited for McAndrew to appear.

The whole Ark was bustling with excitement. Kleeman had made the announcement of McAndrew's incorporation to the Council of Intellects. People who had scarcely spoken to him before stopped us and shook his hand solemnly, wishing him well and thanking him for his devotion to the welfare of the Ark. While I drank an aperitif of glucose and dilute ascorbic acid, preparations for a big ceremony were going on around me. A new Council member was a big event.

When I saw McAndrew threading his way towards me past a network of new scaffolding, I knew his morning had been more successful than mine. His thin face was flushed with excitement and pleasure. He slid into the seat opposite me.

"You found your physicist?" I hardly needed to ask the question.

He nodded. "Up on the other side, in a maximum gravity segment directly—right across from here. He's—you have no idea—he's—" McAndrew was practically spluttering in his excitement.

"Start from the beginning." I leaned across and took his hands in mine.

"Yes. I went out on the other side of the Ark, where there's a sort of tower built out from the surface. We must have passed it on the way over from the *Hoatzin* but I didn't notice it then. Kleeman never took us there—never mentioned it to me."

He reached out with one hand across the table, grabbed my drink and took a great gulp of it. "Och, Jeanie, I needed that. I've not stopped since I first opened my eyes. Where was I? I went on up to that tower, and there was nobody to stop me or to say a word. And I went on inside, further out, to the very end of it. The last segment has a window all the way round it, so when you're there you can see the stars and the nebulae wheeling round past your head.''

McAndrew was unusually stirred and his last sentence proved it. The stars were normally considered fit subjects only for theory and computation.

"He was out in that last room," he went on. "After I'd given up hope of finding anybody in this whole place who could have derived those results we got back through Oberon Station. Jeanie, he looks no more than a boy. So blond, and so young. I couldn't believe that he was the one who worked out that theory. But he is. We sat right down at the terminal there, and I started to run over the background for the way that I renormalize the vacuum self-energy. It's nothing like his way. He has a completely different approach, different invariants, different quantization conditions. I think his method is a good deal more easy to generalize. That's why he can get multiple vacuum colors out when we look for resonance conditions. Jeanie, you should have seen his face when I told him that we probably had fifty people at the Institute who would be able to follow his proofs. He's been completely alone here. There's not another one who can even get close to following him, he says. When he sent back those equations, he didn't tell people how important he thought they might be. He says they worry most about the control on what comes in from the System, rather than what goes out from here. I'm awful glad we came here. God, he's an accident, a sport that shows up only once in a couple of centuries—and he was born out there in the void! Did you know, he's taken all the old path integral methods, and he has a form of quantum theory that looks so simple, you'd never believe it if you didn't see it . . .''

He was off again. I had to break in, or he would have talked without stopping, right through our meal. McAndrew doesn't babble often, but when he does he's hard to stop.

"Mac, hold on. Something here doesn't make sense. What about the Council of Intellects?''

"What about it?" He looked as though he had no possible interest in the Council of Intellect—even though the bustle that was going on all around us, with new structures being erected, was all to mark McAndrew's elevation to the Council.

"Look, just yesterday we agreed that the work you're interested in here must have originated with the Council. You told me you hadn't met one person who knew anything worth discussing. Are you telling me now that this work on the vacuum energy *doesn't* come from the people on the Council?"

"I'm sure it doesn't. I doubted that even before I met Wicklund, up there in the tower." McAndrew was looking at me impatiently. "Captain, if that's the impression I gave, it's not what I meant. A thing like this is almost always the work of a single person. It's not initiated by a group, even though a group may help to apply it to practice. This work, the vacuum color work, that's *all* Wicklund—the Council knows nothing of it."

"So what *does* the Council do? I hope you haven't forgotten that you're going to join it later today. I don't think Kleeman would take it well if you said you wanted to change your mind."

He waved an impatient arm at me. "Now, Jeanie, you know I've no time for that. The Council of Intellects is some sort of guiding and advising group, and I'm willing to serve on it and do what I can for the Ark. But not now. I have to get back over to Wicklund and sort out some of the real details. Did I mention that I've explained all about the drive to him? He mops up new material like a sponge. If we can get him back to the Institute he'll catch up on fifty years of System science development in a few months. You know, I'd better go and talk to Kleeman about this Council of hers. What's the use of calling it a Council of Intellects, when people like Wicklund are not on it? And I'll have to tell her we want to take him back with us. I've already mentioned it to him. He's interested, but he's a bit scared of the idea. This is home to him, the only place he knows. Here, is that Kleeman over there by the scaffolding? I'd better catch her now."

He was up and out out of his seat before I could stop him. He hurried over to her, took her to one side and began to speak to her urgently. He was gesturing and cracking his finger joints, in the way that he always did when he was wound up on something. As I moved to join them I could see Kleeman's expression changing from a friendly interest to a solid determination.

"We can't change things now, McAndrew," she was saying. "The departing Member has already been removed from the Council. It is now imperative that the replacement be installed as soon as possible. That ceremony must take place tonight."

"But I want to continue my meetings with—"

"The ceremony will take place tonight. Don't you understand? The Council cannot function unless there are all twelve Members meeting. I cannot discuss this further. There is nothing to discuss."

She turned and walked away. Just as well. McAndrew was all set to tell her that he was not about to join her precious Council, and he was planning to leave the Ark without fathering hundreds, scores, or even ones of children. And he was taking one of her colonists—her subjects—with him. I took his arm firmly and dragged him back to our table.

"Calm down, Mac." I spoke as urgently as I could. "Don't fly off wild now. Let's get this stupid Council initiation rite out of the way today, and then let's wait a while and approach Kleeman on all this when she's in a more reasonable mood, right?"

"That damned, obstinate, overbearing woman. Who the hell does she think she is?"

"She thinks she's the boss of the Ark of Massingham, and she *is* the boss of the Ark of Massingham. Face facts. Slow down now, and go back to Wicklund. See if he's interested in leaving when we leave, but don't push it too hard. Let's wait a few days, there's nothing to be lost from that."

How naive can you get? Kleeman had told us exactly what was going on, but we hadn't listened. People hear what they expect to hear.

I found out the truth the idiot's way. After McAndrew had gone off again, calm enough to talk of his new protege, I had about four hours to kill. The great ceremony in which McAndrew would become part of the Council of Intellects would not take place until after the next meal. I decided I would have another look at the closed room that I had seen on my earlier roaming.

The room was still locked, but this time there was a servicewoman working on the pipes that led into it. She recognized me as one of the two recent arrivals on the Ark—the less important one, according to Ark standards.

"Tonight's the big event," she said to me, her manner friendly. "You've come to take a look at the place your friend will be, have you? You know, we really need him. The Council has been almost useless for the past two years, with one Member almost gone. Kleeman knew that, but she didn't seem happy to provide a new Member until she met McAndrew."

She obviously assumed I knew all about the Council and its workings. I stepped closer, keeping my voice casual and companionable. "I'll see all this for myself tonight. McAndrew will be in here, right? I wonder if I could take a peek now, I've never been inside before."

"Sure." She went to the door and keyed in a combination. "There's been talk for a while now of moving the Council to another part of Home, where there's less vibration from construction work. No sign of it happening yet, though. Here we go. You won't be able to go inside the inner room, of course, but you'll find you can see most things from the service area."

As the door slid open I stepped through into a long, brightly-lit room. It was empty.

My heart began to pound urgently and my mouth was as dry as Ceres. Strange, how the *absence* of something can produce such a powerful effect on the body.

"Where are they?" I said at last. "The Council. You said they are in this room."

She looked at me in comical disbelief. "Well, you didn't expect to find them out *here,* did you? Take a look through the hatch at the end there."

We walked forward together and peered through a transparent panel at the far end of the room. It led through to another, smaller chamber, this one dimly lit by a soft green glow.

My eyes took a few seconds to adapt. The big, translucent

tank in the center of the room slowly came into definition. All around it, equally spaced, were twelve smaller sections, all inter-connected through a massive set of branching cables and optic bundles.

"Well, there they are," said the servicewoman. "Doesn't look right, does it, with one of them missing like this? It doesn't work, either. The information linkages are all built for a set of exactly twelve units, with a twelve-by-twelve transfer matrix."

Now I could see that one of the small tanks was empty. In each of the eleven others, coupled to a set of thin plastic tubes and contact wires, was a complex shape, a dark-grey ovoid swimming in a bath of green fluid. The surfaces were folded and convoluted, glistening with the sticky sheen of animal tissues. At the lower end, each human brain thinned away past the brain stem to the spinal chord.

I remember asking her just one question.

"What would happen if the twelfth Member of the Council of Intellects were not connected in today?"

"It would be bad." She looked shocked. "Very bad. I don't know the details, but I think all the potentials would run wild in a day or two, and destroy the other eleven. It has never happened. There have always been twelve members of the Council, since Massingham created it. He is the one over there, on the far right."

We must have spoken further, but already my mind was winging its way back to the dining area. I was to meet McAndrew one hour before the big ceremony. 'Incorporation', that was what Kleeman had called it, incorporation into the Council. De-corporation would be a better name for the process. But the Council of Intellects was well-named. After someone has been pared down, flesh, bone and organs, to a brain and a spinal column, intellect is all that can remain. Perhaps the thing that had upset me more than anything in that inner room had been their decision to leave the eyes intact. They were there, attached to each brain by the protruding stalks of their optic nerves. They looked like the horns of a snail, blue, grey or brown balls projecting from the frontal lobes. Since there were no muscles left to change the focal length of the eye lenses, they were directed to display screens set at fixed distances from the tanks.

The wait in the dining area was a terrible period. I had been all right on the way back from the Council Chamber, there had been movement to make the tension tolerable, but when McAndrew finally appeared my nerves had become awfully ragged. He was all set to burble on about his physics discussions. I cut him off before he could get out one word.

"Mac, don't speak and don't make any quick move. We have to leave the Ark. Now."

"Jeanie!" Then he saw my face. "What about Wicklund? We've talked again and he wants to go with us—but he's not ready."

I shook my head and looked down at the table top. It was the worst possible complication. We had to move through the Ark and transfer across to the *Hoatzin*, without being noticed. If Kleeman sensed our intentions, Mac might still make it to the Council. My fate was less certain but probably even worse—if a worse fate is imaginable. It would be hard enough doing what we had to do without the addition of a nervous and inexperienced young physicist. But I knew McAndrew.

"Go get him," I said at last. "Remember the lock we came in by?"

He nodded. "I can get us there. When?"

"Half an hour. Don't let him bring anything with him—we'll be working with a narrow margin."

He stood up and walked away without another word. So he probably wouldn't have agreed to go without Wicklund; but he hadn't asked me for any explanation, hadn't insisted on a reason why we had to leave. That sort of trust isn't built up overnight. I was scared shitless as I stood up and left the dining area, but in an obscure way I was feeling that warm glow you only feel when two people touch deeply. McAndrew had sensed a life-or-death issue.

Back at our sleeping quarters I picked up the comlink that gave me coded access to the computer on the *Hoatzin*. We had to make sure the ship was still in the same position. I followed my own directive and took nothing else. Kal Massingham Kleeman was a lady whose anger was best experienced from a distance—I

had in mind a light-year or two. I was only concerned now with
the first couple of kilometers of that. We might find it necessary
to move out of the Ark in a hurry.

The interior of the Ark was a great warren of connecting
tunnels, so there were a hundred ways between any two points.
That was just as well. I changed my path whenever I saw anyone
else approaching, but I was still able to move steadily in the
direction of our entry lock.

Twenty minutes since McAndrew had left. Now the speaker
system crackled and came to life.

"Everyone will assemble in Main Hall Five."

The ceremony was ready to begin. Kleeman was going to
produce Hamlet without the Prince. I stepped up my pace. The
trip through the interior of the Ark was taking longer than I
expected, and I was going to be late.

Thirty minutes, and I was still one corridor away. The
monitors in the passage ceiling suddenly came to life, their red
lenses glowing. All I could do was keep moving. There was no
way of avoiding those monitors, they extended through the
whole interior of the Ark.

"McAndrew and Roker." It was Kleeman's voice, calm and
superior. "We are waiting for you. There will be punishment
unless you come here at once to Main Hall Five. Your presence
in the outer section has been noted. A collection detail will
arrive there any moment now. McAndrew, do not forget that the
Council awaits you. You are abusing a great honor by your
actions."

I was at last at the lock. McAndrew stood there listening to
Kleeman's voice. The young man by his side—as Mac had said,
so blond, so young—had to be Wicklund. Behind those soft blue
eyes lay a brain that even McAndrew found impressive.
Wicklund was frowning now, his expression indecisive. All his
ideas on life had been turned upside down in the past days, and
now Kleeman's words must be giving him second thoughts
about our escape.

Without speaking, McAndrew turned and pointed towards
the wall of the lock. I looked, and felt a sudden sickness. The
wall where the line of suits should be hanging was empty.

"No suits?" I said stupidly.

He nodded. "Kleeman has been thinking a move ahead of you."

"You know what joining the Council would imply?"

He nodded again. His face was grey. "Wicklund told me as we came over here. I couldn't believe it at first. I asked him, what about the children Kleeman wanted me to sire? They would drain me for the sperm bank before they . . ." He swallowed. There was a long and terrible pause. "I looked out," he said at last. "Through the viewport there. The capsule is still where we left it."

"You're willing to chance it?" I looked at Wicklund, who stood there not following our conversation at all.

"I am." Mac nodded. "But what about him? There's no Sturm Invocation for people here on the Ark."

As I had feared, Wicklund was a major complication. I walked forward and stood in front of him. "Do you still want to go with us?"

He licked his lips, then nodded.

"Into the lock." We moved forward together and I closed the inner door.

"Do not be foolish." It was Kleeman's voice again, this time with a new expression of alarm. "There is nothing to be served by sacrificing yourselves to space. McAndrew, you are a rational man. Come back, and we will discuss this together. Do not waste your potential by a pointless death."

I took a quick look through the port of the outer lock. The capsule was there all right, it looked just the same as when we left it. Wicklund was staring out in horror. Until Kleeman had spoken, it did not seem to have occurred to him that we were facing death in the void.

"Mac!" I said urgently.

He nodded, and gently took Wicklund by the shoulders, swinging him around to face him. I stepped up behind him and dug hard into the nerve centers at the base of his neck. He was unconscious in two seconds.

"Ready, Mac?"

Another quick nod. I checked that Wicklund's eyelids were

closed, and that his breathing was shallow. He would be unconscious for another couple of minutes, pulse rate low and oxygen
need reduced.

McAndrew stood at the outer lock, ready to open it. I pulled
the whistle from the lapel of my jacket and blew hard. The
varying triple tone sounded through the lock. Penalty for im-
proper use of any Sturm Invocation was severe, whether you
used spoken, whistled, or electronic methods. I had never used
it before.

Anyone who goes into space, even if it is just a short trip from
Earth to Moon, must receive Sturm vacuum survival programing. One person in a million uses it. I stood in the lock, waiting
to see what would happen to me.

The sensation was strange. I still had full command of my
actions, but there was also a new set of involuntary activities.
Without any conscious decision to do so, I found that I was
breathing hard, hyper-ventilating in great gulps. My eye-
blinking pattern had reversed. Instead of open eyes with rapid
blinks to moisten and clean the eyeball, my lids were closed
except for brief instants. I saw the lock and the outside as quick
snapshots.

The Sturm Invocation had the same effect on McAndrew, as
his own deep programing took over for vacuum exposure. When
I nodded, he swung open the outer lock door. The air was gone
in a puff of ice vapor. As my eyes flicked open I saw the capsule
at the top of the landing tower. To reach it we had to traverse
sixty meters of the interstellar vacuum. And we had to carry
Wicklund's unconscious body between us.

For some reason I had imagined that the Sturm vacuum
programing would make me insensitive to all pain. Quite illogi-
cal, since you could permanently damage your body all too
easily in that situation. I felt the agony of expansion through my
intestines, as the air rushed out of all my body cavities. My
mouth was performing an automatic yawning and gasping,
emptying the Eustachian tube to protect my ear drums and
delicate inner ear. My eyes were closed to protect the eyeballs
from freezing, and open just often enough to guide my body
movements.

Holding Wicklund between us, McAndrew and I pushed off

into the open depths of space. Ten seconds later, we intersected the landing tower about twenty meters up. Sturm couldn't make a human comfortable in space, but he had provided a set of natural movements that corresponded to a zero gee environment. They were needed. If we missed the tower there was no other landing point within light years.

The metal of the landing tower was at a temperature several hundred degrees below freezing. Our hands were unprotected, and I could feel the ripping of skin at each contact. That was perhaps the worst pain. The feeling that I was a ball, over-inflated and ready to burst, was not a pain. What was it? That calls for the same sort of skills as describing sight to a blind man. All I can say is that once in a lifetime is more than enough.

Thirty seconds in the vacuum, and we were still fifteen meters from the capsule. I was getting the first feeling of anoxia, the first moment of panic. As we dropped into the capsule and tagged shut the hatch I could feel the black clouds moving around me, dark nebulae that blanked out the bright star field.

The transfer capsule had no real air lock. When I hit the air supply, the whole interior began to fill with warm oxygen. As the concentration grew to a perceptible fraction of an atmosphere, I felt something turn off abruptly within me. My eye blinking went back to the usual pattern, my mouth closed instead of gaping and gasping, and the black patches started to dwindle and fragment.

I turned on the drive of the transfer vessel to take us on our fifty kilometer trip to the *Hoatzin* and glanced quickly at the other two. Wicklund was still unconscious, eyes closed but breathing normally. He had come through well. McAndrew was something else. There was blood flowing from the corner of his mouth and he was barely conscious. He must have been much closer to collapse than I when we dropped into the capsule, but he had not loosened his grip on Wicklund.

I felt a moment of irritation. Damn that man. He had assured me that he would replace that damaged lung lobe after our last trip but I was pretty sure he had done nothing about it. This time I would see he had the operation, if I had to take him there myself.

He began to cough weakly and his eyes opened. When he saw

that we were in the capsule and Wicklund was between us, he smiled a little and let his eyes close again. I put the drive on maximum and noticed for the first time the blood that was running from my left hand. The palm and fingers were raw flesh, skin ripped off by the hellish cold of the landing tower. I reached behind me and pulled out the capsule's small medical kit. Major fix-ups would have to wait until we were on the *Hoatzin*. The surrogate flesh was bright yellow, like a thick mustard, but it took away the pain. I smeared it over my own hand, then reached across and did the same for McAndrew. His face was beginning to blaze with the bright red of broken capillaries, and I was sure that I looked just the same. That was nothing. It was the bright blood dribbling down his blue tunic that I didn't like.

Wicklund was awake. He winced and held his hands up to his ears. There might be a burst eardrum there, something else we would have to take care of when we got to the *Hoatzin*.

"How did I get here?" he said wonderingly.

"Across the vacuum. Sorry we had to put you out like that, but I didn't think you could have faced a vacuum passage when you were conscious."

His gaze turned slowly to McAndrew. "Is he all right?"

"I hope so. There may be some lung damage that we'll have to take care of. Want to do something to help?"

He nodded, then turned back to look at the ball of the Ark, dwindling behind us. "They can't catch us now, can they?"

"They might try, but I don't think so. Kleeman probably considers anybody who wants to leave the Ark is not worth having. Here, take the blue tube out of the kit behind you and smear it on your face and hands. Do the same for McAndrew. It will speed up the repair of the ruptured blood vessels in your skin."

Wicklund took the blue salve and began to apply it tenderly to McAndrew's face. After a couple of seconds Mac opened his eyes and smiled. "Thank you, lad," he said softly. "I'd talk more physics with you, but somehow I don't quite feel that I'm up to it."

"Just lie there quiet." There was hero worship in Wicklund's voice. I had a sudden premonition of what the return trip was going to be like. McAndrew and Wicklund in a mutual admiration society, and all the talk of physics.

After we had the capsule back on board the *Hoatzin* I felt secure for the first time. We installed McAndrew comfortably on one of the bunks while I went to the drive unit and set a maximum-acceleration course back to the Solar System. Wicklund's attention was torn between his need to talk to McAndrew and his fascination with the drive and the ship. How would Einstein have felt in 1905, if someone could have shown him a working nuclear reactor just a few months after he had developed the mass-energy relation? It must have been like that for Wicklund.

"Want to take a last look?" I said, my hand on the drive keyboard.

He came across and gazed at the Ark, still set on its long journey to Tau Ceti. He looked sad, and I felt guilty.

"I'm sorry," I said. "We should have asked you if you wanted to come with us before we put you under. But I'm afraid there's no going back now."

"I know." He hesitated. "You found Home a bad place, I could tell from what McAndrew said. But it's not so bad. To me, it was home for my whole life."

"We'll talk to the Ark again. There may be a chance to come here later, when we've had more time to study the life that you lived. I hope you'll find a new life in the System."

I meant it, but I was having a sudden vision of the Earth we were heading back to. Crowded, noisy, short of all resources. Wicklund might find it as hellish as we had found life on the Ark of Massingham. It was too late to do anything about it now. I suspected that this sort of problem meant less to Wicklund than it would to most people. Like McAndrew, his real life was lived inside his own head, and all else was secondary to that private vision.

I pressed the key sequence and the drive went on. Within seconds, the Ark had vanished from sight.

I turned back and was surprised to see that McAndrew was sitting up in his bunk. He looked terrible, but he must be feeling better. His hands were yellow paws of surrogate flesh, his face and neck a bright blue coating of the ointment that Wicklund had applied to them. The dribble of blood that had come from his mouth had spread its bright stain down his chin and over the front of his tunic, mixing with the blue fabric to produce a horrible purple splash.

"How are you, Mac?" I said.

"Not bad. Not bad at all." He forced a smile.

"Ready for that lung operation now?"

"Och, Jeanie." He gave a feeble shrug. "We'll see. Let's get on home, and then we'll see. I've learned a lot on this trip, more than I ever expected. It's all been well worth it."

He caught my sceptical look. "Honest, now, this is more important than you realize. We'll make the next trip out more like what you thought you were getting—maybe to one of the stars. I'm sorry you got nothing out of this one."

I stared at him. He looked like a circus clown, all smears and streaks. I shook my head.

"I got something out of it."

He looked puzzled. "How's that?"

"I listen to you and the other physicists all the time, and usually I don't understand a word of it. This time I know just what you mean. Lie quiet, and I'll be back in a second."

All the colors of the vacuum? If a picture is worth a thousand words, there are times when a mirror is worth more than that. I wanted to watch Mac's face when he saw his reflection.

AFTERWORD: ALL THE COLORS OF THE VACUUM.

In the Afterword to "The Man Who Stole The Moon," I described my confusion when I received a letter from a reader who was pleased to find a hidden reference there to Heinlein's hero, Delos D. Harriman. This story provides me with even more confusing evidence that most of my brain is quite outside my conscious control.

The story was published in the February, 1981, issue of ANALOG. Before the end of the month I received a letter from a reader. He referred me to the works of Sylvester, the 19th Century English mathematician, in one of which he described his first meeting with the French mathematician Poincaré. My description of McAndrew's first encounter with Wicklund, the reader said, was obviously drawn from Sylvester's experience. Even the physical appearance was the same.

Fine.

The only trouble with this idea is that, whereas I had certainly read Heinlein's "The Man Who Sold The Moon" and could well be subconsciously cueing my story and characters to it, I had never to my knowledge read one word of Sylvester that was not in a mathematical paper, and he would not be talking there of an encounter with Poincaré".

I stewed on this for a week or two, without result, and was ready to say the whole thing was blind coincidence. Finally, more or less at random, I went down to the basement and hunted through old books until I found a battered copy of Eric Temple Bell's MEN OF MATHEMATICS. There is a chapter on Poincaré, and in it I found this: "Elsewhere Sylvester records his bewilderment when, after having toiled up the three flights of stairs leading to Poincaré's airy perch, he paused, mopping his magnificent bald head, in astonishment at beholding a mere boy, 'so blond, so young,' as the author of the deluge of papers which had heralded the advent of a successor to Cauchy."

I have read MEN OF MATHEMATICS, so one could argue that this explains the mystery. But not to me. I read the book when I was sixteen years old, and since then I am convinced I have never looked again at that chapter.

When we understand the storage and recall procedures of the human memory, we'll be able to build a very interesting computer.

PERFECTLY SAFE,
NOTHING TO
WORRY ABOUT

"A bit lower on the left. Bit more. There, that's it. Hold it right there."

I held it as Waldo directed and he drove in the last nail, then stepped back. Perfect. We looked at the sign and beamed at each other.

'Burmeister & Carver—Legal Advisors.' The old firm, a long way from Washington D.C., but back in business again.

We went into the office and closed the door. Not much space inside—it cost ten credits a square foot, unfurnished, for rentals in Tharsis City. But we had one respectable-sized office, and a much less fancy office/utility room behind it. We'd agreed to take turns manning the front office until we built up enough business to spread ourselves a bit. As the first and only lawyers on Mars, we were sure that wouldn't take long.

I went back to my desk in the rear office—Waldo was taking the first shift out front. Then I came straight out again. Fifteen minutes earlier there had been a jelly doughnut on my table. I looked at Waldo and began, "Waldo, did you—?"

What was the use? I gave up in mid-sentence. In the twenty years since we left law school I'd seen Waldo swell from a youth of sylphlike elegance to a first-order man-mountain. The time he'd spent (more accurately, done) on the Venus terra-forming project had thinned him, temporarily, but as soon as he reached Mars he'd started to swell again. I'd bullied, insulted, cajoled, lectured and warned Waldo. If he kept on eating the way he did, one day he'd explode. He listened contritely, swore he'd diet at once, implored me to keep sweet stuff out of his reach and thanked me for trying to help. Then as soon as my back was turned—chomp.

As it turned out, we had been over-optimistic about the number of cases that would come our way. True, we were the only lawyers for forty million miles, and Mars did have a population of several thousand. But—no business. I maintain that where a barbarian would pick up a rock or a tree root to settle a dispute, a civilized man picks up a videophone and seeks legal counsel. Measured by that standard, Mars was too busy scrabbling for survival to qualify above the barbarian level. For the first three weeks I had little to do but sit about, watching Waldo occupy a steadily increasing amount of the available office space.

When our first client finally arrived, Waldo was manning the front desk and I was sitting in the back office looking at a lunar travel brochure. Waldo collected them. I was reading a poetic description of a valley of mud, dust and rock when I heard the door of the outer office.

"Are you Burmeister and Carver?" asked an unfamiliar voice.

"We are. I am Waldo Burmeister, at your service."

"I'm Peter Pinton. I've got something extremely valuable here and I'd like to leave it with you to lock in your safe."

Waldo's visitor seemed to be confusing us with a bank. We didn't have a safe, just a big cupboard in the back room with a defective lock. I sneaked a look through a narrow crack in the illfitting and badly made door between our inner and outer offices. Our visitor was very tall and lanky, with brown hair and a pair of innocent and startlingly blue eyes. His dress told me that he was a ranger—probably a geologist, roving around outside the domed city areas. Waldo had responded instinctively to the words 'extremely valuable' and had Pinton already seated in our one comfortable chair.

What would it be? Precious metals, old artifacts, Martian superfluids? I could almost hear the cash registers ringing in Waldo's head.

"In our safe, Mr. Pinton? Of course. Where is your deposit?"

Waldo hadn't missed a beat. Pinton reached into his brown,

bulky jacket and produced a small phial, about the size of a pill bottle, containing a pale, oily-looking liquid. Since Pinton couldn't see me I felt free to register my disappointment.

Waldo looked at the bottle dubiously. "What exactly is it, Mr. Pinton?"

"It's Pintonite, that's what it is." Our visitor smiled happily. "It's going to make me the richest man on Mars. I always suspected there should be something like this here—I've looked in places where the areology is right for ten years, and I've finally found and refined it." He held up the bottle. "The most powerful chemical explosive ever known, by a factor of ten. One gram's enough to blow a ten-meter crater in solid rock. It'll revolutionize mining on the asteroids."

Peter Pinton must have noticed Waldo's lack of enthusiasm at the idea of looking after a super-bomb. "Perfectly safe, nothing to worry about," he added. He shook the bottle with great vigor.

I screamed so hard that no sound came out and clapped my hands over my ears. Waldo, with an equally sound protective logic, covered his eyes with his hands. Pinton cackled inanely. "Perfectly safe. Only explodes under very special conditions. Safe as water."

He reached into his jacket again and produced a five thousand credit note. "Here's a down payment. I'll need your help when the time comes to negotiate on this with General Mining."

Now he was talking. I breathed again, but Waldo still seemed curiously reluctant to touch the phial or the money. I decided that it was time to introduce myself to our new client.

I had second thoughts as I came into the room. Peter Pinton was offering the phial to Waldo with his right hand and absent-mindedly scratching himself around the ribs with his left. No wonder Waldo was hesitant. I've read a hundred theories as to how Earth fleas evaded pre-flight inspection to get to Mars, and I don't believe any of them. But when you've seen how far a flea can jump under a surface gravity only two-fifths that of Earth, and with an atmosphere in the domed cities only one-third as dense, you have no trouble understanding how they've managed to spread the way they have. I could detect ripples of sympathetic itching running up and down Waldo's back. As Peter

Pinton and I shook hands and he gave me the money and phial, I
watched him closely for emigrants.

Pinton seemed relieved to be rid of the bottle. "I told Muriel I
wanted somebody else to look after the Pintonite this morning.
I'm not comfortable carrying valuables in the domicibile. I feel a
lot easier now. Well, I'll be off. See you in a few days. I want to
hear what Muriel says when I tell her you're looking after the
Pintonite."

"Your wife?" I asked politely.

He looked at me curiously. "Now what would a man want
with a woman, out in the red ranges? Muriel's my parrot." And
he was gone without further comment.

Waldo took a big gulp of unsweetened coffee absent-
mindedly as Pinton left the room. His face puckered like a
punctured Mars dome. For the past couple of days he'd been
holding down on his calories and we'd thrown out every temptation. The change so far was imperceptible.

I locked the money in our cash box and went through to the
inner office to put Pinton's phial into the big cupboard, in among
the crockery, stationery, low-calorie food items and legal reference volumes. I put it on the bottom shelf, next to Waldo's
weighing-machine. He'd bought a spring balance, and derived
comfort from the thought that he weighed less than eighty
kilos—his 'college weight,' as he described it. I wondered if he
was looking at lunar brochures for his next stopping-point when
his Mars-weight topped eighty.

In the front office Waldo had a dreamy expression in his eyes.
"If General Mining would pay Pinton a million credits for the
rights to Pintonite, I bet that United Chemicals would offer
double."

I nodded. We discussed it no further. As Disraeli remarked,
sensible men are all of the same religion. And pray, what is that?
Sensible men never tell. Substitute 'financial views' for 'religion' there, and you have my attitude exactly.

The next time Peter Pinton showed up at the office I was on
my own. Waldo had gone off for a meeting 'with an industrial
group' and I had not asked for details. Pinton sat down with the

neat movements of a man who spent most of his life inside a three by four meter domicibile—the standard house/mobile lab/explorer vehicle of the Mars rangers. He took a small jar of white crystals from his jacket pocket and placed it on the table.

"Version two," he said. "Purified, ten times as powerful per gram. Take this for your safe and give me the other one back—I need it for a little demonstration later this week."

I hesitated and he misunderstood my reluctance. "Oh, it's as safe as the last lot. Under any normal circumstances, perfectly neutral. See here." He unscrewed the top of the jar, licked his finger tip, dipped it in the white powder and stuck it in his mouth. He grinned happily as I goggled.

"Perfectly safe. Want a lick? It doesn't taste of much," he assured me. "Sort of yeasty and a bit sweet."

I declined the offer and went reluctantly through to the inner office. I closed the door—so Pinton wouldn't see the non-existent safe—and opened the cupboard to get the phial. Would it still be there? Thank heaven, it was, just where I had left it. Perhaps I had misjudged Waldo's meeting. Feeling much happier I placed the jar of crystal Pintonite in the cupboard and gave his phial back to Pinton. I sat down again behind the desk. Pinton seemed in no hurry and in a chatty mood, and I wanted certain information from him.

"Occurs naturally on Mars?" he said, repeating my question. "Yes, in crude form. Now that's not suprising—Mars has a different geological history from Earth, so we expect some different compounds. Pintonite's an isomeric hydrocarbon-fluorocarbon form—just as diamond is a form of carbon, created under special conditions in the history of the planet."

"You mean you could make Pintonite from other things, the way we make diamonds?"

"Sure—if you knew the chemical structure and were smart enough, you could synthesize it. But why bother? There's plenty here on Mars if you're smart enough to know where to look and what to look for." He preened himself. "You see, the thing that makes Pintonite so powerful is just an unusual hydrocarbon bond. It's like a compressed spring, with a catch on

it. Unhook the catch, and all that energy in the spring is released.
The secret's in the chemical structure.''

"And that can be found by measurement?"

"Sure. Any run-of-the-mill lab could do it. That's why I
wanted to have it here, where it's safe, and not where the
industrial espionage boys could lay their hands on it."

His simple trust in the legal profession was touching. My
suspicions that he was a little cracked were growing. As he left,
those suspicions were given a strong boost by our neighbor
along the corridor. She was a youngish, talkative mother of
three, with a husband who worked the day shift outside the
domes in the open-field agricultural area. According to Waldo,
she fancied me—by comparison, I suppose—but I had so far
survived with my honor intact.

As Peter Pinton departed she came along the corridor and
looked into the office. Her hair had so many curlers in it that she
seemed to be wearing an elaborate bronze headpiece.

"What's old Pete been doing in here?" she inquired. "I
haven't seen him for a year or two."

"Legal matters, Mrs. Wilkinson—I can't betray a client's
confidences, you know. Where did you meet Mr. Pinton?"

"Oh, me and him had a thing going for a while. Never got too
serious, though. He was always too busy during the day—not
like you lawyers." She paused and eyed me speculatively for a
few moments. Gambit declined, she went on. "Anyway, I got a
bit tired of him after a while. He was always going on about his
bloody parrot. No wonder they all called him Looney Pete."

She turned her head back along the corridor, revealing the full
splendor of her ormolu helmet, and shouted a snappy reply to a
child's question. Then she smiled at me alluringly. "I'm just
going to have a cup of coffee and a little something to go with it,
Mr. Carver. Perhaps you'd like to join me?"

As she raised her plucked eyebrows inquiringly, Waldo's
familiar figure loomed over her shoulder. I looked at him with
relief. She gave him a savage glare and then disappeared down
the corridor. Waldo was in excellent spirits. I wondered just
what he'd been up to. Well, regardless of that I had work of my

own to do now, as soon as I could find the right place to help me. But I must admit that I didn't feel comforted by our lady neighbor's report on our client, Mr. Peter Pinton.

Neither Waldo nor I were particularly alarmed at first when the Tharsis City police arrived. Our licenses were in good shape, and our credentials to practice law on Mars impeccable. As the only two lawyers on the planet, we had framed the bar charter ourselves.

Police Investigator Lestrade had with him a saturnine, dark-haired man from General Mining, a double for Bela Lugosi in the classic Dracula 2-D movies, whom he introduced to us as Test Supervisor Kozak.

Like most Martians, they seemed puzzled by what Waldo and I actually *did* for a living. We explained our activities and they dutifully recorded them with a slight air of disbelief. After the general introductions Lestrade cleared his throat, scratched his thinning pate, and got down to business.

"Yesterday, Mr. Peter Pinton gave a demonstration of a powerful new explosive to General Mining. Mr. Kozak supervised the test." Lestrade spoke very slowly, picking his words with care. "Now, we would like you to tell us all that you know about that explosive, Pintonite."

He stopped. We waited. No more words came, apparently he was done. I was puzzled by his accusing manner and wondered again if Waldo had been up to something.

"I think there may be a misunderstanding," I finally replied. "We know very little. We're not geologists or chemists, you know. You want to talk to Peter Pinton himself—he's the expert."

"You can ask him," said Lestrade morosely. He placed a silver box on the desk, about the same size and shape as a portable communicator. I looked at it for the send/receive button but couldn't see it. I looked questioningly at Lestrade, who pressed a catch on the side of the box. The top opened to reveal a layer of grey powder inside.

"There's Peter Pinton, all there is of him." Lestrade looked at the box with a certain macabre satisfaction. "When he brought in his explosive, with his claim that it was superpowerful and completely safe, Mr. Kozak insisted on a controlled demonstration. They put Pinton inside a sealed metal tank to set up the test and watched from outside. Pinton was half right, you might say—it's far and away the most powerful explosive anybody has ever seen. But Pinton hadn't told anybody the chemical formula for it. Mr. Kozak came to see us after the explosion yesterday afternoon, and this morning we went over to see Polly—"

"—his parrot," Waldo interjected, nodding intelligently.

"—Polly Pinton, his ex-wife, now living in Chryse Dome," Lestrade went on. He scrutinized Waldo closely, as though mentally measuring him for a straitjacket. "She told us that Pinton had left a sample of the explosive with Henry Carver and Waldo Burmeister, Lawyers, at this address."

I sighed. So much for a deal with United Chemicals. I looked at Waldo. He shrugged and went into the back room to get the Pintonite sample.

After half a minute of banging around in the cupboard he was back, pale and sweating.

"Henry, it's not there." He signalled his next message with his eyes, as clearly as if he had spoken it: "What have you done with it, Henry?"

I was shocked. "It must be there, Waldo, I saw it just yesterday. Let me take a look."

I went into the back room and did a lightning but thorough search of the cupboard. No jar of white crystals, not a sign of it.

"Henry, for God's sake, don't play games," whispered Waldo from just behind me. "Tell them what you did with it, we can't do any deals now."

I turned back to him. "What do you mean, play games? Aren't you the one who took it to United Chemicals?"

He shook his head. "I was supposed to meet them again tomorrow, with a sample."

We looked at each other in dismay and stupefaction. Finally we went back into the outer office and faced Lestrade. He took the news that the Pintonite was gone with no emotion. It seemed almost as though he had expected something like that. He nodded slowly.

"We'll have to do a deep probe to get information on this. Who was here when Peter Pinton brought that explosive in and discussed storing it with you?"

"I was," Waldo reluctantly volunteered.

"And were you present, Mr. Carver?" asked Lestrade.

"Only at the very end of the meeting." Thank heaven for literal truth, and for the legal definition of present.

"Right. Mr. Burmeister, you'll have to come with us. This examination will take a few hours."

The game was over all right. But thank heaven, too, for my own foresight. I took out my wallet with a sigh and removed a slip of paper from it.

"I don't think that will be necessary, Mr. Lestrade. This contains the chemical anlysis of a Pintonite sample, performed just a few days ago."

I handed it to him. Waldo looked like a man reprieved at the eleventh hour—psychoprobes were tough stuff and a few people came out of them with their brains permanently scrambled. Kozak leapt on the paper with a cry of joy and read it while we watched.

After a few seconds of inspection he began to turn into a vampire. His teeth curled back from his upper lip and a deep snarl came from him. He seemed all set to leap and suck blood.

"Mr. Carver," he finally said in choked tones. "You had a chemical anlysis done. I suppose you are willing to tell us what type of analysis was performed?"

Now I was really confused. "Well, of course I am. I asked them to do the most final and complete one that they could. I forget the exact word that was used on the order."

"An ultimate analysis?"

"Yes, that's it exactly."

"You scientific illiterate," he screamed at once. "You great baboon." My information didn't seem to have pleased him. "An *ultimate* chemical analysis gives the final chemical composition in terms of the percentage of each element. It doesn't tell you a thing about the chemical *structure*." He waved the paper in the air, literally gnashing his teeth as he did so. I'd never encountered that before outside the holodramas. "This just gives the amount of carbon, hydrogen, oxygen and fluorine. I could no more make Pintonite from this information than I could make your friend here—" He glowered at Waldo. "—from a barrel of lard and a sack of flour."

An unfortunate example, I felt, and quite uncalled for. They dragged poor Waldo away to his fate. I hoped he'd be back again, intact, in a few hours. What on Earth—what on Mars— had gone wrong? I was sure Waldo had told me the truth—so where was the Pintonite?

I wandered around the office, looking everywhere I could think of for the missing jar. No sign. I picked up the useless chemical analysis paper—my trump card—and looked at it sadly. Then I crumpled it into a ball and went through to the inner office to throw it into the trash.

I opened the lid of the trash can—and froze. Suddenly, I understood exactly what had happened to the Pintonite. It had never occurred to me to tell Waldo that Peter Pinton had switched the phial of liquid for a jar of crystalline Pintonite. Waldo had been looking for the phial, while I'd looked for the jar. Now I'd found it. Empty. Waldo, in his insane lust for sweetmeats, had used three ounces of Pintonite to sugar his coffee. "Yeasty and sweet," Pinton had said.

When events call for it I can be a man of action. In less than ten minutes I had made reservations for Waldo and myself, immediate departure for Deimos. It was time that Burmeister and Carver found new business offices. I'd write and tell the Tharsis City police all about recent events, but I'd much rather do it from off-planet. I had a clear mental picture of three ounces of Pintonite going into and through Waldo. Tharsis City had, as I recalled, more than thirty thousand meters of sewage pipes beneath it. I could visualize a thin layer of Pintonite spread through every bit. Peter Pinton had said that it was perfectly safe, but his reputation as a reliable authority had diminished considerably in the past few hours. If the Tharsis City plumbing arrangements happened to have the right environment to set it off, it might not be the biggest explosion in the history of Mars, but it would certainly be the most disgusting.

I sat down to wait impatiently for Waldo's return. On second thoughts, I called and modified our space travel reservations. I didn't know how long it took Pintonite to pass completely through the human alimentary canal. Separate flights. If Waldo was about to fulfill my old warning and finally, literally, explode, I would rather not participate in the event.

AFTERWORD: PERFECTLY SAFE, NOTHING TO WORRY ABOUT.

About three years ago our after-dinner conversation turned to the taboos of science fiction. There are, we all agreed, many subjects that have never been written about, not perhaps because they are truly shocking but because they are generally disgusting and awful.

We made a list. Then we worked on it to eliminate duplicates and categories that reflected very personal prejudices ("Frenchmen" and "rice pudding" were in the original set of disgusting things). Then I was given the final condensed list and told to write stories about all the items on it.

Pigs and lice and personal hygiene and fleas and gross fatness and sewage and dental appointments have all been more or less done, and I am steadily working my way through the rest. It is slow going. Writing Parasites Lost *was a real effort, and* Space Opera *keeps trying to convert itself from a short story to a novel.*

I'll be very glad when the list is finished. It is a slow road to literary immortality, and as the tom-cat making love to the skunk said after the first hour or two, I really think I've enjoyed about as much of this as I can stand.

SUMMERTIDE

"Genocide?" My tone showed my disbelief.

Governor Wethel shrugged his shoulders at me in an embarrassed way and turned to his companion without trying to answer me.

"Perhaps you should explain this, Dr. Rebka."

"I intend to." Rebka was a small, thin man, with sharp grey eyes and a long, mournful mouth. His voice was dry and even, with just a trace of accent to reveal that he had not been raised in our System. "Cooperation from both of you will be essential, and I know that I could not command it here for any ordinary crime. Did Governor Wethel tell you where this journey began?"

I nodded. Wethel had time for that and for little else when he had linked through from Cloudside, to tell me that he was flying over, top priority, with a visitor.

"I understand that you were on Lasalle—Delta Pavonis Four. I wondered what a Section Moderator could be doing there. All it has are marshes and Zardalu."

"Not quite right." Moderator Rebka's voice had become flatter yet. "All that Lasalle has now are marshes. The Zardalu are extinct. The last surviving members—two lodges—died two Earth-months ago. The people who killed them escaped from the Pavonis System long before I got there, but I have been able to trace them through four jumps. To here."

I took another look at Sector Moderator Rebka. For the first time, I stared hard at the symbols on the gold cluster fixed to the sleeve of his black jacket. Inside the main pattern was a tiny seven-pointed star. Why hadn't Wethel told me that Rebka belonged to the Species Protection Council? He might be polite enough to ask for our cooperation, but if Rebka wanted to he could do just about anything he liked—including taking over my job or Governor Wethel's.

I looked again at him, but I could see little sign of the exceptional qualities that his position suggested. He was still the same short, thin stranger, with an unimpressive voice and carriage. Now for the real question: what could Rebka's visit here, over on Quakeside, have to do with his search? All the administration of Dumbbell was back over on Cloudside, where he had just come from. They had the police headquarters, the inter-system coordination, and the only interstellar spaceport. I began to feel uneasy. It was less than twenty Days to summertide maximum, and I had no time to spare for visitors, no matter what their mission.

The other two were still looking at me, waiting for my response to Rebka's information. I shrugged.

"I'm shocked to hear about the Zardalu, but I don't see how I can help you. The people who killed them came to Dumbbell, I'm prepared to believe that. But they'll be over on Cloudside, not here. As Governor Wethel could have told you, we have no place for them to hide on Quakeside—all our towns are too small, and the land is all monitored. Are you sure that they landed on Egg at all? Suppose they took off again and were hiding out near Perling?"

Looking at Rebka's baffled expression, I realized my mistake. His accent was slight, but it was clear that he didn't know this System—the names were missing him completely.

All the reference texts outside the System tell the inquirer that Eta Cassiopeiae A has the double planet, Dobelle. It was named after the captain of the ship that made the first scout survey. The components of Dobelle, the twins of the planetary doublet, were logically named Ehrenknechter and Castelnuovo-Kryszkoviak, after the other two men on the scout ship. The records don't tell us how long the first settlers struggled with those jaw-breakers, but well before I was born the two components had been re-named Quake and Egg, and no one in the System ever used their official names—except for formal outside communications. And as soon as the connecting umbilical went in between the two, the name of the planet pair, Dobelle, had naturally slid over into Dumbbell. Only Perling, the gas-giant planet that circled Eta-Cass A seven hundred million kilometers out, had managed to hold on to its original name—probably because no one ever went there.

Governor Wethel jumped into the conversation again, putting all the names I had used back into their official forms. When he had finished, I got another hard look from Rebka and a shake of the head.

"No. They did not go to Perling." He sat down in the chair over by the curved window, his manner stiff and serious. "Please assume that I know how to do at least a part of my job, Captain Mira. Before I came to Dobelle I checked that the fugitives were neither near Perling, nor out by the dwarf companion."

I nodded. I couldn't see anybody trying to hide near Eta-Cass B, there was nothing there but a few orbiting chunks of rock. "But what makes you think they landed here on Egg?"

"No doubt about it," chipped in Wethel. "I looked at the landing records when Moderator Rebka called me. I found we had a jump ship land at Cloudside, twenty Days ago—and it's still there."

"But its passengers are not," said Rebka. "They landed on the other side of this planet—Cloudside?—and they are not there now."

He reached into his pocket and pulled out an ID pack. "Two people were involved in the death of the Zardalu. They were visitors to Delta Pavonis Four, first-time visitors on their way from Peacock A to Sol. They stayed there only one day. Have you seen anyone who looks like this over here in your area? Within the past twenty Days?"

I flicked on the ID pack and looked into it. I had a sudden shock of false recognition. For the first moment, the young woman who smiled at me from the pack was Amy—my Amy.

I looked on, and the thrill faded. The obvious differences were there—how had I failed to see them at once?—and they brought me back to normal. The young woman I was looking at was older than Amy, and she wore a deep tan that no one ever acquired on the cloudy side of Egg. It must have been her clothes—clothes that matched Amy's preference exactly. Dark green and russet, cut low off the smooth shoulders and matching her auburn hair. That, and perhaps something in the smiling eyes, a message of life and laughter that carried through the impersonality of the ID display.

After a few seconds I realized that I had to speak. Rebka was looking at me, and into me, in a way that had to be avoided. I stared back into his eyes and shook my head.

"I don't know her—but if she had been here, I assure you that I would have noticed. Surely this isn't one of the criminals?"

He nodded his head slowly, eyes still locked on mine. "I am afraid that she is. You are looking at Elena Carmel. She, together with her sister, killed the Zardalu."

I couldn't imagine it. Not someone who looked so young and vulnerable herself.

"Could it have been an accident?" I peered again into the depths of the ID image. "I thought that the Zardalu were still in a probationary state—marginally intelligent."

"They were. It could well have been an accident."

"But you still accuse them of genocide—when the Zardalu may not have even been covered by the Species Protection Act."

"Of course." He sighed. "Isn't my position obvious to you? Most of the Zardalu were killed before their potential intelligence was recognized. Killed by humans. A human Moderator is assigned to this investigation—perhaps that was a wrong decision, but it was made. Don't you see that I am obliged to assume the worst? There must be no suspicion on the part of any other Council Member that I sought to cover a crime—even a potential crime—by one of my own species. That would mean the end of the Council. But apart from that, I would pursue them anyway. The death of the Zardalu must be investigated, even though nothing that I do can ever bring them back. They are gone forever."

Rebka's voice was bitter. He was that rarest of all humankind, a man who felt as strongly about the protection of non-humans as he did about his own kind. I was beginning to realize what it took to be a member of the Species Protection Council.

"Do you have an ID pack for the other sister?" I said, breaking a long silence that made us all uncomfortable, but which no one seemed willing to end.

"Of course." Rebka shrugged. "I will show it to you, but it will do no good. If you did not recognize Elena Carmel, you will not recognize Jilli Carmel. They are identical twins."

He handed me a second ID pack. The features were identical, that was undeniable. Yet there were differences, ways in which I thought I would know them apart—and I don't mean the superficial things, such as the styling of the auburn hair. Jilli Carmel had a slightly different expression, a trifle less confident and extrovert than her sister. Reluctantly, I handed it back to him.

"I don't know her. You and Governor Wethel seem confident that they are not on Cloudside. I'm at least as sure that they aren't here, on Quakeside. So where does that leave us? Wherever they are, it's not anywhere on Egg."

"He means anywhere on Ehrenknechter," explained Wethel, then bit his lip.

Rebka had frozen him with a look. Wethel passed it on to me, as a grimace of disgust—self-disgust. He had already explained once to Rebka that the twin planets had been re-named, and the Moderator was not wearing an Ampak at wrist or throat. That meant that he was undoubtedly a mnemonist, with perfect recall—but Klaus Wethel had unfortunately made that deduction a fraction of a second *after* he had spoken.

I gave him a consoling wink, as Rebka went on, "I agree with you. They are not here on Egg. Six Days ago—two Earth-days—they left this planet and went across to your companion world. They are now on Castelnuovo-Kryszkoviak—if you prefer it, on Quake."

He smiled this time at Wethel, to take the edge off his words.

"Never," I said abruptly. Klaus Wethel looked horrified, that I should be so terse with a Sector Moderator, but Rebka did not seem at all perturbed.

"And why not?" he said. "I had a good look at the other

component of this doublet as we were flying in for our approach to the Dobelle System. It is almost wholly undeveloped, is it not? I have no doubt that the Carmel sisters believe that they can hide there safely, perhaps until I am called away for other duties."

I looked over at my calendar and shook my head. Eighteen Days—six Earth-days—to summer maximum. I felt sick inside, a heavy feeling of nausea that the situation could not justify. The ID packs had upset me more than I would have thought possible. I looked back at Rebka, sitting upright and serious in my visitor's chair.

"What is the Species Protection Council punishment for genocide?"

He looked uncomfortable. No one with his degree of empathy for other beings could feel happy at the discussion of penalties.

"The maximum punishment?" he said at last. "For proven intent, which I hope we will not find to be the case here, it would be third level rehabilitation."

He caught my questioning look.

"Erasure," he went on. "In a bad case, of all adult memories."

I nodded. "But never death, even in the worst cases? Even if they acted with full knowledge of their crime?"

Now he looked as sick as I felt. He swallowed and stared off into space, unable to meet my gaze. Klaus Wethel gave me an angry glare.

"No," said Rebka at last. "Excuse me. I had forgotten that many things are different on the frontier planets. The idea of death as punishment is not completely unfamiliar to me, but it is still not something that I can regard without discomfort. It has not been practised in—other places"—I felt that he had almost said civilized places—"for many years."

"Then I'm afraid I must give you information that will make you unhappier yet," I said. I pressed the button that would make the big dome above our heads move to transparency. "Elena and Jilli Carmel must have had the same impression of Quake as you did, that it is an undeveloped area where they could remain in safe seclusion. But if they are on Quake now, and stay there, then it doesn't matter if they are guilty of genocide, or as innocent as you are—they're dead, both of them, within a few Days."

The dome had become completely transparent. I felt sorry for Wethel, with his severe agoraphobia and acrophobia—I was hitting him with both of them at once, but I had to do it. I saw him, as though against his will, slowly turning his head to look upward. He knew what he was going to see, but he couldn't force himself not to look.

It was just past the middle of Second-night on Egg, and as usual at this time of the year the night sky over Quakeside was clear. Directly above us, fully illuminated, hung the bright orb of Quake itself. The building we were in was not far from the center of Quakeside, at the pole of Egg closest to Quake. We were only about twelve thousand kilometers away from the other planet's surface. From where we sat it filled more than thirty-five degrees of the sky, like a great mottled fruit, purple-grey and overripe. It was easy to imagine that it was ready to fall on us. I saw Rebka follow Governor Wethel's reluctant upward look, and flinch when he saw our sister planet.

"Steady," I said. "Don't get alarmed by the way it looks. You know the dynamics as well as I do." I was really speaking for Rebka's benefit—nothing I said could make it any easier for Wethel, he had heard all the logical arguments before and they hadn't helped. "Remember, sir," I went on. "Quake and Egg have been playing roundabouts like this, circling each other this way, for nearly half a billion years. They won't decide to collide tonight for your benefit."

It helped me to know that Rebka had something else on his mind other than seeing through my own psychological defenses. And it said something for the man that he didn't let that first sight of Quake in the sky unnerve him for more than a few seconds. He seemed to focus himself inwards, then dragged his eyes back from the zenith and frowned at me.

"That's an impressive sight. No wonder you keep the dome opaque most of the time. But what do you mean, the Carmel sisters are dead?" He couldn't be distracted from his main interest for long. "I looked at Quake through high power scopes," he went on, "as we were flying in. It didn't just look unde-veloped, it looked like a garden planet. Are you telling me that there are dangerous life forms there?"

"Nothing that you couldn't handle with a hand weapon—and nothing that's dangerously poisonous, either. But Quake's a death trap at this time of the year." I swung the big telescope across towards us and switched on the viewing screen. "Take a look at it for yourself. Compare it with what you saw when you looked a few days ago. Can you see any differences?"

Under a 1000X magnification, it was as though we were hovering a little more than ten kilometers above the surface of the planet. We could see all the rivers and plains of Quake, even the larger of the mines that provided Egg with most of its metals.

Rebka leaned forward and frowned at the screen, while Klaus Wethel did his best not to look at anything—fear of falling was even more intense from ten kilometers than it had been from twelve thousand. It had been a bad thing to do, opening the dome on him. Now I'd have even more trouble than usual to get him to ever come back to Quakeside.

Rebka nodded. "It looks different," he admitted at last. "I have no idea why, but the colors all seem to have changed since we came past it on the way in, more than I would expect from a change in viewing angle or sun angle. How could it have changed so quickly?"

"Did you look at all at Dumbbell's orbit before you came here?" I asked. "I thought not. We're less than six earth-days from perihelion—from midsummer. Our seasons here on Egg, and on Quake, are caused by distance from Eta-Cass A, not by axial tilt the way they are on Earth. Dumbbell sweeps in pretty close—the orbit has an eccentricity better than 0.3. Here on Egg we have good protection from the cloud cover, but Quake doesn't have that. Right now all the vegetation there is getting ready for the summer. The plants die off above the ground, and all the root systems dip deeper for the cooler layers. They go down twenty meters or more."

Rebka was looking sicker than ever. "Are you telling me that the Carmel twins will die of the heat there? What do the native animals do in the summer?"

"They dig deep down, and they estivate."

"Then the Carmel sisters will dig deep down, too. They probably have a good refrigeration pack with them." His expression was now relieved—genocide or not, his first worry at the moment was the survival of his quarry. "They only need to survive a few Earth-days of heat."

"True enough, and they may have counted on that." I hated to do this to him, but he had to know the truth. "It gets really hot there on Quake, but it's not the heat that will get them."

We had seen enough of the other planet, and I cut the transparency of the dome back to full opaqueness. Klaus Wethel drew in a long breath, and began to take an interest in the discussion for the first time in the past ten minutes.

"The heating of the surface goes up like the inverse square of the distance from Eta-Cass A," I went on. "But the tidal forces go up like the inverse *cube*. Quake is smaller and heavier than Egg, and has much more of a liquid core—the radioactives keep in that way. At summer maximum, when the tides hit their peak, the whole surface shakes like a jelly. Why did you think that the first settlers called it Quake? It's the 'quakes and volcanoes that will kill the Carmel sisters."

It took Rebka less than a minute to digest this new information, and factor it into his main objective. The conclusion he drew was one that I was most afraid of.

"So we have very little time before Quake becomes uninhabitable," he said. "We can't leave them there—they obviously don't know any of this."

"But are you sure they *are* there?" I was really playing for time, and Rebka saw right through me.

"I am convinced of it. How difficult would it have been for them to obtain passage along the umbilical?"

"Not difficult at all." I shrugged. "We don't check the outgoing pods, and if a couple of people climbed on board an empty cargo container we would never know it."

"So they are there." He obviously was not prepared to discuss that issue further. "We have six Earth-days to summer maximum, you said. That ought to give a party ample time to go up the umbilical, locate the Carmel sisters on the surface of

Quake, and bring them back here. I assume that you have no bad tidal problems here, even at midsummer?"

"Slight tides," I said. "Nothing to worry about."

My mind was still engaged on Rebka's last words. Up the umbilical, cross to Quake, pick up the girls and back over to Egg—just like that! He had no idea what he was proposing. I had been there, and I knew. He saw my expression, but he misinterpreted it.

"We do have sufficient time, don't we?" he said.

"If we start at once, we may," I replied. "Even so, it would be touch and go. Quake gets less and less predictable the closer we get to summertide maximum. This is the busiest time of the year for me, trying to make sure that we get the mining operations all closed down and packed up the umbilical for the summer."

He ignored that, too. "The party ought to be a small one," he said. "It must have an experienced man, someone who has been on Quake before for the summer."

He turned to Wethel, who was looking at him with horror. "Governor, do you know anyone on the planet who has had summer experience of Quake?"

Klaus Wethel's face turned red—he had never learned how to lie, which is curious when you think that he had reached the position of Governor.

"I'm afraid not, Dr. Rebka," he said, looking anywhere except in my direction. "No one makes summer trips to Quake."

"Thanks, Klaus," I said. "But it's not necessary." I thought again of the happy young faces in the ID packs, and the images of the Carmel twins were overlain with Amy's smile. I turned to Rebka.

"So far as I am aware, Councilman, only one person on Egg has made more than one trip to Quake during summer maximum."

I suppose you don't get to be Sector Moderator without a lot of brains, and you don't get on the Species Protection Council without other qualities as well. Rebka was too sharp for his own good, and he had read something else out of my tone of voice that I didn't know had been in there. He gave me a strange look from those steady grey eyes.

"And how many times have you made that trip, Captain Mira?"

"Three." I took a deep breath. I don't think that I looked down at my hands, but maybe I moved them or something. Rebka was staring at them, at the shiny pink of rebuilt skin and scar tissue. I wanted to put them behind my back.

"I was there five years ago," I said at last. "And I also made visits there four years ago and three years ago."

And since then, I felt like saying, with the help of people like Klaus Wethel I have managed to find other ways to control my misery. But I didn't say that—I had never said it to anyone. In Rebka's case, I'm not sure that it mattered. He had such strong antennae for other people's emotions that I felt he was reading everything out of me anyway.

"I think perhaps you have been there too much already," he said after a few moments. He looked across at Wethel. "Wouldn't you agree, Governor?"

Klaus looked at him gratefully. "I agree completely, Councilman. I do not think that Captain Mira ought to risk another trip. Last time he was very lucky to escape with his life."

That was a matter of opinion.

"I'm going," I said. I stood up. "There will be danger on Quake, and I at least have a good idea where it will come from. But the party should be kept small: I, and my second-in-command. He has not been there at midsummer maximum, but he knows Quake well."

Rebka stood up too. I should have known what was coming.

"No," he said simply. "I cannot permit anyone else to usurp my duties. I must go also." He turned to Wethel. "Captain Mira and I will make the trip. I know you are feeling that you must volunteer too, but I will not accept that. When we return, you and I must spend more time together. The fears you felt when Captain Mira opened the dome are curable. I will show you how to do it."

So he had seen that too, despite his own instinctive reaction to the first sight of Quake in the sky. I wondered how much else he had seen that I thought was hidden.

"I will need a few minutes to prepare myself," went on Rebka. "Then we can go as soon as you like. No arguments," he added, seeing that I was about ready to speak again. "It is my duty, remember, to follow the Carmel sisters, *wherever* that may happen to lead."

I suddenly realized that Rebka was also a driven man. Into the jaws of Death, into the mouth of Hell—it didn't matter where, if his duty told him to go there. I nodded without speaking, and he turned and walked quickly from the dome.

Klaus Wethel was still sitting in his chair. He showed no sign of leaving with Rebka.

"No need to stick around here, Klaus." I knew he would rather be back on Cloudside. "Why don't you head back?"

He stood up and came over to stand directly in front of me. "Marco, you have a chance that you may never get again. Don't miss it."

That was a bad sign. Klaus Wethel never called me by my first name unless he was feeling very uncomfortable. I looked up at him—he was about five centimeters taller than me—and tried to look puzzled.

"Chance for what?"

"Don't act dumb, Marco." His face was getting red again. "You'll probably not meet another Sector Moderator—especially one who is on the Protection Council—in your life. If anybody can sort you out, he can."

"Sorry." I turned around and started out of the room. "There's nothing that Rebka can do for me. Nothing that I want him to do for me, either."

I don't think I lie any better than Klaus Wethel. But I'm not the Governor of Egg, so I don't usually need to. And if I do lie, I hope that my face doesn't go red. I wondered how skilled a Sector Moderator had to be at carefully calculated misstatement. From the look of Rebka, he could do anything that he chose to.

I resolved to watch myself very closely in the Days ahead.

There was more preparation than Rebka had expected. It took nearly two Days—fifteen Earth hours—before we were ready to go over to the foot of the umbilical. Even on Quakeside, the heat was steadily rising. Not enough to be more than slightly uncomfortable, but it was a taste of what was coming.

We took a hover-car over to the umbilical. It would have been quicker to use an air-car, but I wanted Rebka to get used to piloting the hovercraft. I didn't think he would need that skill when we were on Quake, but it's better to prepare for everything.

As we were on our way, noon of the third Day arrived. Rebka watched in fascination as Eta-Cass A swept behind Quake for the midday eclipse, then back out again about forty minutes later.

"Why doesn't it get dark?" he asked. "There can't be much refraction from Quake's atmosphere. It ought to be like another night, but a short one."

"Not at this time of year." I pointed over to the west, which was the first side of Egg to come back to sunlight after the noon eclipse. "You can't see it now because of the cloud cover over there, but Eta-Cass B is above the horizon. Almost ten billion kilometers away from here, but it gives off plenty enough light to throw a shadow when the weather is clear. It never gets dark on Quakeside at this time of year. It won't be dark on Quake, either—there's not much cloud there, except for ash and smoke at midsummer max."

Rebka nodded and continued his tentative manipulation of the car controls. While he did so, I had a chance to look over the records that he had handed to me. They showed the reconstruction of the sequence of events on Delta Pavonis Four that had led to the deaths of the last two lodges of Zardalu—part facts, part Rebka's own deductions.

The more I saw, the less likely it seemed that the Carmel sisters had committed an intentional crime. The Zardalu were big, slow amphibians. They looked like scaly beavers, and they spent their whole lives down by the rivers, damming them and making their complex lodges. From the look of some of the structures, they had a good claim to intelligence. I could recognize cantilevered bridges, all made from the native wood.

That seemed to be part of the problem. With its high silicon content, the xylem of the trees of Delta Pav Four was more like tough, sandy rock than the woods we have on Egg. To chew through that, the Zardalu had developed big, strong teeth, which from the position in their heavy jaws gave them an aggressive, savage look. All human experience with them suggested that they were gentle and herbivorous. But they certainly looked fierce.

According to Rebka's analysis, the Carmel twins had landed very close to the Zardalu colony, and settled in for the night. The Zardalu had come over to look at them, out of sheer curiosity. That was the other problem. The Zardalu were nocturnal—and the Carmel sisters must have awakened to the sight of a circle of grinning jaws, with those grey, razor-edged teeth.

I could imagine that might produce a strong reaction in anyone, even if they had been assured by the life-forms directory that Delta Pav Four had no species dangerous to humans. But it ought not to have led to a blind use of the construction laser, blamed by Rebka as the instrument for the killing. I rubbed at my chin and laid the report down on the hover-car seat.

"I can see how your reconstruction might work, but I still don't understand what put the two women into such a blind panic. Surely they would have come to their senses after a second or two?"

Rebka did not answer for a moment. He was staring out of the front of the car, to where the umbilical was now rising ahead of us. I have grown used to it, but I can still remember my own first sight of it. From the pole of Egg, it rose vertically upward like the trunk of a giant metal tree. Up to infinity, to the point where it became invisible against the sky. At the base it was about forty meters across, and there was no perceptible taper to it as it disappeared from view. Actually, only the load-bearing cable was tapered, and the drive mechanism and power cables dominated the appearance. Above our heads, at the exact center of the rising umbilical, Quake hung in the sky. I noticed that even at noon eclipse the surface was not dark. Already there were the first signs of volcanic activity there, as the tides rose in strength.

Rebka finally managed to get his attention back to the business of driving the hover-car. He gunned the forward motor and took a second to glance around at me.

"I couldn't understand why the women would have been so panicked, either," he said. "Look farther back—go on through the records, all the way to their childhood. That ought to give you some idea why I'm confident that we are looking at pure accident—and panic. But I can't prove that unless we can get them back to Earth for trial and deep testing."

Puzzled, I began to skim backward, into the earlier records of the Carmel twins' life. I had to go all the way, back to where they were just three years old, before I found it.

Their parents had been archeologists, specializing in the artifacts of the Kaneeli, an ancient space-going race whose relics appear on many planets. Their final fate as a species is still a mystery, and the Carmel parents had been pursuing a promising lead. It took them to a planet of Ross 882, an M-4 type star of little interest to human settlers. It had previously been the subject of only one survey, and the native life forms had been reported as small and innocuous.

Quite clearly, the earlier survey had landed in only one hemisphere, or had skimped on the detail of their analysis.

On the second night on the planet, the camp of the Carmel family had been attacked by a large native carnivore, a bipedal reptile that was both quick and ferocious. Elena and Jilli's mother had been killed at once, and their father reached the jump ship with one arm torn off at the shoulder. He had died on the way to Peacock A, after using his last strength to initiate a jump exit. The rescue party had found two small girls, unclear about what had happened to them but with certain memories indelibly rooted.

Were the Zardalu similar to the carnivores that had killed their parents? It was an irrelevant question. They were similar enough, and there was no doubt—to me and to Rebka—that the

Carmel twins had been reliving a terrible period of their child-hood when they awoke on Delta Pav Four and found themselves surrounded.

"But why did they run away?" I asked Rebka. "They must have known they'd made a horrible mistake. There's no way that any Council group would have found them guilty of any-thing but fear."

Rebka was moving us cautiously in towards the foot of the umbilical, too busy to look around. "You are asking the ques-tion that has pursued me as long as I have pursued them," he said quietly. "Why would innocents flee? I can imagine that they might make one jump, in blind panic. But then they should have known why they had acted as they did. Why did they go on running?"

It was some consolation to know that not even Sector Mod-erators, with their combination of native talent, high motivation and specialized training, could explain everything. We climbed out of the car and went on over to the foot of the stalk of the umbilical. The hover-car was small enough to fit into the cargo pod, but I wanted to get one from Midway Station, where they had equipment better suited for work down on the surface of Quake.

It took us about twenty minutes to get settled into the pas-senger car that was waiting for us at the foot of the umbilical. Another five minutes, and the drive train took hold to give us a smooth upward acceleration, away from the surface of Egg.

I had made the trip many times, but Rebka couldn't resist the viewports that showed the scene both ahead and behind the car.

"How long before we can see the whole umbilical?" he asked.

I shook my head. "We never will. It looks thick when we're close to it, but it never gets to be more than about fifty meters wide. And there are twelve thousand kilometers of it, re-member, between us and Quake. We won't see more than you can see right now."

In front of us the umbilical stretched away, thinning out to a fine silver thread that at last vanished into invisibility against the purple backdrop of Quake. Rebka was straining his eyes to follow the silver filament, but it would be hours before we could see it meet the surface of Egg's sister planet.

It was easy to time our progress. Every few minutes there was a vibration and a rumble in the drive train, as a loaded ore car passed us on its trip from Quake to Egg. At this time of year we stopped the transportation of radioactives, even though there were always plenty available on Quake. An accident in the first days of operation of the umbilical had made the use of the transportation system during summertide an activity that always called for caution.

I looked ahead. Hanging there five thousand kilometers away shone the bright knot of Midway Station, marking our halfway point on the journey along the bar between the two spheres of Egg and Quake—the balanced counterweights of the Dumbbell system. I pointed Midway Station out to Rebka and he spent a long time crouching forward, looking out of the front port.

"I've seen a fair number of Stalks in different Systems," he said. "But this is the first one between two planets. Why don't they do it like this in other places? Say between Earth and Luna."

I was fiddling with the scope, trying to get us a better view of Quake's surface. "You need a pair that are in synchronous lock," I said, only half my attention on Rebka—image motion compensation was a problem for the scope at our speed. "Quake and Egg always present the same face to each other. They're so close together, tidal friction has killed off any relative rotation of the two surfaces. In fact, if they were a bit closer together, they'd break apart—they'd be inside the Roche limit."

I locked in the scope, satisfied that it was as good as I was likely to get. The image was crisp enough to let us see the outward flow of lava from a volcano at the terminator, and clouds of blackish smoke were spreading around the sunward side.

"Even with the planets in synchronous lock, this was a tricky job," I went on. "There was a lot more to it than the usual cables and drive train that you're used to back on Earth. Wait until we get to Midway—you'll see what I mean."

Rebka remained silent, staring out of the front screen. I did the same. Quake approaching summer maximum was something I had seen before but never tired of. Tidal forces on the molten interior were steadily mounting and the surface crust was weakening, unable to hold back the heat dragons that would rule the summer land. Already we could see faint blotches of smoke and heat haze, spreading across the purple-grey sphere.

I should have known better than to sit there, doing nothing. Before I knew it all the old memories were streaming back. I could see Amy's face before me as she nudged me carefully along to her own objectives.

"You're the expert, aren't you?"

I was.

"And you have the whole system under control, don't you? All the tether gear and the movement of the cable?"

I thought I had it all under control—everything except Amy.

"Well, then, why won't you take me with you?"

"It's dangerous."

"Not so dangerous that you can't go if you want to. You've been there before."

"I made one trip. I swore I wouldn't make another."

Amy was leaning over me as we lay on the open plain. Above our heads, Quake was still ten Days from midsummer. Even with my eyes shut, I could see its strange beauty. The volcanic action near summertide maximum filled all the upper atmosphere with fine dust and smoke, veiling the surface. The sunsets came every seven and a half hours, and they were a riot of purples, reds and gold. There was nothing like them anywhere else in the known universe—nothing that I had read of or heard rumored.

Amy was watching my expression. She had picked up a piece of fine fern, and was stroking it slowly down my bare chest. She moved in front of my view of Quake, her wide brown eyes unusually serious.

"So you'll take me with you this time?"

I shook my head, rolling it from side to side on the soft earth, too lazy to lift it fully.

"It's not safe there."

"But it would be if you were there with me." She was working on my resistance like an expert climber, sensing and taking advantage of each tiny niche and fractional fingerhold.

"Not at summer maximum," I said at last. *"We couldn't stay through that. I left before that myself."*

She sensed my weakening resolve even before I knew it myself and moved in on it instantly. I could see a different expression in her face, flushed with a new passion and a gleam of adventure. I was staring into her eyes when a new face appeared before me and a different voice broke into our private world.

"I wondered if you were having problems. I thought I'd better check."

I was wrenched back across a four-year gulf. I became aware of Klaus Wethel's anxious face looking in at us over the comscreen, and of Rebka sitting quietly watching me.

"Everything's fine," I said. "We'll be at Midway Station soon."

Wethel nodded. "Then I'll go back to Cloudside. Just wanted to check."

He looked reassured by the fact that the scene in the pod was so peaceful. The comscreen is limited in the amount of information that it will transmit. Klaus Wethel couldn't tell that my shirt was soaked with sweat under the armpits and around the collar—despite the accurate temperature control in the passenger pod.

I couldn't hold out that hope for Rebka. To someone with his sensitivity I would be radiating like a supernova, a rank blend of pheromones: lust, fear, excitement, and anguish.

I managed to keep my face and voice under firm control as we said our goodbyes to Wethel and he vanished from the screen. Nothing that Rebka had said to Klaus Wethel revealed that anything unusual was happening in the car—perhaps nothing unusual *was* happening for Rebka. High empaths must be used to a deluge of emotions from those around them.

After a single, calm look at me, Rebka leaned forward again and set the scope to a higher magnification. Midway Station zoomed towards us.

"I was about to ask you about this," he said. "Why such a big station? I have seen nothing like that structure on other Stalks from surface to orbit."

If he was willing to forget what had been happening to me, I was ready to go along with him. I took in a deep breath and tried to hold my attention firmly in the present. No more trips to the past, until we were safely back on Egg and Rebka had gone on his way, with or without the Carmel sisters.

"That's what I was talking about earlier," I said. "I told you Dumbbell is a tricky system. Midway Station there is four things in one. It's the power center that provides energy all along the umbilical, it's the central maintenance station, plus a very complicated computer system; and it's the Winch, over to the left. Watch as we get closer."

With the scope magnification that Rebka had set we seemed to be only a few hundred meters from Midway. We could see every detail of the Winch's operation. It looked like a flattened disk almost a kilometer in diameter, from which the load cable of the umbilical protruded on both sides, like a thread through a bead of greenish glass. We could follow the cable for the first few meters inside the Winch, then its outline faded to a delicate branching pattern that baffled the eye. I set the zoom higher and moved our view in to the entry point of the cable.

"Look at the movement there."

As we watched, the umbilical on the side facing us was in continuous motion, reeling in meter after meter to the mysterious interior of the Winch. It seemed to be gobbled up endlessly by the dark mouth. Rebka looked at me in alarm.

"I thought the connection between Ehrenknechter and Castelnuovo-Kryszkoviak was a permanent one? Won't we lose contact at the other end if it keeps in reeling in the load cable like that?"

"No. Look." I changed the scope setting, so that we had a view of the far end of the umbilical. It was still firmly attached to the surface of Quake, six thousand kilometers ahead of us. "See? We're still connected at both ends. The whole assembly is permanently tied—except for a few hours near midsummer maximum. But the length still has to vary, to allow for changes in the distance between the two planets. Their orbits are almost exactly circular about each other—as near as can be. There are still perturbing forces, though. They depend on the distance of Dumbbell from Eta-Cass A, and on the changes in the tidal forces. And don't forget the wobbles in Egg and Quake. Quake is almost a perfect sphere, but Egg fits its name—we have a two hundred kilometer difference between polar and equatorial radius.''

Rebka was staring hard. ''But how does it do it? How do you know how much load cable has to be picked up or let out?''

''All computer-controlled. I told you we have a fancy set-up at Midway Station. The Winch is programmed to allow for all the perturbing effects—otherwise we could never hold a connection between Quake and Egg for more than a few minutes. We'd break the cable, or have it flopping loose between the planets.''

As we were speaking, we had swept closer and closer to Midway Station. Just before we came to the Winch, our car was detached from the load cable and followed the drive train around the outside of the Winch. After a couple of minutes, we reconnected at the other side, and began the long fall towards Quake, once more securely attached to the drive—which soon had to slow our fall rather than driving us upward away from Egg. Midway Station was set at the mean center of mass of the Dumbbell system. A point of equilibrium, but an unstable one. Only the tension in the umbilical kept the whole assembly in overall balance.

The complexity of the mechanical structure we had just passed seemed to have quietened Rebka. I felt that he was perhaps beginning to realize that a trip to Quake, for any reason, was not the same as taking a simple air-car flight. The umbilical was as simple as it could be—but that didn't make it simple. We settled into an uneasy silence, and watched the steady approach of the surface of Quake.

In the two days since Rebka had first looked at it from my office, there had been changes. It was now daytime below us, and the purple-grey-green of our earlier view had dimmed to a general subdued grey. The plants were diving deeper, letting the top foliage die off and dry out. That would be sacrificed to the summer heat and widespread brush-fires.

As the vegetation retreated from the surface, the scabs of recent wounds were revealed on Quake. I pointed to the long rifts and cuts that marked the planet beneath us.

"See those? When we get a couple of hundred kilometers closer you'll see more of them."

"Lava flows?" Rebka's voice was calm. I wondered what he had seen already, in his years as Sector Moderator. Whole planets wasted, and star-going civilizations wiped out? Probably. The Council was reluctant to tell of the worst side of its work. Perhaps Quake at summertide maximum was something he would take in his stride. In that case, I hoped he could teach me the trick. I zoomed the screen in on one of the longer rifts.

"Lava, and fractures in the rock," I said. "Every year at perihelion, about two percent of Quake's surface gets covered with lava and hot ashes. That may not sound like a lot, but even the parts that don't get covered are affected by the eruptions. What you're looking at is one of last year's, or maybe the year before. The plants haven't had time to grow back yet. They'll do it all right, and they find rich soil there when the lava decomposes, but it takes a few years. Come back in ten years and there'll be a whole new set of scars, in many different places. That's one of the problems with Quake. The eruptions seem to come in different places each year."

Rebka was looking suitably chastened. "What's the radius of Quake?"

"About fifty-four hundred kilometers—the Carmel sisters could be anywhere in three hundred and fifty million square kilometers."

"Yet you are still convinced that you can find them?"

"We have a good chance. I'm betting that they have stayed within hover-car range of the foot of the umbilical. And they will want to be near water. I think that tells us where to look—if we can look there in time."

He nodded thoughtfully. "You were quite right. This would be impossible without someone who knows the summer surface of the planet. I would be useless alone."

So he had considered that option. That proved he was either

braver or more foolish than anyone else I knew—perhaps both.

"Suppose we don't get to them," he went on. "There must still be a chance that they would survive perihelion. How good would that chance be?"

I had to think hard about that one. Could they survive summertide maximum? I had, in a manner of speaking, but that could be put down to blind fortune.

I shrugged. "I'd give them maybe five percent. No more, and probably less. What will you do if they get killed there?"

I should have realized that my question would upset him as much as my answer. Rebka winced at the thought.

"I will blame myself," he said. "I am the one who has pursued them across four systems. If I had been less clumsy in pursuit—in signalling my approach—perhaps they would not have fled to Dobelle. We must save them, if they cannot save themselves. How do the native animals survive—can you give me any details?"

No comfort for him there. "Most of them don't," I said. "They all dig deep down, but the biologists who've looked at the fauna here reckon that at least half of the animals are killed off each year. They can breed fast enough to keep up, but overpopulation doesn't ever seem to be a problem on Quake."

He nodded again and fell silent. He was acting more like the guardian of the Carmel sisters than their pursuer, but it suited me fine if he would keep his mind on them. In a miserable silence, we approached the foot of the umbilical. When we got near enough to see clearly where it joined the surface of Quake, Rebka saw something that brought him out of his introspection.

"What's going on there?" he said, as we reached the end of the drive train and prepared to descend to the surface.

He was pointing off to one side, where the first stage of loosening of the tether had begun. The heavy cables had already been deployed around the tether end, as it lay like a broad inverted mushroom on the surface.

"They're getting the tether loose, ready for midsummer."

"I thought you said that the connection with the planet was permanent?"

"It is. It always provides the tension we need to stabilize the load cable. But at midsummer maximum we can't risk a simple mechanical contact, the way we have over on Egg. In a few more Days we'll draw the end of the umbilical up to about three thousand meters from the surface, well away from danger of real damage during the eruptions at tidal maximum. We have to be back here long before that happens."

"So you are telling me that there is no permanent coupling?"

I shrugged, and opened the door of the passenger car. We had reached the end of the line, the surface of Quake. So far, everything about us looked peaceful, with no obvious signs of seismic activity. We had to get the hovercar ready and be on our way as soon as possible.

"It depends what you call a coupling," I replied. "We keep the tension in the cable through midsummer with a magnetic hold. Quake is full of ferromagnetics, and the umbilical has a generator in its tether. We just use Quake as a big lump of iron. The bond is as strong as a mechanical one, and it doesn't need a contact with the surface. You'll see, it works fine."

"And how do you get off the surface when the umbilical is drawn up?"

I looked back at him before I set my foot down onto Quake's surface. "That's what I've been trying to say. You don't. That's why we have to be back here in twenty hours or less."

I was getting through to him. It was no good getting back to this point, unless we could do it in time. I went on with the unshipping of the hover-craft from the cargo pod that had followed us down, while Rebka walked over to the cables that hung loosely by the edge of the tether. He was inspecting them closely.

"We could still use one of those, couldn't we?" he said. "It looks as though they will still be hanging down to the surface. Couldn't they serve as an emergency hoist to the bottom of the umbilical?"

I went over and took a look for myself. He was right, the cables would hang down to the surface, even when the umbilical was high in the sky. I looked at their size and weight, then went back to the hover-car.

"Rather you than me, but I suppose you're right. In fact, I

think that if you look at the specifications on the umbilical, you'll find a statement that says the cables can form an emergency system.''

"I gather that you do not regard them as such."

I shrugged and climbed into the driver's seat on the hover-craft. "It all depends what you define as an emergency system. If I open my shirt and look at my chest I find I've got two nipples, and I guess they're my emergency system in case I ever get pregnant. I'm hoping the idea that we'll have to shin up those cables is somewhere about the same level of probability. I never thought of using them before, and I handle all the shipment of materials from here to Egg and back.''

"Do you like your work?"

I didn't care for his change of subject.

"It's a good job. It passes the time."

Since we had nothing else to do for a couple of hours, while we drove off towards the lake side, it looked as though Rebka was proposing to try his hand on me. I felt I had to improve on my last answer.

"I wouldn't change it for any job on Egg or Quake, so I guess I like it.''

Leave me alone, Rebka, my tone said. Not a chance.

"Do you realize how fond Governor Wethel is of you, Captain Mira?"

"Wethel? I always thought he felt uncomfortable with me." I had set the speed to forward maximum, and was skimming us across the quiet surface of Quake. It was hard to believe that all this peace would soon be broken.

"He is uncomfortable with you. Most uncomfortable. Do you know why?"

Wethel wasn't any more uncomfortable than I was. How rude could I be to a Sector Moderator?

"No, I have no idea why."

"Then I will tell you. He is uncomfortable because he is convinced that you could do his job much better than he can.''

I was tempted to look round at him, but at the speed we were going it could be fatal.

"I couldn't do his job at all. I couldn't stand it. In fact, if you want to know the truth I once refused it.''

"I know. Three and a half years ago, after your second visit to Quake in summer, and before your third visit.''

Damn the man. I didn't know just how long he had been in the Dumbbell system, but he seemed to have found out everybody's whole life history.

"And that's exactly why Wethel feels it's really your job,'' went on Rebka calmly. "You refused it—so he feels like a second choice, with the first choice there to prove it.''

I was holding the controls so hard that I thought they ought to snap off in my hands. This type of conversation may be nothing to Rebka, but I couldn't take it—and where it was leading. The sudden orange glow in the sky ahead of us was exactly what I needed. I switched the screen to maximum transparency.

"See that?'' As I spoke, the tremor shook the car. We were travelling on a meter-deep cushion of air, but we were also skimming forward at forty kilometers an hour. The ground ahead was moving in smooth, linear waves, rippling out from the quake center. Driving the hover-car over them was like sitting in a power boat and shooting the Grand Rapid on Egg's eastern limb.

Ten seconds after the land waves we heard the deep rumble of the eruption. Rebka had moved forward to sit next to me, craning closer to the front screen.

"Is that a big one?''

"Medium size. I'd say it's fifteen kilometers away. You'll see break-outs ten times that big in another five hours, when we're really getting in to the maximum tidal force. Hold tight now. We'll hit the secondary wave front in a second, and that'll be choppy.''

As we came to the region where surface and body waves had created their complicated interference pattern I had to slow our speed. The hover-car was rolling and yawing, even when I cut us to walking pace. It wasn't a bad quake—for Quake—but it had given Rebka something else to think about. We were going to see more and worse before we reached the Carmel twins.

The early records of the Dumbbell System make interesting

reading. The first settlement party had arrived at Eta-Cass A in the winter months of Dumbbell, and had the choice of landing on Egg or on Quake. It looked like an easy decision. Quake was more fertile, it had lots of metals and available radioactives, and it was less humid and muggy than Egg. I'm used to the Egg climate, but I must say I wouldn't care to live over on Cloudside.

The settlers put small camps on both planets, but they made it clear that Egg would be a temporary facility, only to be used for general exploration.

The tone of the old records on Quake gradually changes as their first summer approached. They knew it would be hot, because the orbit of Dumbbell had been known since the first scout ship came through. What worried them was something else. They could see recent evidence of widespread vulcanism, even though there had been no signs of volcanic activity when they landed.

Dumbbell swept in closer to the sun. The temperature shot up, all the plants began to die off and root deeper, and the earth tremors began. Even then, no one seemed to realize how bad it would get.

One colony camp stuck it out until three Days before summer maximum, before they finally gave up and ran over to Egg for shelter under the clouds.

Reading between the lines, you can detect another tone in those old records. It is almost one of disbelief. If Quake is as inhospitable to life as this, they seem to say, how could life ever have arisen here in the first place?

It took several hundred years before anyone could definitively answer that old question. The gas-giant, Perling, orbiting Eta-Cass A seven hundred million kilometers farther out, emerged as the villain of the story. Dumbbell had circled its sun peacefully for several billion years, not changing much in climate or distance. Life had emerged and developed on both Quake and Egg. It had been a tranquil environment on both members of the planet pair, until a third component of the planetary system, perturbed by the gravitational forces of the dwarf sun Eta-Cass B, had suffered a close encounter with Perling, two hundred times its mass. The giant had thrown it into a close swing-by of Eta-Cass A, from which it should have emerged with an eccentric but stable orbit. But Dumbbell lay in its path.

The stranger had done a complex dance about the doublet, moving the components closer together and changing their combined orbit to one that now skimmed much nearer to Eta-Cass A at perihelion—the present orbit. And the other planet had been slung clear out of the system by the encounter. Somewhere in interstellar space there was a solitary planet on an endless journey, waiting for encounter with and possible capture by another sun.

I couldn't help wondering about the old Quake, the planet before the encounter that gave it its present orbit and unruly surface. Had it been a true garden planet, with tranquil streams and clean, fragrant air? The present atmosphere was breathable, but near summer there was always a faint sulphurous smell to the air, a reminder that new eruptions were on the way to buckle and scar the face of Quake. I didn't mind it, but Rebka had reacted strongly when we first encountered that faint smell. He was sitting near a side window that had been left cracked open—everything would have to be closed as the sun rose, so that the air-cooler could do its job, but near dawn the temperature was still tolerable.

When the breeze carried in its trace of sulphur, Rebka had stiffened and sniffed. He seemed like a hunting animal, turning to track a scent. It took his mind off the thought of the eruptions ahead of us.

"You all right?" I asked. He was acting strangely, head rigid and cocked to one side.

He leaned back, and nodded. "That smell brings back old memories too clearly. I had an experience on Luytens, a long time ago. Curious, how strongly the stimulus of smells can affect our recall."

So I was not the only one who could be troubled by my memories. I didn't know if I was pleased or worried. It was easy to think of Rebka as a superman, the image that the words 'Sector Moderator' carried with them. If he was as frail and human as I was, it was good to know that. We might need a superman in the hours ahead, but if we didn't have one it was better to know it ahead of time.

Rebka reached out and closed the side window. The thermometer was beginning to show a rapid rise outside the car, and we might as well enjoy cool air while we could—I knew that soon enough we would have to go outside.

We were traveling now across a sea of dry spiky plants that cracked and powdered beneath the skirts of the hover-car. It was hard to believe that the brittle stems had been healthy and growing less than ten Days before.

"I don't understand how life survived here," said Rebka, peering out at the dead landscape. "After the orbit changed, everything else must have changed too. Temperatures, seasons, even the atmosphere. How could the life forms have endured?"

"I'm sure most of them didn't." I was skimming us along into a dry ravine, where we could make better speed. It was going slower than I had hoped. "Look at the plants that you'll see in a few minutes in the valley bottoms. Most of them are primitive forms, nothing like as complex as you'd expect on a planet this old. And there are a lot less species than you find on Egg. It must have been touch and go here. Egg was lucky, it had more water and it's less dense."

"You think it was simple adaptation of existing forms?"

"What else could it be?" I skirted us around a smoking patch of black rock. We could probably have gone over it without damage, but the underside of the hover-car was its most vulnerable part.

"Talk to the biologists when we get back to Egg," I went on. (If we got back?) "The forms that were already here and adapted to summer inactivity and deep rooting took that trend further. You won't see any animals at all at midsummer—they've found their hideaways. Quake has no viviparous forms, and all the eggs are tucked away ten meters down. Some of those will survive almost any violence on the surface."

While we were talking, the face of the land around us had been changing, slowly becoming flatter and less dried-out. There was only one body of water of decent size within two hundred kilometers of the foot of the umbilical, and we were getting close to it. Even in the worst earthquakes, I had never known it to dry up. I had come here on each of my summer visits to Quake. The first time had been pure exploration. On my second trip, Amy had wanted to see everything, but I had carefully chosen areas that I already knew, where the dangers would be reduced. I was sure that she would behave in her usual way, dancing on ahead of me and revelling in every new sight. I couldn't control her, had never been able to. Now we were tracing back over the same familiar ground, heading for the side of the lake. As we curved around a deep caldera, I halted our craft completely and let us settle to the ground. I remembered this spot from my previous visits—it had been inactive for at least five years, and that was unusual for Quake.

I opened the door. The heat sprang in at us, as though it had been waiting outside for its chance. We were still many hours from midsummer, and more than that from maximum temperatures. I breathed shallowly, reluctant to impose that sulphurous hotblast on my unprepared lungs.

"See those, Councilman?" I pointed down the steep caldera side. "At the bottom there. This is one place that Eta-Cass never shines. You might expect it to, at noon, but that's when Egg eclipses it. Those places, the bottoms of the steep craters— that's the coolest place on Quake in midsummer. If anyone wants to survive summertide here, that's where they ought to go."

Rebka peered gingerly down the steep slope. "So you think that's where we'll find the Carmel sisters?"

"Not in this particular one—in one nearer to the lake. We have time to look at maybe three of them before we have to turn back. But it's still our best bet. We have to keep moving and hope that Quake doesn't decide to fill the bottom of the one we want with molten lava."

Now it was Rebka's turn to look anxiously at his watch. He nodded. "We ought to be able to look at more than three, we've done well."

"Less well than you might think. I expect we'll be slower going back. Quake will be a lot livelier then."

I slid the door shut, turned the air-cooler to its maximum

setting, and started the lift and forward motors. As we moved closer to the lake, Rebka studied again the images that we had made from the umbilical. They were high-resolution, and he was looking for any signs of unusual activity in the craters by the lake.

"See anything on those?"

He shook his head. "I'm not used to looking at pictures of Quake. You'd do a better job."

"I think it's better if I stick with the driving. Time is the most important element of all now. Are any of the craters more heavily vegetated than the rest?"

He puzzled over them for a couple more minutes. Outside, it was again growing dark, but we had to press on through the night—not too difficult, thanks to the steady light from Eta-Cass B.

"I think three of them have more growths in the bottom than the others," he said at last.

I shrugged. "That saves any tough decision-making. Mark them up, and pass them over. I'll try and pick us the best path to them."

There was no point in trying to be too fancy. As Quake became more turbulent, we would have to make course changes to accommodate that. With old memories running on ahead of me, I set our speed as fast as I dared and threw the hover-car on and on, across the lava-lit, smoke-veiled landscape. Black and orange-red, heaving and moving like a wounded animal— Quake summer, the season for nightmare.

I was glad to be back.

The Winch controllers had promised me an extra four hours. That was my margin for error, as much as they dared grant us without risking huge damage to the umbilical. Rebka had no idea how much that four-hour dispensation would cost in possible recriminations if things went wrong. I did, and I was horrified at how much the controllers were willing to put on the line for my benefit—I knew it wasn't for Rebka or the Carmel twins, they were strangers. If we got back in one piece, I owed the group of engineers a debt that I would have trouble ever repaying. How much is four hours worth? At midsummer maximum, the price was too high to calculate.

We were approaching the first of our selected craters, moving in on it to the irregular accompaniment of distant thunder. Part weather, part volcanic eruption. As Quake trembled, atmospheric storms grew in intensity.

Our timing was bad. Quake's three-hour night was rushing in on us, and there was no way that Eta-Cass B could shine into the depths of the crater. I handed the controls of the hover-car over to Rebka, and took a last look at the dark pit-depth in front of us before I opened the door.

"Hold us steady right here. Don't move, unless you have to because you see a lava-flow getting too near. Sound the siren if that happens—I don't want to come back up and find molten rock coming down to meet me."

The air outside was stifling. I guessed that it had heated up another five degrees since we had last opened the door. It took me only a few seconds to walk over to the lip of the crater and begin the slither down its steep sides. In that short time I felt perspiration start out onto my face and arms. It took me another couple of minutes to stumble and scrape my way to the bottom, to the place where the head-high purple ferns marked the area shielded from the direct sun. The flashlight that I carried was not much use. It allowed me to avoid the worst stumbles, but I still had a number of semi-falls on the way down.

After a few minutes of thrashing around in the crater bottom, I was confident that it held nothing but plant life. No one could have forced their way into the ferns without leaving a trail of broken stems behind them.

I turned and began to scramble my way back up the steep sides, noting that the bottom of the ferns had managed to slash through my pants and leave lines of itchy cuts all over my lower calves. I could feel a strong reaction there, a quick swelling caused by the irritant sap. By the time I reached the car the pain and itching were all I could stand.

"Nothing?" said Rebka, as I swung open the door. It was a rhetorical question. I dropped into my seat and waved at him to get us moving again. While I sprayed my legs with a coagulant and anesthetic, Rebka started us cautiously on our way to the second crater. As soon as I was in reasonable shape I went over and took the controls.

"We have to go faster. I took too long down in that crater." I risked opening the throttle one more notch, remembering that the path towards the lake side held no major rock outcrops that might cripple the hover-car. "Good thing it's getting light again. We'll find the next one easier with the sun shining. I lost time in the bottom of that one splashing in a sort of messy bog. If I could have seen it from above I'd have known ahead of time that we wouldn't find them in that."

After a couple of minutes I had to decrease speed again. Rocks or no rocks, there was no way that I could hold our pace. Quake was feeling the full power of the solar forces. The ground that we moved over was in constant motion, an uneasy, irregular stirring. I increased the pressure of the under-blowers, to move us fifty centimeters higher from the ground, and ran us along as fast as I dared.

Before I went down into the next crater I borrowed Rebka's knee-high boots. They were two sizes too small, but I could stand a couple of blisters and cramped toes better than lacerated calves. Dawn had arrived as we drove. The sun had risen through a red, smoky screen that made everything in the air of Quake diffuse and incredibly beautiful. Dust in the upper atmosphere offered some shielding from the solar rays—not much, but anything was welcome.

This time it took me only a minute to determine that no one was in the crater. All I had to do was make a quick circuit of the stand of vegetation at the bottom, and confirm that its perimeter was undisturbed. On the way around it I saw a small shape fleeing in front of me. Some native animal had lost the battle with the planet. Something must have gone wrong with its time sense, and now it was too late to estivate. There was a tiny chance that it could survive summertide by crouching deep in the vegetation. I wished it luck as I scrambled back to the car, using my hands to help me in the ascent. The crater walls were perceptibly hotter than the air. That didn't look good for the little animal.

A few more hours, and this pit would probably see a lava breakthrough. The plants and animals would be buried beneath the molten flow. Ten years from now, wind-borne seeds would begin the recolonization, rooting in the mineral-rich surface of hardened lava. Twenty years, and the animals would return.

It occurred to me that we could adapt to life on Quake, if we really wanted to. All it needed was a change in attitude. We would have to accept a more rapid breeding rate, and the idea that we would lose one-fifth of the population each year. Maybe we had just become too soft. Random, violent death had gone from our lives—look at Rebka's reaction to the possible death of the Carmel sisters. We had no plagues, famines, or natural disasters to thin our ranks—unless we chose to seek them out in places like Quake.

Rebka was looking anxiously at his watch when I finally got back to the car. I dropped into my seat and sat, head down, for a full minute while he again got us moving on our way.

"We're going too slowly," he said. "We'll never do it in time. Four more hours, and we have to turn back."

His face was pinched with tension. I at least had the chance to work some of mine off, scrambling around the crater bottoms and burning up the adrenalin.

"One more crater," I said, as soon as I had enough breath to speak. "The next one is closest to the lake. I give it a better chance than the other two we've done."

After the outside heat the inside of the car felt freezing. I gulped down fruit juice and a stimulant and took over the controls again. Now I drove with one eye on the sun—I wanted to reach the final crater in full daylight. Eta-Cass A seemed to be racing across the sky, a reddened, dust-dimmed blur that occasionally broke through to send bright spears of yellow light onto the heaving surface of Quake. I was racing against the sun, and I was losing. Noon eclipse came when we were little more than halfway there.

Close as we were to perihelion, I knew that the outside temperature was still far from its peak. Fractures on the surface of Quake were still releasing the inner fires, at the same time as Eta-Cass A poured in more solar flux.

We came to the third crater as night was again falling. The orange glow around the horizon was continuous now, reflecting from the high dust clouds. As I climbed out of the car there was a violent burst of crimson light directly in front of me, not more than a kilometer from the other side of the crater. As the lava burst from the volcano summit, I saw Amy.

She was watching the eruption, clapping her hands as the crimson was replaced by the glow of white-hot lava. The stream crested the cone and began a quick march towards us, sputtering and sparking where it touched the cooler earth.

I turned and looked closely at her face. There was no fear there, only the rapt entrancement of a child at a fireworks display. The caution had to come from me—there was no place for it in her view of the world.

I tugged at her sleeve. "All right, that's the high spot of the show. We have to start back to the Stalk. It's a five-hour journey, and by the time we get there they'll be thinking about loosening the tether and moving it up."

She turned to me. I knew that pout very well. "Not yet. Let's watch until the lava gets to the water."

"No. I'm not taking more risks. We have to get out of here. I'm beginning to boil."

I was, too, despite the air curtain that kept a sheath of cool air blowing about us. My heat came from inside, the burning of my own worry.

"In a minute." Amy turned all the way around, looking over the whole horizon. There was, thank God, no new eruption emerging near the lake. "All right, then. Marco, you've got to learn how to have fun. All the time we've been here, you've been sitting there like a block of stone." She took my hand and pulled me closer. "You have to let yourself go and get into things."

I felt relief as we began to walk back to the car. We still had plenty of time. From the lake side, we went back to the high point where we had first parked to overlook the arrival of summertide. I had wanted to stay there, but somehow we had found ourselves outside, halfway to the lake. I didn't want to be too near when the lava met the water behind us.

And now I was again at the same lake—my fourth visit during

Quake's summer. This time, I was hurrying into the shaded depths of an old crater, closer to midsummer maximum than ever before. Quake's brief twilight was over and the pit below me was black and unfathomable. I shone my light close to the ground in front of me and half slipped, half fell down the steep slope.

At the bottom there was no sign of the lava glow, but I could still hear and feel the broken percussion of seismic movement. When I put my hand to it, the ground was at blood heat. This crater too was probably due for drastic change.

Then I shone my torch on the central clump of plants, and knew that our search had changed its character. The stems along a two-meter stretch were broken off at the base.

I knew that no native animal was large enough to make that opening—and such life as there was on Quake should be long since deep down in the cooler earth. I hurried forward. Ten paces in, close to the center of the clump, I found them.

Rebka's description of the twins, added to the ID pack images, should have given me a complete picture of them. But it's always hard to convert meters and kilos to flesh and blood. When I first saw them, sitting back to back in the clearing they had made and touching all the way from hips to shoulders, my first thought was how small they looked. I am not a tall man, but they would not have come higher than my shoulder.

My blundering approach must have been noisy but it had been lost in Quake's summer turmoil. The Carmel twins were unaware of my presence. Rushed as I was, I stood for a second before I entered the air curtain that marked the edge of their camp. Within that two-meter radius I knew that it would be cool and comfortable, even if the temperature outside went up another fifty degrees. The danger came from below. The ground beneath my feet was shaking and trembling, moving every few seconds with an upward flexing like the clench of a birth contraction.

The girls were twins, and identical twins—but they were not identical in all ways. The moment that I saw them I knew that the one closer to me was Jilli. Some subtle difference—*was* it an air of dependence?—had been captured by the ID pack.

I stood there much too long, mindlessly watching, until finally I forced myself to move forward, in through the air curtain.

Both girls turned in alarm at my sudden appearance. They must have decided that there were no large animals on Quake, but I wasn't risking the beam of a construction laser. I spoke as soon as they saw me.

"Don't panic. I'm here to help you."

I kept my voice calm, but there was no mistaking the terrible fear that showed on both their faces. Elena turned and began to grope in the case by her side. I sighed and lifted the stunner. It wasn't going to be easy.

"Don't move, either of you, or I'll have to put you both to sleep for a while. That won't help anybody—we have to get up that slope and out of here as fast as we can."

While I was speaking I groped in my jacket with one hand and pulled out my official ID pack. I tossed it forward to lie on the ground in front of Jilli. She picked it up.

"Look inside that," I said. "I'm here on official business." Still neither of them spoke. "On behalf of the Government of Dobelle," I went on, "and on behalf of the Office of Species Protection, I arrest you as suspects for the genocide of the Zardalu species. You will be taken to the planetary center on Ehrenknechter, formally charged there, and transported for testing and interrogation on Sol."

That was the formal piece, but I added, "Unless you both want to die here when summertide hits, we'd better get out of this crater. Let's go, the sooner we do it the better our chances are."

I didn't expect resistance. There was no rational way in which they could hope to disarm me, or if they did there was no chance that they would survive on Quake. But neither girl moved.

Finally Elena spoke. She did not look at me, but she took Jilli's hand.

"We won't go," she said. "Leave us alone here. If we die,

that ought to be enough punishment. We'll take our chances here.''

I looked at Jilli. She nodded agreement. I was in trouble, and it was of a type that I had never expected. I could make both sisters unconscious easily enough—but could I get them back to the lip of the crater without assistance? The heat was getting worse and worse, even though they were not aware of it inside the conditioned air of their camp. And I was slowly becoming aware of Quake's higher gravity—not much more than Egg, about ten percent, but that would be important if I had to carry anything up the steep slope.

"You don't have the choice," I said. I still kept my voice as gentle and reassuring as I could. "If I have to, I can take you both in unconsciousness. You know what this is?''

I waved the stunner, and both sisters nodded.

"I don't want to use it unless I have to," I went on. "It would take time to get you up there, and we don't have time. Make me do it that way, and you'll make my chances of living through this a good deal less.''

Jilli put one hand up to her face. I couldn't stand the look in her eyes. It was despair, final and hopeless, the knowledge that something worse than death was coming to her. I swallowed my own bile and stood there, waiting. Around us, frequent thunder marked the passing of precious seconds. Unless they could be persuaded quickly, their final decision would be irrelevant.

Jilli looked around at her sister, questioning. "It's not just us, Ellie," she said. "We can't make it more dangerous for him. He hasn't done anything to us.''

I didn't see Elena Carmel's expression change, but her twin could read signs that were invisible to a stranger. She turned back to me.

"You can put away your gun. We'll come with you.''

They began to break camp, but I stopped them.

"No time for that. Just bring what you absolutely need.''

Two nods, in unison. They picked up one bag each and we stepped outside the air screen.

Away from the protective curtain of cool air, perspiration seemed to burst out of our skins. Static conditioning areas were easy, but we had no way of providing a mobile one that could move along with us. I motioned for them to go ahead of me up the slope. It would have been better if I had led them back along the way I came, but even now I couldn't be sure there would not be a change of heart. Close as we were to our deadline, it was still better to take a few extra minutes to make sure that I reached the hover-car with the Carmel sisters safely in tow. As we climbed the rough slope, I noticed that Jilli and Elena moved side by side, closer together than I would have chosen. If one fell, both might slip back down.

By the time we reached the top I was feeling crushed. Rebka and I had gone a long time without rest or sleep. The combination of higher gravity, fatigue, heat, tension and troublesome old memories was beating me down. I longed for a chance to collapse into the hover-car chairs. The cuts on my legs had opened again, and I could feel the blood trickling down into Rebka's borrowed boots.

The relief on Rebka's face when we appeared over the top of the crater lip lifted me a little, enough to grin at him as he swung to the ground and helped the two women inside the hover-car. They looked at him, once, then turned their eyes down. He was the Inquisitor, the Tormentor, pursuing them remorselessly across the space between the stars.

If I could read their look, Rebka could analyze it in detail. He was thoughtful for a second.

"Sit there, in the back," he said. "The worst is over now."

He left them to their own thoughts while he secured the door and turned the car around for the return journey—with more experience, he would have done that while I was gone and saved us some precious time. Then he handed the controls over again to me and went to sit opposite the Carmel sisters. I would have preferred to take a few minutes rest, but we had no choice. We were too late already, half an hour past my own mental deadline for the return. I set the forward motor. Too fast for full safety, I hurled us across the heaving, smoldering surface, back towards the foot of the umbilical.

Fatigue and tension; they can combine to produce strange

effects. I felt as though there were three of me in the hover-car.
One was piloting us back to our starting point, automatically
skirting dangerous spots on Quake but still trying to hold as
close as possible to a straight line on the ground. The second
man inhabiting my body was listening to the conversation behind me between Rebka and the twins. Their voices seemed to
cut in and out, disappearing completely when the way ahead of
us required total attention. The crust of Quake was full of new
fissures and fractures that had appeared since our outward trip.

Who was the third man? He was a shadow, a pair of eyes and
ears looking out on Quake—the Quake of long ago, the garden
planet that existed before Perling threw a planetary ball across
the inner System. The third man watched and listened, while a
young, auburn-haired woman danced and skipped her way
across the sunny plains, smiling wide-eyed at the noon eclipse
and breathing in the fragrance of dawn and evening. By careful
concentration, he could banish the drab reality of the present.

I would like to have stayed with the third man, but the other
two intruded. First it was a stream of lava, dull black-red across
our path. I had to swing a kilometer left to clear it. Four more
minutes had been lost. And I had to hear what was being said
behind me, because part of the young woman that danced across
my sight was Jilli Carmel, the happy Jilli who had looked at me
from the ID pack.

"There is nothing that I can do about that part of it," Rebka
was saying. Somehow or other he had broken through the dark
despair that had climbed out of the crater. The two women were
talking to him, low-voiced and intense.

"You must go back to Earth with me," he said. "I have no
latitude in that area. Perhaps if you were not human, or I were
not human, I could take greater risks. But we must let you prove
conclusively, to every species on the Council, that you were
controlled only by fear and early experience when you killed and
fled on Lasalle. I have seen the record of your childhood. I know
what drove you to act as you did."

Not true, said a small part of me. You told me that you
couldn't understand why they fled, any more than I could.
Rebka was playing his own game, making the conversation

behind me follow some predetermined pattern that he had established.

"We were terrified," said Jilli Carmel softly. "They came so quietly. I had the beam disperser close to me, and I fired it without thinking. There was nothing that Ellie could do to stop me—it was all done in a second."

"But I would have done just the same," said her sister. "I woke up a second after you, that was all."

"And then we ran," said Jilli simply, as though she and her sister were one person continuing a monolog. "We ran away, and jumped to Kirsten."

"But we knew someone would be pursuing us," said Elena. "Someone from the Council. So we kept going until we reached Dobelle. This planet seemed safe, there was no one here to betray us to you."

There was a long silence. In front of us we faced the long, slow hill that led to the foot of the umbilical. I strained my eyes through the smoke, but we were still too far away to see anything. I did not mention it to anyone behind me, but the deadline had passed fifteen minutes earlier.

"I don't understand," said Rebka at last. "You killed by accident, when you were still half-asleep. You killed beings who looked like those who had killed your own parents. Our tests would have shown that, as soon as we began them. The Council will not offer punishment for an accident. We would have given you a rehabilitation treatment, but only to cure the things that caused you your fear." His voice was baffled and disturbed. "We are not monsters on the Council. We would never do more rehabilitation than is necessary for your own good."

Another long silence. I concentrated on steering us across a charred and smoking landscape and waited for some response from the Carmel twins. There was no time to spare for my third self. We were just hours away from summertide maximum, and it took full attention to move us safely across the tide-torn, dragon-haunted surface of Quake. The ground moved constantly, hot vapors breathed from fissures in the rock, and the sky above was a rolling mass of fine ash and bright lightning.

We skimmed through occasional downpours of warm, sulphur-charged rain that steamed as it touched the hot earth.

"For our own good," said one of the girls at last. Her voice was bitter and accusing. "You'll give us rehabilitation necessary for our own good. That is exactly what we are afraid of. We don't want your treatment, any of it."

I couldn't tell which of the twins had spoken, and I had my hands too full with the controls to risk turning round to look.

"It wouldn't hurt you," said Rebka. I felt sure that he was staring at them with his intense, deep-probe look, trying to see through into the working of their souls, as he had done to me. "How could you think we would hurt you? Doesn't the Council have a good reputation? We want to make you stronger, saner people—you will be much happier after treatment than you could be before it."

"You can't guarantee that." Again, which twin was speaking? I thought it was Elena. "That means you'd remove our problems, doesn't it? Make us 'saner'—but we know what that would include."

"It would mean that you'd remove the thing that is more important to us than anything else," said the other sister. "You wouldn't consider it at all—except as one of our 'problems.' "

"We would remove *nothing* that was right for you," said Rebka. He was beginning to sound baffled—even irritated, which would never do for a member of the Species Protection Council. "We'd make only minor changes, enough to let you live normal balanced lives—without those terrible childhood memories."

"Of course. Normal, balanced lives. We knew that's the way the Council would work." The voice was low and intense.

"But you see, we're *not* normal," said her sister. "Your treatment would make us like other people. Does the Council have other human members?"

"No. We have only one of each species—but every species is represented," Rebka's voice was puzzled now. "Why do you ask that?"

"Because to us there is one species that is not considered by the Council—its needs are ignored. No other species has *twins*—and we are different from you.''

"You'd change us''—I felt sure that was Jilli speaking. "You'd make it so we were not dependent on each other, the way that we have been all our lives. Did you know that one other pair of identical twins was given Council treatment? They lost their closeness.''

There was a sudden grunt from Rebka, like an in-drawn breath of pain. The sisters kept up their attack.

"Can't you see that to twins like us, what you'd do is the worst thing that we can imagine? Worse than killing us, worse than putting us into a prison—if we were together. But you'd do it to us and think you were helping—and not one of the other species on the Council would help us, because they have no idea what it means to be identical twins.''

Rebka grunted again, but he had himself under control. "I've been blind," he said. "Blind for years. I've been conceited enough to think that I can empathize with any creature, from any world. Now I find that I don't understand my own species. No single individual can every truly understand a compound being, that's obvious. That's why you fled from Delta Pavonis?''

"Of course." Both spoke together.

"We would have treated you," went on Rebka, as though to himself. "We *would* have broken your dependence. Of course we would. All our psych profiles would tell us that it was unnatural. In anyone else, it would be.''

"But not for us. We would rather die.''

"I understand. Your pain is my pain.'' Rebka sounded as though he were repeating some familiar litany, some phrase that he had used many times to soothe himself in his work. But it was true, I was sure of it. Their pain *was* his, and he felt it all the more keenly because he had missed seeing it for so long. I knew that the rehab procedures back on Earth were due for a big shake-up as soon as Rebka got back.

If he got back. The view from the front screen grabbed my attention. Ahead of us, dim through the smoke, I could see the great column of the umbilical. It was about a kilometer and a half away—but it was no longer attached to Quake at its base. I looked at my watch. We were more than an hour after our last deadline. The controllers must have waited as long as they dared, held it well past the promise they had made to me. But at last they had been forced to begin the lift. Worse yet, dead ahead of us I could see a ribbon of red-hot lava, winding between us and the foot of the umbilical stalk. I could find no way around it—the top of the hill that we wanted was surrounded by a moat of fire.

I killed the engine that gave us our forward motion and we remained hovering on the air cushion. I tracked the lava with the scope, confirming that our way ahead was blocked, then turned to the others in the rear of the car.

"Problems," I said. "There's a lava flow ahead, about thirty meters wide. We have to make a choice. I don't see any way across it, but we could look all the way around and see if there's any sort of break. That will cost us a good deal of time—and we'll risk more eruptions here while we do it. We're right at summertide maximum."

Rebka had been sitting with his head down, concentrating on his own problem. He slowly looked up. "And what is our alternative? So far you have offered no choice."

"We can shoot the lava. I think I can get the car across it all right—it's not impossibly wide. But I think the heat will burn through the skirts around the base, and we'll lose all our lift. We might have to get out and go the rest of the way on foot."

He came forward and looked ahead, noting that the umbilical had been raised but apparently seeing no point in mentioning anything that would further worry the Carmel sisters. "It would only be about a kilometer," he said.

"A bit more than that. But take a look at the outside temperature. It's a furnace out there. I don't see how we could take more than ten minutes of it."

"Are you sure that the lava will burn the skirts on the car?"

"No, we might get lucky. But even if we're not, I think it's the best bet we have. Feel that tremor? Quake's getting more restless, will do until we're past summertide. We don't have much time to think about this."

Rebka turned and looked at the twins. He seemed to be able to read their faces and the look that passed between them. I was beginning to feel like a blind man—Elena and Jilli could read each other, and Rebka could read both of them, but I couldn't even track my own emotions. I looked back at him, and he nodded.

"We agree. It's the best hope we have. Let's go over the lava, and hope that we will reach the foot of the Stalk before the skirt burns through."

It was not a time for debate. I nodded, turned, and pushed the forward power control to maximum. We jerked forward, accelerated to our top speed, and lurched up onto the river of lava.

After the first second, I lost sight of the path ahead. The view was blocked by a thick black smoke that rose from the burning skirt of our car. I had no idea what lay in front of us, but I held the speed to maximum—we had nothing to lose. We ploughed on, shaking and swaying, and after a few more seconds there was another lurch, this time downwards. We were over the molten river with no obstacle between us and the foot of the umbilical.

But we were sitting in a dead hover-car. I applied maximum forward power and it produced nothing but a rough grating sound. The under-skirt was gone. I cut all power and stood up.

"Come on. We have to go on foot. The faster we do this, the better."

I swung the door open and stepped out onto the surface. The lava lay behind us, ten meters away. After the cool interior of the car, the air of Quake hit me like a solid wedge of heat. I held the door for the others to step through, as faucets turned on inside my skin. Ten minutes? I doubted that we could stand more than five. Elena came out first, then Jilli. I helped them to the ground—the contact with Jilli's hand made my skin tingle, as though there existed a big potential difference between her skin and mine.

Last of all came Rebka, stumbling down and heading for the base of the stalk at a shambling run. I realized that I had shown more speed than sense. I was still wearing his boots, that he had lent to me when I looked at the second crater, and he was wearing my shoes—two sizes too big for him. We were like a couple of cripples, hobbling and staggering along after the Carmel sisters.

They were making good speed, about forty meters in front of me. They were running side by side, almost holding hands, but as I watched Jilli had to slow a little and turn in her path to avoid a patch of jagged rock. And in that same moment I saw, five meters ahead of Elena, the odd blurring of the flat surface.

It was like a slight shimmer, a hint of loss of focus in my view of the ground. I had seen it once before, four years earlier. I stopped and screamed. Even as I shouted my warning, the scene before me was dimming, over-written by memory so intense that it had never faded.

Amy, laughing and playful in the heat, ran on ahead of me, back to the foot of the umbilical. It was just a few hundred meters away.

"Hey, slow down. I'm the one that has to carry the equipment."

She spun around and laughed at me. "Come on, Marco. Learn to have fun. We don't need all that stuff–leave it here."

Her tone was teasing, making me smile in spite of the heat. "I can't just leave it–it's official property. Wait for me, Amy."

She laughed, and danced on, on into that blurring of the surface, the shimmering ground of summertide.

There was less than a centimeter of solid crust. Beneath it lay boiling, pitch-black slime. The surface bore her weight long enough for her to get beyond my reach, then it broke. While I watched, she plunged screaming into the bubbling mud.

Before I could reach the edge she was gone, down into the seething pitch. I threw myself flat and plunged my hands down into it, up to the elbows in the boiling blackness. I could grasp nothing solid. All that I could take back from Quake was pain, physical and mental. The scars were inside and out. The grafts could replace my skin, but nothing could replace Amy; not work, not sex, not even another visit to Quake at summertide.

I stood, screaming and screaming, as Rebka came alongside me. He looked at me for one split-second, then hit me savagely across my left cheek. I jerked back to the present.

Elena, chest-deep in the boiling pitch, was writhing in agony. Four paces from her was Jilli, running towards her. Rebka and I threw ourselves at her, falling as we did it. I managed to get a hold of her waist and he grabbed the back of her boots. One more step and she would have joined her sister, as Elena disappeared beneath the seething surface.

Whose screams was I hearing? Not Elena's, she was gone. Jilli's, certainly, and probably my own.

Working together, Rebka and I managed to drag Jilli away. She would have gone back, to plunge herself after her sister, but between us we managed to hold her and work our way along to the foot of the umbilical. The main tether was well above our heads, seven or eight hundred meters and still rising steadily.

I let go of Jilli with one hand, relying on Rebka to stop her pulling free. I took the thick cable that hung from the umbilical, wound it about the three of us, and pressed the activator at the end. We were hauled aloft, crushed together by the tension in the cable—it had been designed to accommodate only one person.

Up we went, into the smoke-filled sky of Quake. All about us, the summer lightning flickered, and the ground beneath swayed and shuddered like a drunkard. Jilli was weeping desperately, and Rebka was beyond tears. The loss of Elena was doubly affecting to him—he felt his own loss, and shared Jilli's.

And I? Selfish as ever, I was back again in my own past, four years gone, watching Amy sink into the boiling mud. But now Amy was Elena, and Amy was Jilli. And I was Amy, sinking forever into the molten interior of Quake, while we slowly ascended, swinging and turning, to the safety of the foot of the umbilical.

None of us was aware of our danger, dangling from a system strained beyond its safety limit, five hundred meters above the ground. How could we feel danger, when each of us was ready to welcome death? Perhaps not. Perhaps Rebka's control still existed even then. There are stories about Sector Moderators—perhaps I ought to call them legends—stories of Moderators cut in half by lasers, and still able to discuss terms logically with their attackers. I can't believe those stories—the body control needed to maintain the blood pressure and keep the heart pumping would be too much. But I do know, from my own observation, how much pain Rebka could stand, and still run, think and work. My proof?

The crew who received us into the Emergency Entrance of the umbilical took one look at us and at once called ahead to Midway Station for complete physical support functions in the hospital. All of us had been burned by hot ash and spatters of boiling mud. Most of Jilli's long hair had been burnt off, and I had plunged one of my legs above the boot top into the molten pitch. But Rebka had fared worst of all.

He had lost both my shoes in our final struggle to the umbilical, and the underside of both his feet had burned through to the bone. I saw them when we reached the umbilical, bloodied slabs of raw meat, oozing lymph and crusted with burnt tissue. Rebka had carried Jilli on those, for more than a kilometer—and was able to comfort Jilli as we were hoisted up by the cable.

That I saw, and nothing more before heavy sedation plunged me into a sleep too deep for dreams.

It took two days to get us back to the hospital on Egg. I drifted, always on the edge of consciousness, as we were carried carefully back along the umbilical. My first real memory came when I awoke in my hospital bed. It was night and the dome was transparent above me. I must have somehow operated the controls myself.

It was after perihelion now, and close to midnight on Egg. The daylit face of Quake hung above me. It was blackened and smoking, with ash clouds hiding most of the surface features. I watched and watched, until the surface lost the sunlight and glowed on, a dull and savage red. Then I turned my face to the wall and waited for another dawn.

Before it came I awoke again and found Rebka by my bedside. He was a tough specimen. His legs ended in giant swollen balls of padding, but he was up and about and fully alert. He was still a small, thin man with a sad mouth, but I was under no illusions. I watched him warily.

"Jilli is doing well," he said. "I wish I could say the same for you."

"I'm fine."

"No you're not. Did you realize that you had been losing blood ever since you went down into that first crater?"

I shook my head. "No. I put coagulant on my legs. The bleeding didn't begin again until I was climbing out of the crater with the Carmel sisters. There was no time to bother with it after that."

"You were lucky to make it to the umbilical." Rebka smiled.

"I suppose I'm lucky too. I don't think I could have handled Jilli on my own."

He sat down on the end of my bed, watching me with steady eyes. I glowered back at him.

"Jilli and I will be leaving in three more days," he said. "She will be fit enough to travel by then."

"To Earth?"

He nodded. "She'll need more rehab than ever now. For her childhood and for the Zardalu. And for Ellie."

I didn't like to hear that. I began to replay everything again inside my head. Elena and Amy were tangled up there—I could no longer separate the two deaths.

"Can you help her?" I asked after a few seconds.

"Of course. We can help anyone. In her case, the punishment will be waived, but she will badly need the rehab treatment. The death of the Zardalu is merely my guarantee that she will be obliged to take it. In some cases I have no powers of coercion."

I looked up, out of the transparent dome. "You can only force someone to treatment if there has been a crime."

"It is worse than that." He shrugged his thin shoulders. "There are really two kinds of crime. I can pursue and bring to justice—and to rehab treatment—one type of criminal. The one who commits an act of savagery or injustice against another sentient being. But I am not allowed to do anything about a person who commits a crime against himself."

"It's not easy to rehab a suicide." I said it intentionally, to see if he would wince. He did, but then he smiled. I knew he had seen through me again.

"Not suicide. I didn't mean suicide." (He was proving to me that he was tough enough to use the word). "What kind of crime is it if a man blights his own great potential? I feel just as badly if a man cripples his own hopes and dreams, as if he does it to another.'' He leaned forward. ''Captain Mira, when Jilli Carmel and I leave for Earth, will you come with me?''

''For rehab?''

He nodded. ''First level erasure. You'll lose memories, but little change to your personality. You'll still be you.''

I lay back on my pillow and looked up at Quake again. Memories, those I certainly had. Rebka knew his job better than anyone. But it seemed to me that memories were all that I had. Take those away, and what was left? Nothing.

I shook my head. ''I need no rehabilitation. I'll stay here on Egg, and keep an eye on the traffic with Quake.''

He did not appear at all surprised. ''Very well,'' he said quietly. ''I told you, I have no control of that. You have committed no crime that I can document. We will go, Jilli and I.''

He stood up, gingerly on his swaddled feet.

''She will be cured?'' I said.

He nodded. ''She will be in treatment for one hundred Earth-days. When that is complete, she will be very confused about everything. In order for her rehab to succeed completely, she will need help in the year or two after that.''

I lifted my head up from the pillow so that I could look at him properly. ''I'm sure you will succeed.'' It was hard to believe that he had given up on me.

''We may succeed with Jilli.'' he said. ''I hope so. But I cannot be involved in that phase of her treatment. I must go to another case on Peacock A—a bad one. I will go with Jilli as far as Earth, for the first rehab phase, then I must leave her.''

I looked down at his bandaged feet. ''No rest for you, eh? When do you get your own rehab treatment, Councilman? No one is more driven than you.''

He smiled. I had tried to get in a low blow, and it had bounced off him. ''Drives in a good cause are all right,'' he said. ''In any case, I am not the subject of the discussion. I want to talk about Jilli Carmel. As I told you, I have authority only in certain areas, but one of those is the decision as to where subjects who have been rehabilitated will receive Phase Two of their treatment. On that, I have full authority. I have decided that Jilli will spend that time here, on Quakeside.''

"You can't do that," I said. My throat was constricted and I had to choke the words out. I had enough problems already.

"I'm afraid that I can, Captain," he said. "Check it if you wish, but you'll find that your cooperation is obliged by Sector law."

"You can't go away and dump this in my lap," I began, but Rebka had turned and was walking towards the door.

"I can," he said. He turned in the doorway and pulled something from his pocket. "By the way, you might want to keep this." He lobbed it through the air and it landed lightly on my chest as he walked out of the room.

I picked it up. It was the ID pack of Jilli Carmel, smiling as she had been before they had landed on Delta Pavonis. I stared at it for a long time, then put it under my pillow. I wondered just how well Rebka knew his job. Was it possible that he knew it so well that the rehab center on Earth was something that he could dispense with if he had to?

I moved the dome to its opaque setting and the image of Quake slowly dimmed above me and disappeared. I couldn't answer my own question. Not yet. Did Rebka know me, after a few Days, better than I knew myself? Perhaps in another year I might have some kind of answer.

AFTERWORD: SUMMERTIDE.

About a year ago I was sitting in a bar in Brighton, drinking beer with Bob Forward. His first novel, ''Dragon's Egg'', was finished but not yet published, and we were chatting randomly about exotic stellar and planetary settings for stories. We had known each other long before either one of us published a word of fiction, so we tended in our conversation to dwell on the science side of sf plotting.

Bob mentioned that he had come up with a rather interesting planetary system and he was going to build a novel around it. Naturally, I asked for details. He didn't want to give them. He said that he preferred not to talk until he had everything plotted out to a conclusion. I quite understand that attitude—some writers go further, and will never say a word about a story until the last sentence has been typed and the finished story is away in the hands of an editor. So I just nodded, and instead I started to describe the planetary doublet system that I developed for use in ''Summertide,'' which I had finished and sold just a couple of months earlier for publication in DESTINIES.

I described the twin planets of Quake and Egg, rotating just outside the Roche limit, and I mentioned the big tidal effects that would be generated if we had a highly eccentric orbit for the pair about their sun.

Bob didn't seem too responsive, so at last I stopped talking. Long silence. Then he said: ''I was thinking that my novel would probably be called ROCHE WORLD.'' It would be about— you are allowed one guess—a planetary pair that rotates about each other just outside the Roche limit. The eccentric orbit of the doublet around their sun would produce huge tidal forces . . .

So of course we had to talk plots, and it fortunately turned out that they were completely different. Thank Heaven. I had just been through a similar experience a few months earlier, with

THE WEB BETWEEN THE WORLDS and Arthur Clarke's *THE FOUNTAINS OF PARADISE*. Coincidences lose their charm if they begin to happen regularly.

I really shouldn't have worried. A system like Dumbbell has enough strange properties to provide a hundred different story settings. Keep your eyes open for *ROCHE WORLD*, it will be interesting.

THE MARRIAGE OF
TRUE MINDS

It was one of those mornings where Nature seemed to have gone overboard in her desire for perfection. The sun was shining cheerfully from a sky of cloudless blue. Summer flowers nodded their heads with proper appreciation of the light breeze, birds sang, bees droned smiling in and out of the blossoms, and lambs skipped through the long grass. A morning, in short, where man and setting were in tune. So it seemed to Clarence, ninth Earl of Emsworth, as he leaned over the side of the pigsty, silent and admiring.

The object of his devotion looked to be full of the same blithe spirit. She was standing contentedly at the trough, busily working her way through the fifty-seven thousand, eight hundred calories that Wolff-Lehmann assures us is the appropriate daily intake for any pig who insists on the silver medal and will not take no for an answer. Turnip tops, bran mash, potato peelings and windfall apples were falling before her onslaught, like the Assyrian after a bad night out with the Angel of Death. The Empress of Blandings was in rare form, and the Earl watched in fascination. With that inspired attack, he felt, next week's contest in Bletchingham would be no more than a formality, a simple matter of a rubber stamp on an already assured decision. God's in his Heaven, all's right with the world, thought Lord Emsworth; or at any rate he might have, if his memory for poetry had been a little better.

Which shows that even ninth earls can be wrong and that there may be a worm in the most attractive apple. The Blandings worm, in fact, had just popped his head up over a hedge forty yards from the sty and was watching closely. Observers familiar

336

with the local scene might point out that the newcomer, worm or no worm, bore an amazing physical resemblance to George Cyril Wellbeloved, late pigkeeper at Blandings Castle, and but recently removed from the Earl's employ for the ghastly deed of pig nobbling. George Cyril, although he had encountered no difficulty in finding alternative employment, did not look happy with his new position. All may have been sunshine and brightness in the world at large, but in the heart of the pig man there was no light, save what from heaven was with the breezes blown. He had the look of a man whose employer had ordered him to win the Bletchingham Fat Pigs' Contest with a mere shadow of a pig, a puny porker whom the Empress of Blandings outweighed by a good ten stone.

It could not be done, thought G.C. Wellbeloved. Judging from the sounds that came from the sty, the contest was becoming more one-sided every minute. He ducked below the hedge and snaked back to the gate, where his new employer, Sir Hamish Mackay, was awaiting his return.

"Noo, whut's 'a seetuation, mon?"

Sir Hamish had spent most of his life harassing the unfortunate natives on the Afghanistan border, which was doubtless character-building but offered a Highland Scot no opportunity to learn more than a feeble approximation to spoken English.

"No."

"Nae what?"

"No." George Cyril was not a man to waste words.

"Ye mean we canna win?"

"Yes."

"The Empress is fatter than the Jewel o' Kabul?"

"Yes."

Sir Hamish was also sparing in his words. He retreated briefly behind his substantial whiskers for a moment's thought, then stepped closer to Wellbeloved. He faltered before the effluvium of pig manure that clung to George Cyril like a guardian angel, then firmed his resolve and pressed closer.

"Ye see whut that means?"

"Yes."

"We'll hafta pinch her."

"Yes."

Wellbeloved considered his last response for a moment. It was missing an important element.

"But I'll need a hundred pounds. Service beyond the usual duties."

"A hundred!"

"One hundred."

"Poonds!"

"Pounds," corrected George Cyril.

Sir Hamish looked at the pig man's stubborn countenance and fought a mighty battle within himself. To understand the baronet, it is first necessary to realize that he had not been a lifelong admirer of pigs. Most of his existence, he would frankly admit, had been a sordid waste, pottering about collecting medals and honors. Only recently had the overwhelming attraction of black Berkshire sows pierced his heart, and now he was trying to make up for lost time. If money were needed, money would be used. After all, what else was money for? But that decision had to win out over the native thriftiness of a true Scotsman, and the battle was of epic proportions within his sturdy breast.

"Fifty," he said at last.

"No. One hundred."

Sir Hamish sought to look Wellbeloved straight in the eye, with the expression that had in the past quelled the playful spirit of wounded Bengal tigers, but he was defeated by the pig man's sinister squint, which never permitted him to look into more than one eye at a time.

"Grrarrr," said Sir Hamish.

"Right," said George Cyril, recognizing a growl of assent when he heard one. "Eight o'clock tonight, after she's had her linseed meal. She gets quiet then. Money in advance. Don't forget it. I'll bring the van."

He turned and hurried away along the ditch, before Sir Hamish could offer a counterproposal. The latter stood there, fists clenched and whiskers vibrating. Like the poet Keats, he could not see what flowers were at his feet, or what soft incese hung upon each bough. He was thinking of his hundred pounds, and already he was suffering separation pains. No bloodthirsty Pathan, seeing Sir Hamish at that moment, would have risked an appearance before him; and in fact the head that popped up from behind the nearby hedge was not that of an Asian warrior. It belonged to George, the eleven-year-old grandson of Lord Emsworth, and it was clear from his expression that he had overheard the lot.

Under normal circumstances, the lad's reaction would have been to lie low until Sir Hamish had gone, then run off to spill the beans to his grandfather. He got along famously with Lord Emsworth, although the latter sometimes seemed unsure who he was.

Today, however, George had retired behind the hedgerow to brood over the unfairness of the world in general, and of Lord Emsworth in particular. When the editors of a recent issue of the *Champion Paper for Boys* gave full and explicit directions for the construction of a bow and arrow, presumably they expected their readers to follow them. And having followed them to the letter, it was not reasonable to suppose that an enterprising youth should leave the bow untested.

It was blind fortune that decreed that the household cat, after receiving an arrow amidships (fired, George estimated, from not less than twelve paces) should have chosen to leap through the open window, demolishing in transit three potted begonias and a china bust of Narcissus.

Lord Emsworth, under strong pressure from his sister, Lady Constance, had confiscated the bow and a bag of toffees and garnisheed George's allowance until the plants were paid for. The lad had retired to the hedge to seek solace from the latest copy of the *Champion Paper* and had been there, alone and palely loitering, when Sir Hamish and his pig man appeared on the scene.

What, you may ask, could an eleven-year-old do with the information he had overheard, other than take it to his older and wiser relatives? Setting aside any question of Lord Emsworth's wisdom, the problem is still a good one. It was pure coincidence that the latest issue of George's magazine should contain an article on becoming a millionaire in six months or less. The men who write for the *Champion Paper* are of catholic tastes—today the key to great wealth, tomorrow perhaps a novel and improved method of catching rats. The fact that the author of the latest article had never managed to make more than twelve shillings and sixpence a week was not mentioned in the magazine.

George's recent studies had told him exactly what to do. He stood up straight and looked calmly at Sir Hamish Mackay.

"I heard everything," he said. "The price for my silence is ten pounds."

Logically, George should have asked for more. Wellbeloved had set his fee at a hundred. On the other hand, ten pounds was the largest sum of which George had any personal acquaintance, and amounts beyond that felt vague and insubstantial. One hundred pounds would have raised questions within him, that logically should have troubled seekers of the Holy Grail, but apparently never did; to wit, what would one do with it if he had it? Ten pounds, on the other hand, would buy an excellent airgun and leave enough over for riotous living. More than that, despite the written advice he had just received, would make George uneasy.

"Grrrrrrr," said Sir Hamish.

It was not this time a growl of assent, but one of frustration. One does not make arrangements for a criminal act, only to have them overheard by a small boy who is the grandson of the victim. Sir Hamish would have sworn that there was no one around when he and George Cyril Wellbeloved had begun their brief conversation, and the boy's ectoplasmic manifestation had been a nasty shock.

Sir Hamish knew he would have to act quickly. However, the Mackays had survived in the highlands of Scotland for hundreds of years, and that called for a certain basic cunning.

"Aye. Hmph. Ten poonds. Ah," said Sir Hamish.

He reached into his pocket as though seeking his wallet and drew out a curiously carved ebony disc, to which a number of leather tassels had been tied. He handed it across the hedge to George.

"Here, houd this while Ah see if Ah ha' the poonds. Houd it soft, noo."

George looked curiously at the carvings on the disc's face.

"I say, what are these markings?"

"Spells. Dinna ye worrit ye'sel aboot them."

George had understood only the first word, but it was enough.

"Coo. Magic spells?"

"Aye. Yon's a giftie fra' ma auld serrvant, Khalatbar."

"Coo. What does it do?"

Sir Hamish pulled a much wrinkled piece of paper from his pocket. It seemed to have suffered diverse fates before being used to transmit a written message. The baronet looked at George with a cunning eye.

"D'ye read Pushtu?"

The lad shook his head, and Sir Hamish nodded in satisfaction.

"So Ah'll have tae translate fer ye."

He ran his eye quickly over the document, making the throat-clearing noise that in a Scotsman often passes for reasoned speech. At last he nodded.

"A verra valuable giftie. It turrns a mon tae a creature, when ye gie it a wee bit rubbit."

"Coo." George looked at the amulet reverently. "Any man? Why did he send it to you?"

Sir Hamish peered hard at the paper.

"Aye. Any mon, it's guid for. Ma serrvant used yon tae alterr his wifie's mother tae a croco-dial. He doesna' want her back noo, and he's sent me yon talisman tae pree-vent it bein' used agin."

"Coo."

George looked again at the ebony disc. Compared with that, a mere airgun seemed like an infant's plaything. His eyes gleamed at the possibilities. Fatty Parsons could be a hippo, and Cousin Juliet a horned toad. And what about Spotty Trimble? The potential was enormous.

"Would you sell it? I'd take it instead of ten pounds."

Sir Hamish rolled his eyes, wiggled his whiskers, bared his teeth and otherwise registered shock.

"Sell it? Ma laddie, yon's worrth a forrtune. Sell for ten poonds? Ah'd be gie'in' it awa'."

''Then I'll just have to go and tell grandfather what you'll be doing tonight.''

''Houd on.'' Sir Hamish held up his hand. ''A' right, ye win. Ye can tak' it. But mind noo, nae worrd aboot ony o' this. Gang awa' wi' ye.''

George grabbled the amulet and did his instant disappearing act behind the hedge. Sir Hamish breathed a sigh of relief at his wallet's close escape, smiled a horrid and whiskery smile, and set off for the gate. As he went, he threw away Khalatbar's request that Sir Hamish obtain for him a commission in the Coldstream Guards. It had, contrary to all logic, served a useful purpose. Now there were serious pigpinching arrangements to be considered, if the Empress were to be in his possession before the day was done.

* * *

George was Lord Emsworth's flesh and blood, and it was no more than natural that they should share a few traits of character. The lad had avoided the general dottiness and absentmindedness of the ninth Earl, but he had inherited his singleness of purpose. When Lord Emsworth went over to the pigsty to look at the Empress of Blandings, that is exactly what he did. If there were no interruptions, he would stand there happily until it was too dark to see, then stay to listen. In the same way, George now had his mind set on a fair test of the talisman, and he proposed to employ it, like Oberon's love potion, upon the next live creature that he saw. Fatty Parsons, Cousin Juliet, and Spotty Trimble were perhaps more intriguing targets, but the figure of Lord Emsworth, still bending over the sty, had the great advantage of immediacy.

George hurried closer, rubbing the talisman against his pullover.

The Empress had inexplicably stopped eating. Lord Emsworth was mentally urging her on with all his inadequate powers of mind, and at the same time he had thrust one hand into his jacket pocket. Encountering George's bag of toffees, some primitive childhood instinct led him to remove one, unwrap it. and lift it to his mouth.

The life of a prize pig is not particularly exciting. The high point of the Empress' week was likely to be signaled by the discovery of an unusually juicy turnip, or a better-than-average pail of potato peelings. But in that bland catalog of days, unenriched by strange events, one stood higher than the rest. A visitor had once thrown into the sty a bar of Devon toffee that had accidentally been dropped in the mud. Now, that ambrosial fragrance was again wafting to her nostrils. The Empress yearned towards it, as the hart after the water-brook, at the same time as Lord Emsworth, toffee poised before his lips, willed her to eat. George rubbed the talisman.

Nothing happened. His grandfather stood there still, in human form. George felt that old sinking feeling. For the first time, he began to appreciate the meaning of the phrase *caveat emptor*. Sir Hamish, the cunning haggis-eater, had tricked him into accepting a useless bit of carved wood instead of ten pounds.

George turned and ran back towards the gate. It might be too late to reverse the decision, but he had to give it a try. At the very least, he would have to learn Pushtu to make sure this sort of thing did not happen again.

Back at the sty, matters apparently ran on much as before. It may be, as the gents who specialize in studies of animal intelligence assure us, that a pig has no capacity for abstract thought. Its perceptions of matters intellectual, they assert, are dim and confused, and it can think of only one thing at a time. But for many years, friends and relatives had been saying much the same thing about Clarence, ninth Earl of Emsworth, and in rather stronger language. From a line purified by centuries of inbreeding, no one expects too much in the way of brains. Even so, many people felt that Lord Emsworth, with a power of mind that had on occasion been compared unfavorably with that of a boiled potato, took the matter to extremes.

This mental lack now stood the ninth Earl in good stead. Many men finding themselves on all fours inside a pigsty might be perplexed, even alarmed. Not so Lord Emsworth. Two feet in front of his snout stood a cornucopia of interesting food, and it all smelled delicious. A few turnip tops as hors d'oeuvres, he thought, and then perhaps twenty or thirty pounds of bran mash

as a nice entree. Deep within, Lord Emsworth sensed the vast
eating potential of his new form. He pushed his head forward
and took the first mouthful.

It was exquisite; better, in his judgment, than the *cordon bleu*
of Alphonse at the Astoria on even a very good day. The sun
shone warm on his broad back, and from the corner of his eye he
could see a patch of squishy mud that looked ideal for a post-
prandial wallow and nap. The peace that passeth all understanding filled his soul. He was perfectly happy.

The Empress, on the other hand, was a good deal less contented with her lot. Although the Earl, never a slave to fashion,
was dressed for comfort, the clothing felt strange against her
skin. She wriggled about uncomfortably inside the itchy shirt
and trousers. Then there was her new shape. It was wrong in a
number of ways, shorter here and longer there. If Richard III had
popped up next to her outside the sty, to complain that Nature
had shaped his legs of an unequal size and disproportioned him
in every part, the Empress would have applauded and joined in
the chorus. The only advantage of her new posture was a view of
the kitchen garden, denied to her from lower levels. It was a
sight that no prize pig, however transmogrified, could ever
resist. She turned and slowly made her way towards a laden
plum tree.

It was there, twenty-seven plums later, that Lady Constance
found her. Lord Emsworth's sister was not dressed for comfort.
She was heading for London, and her hat alone had denuded the
ostriches from a large portion of the African continent.

"There you are, Clarence," she said benevolently. There
was nothing like a trip to the big city to tone up the system. "I
see the plums are ripening nicely, but it looks as though the birds
have been at them."

The Empress grunted companionably. Lady Constance had
never been one to stand there and dish out the rotten potatoes
with her own fair hand, but her tone was friendly and the
Empress was of a naturally kindly disposition.

"I have asked Beach to serve tea on the terrace," went on
Lady Constance. "With the weather so beautiful, it seemed a

shame to remain inside. Come along, Clarence. I'm afraid I will not be able to join you, since my train leaves in thirty minutes.''

The Empress grunted.

"And remember," said Lady Constance, "you must be careful about the house tonight. Lock all the doors. I have asked Beach to do the same and to check everything before retiring. Julia called me this morning, and apparently the burglars are still at work in the neighborhood. The Bishop lost all his silver just last night.''

The Empress grunted again. When Lady Constance took her arm, she allowed herself to be led out of the orchard and over to the terrace, where an ample tea had been set out. Lady Constance looked at her watch.

"I'm afraid I'll have to leave you to it. I'll see you tomorrow afternoon.''

The Empress gave a final grunt and watched as Lady Constance hurried off through the French windows that opened onto the terrace. To some people, grunting might seem an inferior form of conversational response, but not to Lady Constance. She knew her brother well, and he would not in her opinion be easily mistaken for Oscar Wilde. She could recall occasions when Lord Emsworth's contribution to a dinner party had been the single word "Capital," repeated two or three hundred times, and another when he had described the care and feeding of prize pigs in such relentless and graphic detail that a lady guest of neurasthenic temperament had been led from the room in hysterics. Lord Emsworth had many sterling qualities, and his sister found a grunt to be quite satisfactory.

Left now to her own devices, the Empress found much at the tea table to interest her. Apart from sandwiches, potted shrimps, and several varieties of cakes and jams, the thoughtful Beach had set out a selection of hothouse grapes and peaches. Although rather hindered by her unfamiliar form, the Empress had a fair go at all of these delicacies and pretty much managed to sweep the board. It was only when the last mustard-and-cress sandwich had followed the final dollop of clotted cream down the hatch that the Empress became aware of the answer to the old riddle: What is the difference between the digestive system of an aging peer and that of a pig who has three times won the silver medal in the Shropshire Fat Pigs competition?

A little contemplation of the infinite seemed to be called for. She staggered back to the orchard, lay down full-length beneath the shade of a pear tree, and was soon fast asleep. The servant who came out to collect the remnants of the tea noticed the recumbent form of Lord Emsworth, but her main attention was reserved for the carnage on the terrace table. The *Shropshire Herald* was apt to miss some news items, that she knew, but an invasion of the district by a Mongol Horde ought to have drawn at least a paragraph. So she mused, and returned inside as the shadows lengthened across the rolling lawns of Blandings Castle, and the calm of evening descended over house and garden.

Descended outside the house, that is. Inside it, there was a certain amount of ferment—most of it within the breast of young George.

The lad had been thinking about his recent encounter with Sir Hamish, and it was becoming increasingly apparent to him that he had been manipulated, as clay in the hands of the potter. He realized that would not do. The *Champion Paper* had been quite firm on the point; millionaires-to-be never allow themselves to be separated from their earnings by the mere blandishments of a honeyed tongue.

Fortunately, it was not too late. George knew now what he had to do. At eight o'clock, Sir Hamish and Maestro Wellbeloved would observe their tryst by the pigsty, for the purpose of abducting the Empress. Clearly, if George were to turn up there also, return the talisman and again demand a tenner as the price of his silence, the baronet would have no choice but to give it to him. George had heard the yearning tone in Sir Hamish's voice when he spoke of the Empress, and it had sounded familiar. Like Lord Emsworth, the man would be putty where pigs were concerned.

George picked up the talisman and sneaked out of the back door of the castle. The shades of night were falling fast as he approached the Empress' sty, ready for the confrontation.

His timing had been excellent. Sir Hamish had just arrived but had not yet begun the operation proper. For one thing, his accomplice had been slightly delayed by a desire to make the first dent in his pig-pinching earnings. George Cyril Wellbeloved had just emerged from the Emsworth Arms, weaving a little but clearly feeling no pain, and was now making unsteady progress towards Blandings Castle. The other factor that had slowed Sir Hamish was the first sight of the Empress herself. He felt like some watcher of the skies, when a new planet swims into his ken. The Empress made the Jewel of Kabul look like the runt of the litter. Earth, thought Sir Hamish as he looked on her, had not anything to show more fair. What was that other Wordsworth poem that had helped to make his schooldays miserable? My heart leaps up when I behold, the Empress in her sty. Something like that. He gazed on.

In the sty itself, Lord Emsworth had just awakened from a blissful sleep. He had eaten until even a champion fat pig could hold no more, then enjoyed a refreshing mud wallow and nap. The only cloud on his horizon was the horrid object that had appeared over the side of the sty. Sir Hamish, taking his cue from the wily Pathan, had covered his face with boot-blacking before venturing forth on his ill-deeds. He would have reaped applause in the minstrel show on Brighton Pier, but he fitted in poorly with native customs in central Shropshire.

This was the tableau, Man and Pig, that presented itself to George as he approached the Empress' abode. He paused twenty paces short of the sty. Sir Hamish, eyes and teeth gleaming from a coal-black countenance, was a trifle off-putting. Although George was a brave lad, he decided he ought perhaps to give the talisman another chance before taking the next step. He pulled it from his pocket, rubbed it feverishly on his sleeve, and closed his eyes.

It was no use. When he opened them, Sir Hamish still stood there, black and fierce as ever. George girded up his loins, walked forward, and held out the amulet.

"You can have this back," he said. "I want my ten pounds instead."

The sudden appearance of his grandson startled Lord Emsworth. He was already feeling a little dazed by his abrupt

return to human form, if that term may be stretched to include
Sir Hamish.

"What?" he said. "What what?"

"Ten pounds. You agreed to give me ten pounds."

"I did?

"Yes."

"Are you sure?"

"Yes."

Lord Emsworth was struck by a sudden thought.

"Is it your birthday?"

"No."

George was beginning to feel a lot more comfortable. Sir
Hamish looked fierce, no doubt about it, but the conversation
was running along lines already familiar to George from frequent discourse with his grandfather.

"Ten pounds," he repeated. "You owe me ten pounds."

"Right. Ten pounds. Do I have ten pounds?"

"Why not look in your wallet?"

"Of course." Lord Emsworth warmed to the lad's quick
intelligence. "Capital idea. You're quite right, there's more
than enough here."

As he peeled a couple of fivers from Sir Hamish's wad, Lord
Emsworth heard an anguished squeal from the sty behind him.
Normally, he would have responded to it instantly, but just now
an odd feeling was creeping over him. Even to an intellect as
limited as the ninth Earl's, recent events were beginning to seem
a little odd. It was, he realized, time for some peace and quiet. A
couple of chapters of Whiffle's masterpiece *The Care of the
Pig,* accompanied by a beaker full of the warm south with
perhaps a splash or two of soda, would go far to restore him. He
pressed the money into George's hand and set a determined
course for Blandings Castle. Whiffle's book and the decanter
were both in the study, and the sooner he could be with them the
better he would like it.

"Here, wait a minute." George was pleased by the smooth-
ness of the operation, but he was an honest lad. "I didn't give
you back the amulet. It's yours now."

He pressed it into Lord Emsworth's hand, shuddered again at

the blackened and bewhiskered face, and made a rapid exit before Sir Hamish could tell him that he had changed his mind.

Lord Emsworth looked at the talisman for a moment, but his attention was elsewhere. He again set his legs in motion towards the castle, and again he was detained. The figure of George Cyril Wellbeloved now stood before him, clutching at a convenient fence post in an attempt to stop the ground from moving around beneath his feet.

"'s all ready." he said.

"What?" said Lord Emsworth, regarding his former pig man with little favor.

" 'sready. 's all ready to pinch the Empress.''

"What!!"

It occurred to George Cyril that, since his own speech was impeccably clear, Sir Hamish must be hard of hearing, or even perhaps inebriated. He leaned forward and put his mouth close to Lord Emsworth's ear.

"Ready to pinch the Empress!" he bellowed, forgetting that pig-pinching is usually regarded as a silent sport.

Lord Emsworth recoiled. There was a certain something in the pig man's aura, overwhelming the usual pig-related smells.

"Wellbeloved, you're drunk. Stop this silliness and get along home at once."

It seemed at first as though George Cyril had found a way to obey the instruction instantaneously. He had immediately disappeared from sight. His big mistake, he realized as he fell into the warm bosom of the ditch, had been to release his hold on the fence post. Shortly before he lapsed into the arms of Morpheus, it occurred to the pig man that the aristocracy follow very inconsistent behavior patterns. In the afternoon they harass you to pinch a pig, and that same night they have lost all interest in it.

With Wellbeloved out of the way, Lord Emsworth set off once more for the house. On the way, he became aware of the amulet that young George had thrust into his hand. It was of no special interest to him and a nuisance to carry. He threw it from him into the orchard and proceeded to the front door. It was locked, but that was nothing to a man of his resources. In a few moments he had fished out the spare key from its hiding place

behind the rose trellis. He went inside, and continued steadily to
the study and to the combined restorative powers of Whiffle and
a glass of liquid refreshment.

And it was there that Beach saw him a few minutes later, as
the butler made his rounds of the house in accordance with Lady
Constance's parting instructions.

Young George had retired to his room immediately upon his
return from the sty. He was happy to have his ten pounds and did
not contemplate any further action that night. Something attempted, something done, has earned the night's repose, he
thought. It was with some surprise that he soon heard a knock on
his bedroom door and saw Beach enter. Relations between the
two were pretty good, but they did not extend to evening soirees
in George's bedroom.

Beach's manner was never exactly festive, but now he looked
positively grim. He was carrying a large iron poker.

"Excuse me, Master George," he began. "But are you aware
of Lord Emsworth's whereabouts?"

It seemed an odd question. The Earl was not in the habit of
leaving an itinerary with his grandson. George shook his head.

"It is most important that we locate him," went on the butler.
"In making my rounds of the castle a few minutes ago, I
observed a burglar in His Lordship's study. He was unaware of
my presence and had even had the audacity to help himself to
certain potables there. I have left Jarvis guarding the study door,
but I would like to have Lord Emsworth present when we
apprehend the malefactor."

George's eyes opened wide at Beach's words. If the *Champion Paper for Boys* had a fault, it was a tendency to dwell on
sensational crime.

"Did you recognize him?"

Beach shook his head. "My acquaintances in the criminal
community are regrettably few, Master George, and the man
was wearing an excellent disguise. I would much appreciate it if
you would run along to the Empress' sty now and see if His
Lordship is there."

George started guiltily. "He's not there."

"Indeed. Are you sure? I have not seen him since before tea."

And there, of course, he had George. To reveal one thing to Beach might lead to revealing all, including George's own role in the purloining of the pig. George's reading had made him well aware of the dangers of being an accessory after the fact.

"I'd better just go and look," he said and escaped before further questioning could be applied.

We left the Empress, you will recall, asleep in the orchard. So it may seem unlikely that George, heading for the sty, would encounter anything that looked like his grandfather. The Empress, we might argue, should have stayed put. Pigs, and especially prize pigs, can sleep almost indefinitely, even if they look like peers of the realm. That does not hold true, of course, when they are struck hard on the nose by flying objects. The amulet that Lord Emsworth had cast into the orchard had given the Empress a good one, and she came to a rude awakening.

It took her only a second or two to pick up the talisman, decide that it could not be eaten, and begin to look for other diversions. Gadding about is all right for the daytime, but as evening shadows fall the right-minded pig yearns for the comforts of the home sty. Somewhat stiffly—for the ground beneath a pear tree is not an ideal couch for anyone over fifty—the Empress rose and made her way back home. She came to the fence that surrounded the sty and looked in. To her great surprise, she found it already occupied.

The change to porcine form had not pleased Sir Hamish. Putting aside the fact that it may have improved his appearance, we must admit that he had a point. A man who has come to snaffle a pig must be ready for certain surprises, but a change of roles with the swag is not one of them. Sir Hamish had concluded that Lord Emsworth arranged it and somehow turned the tables on him.

His suspicion seemed to be confirmed when, after some minutes of standing in the sty, he saw Lord Emsworth's face peering in at him over the fence. He fancied that he could detect a smug look of triumph in the Earl's expression. A man who had trained his stomach to accept Madras curry for breakfast would never know it, but lingering indigestion can produce just such a look. Twenty-seven plums in five minutes would be nothing to the Empress under normal circumstances, but now she was handicapped by the inadequate alimentary canal of a mere human. She did not like the feeling inside her. All she wanted was her straw bed and a few hours of meditation.

And for real satisfaction, she would like to be rid of Lord Emsworth's clothes. They itched and chafed. She reached behind her and scratched at her back with the amulet she was holding. It was nice and sharp, and rather like the pumice scraper that George Cyril Wellbeloved had applied to her in the happy days before his disappearance from the Blandings Castle environs.

George, approaching from the side, did not notice the amulet with which his grandfather had been rubbing his back. His mind was mainly taken up with the odd fact that Lord Emsworth was at the sty, while Sir Hamish was not. Then reason asserted itself. Clearly, the Earl has pottered down there for a late night worship of the Empress, and Sir Hamish was not stupid enough to try and steal the pig under the very nose of her owner.

He tugged at his grandfather's sleeve. "I say. Beach wants you to come back to the castle."

"Mph?" said Sir Hamish.

Not a sparkling reply, but George knew his grandfather's style. He tried again. "Beach wants you to come to the castle."

"Mph?" repeated Sir Hamish, still feeling slightly dizzy from the switch.

It occurred to George that he was certainly earning his ten pounds. If Sir Hamish were within earshot, he ought to be ready to double the fee.

"Beach says there's a burglar in the study, drinking your whisky. He wants you to come back and help to arrest him."

Lord Emsworth, approached in this fashion, was likely to ask why Beach wanted to be arrested, but Sir Hamish responded differently. He had been in a pigsty for hours, then suddenly shifted to a body that had recently done awful things to its digestive system. Only one word of George's remarks had penetrated his clouded brain.

"Whisky?"

"That's right, drinking your whisky. In the study. Come on."

George turned and led the way. Sir Hamish trailed along behind him, still clutching the amulet. He felt like one that hath been stunned and is of sense forlorn, but if it were all a dream, at least it was a superior dream, one with whisky in it.

As they left the sty, there was stirring within. The Empress was home again and feeling as though a late-night snack of linseed meal and buttermilk might go down well. She did not see the two visitors approach the castle, where Beach stood on guard.

As a butler, Beach had few equals. If you wanted a man to shoot the crusty rolls around the dinner table or put a baronet in his place with a single raised eyebrow, you should look no further. He had it all. About the only criticism that one could make of that super-butler was of his odd reading habits. Beach was an insatiable consumer of those lurid volumes that one sees on sale in railway bookstalls, with daggers, drops of blood, white gloves and black masks displayed prominently on the cover. The arrival of a burglar at Blandings Castle offered a once-in-a-lifetime opportunity. Within minutes, Beach had footmen guarding doors, windows and chimneys, and another by the fuse box. He had already ascertained that the telephone wires had not been cut—much to his surprise. He tiptoed towards Sir Hamish, as the latter followed young George into the castle.

"He is still in the study, Your Lordship," he breathed softly, in a whisper that suggested an advanced case of laryngitis. "Drinking whisky."

"WHISKY!" replied Sir Hamish, getting at once to the heart of the matter.

His voice had been trained on the parade grounds of northern India, where it had learned to compete with the trumpeting of bull elephants and the roar and boom of field cannon. It rang now through the whole castle. So it was not surprising that Lord Emsworth should appear promptly at the study door, a glass of liquid comfort in one hand and Whiffle's masterpiece in the other, to discover the reason for the uproar.

Sir Hamish was vaguely aware of a man of dark complexion standing before him. He was much more aware of the full glass of whisky that the burnt cork character was holding in his hand. After what Sir Hamish had been through, he yearned towards it like Moses approaching the Promised Land. The talisman dropped to the carpet from his nerveless hand. Beach bent to retrieve it and, with the instinct of the true butler, whipped out a muslin cloth from his pocket and gave it an absent-minded but thorough polish to free it from dust.

The most surprising thing of all was the calm way that the intruder was behaving. He had shown no sign of alarm when he appeared, and now he was quietly drinking whisky. Sir Hamish, finding himself after a moment's dizziness in possession of a full glass of heartsease, had not waited to discuss its origin. He stuck his nose in and started sucking it down like a thirsty camel before anyone else in the room could move. Beach realized that he was dealing with what the authorities would term a cool customer.

"Do you wish me to apprehend this man, My Lord?" he asked, taking a firmer grip of the poker.

Lord Emsworth did not reply. He walked steadily forward, past Sir Hamish, and on into the study. During a brief moment of disorientation, his glass had somehow gone from his hand, and his first priority was to remedy that lack with a sizable replacement. He wasn't going to worry about lesser matters until that was taken care of.

Beach lowered the poker. If Lord Emsworth wished to delay action, that was a relief. The felon looked fierce and of muscular build, and grappling with him would be a task better suited to a chucker-out at a London night club than a well-trained butler. In any case, the visitor showed no wish to escape. He had seated himself in a comfortable chair, opened Whiffle, and appeared to be reading it between swallows. Sir Hamish had confirmed the fact that he was dreaming, and since he was now in one of the good bits he had no desire to wake up.

Clearly, it could not last. Lord Emsworth had reappeared from the study holding another full glass, and now he was ready to repossess Whiffle and continue his studies. Inexplicably, it was in the hands of a large, hairy gentleman who had apparently just come from an audition for the part of Othello, Moor of Venice. The Earl advanced and stood before the newcomer.

"Whiffle," he said courteously, holding out his hand.

"Aye, Whiffle," agreed Sir Hamish.

"I mean, I would like my copy of Whiffle. I was reading it."

To Lord Emsworth's great surprise, he perceived that the visitor had been reading it too. He had made many attempts to persuade others of his own household to peruse the work in detail, but had met with no success. But here, apparently, was a man who was studying the work without coercion.

Sir Hamish looked up from the book and shook his blackened head.

"Nae doot aboot it, this mon's a gee-enius. Would ye see this noo, his deescussin' o' the feedin' mix."

"You read Whiffle?" asked Lord Emsworth. He was a man who liked to be sure.

Sir Hamish nodded. "Aye. Morn an' eve. He's the Masterr of us a'."

There was no mistaking the reverence in his tone. Lord Emsworth felt the sudden thrill of communion with a fellow spirit. Sir Hamish had expressed his own sentiments exactly.

"Did you ever—?" he began, but Beach had appeared annoyingly in front of him.

"Excuse me, My Lord, but I wonder if you wish me to arrest this intruder."

"Arrest him?"

"Yes, My Lord. For illegal entry."

"Certainly not, Beach. This gentleman is not an intruder. Didn't you hear what he said about Whiffle? Tell me," said Lord Emsworth, turning his attention again to Sir Hamish. "Do you by any chance raise pigs yourself?"

Sir Hamish hung his head in shame. It was a question that seared his soul. "Ah'm tryin'. But it's nae use. Ma piggy's as thin as a wheeppet. Ah canna mak' the Jewel tak' tae the bran mash."

"Ah." Lord Emsworth looked grave. He knew how such problems could bring a strong man to the brink of despair. "I wonder, have you tried adding a spoonful of malt to it?''

"Malt?"

"One tablespoonful to two pounds of mash."

"Ye think it'd perr-suade yon tae tak' her fodder?"

"The Empress of Blandings put on ten pounds in the first week I tried it."

"Ten!"

"Ten."

"Poonds!"

"Pounds," corrected Lord Emsworth.

"Ah'll try it," said Sir Hamish. Then he hung his head again. The scales were falling from his eyes, and he realized that only a man of saintly mind would reveal the secrets of superpig raising to a rival.

"But Ah hafta mak'a confession tae ye. Ah was after tryin' tae steal the Empress."

"Stealing her?"

Sir Hamish nodded glumly. "Aye. She's a queen o' pigs. Ah wanted t' tak' her."

"Very natural," said Lord Emsworth charitably. "If she didn't belong to me I would feel the same way myself. But now, about this important matter of the feeding mix. What do you think of the Petrovsky masher? That's what I've been using, but there are still lumps in the feed."

"Aye, Ah ken that. Ye ha' need o' the McGillicuddy Mix-Master, afore the mash. Then there's niver ony deeficulty wi' it."

Lord Emsworth blinked with excitement. It sounded like the instrument he had been looking for. He wondered how he had failed to meet this excellent man before, one who knew his Whiffle thoroughly and who, despite a penchant for burnt cork and an apparently incurable speech impediment, was willing to dispense good advice so freely.

"I'll buy one immediately. Beach, get me Whister's of Bond Street on the telephone."

Beach coughed politely. "With respect, Your Lordship, it is now eleven o'clock at night. I am not sure they will still be open."

"Eleven o'clock? Good Heavens, then it's time for the Empress to have her bread and molasses." He looked at Sir Hamish diffidently. "You know, there is a Fat Pig Contest over in Bletchingham next week, and I will be unable to attend in person—there's this silly nonsense in the House Of Lords, and my sister will make me go to it. I was wondering. Is there any chance that you would be willing to show the Empress for me? If it wouldn't be too much trouble."

Sir Hamish, overcome with emotion, picked up a priceless Elizabethan embroidery and wiped at his eyes with it. Three woven members of the English nobility were transformed to chimney sweeps.

"Ah canna think o' anythin' finer. Ah'm no worthy o' the honor, Ma' Lorrd."

Lord Emsworth put his arm around Sir Hamish's shoulders and led him to the door. It went without saying that his visitor would want to share the excitement when the Empress embarked on her last meal of the day.

"Call me Clarence," he said.

AFTERWORD: THE MARRIAGE OF TRUE MINDS.

As they say, one pig leads to another. After Judy-Lyn del Rey bought "The Deimos Plague" for STELLAR 4, we sat in her office and talked of our shared admiration for P.G. Wodehouse in general and the Empress of Blandings in particular. She remarked how nice it would be if there were a story in which the Empress starred in a fantasy or sf setting, complete with the other occupants of Blandings Castle.

I agreed completely, went back home, and wrote this story with much enjoyment and even more effort. The Wodehouse style is unique and it is beyond hubris to try to match it.

By the time this was finished I had sold a different story ("The Subtle Serpent") for STELLAR 5, and anyway this wasn't right for that series. However, Judy-Lynn helped me to obtain permission to publish from the Wodehouse literary executors, and I sold the story to FANTASY AND SCIENCE FICTION. For a week or two after the sale I was riding high. I must, I felt, have captured that delicate and elusive Wodehouse touch.

I came down in a hurry. I received a letter from Ed Ferman, editor of F&SF. He had not, he explained, read any P.G. Wodehouse. Would I therefore send him some appropriate background for the story's lead-in?

Oh my prosthetic soul! I sent background material, of course I sent it. But if not actually disgruntled, I was (to borrow from the Master) far from being gruntled.

About the Author . . .

President of the American Astronautical Society and Vice President in charge of Research & Development for the Earth Satellite Corporation, Charles Sheffield first began writing fiction in 1976. Since then he has published two novels, SIGHT OF PROTEUS and THE WEB BETWEEN THE WORLDS, and another short story collection, VECTORS. A third novel, tentatively entitled ERASMUS MAGISTER, is forthcoming from Ace. Currently residing in Washington, D.C., Sheffield was born in England, where he received his B.A. and M.A. in mathematics from St. John's College, Cambridge, an achievement he capped with a Ph.D. in theoretical physics.